The Quiet Government Men

Chris Cauwood

New Generation **Publishing**

The Quiet Government Men

'You have a choice, Taylor. Become one of our quiet government men, or remain accused of murder.'

London. Westminster. 2015.

The Environment Minister's personal private secretary leafed through the report before him. He muttered to his assistant,

'I wonder what his lordship will think of this?'

'Not invented here, would be my guess. Do you need me? I've got a mile high in-tray.'

'No, you go. I'll break it to him.'

The Minister breezed in, his charisma on a high setting. The PPS imagined dust and loose papers settling behind him. He suppressed a groan.

'Three minutes, PPS, that's your lot. I'm nearly late. What do you have for me?'

'An environmental proposal document, Minister. Melting ice caps; weather upsets; the effects of sea level rises on the lowlands… titled –

When the Storms come: Never mind what if, what do we do when?

- by this man, Cartwright, he is highly thought of, an expert. The P.M. is keen. The Press are running Sunday glossies on it. You may be called on to comment sooner rather than later…'

'Bah! More green nonsense! Go on, what are these devilish clever plans for the new drowned world? Polar bear hotels? Gardening grants for rainforests in suburbia?'

'They say we can grow algae in bio tubes, sir. The algae will flourish in the new tropical climate. The climate they predict will descend on what remains of Europe. Algae can make food, ethanol for fuel, and building materials apparently. They say it will seize excess CO_2 back from the atmosphere…'

'How big are these bio tubes? Where will they go if the sea, as they predict, reclaims the land?'

'They will float on the new inland sea… big enough for an average person to stand up inside, it says here…'

'Fabulous imaginations, some people. What else is on the menu?'

'Well, there's the bamboo for building, thicker than your wrist, grows up to a metre a fortnight. Nettles for clothing…'

'Bamboo? Nettles? Are we going back to the Stone Age?'

'Their introduction says both the Kaiser in 1914 and Napoleon in 1805 clothed their armies in nettle cloth. We can eat; we can build with these and other plants; medicine, tea, antiseptics, the list goes on. Do you believe in higher entities, Gods, pre planning, fore-ordained things, Minister?'

'That's my business but why do you ask?'

'They say one could be swayed with these two plants. It's almost as if they were a gift, a plentiful resource we ignore.'

'Hmmm – I'm meeting the Environment Committee this morning, better get weaving. Hah! Weaving! What's the bottom line? Get your assistant to write me up a précis – bullet points and so on, you know. Don't email it, the place is still leaking like a sieve. I'll read it tonight. Right! I'm off.'

***

No papers floated down but the image persisted. The PPS subconsciously held the file down firmly on the table until he'd gone. Peace. He sat alone, fingered a document that could change the world. He spoke softly to himself.

'The Stone Age. That's the bottom line; no alternative if we don't adopt these ideas...and we won't. Should I whittle myself a club this weekend?'

He went into his assistant's office.

'Wendy, see if you can get hold of this Cartwright character for me. Under your hat for now, yes?'

***

Chapter One

Eastern England. Ten years on.

In an old school assembly hall crowded with frightened angry people, one red faced farmer bawled.

'What about our livelihoods? What about the animals you've put on trucks and taken away with no compensation? We've been here for generations! They did this to the Scots two hundred years ago!'

Cheers added to the excitement in the room. Chairs were set out but few sat down. Up on the stage, a group of officials headed the impromptu meeting. A Police chief took his turn to speak. Supporting him were a Royal Engineer Colonel, here to blow up the dam with his two civilian demolition experts, Bernard Samuels and Mark Taylor. On his other side, two councillors and the government agency man. No one seemed clear on exactly which agency. The chief cleared his throat.

'Ladies and gentlemen, we must destroy the dam to relieve pressure, to save the rest of the area. They built the dam to act as a safety valve. The reservoir water is escaping and flooding the villages all around. You must see the sense of it. The sea will rise and flood you anyway.'

'You'll destroy the dam over our dead bodies,' shouted the self-appointed leader, shaking his fist to a low roar of agreement.

On the stage, the quiet government man bent to the microphone.

'These aren't winter flash floods. This is climate change, disaster. Please listen to reason.'

The crowd quietened to an angry murmur, struggling to come to terms with it all. They were a mob, uninformed and frightened. The Royal Engineer Colonel reached for the mike.

'Hurricane Noah has hit us once already. It is wreaking havoc over Europe just now. It is the culmination of three hurricanes coming in across the Atlantic. A Super Storm, which may swing back any time. We must get our heads down until it all blows over...'

'What the bloody hell do you know? You're just a soldier,' shouted one woman.

'I may look like a soldier, Madam, but I'm a civil engineer. I specialise in hydrology...'

'Madam? Madam?' she sneered.

The quiet man stood again.

'Please, please, arguing who is who and what they do is not the

5

point. The world is in some imbalance. This is not just a big storm. The North Sea, the oceans, are all rising. We thought it a storm surge like 1953 but this time it does not look like the waters will recede…'

'And?' said the farmer.

'We must evacuate you. You are the last few.'

'So you say, with the news switched off; bloody government!' 'The last lot were bad enough - now this…' said another.

The government man saw bags of belongings lining the side of the hall. Pride stopped them going without a fight, but they would go all the same.

***

They deny the inevitable, Mark Taylor thought. Their livelihoods are finished. It's over.

He sat off to one side near the edge of the stage. A stranger in the village, like most on the committee, he'd watched the storm rage for days, heard terrifying news of power cuts, flooding, refugees, no Internet, and no TV. Then, no more news; his car radio only ran repeated advice to flee to high ground and report to police and army authorities.

He saw Bernard, head of their demolition company, Demolition Solutions. Sat between Bernard and the colonel was a man introduced as from a government agency.

What's he doing out here, away from London? he wondered and then put him aside at the lingering irritation with Bernard for renaming the company Demolutions.

***

Taylor saw Bernard trying to catch his eye. He nodded their prearranged signal. Time to break up the meeting, an end to token democracy, these good people would have decisions forced on them, agreed or not. Taylor got up and stepped to one side. The charges were set and wired. A matter of connecting the wires to his box of tricks, setting the timer - the dam would be history. He started to make his way out of the hall.

'Where's that bugger think he's goin'?' someone shouted. The Colonel spoke into a hand held radio. Half a dozen soldiers forced their way in and Taylor found himself surrounded; bundled out of the hall. He shrank from mean vicious attempts to grab and hit him, some by women. The soldiers fared worst. He admired their self-control and discipline. He was sure he would have lashed out at a few faces. Police officers with clear plastic shields burst in through the double doors and forced the crowd back to allow their exit.

Outside, he gasped the fresh air. He jumped into his Jeep. Waves of relief washed over him – he was free of the crowd, heaving and pushing, trying to smother him. The last he heard was the Colonel's voice,

'…we have tried to reason with you. What happens now is for the greatest good of the greatest number. A state of martial law is in force. Transport to safety awaits you. Please leave the hall in an orderly fashion…'

Slamming the door shut, Taylor started the engine.

Crowds, thought Taylor. Not a "people person", he loathed their sheep like qualities. If we left them to starve or drown, any survivors would blame him and his team immediately they had the chance. Like baby bird chicks – "me, me, me," with their beaks wide open.

***

Peering between smearing wipers, he followed the Army Land Rover's tail lights out of the school grounds and up a small hill to the firing point. Driving past a dozen coaches, sat with engines running, he saw a few resigned but realistic people wiping condensation from the windows. They stared out at him with hollow eyes. Full or not, these coaches would be leaving soon. Many had already left.

The dam was ahead in the rain and dark; he could sense it if he couldn't see it. Below the dam were the doomed fields.

Devil from the government, am I? I'd like nothing more than to wave a magic wand, hold back the waters; turn the clock back, he thought.

He stopped just past the temporary canvas shelter of the firing point and parked facing the other end of the dam.

'Don't you want to turn your Jeep the other way, for a quick get away?' said the young Royal Engineer corporal, opening his door for him.

'Bags of time, there's bags of time. There's a fifteen minute delay built in; after your Boss gives the order to blow,' Taylor said.

They strolled along the top of the dam. Too warm for February, he felt the rain and wind buffet at them. Another flash of lightning; he glimpsed a wide avenue, a boulevard paved with those concrete slabs that allow grass to grow up between the small squares. It reminded him of a similar water near home, designed for pleasant walks for

7

people who liked to see the water on one side and view the landscape of patchwork fields on the other. Demolition cables snaked away, disappearing at intervals down manhole covers. A pleasant place whose time was up, the explosives lay below, waiting to exert massive forces on the weakened points of the dam.

The army man by his side - was he thinking the same thoughts? - a bright keen active young man who hadn't fallen to the weary cynicism Taylor suffered from these days. They found themselves in a sheltered spot, some freak of the construction stopped the flurry of wind; the acoustics allowed normal conversation.

'What's going to happen to us? It feels like the end of the world. I joined the Army to see the world. Not the end of it.'

'I know,' Taylor said. 'You're more likely to come out of this than those civilians. They don't understand. Their lives are shattered already.'

'You're a civilian, you don't seem to be losing your head; just getting on with it.'

'I had a few years in the RAF. That's how I got interested in blowing things up. I don't feel like a civilian, even now.'

Both looked out over the dam wall. Lightning flashed again and lit up the waterlogged landscape. Taylor could imagine, almost feel the solid ground giving way beneath them, washing them away in a frantic helter-skelter to lower ground.

'I'm Jack, by the way.'

'Most people just call me Taylor.'

'How do you do, Taylor.' They laughed at the oddness of the formality. Below their feet were enough explosives to atomise them.

'How old's this dam? Thirty, forty years? I bet they moaned about it being built. Are you married? Kids?' Taylor said.

'No, divorced; the other married lads' wives and kids were taken to a central emergency unit, an old nuclear bunker up in the Dales. The Army looks after its own; so we're not always looking over our shoulders, I suppose. Running off to go find them and protect them, sort of thing.'

He looked at Taylor.

'You?'

'Yes. Two kids, boy and a girl.'

A clap of distant thunder jarred the ground under his feet; that, or his imagination.

'Time to go, I can feel the dam giving way already.'

This Jack; Taylor felt he could be a friend. He wished one didn't have to be thrust into dire circumstance to find true people. Taylor struggled with humanity. His major weakness, he often felt he didn't belong here on Earth. He grunted cynically to himself. The weather, Mother Nature, Gaia, the Earth Goddess, all seem to be of the same opinion; we don't belong here maybe.

As they walked back to the firing point, Jack said,

'I'd want to go and find the family if I was you.'

Taylor didn't answer.

***

He watched the now subdued people from the meeting. Dragging weary heels, they filed aboard the coaches, the red faced farmer included. Soldiers helped shove their bags into the spaces below. He shuddered in distaste. Some package holiday! He could no more get on one of those buses than jump to his death over the dam. He thought of one of his old friends who had a theory that all people follow the inside of a tunnel in life. Most just went along the tunnel with the rest. Some, a select few, knew the secret hatches in the roof and walked along the outside; along the top. All must follow the tunnel direction. At some time, all must rejoin the others inside.

Taylor was ready to get out through one of the hatches. No intention at all of going with the convoy or inside the bus / tunnel along with the soldiers or the mob. His spine crawled with anticipated claustrophobia at the prospect. His route home across country was already planned, away from the strangled main roads and the panicking refugees. The Jeep was ready with every off road accessory he could find. He would fire the dam charges with a much-reduced delay and then light out of there, over the doomed grass patterned concrete road to where they dare not follow. He was going home to get her and the kids, the only important things in his life.

***

He arrived home in the dark, twenty-four hours later. Rain lashed against the Jeep, the wipers barely clearing the screen before it was awash again. The wheels gushed through deep puddles, the Jeep slowing and then running free again. The streetlights were off. The storm centre had moved away but the horizon lit up with lightning every few seconds. He'd never seen weather like it; nobody had.

He turned into his street and parked outside the house. Nobody about; a ghost town. He ran down the side path and hammered on his back door. No one in. He unlocked it and groped for the torch that usually sat on the windowsill. Not there. Fumbling in a drawer found a puny key ring novelty torch; then the wind up torch in his filing cabinet. His "green" torch; some decent light.

The note on the table read:

"Gone to shelter up above the reservoir. Everyone must go to high ground where evacuation will be organized. Kids missing you, and me – hope you catch up. Love S xxx"

His heart thumped in his chest. Feelings of panic rose up making his breathing shallow. He cast about, gasping. What to do? Away from home a week longer than planned, he thought his hometown was on high enough ground to be safe from flooding. As they retreated inland with the Army and Civil Defence teams, as first one sea defence and then another succumbed to the North Sea, he thought they were safe. Then he began to really worry.

His mad dash across the countryside; he would have nightmares forever, of getting stuck or being intercepted by officialdom, his only goal to get home and be reunited...

Reservoir? After helping empty one reservoir on the command of the emergency authorities, he didn't want his family near or in the hands of a selfish frightened mob like that last one. He calmed himself, counted to ten, took deep breaths; this panic attack wasn't going to help anything. There would be no benefit from emptying the local reservoir, little threat from it overflowing, he thought. It was up high and fed by the two controllable river branches which could be closed or diverted; two rivers which led to the sea. In full spate, they could bear reasonable sized barges. They must be evacuating people by sea! By sea to where?

In his agitation, he nearly jumped out of his skin as a flash of lightning lit up an apparition in the doorway. Only old George from two doors away. He wore an oilskin coat and a waxed cotton hat. They dripped all over the floor. If Sal were here, he'd be scolded.

'They've gone, son, they were taken by the Special Police. The whole street, the whole town I reckon, though most left ten days or so ago, in their cars,' George said.

'Special Police? What Special Police, George?' he said, startled.

'You'll know them soon enough, if you follow them up there.'

Taylor felt like exploding. Did the old fool think he wouldn't follow, would stay here in the dark empty house without them?

'Look George, I haven't got time for guessing games, why are you still here?'

'I remember secret police from the war. If they took you, you didn't come back.'

- George is old, but not that old; some stories he'd picked up no doubt.

Taylor waved the note. 'It says they've gone up to the reservoir, to high ground. Come on old boy, let's go. You'll die here. What you going to live on?'

George made to leave in the opposite direction.

'I can catch him quick enough,' Taylor muttered.

He went to the phone; dead. Mobile phones stopped working days ago, the lightning played havoc with the phone masts. His mind's eye saw silhouettes; the dark cloaked soaking wet figures of Sal and the kids, Rachel and Andy, being led away by dark men with guns and helmets.

Looking wildly round the room, he mindlessly sought a memento, some reassurance, some comfort, something to carry with him out of this hell. Over the TV, on a shelf where he sometimes dumped the contents of his pockets, he saw the fob watch. A Christmas present, he never found a waistcoat to wear with it. Clockwork, not batteries, he could wind it. He pocketed it, and then undid the backs of a pair of family photo frames seized at random. He took out the photos. His fingers fumbled, glass shattered into shards on the tiled stone floor glinting their omen up at him.

Control! Calm down man!

Into the study, the dead computer; all that information; with no power, useless.

He lifted a tape drive backup then discarded it. Instead, he picked up his handful of USB memory sticks from a drawer. All his digital photos and quite a lot of music must be on one or other of them. One of them held local ordnance survey maps for his sat nav. They may come in useful one day, don't know why, he thought. Securing them all, including the scribbled note, in a dry inner pocket, he shot upstairs darting his head into the bedrooms. Small pale ghosts giggled with mischief – Ha Dad! Fooled you! We would have called you back, really!

The ghosts dissolved into crumpled, hastily abandoned, duvets.

Back downstairs, he went outside, through the front door this time. He didn't lock it; something told him he would never return.

There he was, old George, down the street, waving his stick at the storm. Climbing into the Jeep, he turned the key; quarter full of fuel. That was it, no electricity; no fuel pumps. If necessary, he could siphon fuel from an abandoned car. He had the necessary in the back.

Starting the engine, he moved off, edging the passenger window down as he came alongside George.

'Get in George, come on man.'

George dithered for a few seconds then got in and slammed the door shut. Much to Taylor's wonder, he put on his seat belt.

'Let's have a look see; anyone about down in the town centre.'

Elongated drops of white rain, lit up by his lights, swooped towards them. "Back! The other way! Not here," they seemed to tell him. The main beam flared and bounced dazzle back into his eyes. Something wasn't right ahead, at the bottom of the hill near the river. Taylor squinted and strained to see ahead with lights both on and off. Weird, but it looked like the centre of town was under water. Getting out, he peered through the rain. Not only was the lower town underwater but the level was rising.

His sixth sense alerted him. Something was wrong. He edged backwards to his door.

Out of the dark, a surging frothing wave headed towards him. Jumping back in, he reversed retreating up the hill, water lapping at his front bumper. Swinging the Jeep round, he jammed the gears into forward and accelerated away. It was head for high ground but, why the reservoir? Nothing there; just farmland.

***

'Now, George, tell me about these special police.'

'You don't believe me do you? Think I'm potty…'

'No, it's just new to me. I was stuck up in the Wolds. I had to drive off road on tracks, railway lines and stuff. All the roads were blocked with refugees in their cars. It's taken me a day to drive thirty miles. There are no cars here though, it's very odd.'

'How d'ye find your way then?'

Taylor tapped at the sat-nav.

'One of these things for hill walkers and off road types.'

'Best you ask it for another way then,' said George, pointing ahead.

Ahead the road was more or less straight but with dips and hollows all the way to the reservoir. Taylor remembered bright summers' days, a pleasant roller coaster ride with the reservoir appearing on the high parts, disappearing with the lower parts and reappearing again, tantalizing picnic intent families, windsurfers and leisure sailors alike as they drew nearer. He stopped for the second time in ten minutes, the way ahead blocked by water filling the dip.

The rain had eased but there were still rumbles of thunder from behind them. He eased himself out. He began to feel paranoid. So near yet so far, his decision-making reserves were fading with exhaustion. No driving through the water in the dip; it must be a metre or so deep. It didn't seem to be rising. He looked back the way they had come. A flash of lightning lit the horizon again. He could see the sea, as if he was on a beach at night during rough weather. No, his imagination was in overdrive. The sea was eighty miles away. George joined him.

'Town's gone.' He nudged Taylor and pointed over the flattened hedge to their right. Taylor shone the torch. A jumble of dozens of wrecked cars piled up in the fields. Looking down, Taylor saw the muddy marks left by tracked vehicles.

Bulldozed off the road.

George gave him a knowing look and then pointed to a slight rise to their left.

'There's a track to Top Farm yonder. It will circle us round to the village, Eltham village, by the dam.'

'Looks like we have no choice, eh George?' They got back in the Jeep; Taylor turned around, found the track and drove off the road. The way was blocked. By a five-barred gate.

'Can you...?' but George was out and heading towards the gate without prompting.

'I'll shut it behind us. Keep the animals in,' he said.

This is no time to worry about the country code, you daft old man, he thought, but he was glad of the company all the same.

George was back at Taylor's window. 'Locked, with a chain and a hefty padlock.'

He got out, rooted around in the back of the Jeep and pulled out a steel towrope.

'Hold the torch, George.'

'Whatever you're going to do, you'd best hurry,' Taylor looked over his shoulder. The hairs on the back of his neck stood on end. Behind them, the road they had just left was swimming with water and filling up under the hedge. He had not imagined the night beach scene. Was it following him; biding its time? Watching, waiting, until he was trapped, back against a wall with nowhere to go?

He hissed and hooked the towrope through the chain and ran it back to the Jeep's front strongpoint.

'Get in George, if it snaps it'll cut you in half.' He selected reverse, revved the engine and dropped the clutch. The wheels spun then gripped and the Jeep shot backwards to be arrested by the rope. Something snapped and the Jeep was free. He got out again. The chain had broken. Breathing a sigh of relief, he dragged the gate open and, about to disentangle the rope, he saw the water was now up to the

Jeep's back wheels. He undid the rope, flung it away and climbed back into his seat. They shot through the gate and on up the steep hill.

Glad he kept the Jeep now, he would never have made it back tonight in an ordinary car. He'd fancied something comfortable, greener; without rattles. As it was he was too late, he'd missed them. In his frantic cross-country dash he'd turned off the radio – a single repeated recording;

"Do not, repeat not, try to find friends and family. Go straight to a police or army checkpoint. They will take care of you…"

***

Top Farm was a huddle of buildings with its barns and sheds scattered around. It was deserted or at least, with the lights off, no one came out to meet them.

'Black uniforms,' said George, picking up the conversation from earlier. 'Like riot police but not, like something from the Space Wars films. They shot your mate with one of those Taser guns. He was calling them all sorts. They just fired at him once and he went down. They carried him to the buses. No argument from the rest after that.'

'Stupid old hippy,' Taylor said, 'Wish I'd seen that. What's happening over there by the reservoir?'

They could see flickering lights ahead on the peninsular in the distance. Bright lights like the ones used on night time road works. Judging by the moving headlights of vehicles, a lot of activity. They had less than a mile to go but the lightning flashes seemed to reflect more water than land. No obvious route suggested itself in the dark.

'Let's wait until daylight, George, eh?' Driving the Jeep into a hay barn he switched off.

'You OK?' George said.

'Frantic rough cross-country rides are no good for my back these days. It's sore as f...'

His head thumped with tension. Scratching around in the glove locker found him some paracetamol. The hay looked so inviting.

'I'll go and find some water,' George said.

***

At dawn Taylor awoke to the smell of hay, farmyard manure and diesel fuel. He heard the chatter of rain on tin roofing; no sign of George. He looked around, only half aware of his predicament. Outside, the rain came down in a steady drizzle. The storm centre must be elsewhere. He wandered over to the Jeep, poked about inside, found a battered paper cup wedged under his seat; dunked it into the bucket George must have found last night and filled with water. He drank deep. I should drink water more often, this is nectar, he thought. A half melted chocolate bar lurked in the armrest bin and he devoured half of it. -

Where was George? Has he cleared off in his fear of the police?

A voice came from behind him. 'Don't move.' He turned and received two sharp barbs in the chest and a fierce jolt of electricity. It threw him to the ground; he banged his head hard on the hub of the Jeep's front wheel.

- *Special Police* - flashed through his mind as he passed out.

***

'Which part of "Don't move" didn't he understand?' said the black uniformed trooper to his three colleagues.

A sergeant pushed forward. He looked down at Taylor.

'You're too trigger-happy with that thing Collins. He was no threat; nor was that poor old man you killed on the way in.'

'I didn't kill him. He had a heart attack.'

'Thanks to you.'

The sergeant glared Collins down then kneeled to take Taylor's pulse.

'He's lucky and so are you. We'll have one of our little chats when we get back. Load him up. Let's go; we won't be driving round here in twelve hours.' We won't be here at all in twenty-four, he thought.

***

Taylor came round inside a dark functional vehicle, alternately bouncing up and down one minute, drifting serenely the next. His head was sore and he reached for the bump on his head. He was manacled with one of those plastic cable ties. Please let me wake up in my own bed, he prayed. A light shone in his face.

'You're awake then. What were you doing at the farm?'

'Who are you? Why am I tied up? What's this coffin we're in?'

'We are SP. You had to be restrained for your own good. An amphibious vehicle, if you must know. Now, it's your turn. What were you doing at the farm?'

'OK Collins, back off. Not everybody wandering around the countryside is a criminal,' said the one with three stripes as he

15

shouldered Collins aside.

'He could be a looter. We were told we could shoot looters.'

'Look Collins, we were told it may be necessary to shoot them, not shoot them if we feel like it. Now, clear off out of my sight before I shoot you.' He turned to Taylor.

'Sorry, he's a tad over zealous. Worse, he's on my squad today. Were you looting?'

He winked.

A human, thought Taylor. They still exist.

'Of course not, what's to loot from a farm? Unless there's a black market for cattle fodder in the new age.'

The man laughed at his bitterness.

'I like a bit of dry sarcasm. Don't try it on Collins though. He just pulls his trigger and never asks questions afterwards. Anyway, Mr Taylor, my name's Sharpe. Nick Sharpe. Have some water and a biscuit.'

'How do you know my name?'

Sharpe held up his wallet, leaned over and tucked it back into Taylor's jacket pocket.

He held out his wrists for Sharpe to cut his bonds. Another trooper passed him back a water bottle. The biscuits were wrapped in dark blue plastic with the label: Z rations – Field Ops - Biscuits.

He gave Sharpe a rough outline of his past thirty-six hours. Sharpe grunted; 'You could come in handy in all this.' He turned to glare at Collins; 'unlike some.' He continued.

'You wouldn't have made it last night. You'd have bogged in and we wouldn't have seen you. We saw your lights up on the hill last night and came for a reconnaissance this morning. The water's much higher now. You were well stranded without us.'

'What happened to old George?'

Sharpe paused.

'We only found you. Was he a friend?'

'More of a long term neighbour, but yes, I suppose he was. Nice old guy. Can't we go back and look for him?'

'I'll send the next patrol out if the conditions allow. Time and, as you see, tide, wait for no man. The water won't reach up there – I hope…'

Taylor's head hurt and he failed to detect any evasion. He did note an evil gleam in Collins's eye though.

We live in desperate times, he thought - I owe you several thousand volts and a bump on the head, Mr Collins.

Chapter Two

The vehicle lurched to a halt, throwing them all forward. Taylor peered through slotted windows to see a checkpoint guarded by regular soldiers in waterproof camouflage gear. A barrier went up and they moved further on into a well-lit area and stopped. He realised they must be undercover; the rain no longer drummed on the roof. The back door was heaved open from outside. Another black uniformed trooper reached in to help him climb out.

'Only one, Sharpey? Must be royalty this one...?'

'Anyone left is either hiding up a tall tree or underwater,' Sharpe said. 'When's the next boat in?'

'Midday, they said. Probably the last one. There won't be room for...'

Sharpe held up his hand to silence him. He turned to Taylor.

'Maybe best if you didn't hear that. There are only so many berths before the landing stage floods. Harsh decision times.'

'My family, I'm worried sick about them. Are they subject to harsh decisions? They were brought here,' Taylor said.

'The last civilian women and kids shipped out yesterday at noon, don't worry,'

'Where to?'

'High ground proper; I don't know where. They'll be safe, unless this goes on like Noah's Ark. This water level rise has well caught us with our pants down. It's chaos. Anyway, come. I'll see you are processed as an active.'

'An active?'

'You'll see, let's go.'

***

Collins tried to trip Taylor as he went past. A mistake. Somehow, it was Collins in a stranglehold, face forced down into the mud gasping for air. Nobody moves that fast, he thought as he began to black out. As his swimming senses recovered, he heard the scornful jeers of his unsympathetic colleagues.

'Had a fall, Collins, mate?'

'He had you. Never seen a move like that. He'd have tied your knees round your neck in a bow if Sharpey hadn't hauled him off – brilliant show.'

'Try and trip him again later. I want to see it again.'

They kicked him into a kneeling position. 'Get up, yer bleedin' psycho.'

***

'Neat trick you have there, Taylor,' said Sharpe as he led him into a medical tent. They were in a huge temporary hangar. He could hear engines and pumps running outside nearby. The hangar was kept rigid by compressed air. Big enough for a passenger jet, Taylor thought. He answered Sharpe;

'I took up Judo once.' Good enough for now.

He winced as the army medic probed and peered at the scalp wound. The man sniffed, dabbed some iodine on the area and gave him a field dressing to hold over it. 'You'll live,' he grunted and turned away to attend to the first aid kits he was assembling into canvas bags and flinging into a net hanging from a hook.

'Thanks. Hell of a bedside manner. Got anything for a headache?'

The medic thrust a foil sheet of twelve paracetamol at him. 'Take two every four hours and keep away from children. They all shipped out so ignore the last advice.'

Taylor could see the hangar was divided up into sections made up of tents and separate smaller inflatable rooms. The inflatable ones reminded him of children's bouncy castles but serious in their army green. The thought of children wrenched at him. Were they safe? Where were they shipped out to?

He followed Sharpe up some scaffolding steps to a reception desk manned by a woman in a dark green uniform. Her back was turned to them.

'Think we have an active here,' Sharpe said.

The woman turned and glanced up at Taylor. She looked tired and drawn. The corners of her mouth were turned down but she brightened a little at the sight of them both.

'He looks like he's been active, covered in mud and blood and shit like that.'

Taylor smiled as she inspected him.

'You're supposed to bring in people, Sharpey. Not scarecrows. Hmm. Tall-ish. Fit looking. Semi-intelligent. Suffering from borderline shock like everyone brought in lately. Nice dressing, mate. Still, there's a cheeky face with blue eyes peering out of your scarecrow head. About time, some of the scallie scum we got in the compound,' she said; the last aside to Sharpe. She produced a paper pad and tore off three pages.

'Here, Active man, fill in this form and report to the Imperial Storm Troopers. Keep the obvious quips to yourself. Humour's not an option.'

He sensed her watching him as he filled in his details. One page with two non carbon copies.

'I'd have worried if you'd filled in your phone number.' She smiled, kept the back page, nodded towards Sharpe lolling against a tent pole. 'Take the form with you, don't lose it. Go with him. Good luck,' she said, turning back to whatever she was doing earlier.

***

He followed Sharpe's burly figure along a series of wooden boardwalks that bounced if they went too fast, threatening to pitch them down to the ground. Ahead lay more tents on this floor, all supported by everyday scaffolding covered in wooden sheets. They overlooked the groups of smaller inflatable and canvas covered areas below.

Across the hangar open area, he saw a chain link compound full of refugees who were yelling clawing and snarling. They demanded their release from the armed regular soldiers on the other side of the barrier. Young men and women soldiers barely out of their teens faced them, stationed at intervals with guns ready. Proper guns, not Tasers, he noted.

In another area, a doorway of rubber flaps pushed open for a few seconds, long enough for him to see half a dozen patients in hospital beds with drip stands and medical paraphernalia. Medical staff in surgical green outfits went in and out with a purpose.

They came to a gap where the fabric roof ended and corrugated skin panels made up the walls. An existing building, a factory or farm unit. The drumming rain sound started up again. Below, out of sight of the people at floor level, he saw a fork lift truck moving a pallet of body bags – full body bags.

***

On a landing above the hospital now, Sharpe pushed aside a tent door flap and ushered him inside. Taylor gaped at the sophistication of the equipment around the walls. Men and women sat at big screens showing radar weather, satellite view of the sea encroachment; satellite communications; a serious command centre. He glimpsed the overlay screens. The area around Norwich was becoming an island.

Cambridge was practically a dot.

Shocked, he allowed Sharpe to pull him through another set of door flaps.

Another sergeant in black sat alone at a ruggedized computer. One of those laptops that don't break when soldiers drop them.

'Who you got Sharpey?' he said without interest.

'Possible active, been doing government work, assistance to the civil powers; demolition, that sort of thing.'

Taylor offered his application form.

The desk man shrugged and nodded towards the far end of the tent.

'Take it with you when you meet the Z4.'

Sharpe gestured to a further inner door. Taylor approached it, edged it open.

'He doesn't bite. Good luck, see you at sea,' said Sharpe, shoving him in the back.

Taylor blinked his eyes to adjust to what at first seemed a dark empty room. A tall man rose from a desk, flicked a lamp on and came round to greet him. He took the form, glanced through it and put it down.

'Dreadful times Taylor. If there is a future, it lies with us. We are part of the Earth Survival Organisation, ESO. This was foreseen and planned for. It's come earlier than anticipated. We need clever practical survivors. People who can help rebuild; adapt to new circumstances. Is that you?'

'Yes,' Taylor said.

'You will be processed as a raw recruit. You will be on probation for a while, a labourer; Scale 'D'. It's not personal. Me? I was recruited some years back as an administrator. I was a Justice of the Peace up until a few weeks ago.'

He strode across the room and drew a canvas curtain flap aside allowing green light and sounds in. He nodded for Taylor to join him. The man turned to make space for him at the window. Now he could read the name tag; Livingstone. Down and adjacent, they looked out over the caged compound. Every now and again, a concerted chant rose up, a hooting football crowd chant, as the prisoners around the forward edge danced like lunatics and stabbed angry aggressive fingers in unison at their guards.

'Let us out! Let us out! Let us out you bastards!' they bawled over and over again until they tired and a new cheerleader could be found. The chant stopped. More subtle threats were probably being made to the soldiers, Taylor thought.

To the rear of the cage, he saw much quieter groups huddled, squatting together in horror and dismay at their circumstances. In between, a drunken mad woman with a shock of dyed blonde hair and one of her breasts almost hanging out screeched for no apparent reason. She upended a bottle of some amber liquid into her mouth.

He turned away to see Livingstone waiting for his reaction.

'Hieronymus Bosch's Hell or something, needs a few devils and flames for the full effect,' Taylor said. Livingstone gave him a measuring look.

'You're not the wild barbarian you appear. I'm not a man of God but we are seeing the other one, Satan, in these times. Looters and people who refuse to cooperate are locked in down there. I've probably put some of these men and women in prison. If not already, I would have done one day. Look at them. Somehow, some have managed to get drunk. What would you loot first, Taylor?'

'A boat with a sail, an outboard motor, camping gear... rations...'

'Not an off license then? Some of them had bags full of whisky, vodka; some had stolen music disks and DVDs.' The tall man did not wait for an answer.

'If you had to decide who reaches safety; who steps across the divide into the new world of the future, which of these would you take?'

Taylor was relieved, a rhetorical question. He assumed he referred to the people not the stolen goods.

'They are frightened, they don't know what will happen to them,' he said in some part defence he didn't really feel.

'I'm frightened Taylor. So are you. Shall we dance and hoot and roar together? Drink ourselves senseless at the end of the world?' He glared down at the cage people, giving Taylor a chance to study him in the light.

His shoulder bars each bore a single crown. A Major? A Major who now flung the curtain closed with contempt. Taylor watched him go through the application form. He added a few remarks then asked:

'Admin or Practical?'

'Practical.'

'Supervisory experience?'

'Yes.'

'Ex military?'

'Yes, Air Force. Weapons and stuff.'

'Any other skills?'

'Demolition, both military and civil. Carpentry. Single engine pilot. – hobby, not serious. Halfway through helicopter course, went solo. Got too expensive though.'

Livingstone turned to him. 'Hmmm, handy if there's anything left to fly. Then there's the weather. We can use you but not, I think, as an SP. I'll put you down for Logistics and Recovery, O.K?'

'Fine by me, Major.'

'Not Major. Z4. I am part of the organisation we call Zero Interference. Plant the seeds, let them grow but let no one dare tread on the seedlings. We are leaving here for now Taylor but one day we will come back. You may be one of the doves we send to find dry land.'

Taylor considered whether to ask the man if he saw himself as one of Noah's family but thought better of it. Something strange here, he thought. Who are these capable organised people? Where did they spring up from like some secret army?

Instead he queried, 'Z4?'

Livingstone smiled. 'At least we don't have to argue about how to say or spell "lieutenant". Yes, Z1 to Z6 are a bit like Army Officer ranks; Z7 to Z9, like NCOs. I'm top of the field officers at Z4 – those above are higher beings. Clever idea is you will rarely find a Z4 and 5 together; always two ranks apart, for that certain distance maybe. Does that answer your question? I doubt you'll be meeting Zs 1 to 3 any time soon.'

The sergeant came in with a print out for Livingstone. He brushed past Taylor as if he wasn't there, handed over the note and left in the same manner.

Livingstone looked up from the note and handed it to Taylor.

--Evacuation Convoy: Levington Dam; lost in mudslide.--
-Survivors:
-Brittain; Lesley. Lt Colonel. RE.
-Saunders; John (Jack). Corporal. RE.
-Samuels; Bernard. Civilian contractor, Demolutions Company. Assisting Civil Powers.

Ten names. He breathed a sigh of relief. Bernard! Jack! He didn't know the other names to feel happy for them. Looking down the list for his own name, he imagined the red-faced farmer, fist still waving as he was sucked down into the mud. He shook his head; saw himself.

-Missing.
-Taylor; Mark. Civilian contractor, Demolutions Company. RAF Reserve. Assisting Civil Powers. Did not accompany convoy. Thought to have headed home to find family. Presumed caught up

in refugee chaos. Assume lost for evacuation purposes.

Livingstone made notes, entered data into one of the ubiquitous rugged notebooks, signed the form and handed it back to him.

'Lucky man; desirable quality nowadays. Looks like you were destined to join us anyway. Good job you came by a different route. Have you any questions for me?'

'Who's in charge of all this? I get the idea you are some disaster team set up waiting for this but, where's the government? What plans are there for sixty million people? What's happening in the big cities?'

Livingstone said nothing for a few seconds, ordering his thoughts it seemed, then,

'Many were moved to higher ground over the last two weeks or so. Empty warehouses, shared housing enforcement... the government declared the state of emergency then went to ground. There were limited coastal flooding plans. When they failed, only thing left was the nuclear war contingency plan. They were acting on that.'

'Were acting...?

'No communications for thirty six hours now.'

'So those who don't make it to shelter...?'

'Quite, the food will run out fast, the means of distribution is breaking down already. There are riots in the cities, like Birmingham and the North. The motorways are blocked with cars, some with stranded families, some abandoned. No power, no fuel, no trains. Planes are grounded by weather; helicopters are hit by lightning. This lightning is indiscriminate, vicious, setting fires, blasting into crowds out in the open. An impossible mess; it's a disgrace.'

'And you people...?'

'As I said, this was foreseen, planned for. But with much more government involvement, which has dissolved. They allocated some military and police to us as they saw their grip slipping. Mainland Europe have embraced ESO, even the French who are notorious for being independent. We warned the governments we could save only so many.

We have food laid down and accommodation planned in Europe but not enough for all. Your arrival and proximity was fortuitous; for you. This is a disaster of biblical proportions, Taylor. Are you a man of God yourself?'

'Not at all; not for me. Let people believe what they want, I say.'

Livingstone looked at him again. Taylor couldn't work out if Livingstone couldn't make up his mind about him or maybe thought he'd seen him before.

'I saw a vicar, or maybe a priest, struck, burnt to a cinder by lightning a few days ago. Dark days. Dark days.'

He called through the door.

'Get him tidied up and processed. He'll end up in the cage looking like he is.'

He shook Taylor's hand.

'It will get worse before it gets better. Good luck with your seeds Mr Taylor.'

He turned away. Taylor was dismissed.

***

He would remember his induction as brief and hurried and sparing him no blushes. An anonymous group of attendants processed him. Not one looked him in the eye. As far as he could see, they didn't look at each other. He braced himself as his clothes were cut from him, grimaced as they shaved his head like a Marine and began to feel like a herd animal as he was thrust into a scalding shower unit. He saw antiseptic soap dispensers and started to soap himself, hopping painfully in and out of the water jets.

'Turn the wick down a bit for Christ's sake,' he yelled. It settled to a more bearable heat. A voice called, 'Wash everything twice, and I mean everything, Mr Taylor, or you go back round again, cold next time.'

Beyond the shower unit, a pile of clean clothing awaited him on a bare wooden table to one side with a green towel, a pair of black coveralls, socks and some army green underwear. He wrapped the towel around him. In the next compartment, he re-joined his torn clothes. An attendant emptied the pockets, gave the contents a cursory glance, decanted them into a re-sealable plastic bag and handed it to him. The man dumped his clothes into a rubbish bag but returned his outdoor jacket and boots.

Clutching his new life, he was pushed through into yet another medical tent where a scowling doctor took his temperature and blood pressure, made a rough guess at his height and weight, muttered, '185 – 90' and wrote it down. Taylor hoped it wasn't his blood pressure.

The medic peered with a torch into his eyes, ears and throat and made him bend over for a rough prostate examination that made Taylor frown in dismay.

'Think positive, if I'd found anything I didn't like up there, you'd be last in the queue for the boat,' he said.

Grabbing Taylor's upper left arm, he swabbed it with alcohol and injected him with a multiple inoculation gun. He thrust two pills and a paper water cup at him. For a second he was nearly human again as the man watched to make sure he swallowed them.

'Dysentery, cholera, typhoid. All that sewage afloat. We can't trust the water. Three quarters of those in the cage won't see the first month out. You must have ticked the right boxes. They didn't.'

He rattled an aerosol paint can. 'Hold out your left hand.'

The luminous green paint spray was freezing. The medic held his wrist, blew on the paint to help it dry and then marked a red cross across the back of his hand.

'Get dressed, you'll do.' The medic turned away, already losing interest in him.

In the next partition, he re-joined his paperwork. A hard faced woman in the same black uniform as Sharpe entered details into her computer. Her uniform was tailored to fit with the letters, ZI - SP, stencilled in blue on her right breast pocket, her embroidered nametag with CULSHAW, on the other side. All such small details argued preparation, readiness for this dire situation.

He watched her save his profile onto the USB memory stick she snatched from a box of dozens. She leaned close and attached it with a string loop round his neck.

'Electronic dog tags,' she said. Another for my collection, he thought.

Staying close, she wrote his name in marker pen on a bare patch on his left breast pocket. T-A-Y-L-O-R. She smelled of mothballs and canvas, her breath of coffee.

'Can you find my family on that thing?' he said, nodding towards her computer, desperation creeping into his voice. The woman paused, blew out through her nostrils.

'Give me their names then,' she said at last. He did so and she typed and clicked away.

He could not see the screen and she did not encourage him. Her eyebrows rose at whatever she found.

'They are at a holding area in Wales. They can't stay there long, they'll be shipped out on something ocean going to a pre-planned reception area, most likely Europe somewhere. They're fortunate. UK is madness. That's all I can say for now, they are safe.'

Taylor's eyes prickled as he blinked back tears. The woman touched his forearm in a gesture of sympathy.

'You're bleeding, here,' dabbing at his head with a tissue. Pausing, she wiped around his eyes. Taking an adhesive plaster from her belt pouch, she slapped it over his head wound. She smiled at him then hardened behind her professional shell again.

'This is you from now on, mate. You are now a member of ESO. The storm is getting worse, the icecaps are melting; all must pull together. Your personal ambitions aren't worth a shit. Lose the dog tag, try and disguise your hand colour and you could be shot for a looter. Worse, you could end up in a cage like that one out there. Z4 liked you – thinks you're good for 'C' or 'B'. Keep your head down and your mouth shut for now. Got it?'

He nodded his understanding. These people had a plan, obvious long laid down plans for the end of the world. He wasn't in any position to circumvent it. At least not for the time being.

***

Sharpe met him on the ground floor.

'Hungry?' he said and without waiting, led him to a canteen. A small cheer went up as they went in; a minor fan club following his brush with Collins.

'Hey, Collins! Your pal's here! Try a bit of friendly wrestling again,' shouted one.

At a stainless steel servery they helped themselves to some nameless stew and slices of home baked bread. Taylor spilt gravy on his green hand.

'Dare I lick it off?'

'Well I'm not,' said Sharpe. 'Come on, let's sit down. How's your prostate?'

'I can still feel it...'

He devoured the food. Wiping the stew off the paper plate with the bread, he sat, quivering, wondering if he could go round again. Sharpe nodded him to go ahead. Eating at a more measured pace he took more notice of his surroundings. Collins wouldn't meet his gaze and made a hasty exit. Sharpe got up.

'Wait here, Judo man,' and left the canteen. The other two from the patrol came over.

'You asked Sharpey about your friend. Sharpey didn't want you upset – you were wounded, in shock but...'

***

Taylor remembered well his time in the military. Part of NATO exercises. They always eventually stopped and everyone went home, in time for tea. The enemy was here now and they were on the run.

26

The water was well up over the door of 10 Downing Street. Home was disappearing fast. No negotiation, no surrender, just retreat.

Now, standing under a canvas shelter on the boat's rear deck, he watched the big hangar on the shore fade into the distance. Rain drummed on the tight canvas above him; hissed into the lake like machine gun fire. The black sky was overbearing; the clouds never short of reinforcements.

Under the feet of the sailors who rushed about below, he'd found his way up here. He took out the snatched photos he'd ripped from the frames the night before. Sally, on her own, when they'd first met. Taken by this very reservoir. The two kids; Andy and Rachel. They were older now but there they were laughing at some forgotten joke. He'd not had a minute to look at them. The future and how he would get them all back together was an impenetrable fog. First, he must assert himself in his new, unplanned for role in this new organisation.

Below him the shallow draught landing and assault craft's wake churned and bubbled in a brown frenzy; the craft that arrived as promised, at midday. Designed to work in shallow coastal waters, only the risen water levels allowed it inland. Smaller landing craft bearing the last soldiers and police bobbed up and down in their wake and took the brunt of the rain. It reminded him of film of the D Day landings.

He'd seen a few rubber boats and the last of the supplies left behind for the ones in the cage. There just wasn't room for all, let alone crazed drunks. He recognised some of the quieter caged ones on the deck below, segregated and watched by SPs. Sharpe said an electronic timer would release the gates of the cage back at the hangar in an hour or so. The cage folk still had a way out by land. Just. Going on the medic's few words, their problems would come as the diseases took hold and they tried to rebuild a rudimentary society after the supplies ran out. He doubted the discipline and leadership in those left behind.

We'll regret leaving them one day. The ones who survive this are going to be mean and hard. And they won't forget.

In spite of the humid warmth he was sick and shivery from the whole shock and suddenness of it all. Maybe the rudely applied inoculations weren't helping.

Sharpe joined him at the rail. He glanced at him and looked away. Sharpe knew his men told him about the old man. Shamefaced, they'd said they didn't think Collins should get away with it. Taylor resented Sharpe evading the question of George's fate.

'Look, I'm sorry about your friend,' said Sharpe. 'Collins is a bastard. He will be disciplined for it…'

'Yes, the lads told me. He's not popular it seems,' Taylor said in a distant way, looking back along their wake.

'We found Collins tied up in one of the stores tents. He was terrified. He wouldn't say who did it. Said someone jumped him from behind. He was gibbering; we called the medic to sedate him.'

Taylor shrugged.' I bet he wasn't popular with those wild boys in the cages. I bet he stung them with his toy gun a few times.'

Sharpe's eyes narrowed. 'Are you trying to tell me something?'

Taylor turned to look him full in the eye.

'Awful to be left behind with that rabble. Awful to think you'd miss the boat and be found by that angry mob, just after the timer locks freed them. Awful if there was reason to remember you with unpleasant associations; or so I would imagine.'

Sharpe held his gaze for a second or two then looked away. Taylor watched the play of emotions on the man's face. Sharpe had his answer in so many words. He could see Sharpe, the sergeant, torn between the duty of keeping discipline and Sharpe, the human's acceptance that rough justice may have taken place. He watched his decision process come to its conclusion; watched the man's shoulders slump in resignation as he started to walk away.

Over his shoulder, he left a parting remark.

'Collins is a sadist. I hope it's not catching, Taylor. Don't get a reputation for being…scary. You proved yourself at the entrance. Enough, OK?'

Taylor had only seen two dead bodies in his life. His parents, at different times and in different hospitals. He couldn't kill a man but maybe he could condemn one to death.

How do I feel? Would I feel guilty if they'd not found him in time?

He was numb, indifferent about Collins. Sorrow for old George. For now, he'd settled some of old George's score.

Chapter Three

Switzerland. Geneva. The storm is overhead.

Cartwright's rocking chair creaked under his weight on the timber floor. He looked out over the lake from the safety of the bay window of his sheltered eyrie. Dark clouds scudded low across the water like bombers, dumping their rain and obscuring the far shore. Lightning flashes and rumbles of thunder completed the effect. He was safe from them up here.

Here it comes, he thought. We have worked to prepare for this.

He heard the door open behind him.

'Only me, your darling Brigitte. What are you dwelling on, sat there watching the storm? I heard your chair creaking. Agitated creaking. I can read your mind when you sit in that silly old bamboo thing.'

'I was thinking. I like to think to the creak of bamboo. It was the first bamboo thing I ever made.'

Strong thumbs ground away at the tension in his neck and shoulders.

'So now I can't tell the difference between 'thinking creak' and 'agitated creak' after eight years together?'

'Oof, don't stop, that's just right.'

'Much quieter for me as well. That's enough, got things to do.'

'I was wondering if I am right, or just some arrogant son of a bitch who got lucky.'

'There would be no ESO without you – well there might, but a shadow version. You can see into the future where they are blind.'

'Some put it down to lucky guesswork if they credit me at all.'

'Guesswork! We spent three years looking at weather trends, the worst case effects of global warming. Depressed the hell out of me. Then five years planning for the worst. What did the government committees and scientists do? Argue back and forth but no plans. Don't you ever forget. Here, remember this?'

Cartwright looked down in his lap at the file she'd dropped there. His learned paper.

When the Storms come. Never mind what if; what do we do when?

'I suppose it attracted some critical acclaim.'

'Suppose? You'd never have met those others and be where you are now. I'm going to the Comms room. Shams Siddiqui and Mark Llewellyn are due to call. Satellite's almost in position. Don't go too far. Oh, and Benson's bringing his new girlfriend for dinner so put Mr Grumpy away for a few hours, OK?'

***

What's happening in the lowlands? he wondered. We've mobilised the teams. The ZI and the quiet government men.

His quiet government men who got the contingency plans into the chiefs of Police through the Masonic lodges; the quaint old-fashioned gentlemen's clubs in London for the military. Thanks to the Eton and Oxbridge brigade who put pressure on MI5 and MI6 to leave his men and women alone. Then the trade unions, he'd thought them a spent force.

They jumped for joy at the chance to lay false trails to confuse the security services. With all their help, his ESO was not investigated, hindered, broken up before it had chance to grow.

He tried to imagine what it must be like now over there. The panic and upheaval for the fleeing people. The sea pressing ever onward, driving them to high ground. An uncompromising enemy sweeping all before it.

He paused in his reverie; Lake Geneva swam back into focus. Just maybe they could save some lives, maybe help put the new world on some sort of recovery footing.

I feel like an underground train driver, hurtling, boring through a dark tunnel to the future with the rest of Europe as passengers behind me. I hope I'm right. I hope we are right, he corrected himself.

Our five year plan; almost ready; could have done with another year or so, thought Cartwright. Our Earth Survival Organisation; ESO. Now the flooding and the storms were here. Holland, Belgium, Denmark, Ireland and the East coast of England evacuated. Scotland nearly cut off from the mainland. Twenty metres sea rise was an optimistic forecast - nearly there already, no sign of it abating.

Too late to save the status quo. Time for a new beginning. The core decision makers were installed, safe in the high shelters; safe from the storm. Only time would tell.

He started at the shrilling noise behind him; turned to deal with the incoming satellite phone call.

Mr Grumpy? Bah!

Chapter Four

Leaving England, Taylor would remember it as a nightmare of heaving tossing seas. He was berthed on an ocean-going tug; part of a small fleet commandeered by ESO.

'Will we make it?' he asked one of the crew on the first day out at sea.

'Seen worse than this. Towed tankers off rocks in worse than this,' the man said.

'It's working back into land worries me, the whole of Europe is a lee shore battered by the Atlantic.'

The tug, the *Vaca Amarilla*, growled, heaved, shuddered, plunged and battered its way out into open ocean. The horizon was a swooping dark line of black lead with white spattering spray and spindrift. Taylor was more a creature of the land and air and, while not seasick, thought better of eating with the same gusto as the crew. He shared the ride with a platoon of SPs and some soldiers still in their combat uniforms but preparing to move over to ZI. Below decks, double bunks were crammed in like a warren. In the gaps remaining, hammocks swung through wild arcs. Many remained occupied, their occupants' heads buried in fear and seasickness under coarse blankets. The blankets were a strange weave, thought Taylor. Coarse on one side, smooth on the other. He asked another crewman.

'The Z people issued them. Amazing, warmer than a quilt, one said they were made from nettles. Probably taking the piss. Strange people. Like they weren't from this planet.'

They were to rendezvous out at sea with a cruise ship two days out into the Atlantic. Taylor went about in a dream, fingers of both hands crossed he might rendezvous with his family.

He summoned courage enough to visit the bridge, negotiating the never horizontal gangways and ladders. The Captain said,

'The eye of this new storm, we're calling it Noah Four, is out past Madeira. We'll have sea room and calm enough to get you on board,'

'How are you navigating? I mean with all this atmospheric disturbance and so on.'

'The European GPS system – EGNOS, plus some relays and beacons our mysterious friends, ESO, have seen fit to provide. Provided in such convenient time you'd think they'd known it was going to happen. We know where we are from our own gyros. Inshore the satellites work some of the time.'

'What then for this boat?'

'Back and forth until we've got a few more off. We can only take the disciplined. The mobs are going crazy, ransacking everything, stealing food, murdering anyone who looks like they work for government or dressed in black – like these Z boys. It's like a bad disaster movie. Hard to believe civilisation could crumble so fast. Fuel's going to be a problem soon. Once that's gone, well…'

***

The rendezvous. They hove close to the cruise ship's side loading door, open on the lee side away from the Atlantic swell and the wind. Exhilarating to jump across; even with a harness. One SP slipped. He was snatched up and whisked up and aboard without comment by either crew.

Taylor went up on deck with some idea of waving to the *Vaca*. It was a vague ghost, a shadow fading in the rain by the time he found his way to a vantage point.

He was allocated a bunk with three other men. One, Ben, a friendly young man, a horticulture student of medium height with a shock of brown hair, a mischievous grin and wide eyes giving him a constantly curious expression. The other two kept to themselves, hollow eyed with grief and their changed world, they left no positive impression on Taylor. He hardly recognised them from one exposure to the next.

As an ESO recruit he found himself apart from the mass of the passengers, the non actives who were herded and kept under strict control by particularly mean no-nonsense SPs. Any indiscipline or rowdiness was met by overwhelming force; the zap-zit sound of Tasers a familiar sound.

Sent to a stateroom for a briefing, he found the room packed with a mixture of races and types, men and women of all ages. Half wore grey green issue coveralls which Taylor now recognised as the same material as the blankets on the Vaca Amarilla. Warm in a cold breeze, cool in a warm room, they said.

To his surprise the briefing was conducted by his inducting Z4, Livingstone. He rapped on the microphone.

'Ladies and Gentlemen. Welcome to the *SS Muscovy*. You'll be anxious for news. Those with families evacuated by sea, we can be positive about their safety but not yet their whereabouts. Those who remained in England, I can give no such guarantee. I think we all know the state of anarchy developing. I am sorry but the time for reconciliation and repatriation is some way off and you must consider yourselves, we all must consider ourselves, servants of the recovery programme. There will be dire consequences for desertion. Not imposed by us, I might add. We have video of riots and anarchy for those who are considering going it alone.'

He paused for effect; went on.

'I will say no more other than we will feed, clothe and give you shelter; a life denied to many left behind in England and all across Europe. In return we require commitment, loyalty, hard work and possibly, exposure to danger.

Why are we at sea? Someone once said, " the safest place to hide from the sea is on top of it" '

Some wag said, 'Or under it!' to a murmur of nervous laughter.

'Submarines are in short supply I'm afraid, and the world's governments neglected to invest in undersea cities,' Livingstone said.

Thanks be, thought Taylor. The idea of either made him push his elbows out to ward off the imagined confinement. Livingstone seemed to have his audience on side. He continued.

'Where are we heading? Eventually Switzerland. Why? Switzerland is ESO HQ and because of the old UN and its high ground was considered safe as a launch platform from which to begin the recovery. The trainers, the resources, the stockpiled tools and equipment and naturally the genius of planning and preparation for this disaster; all lies there. This ship will sail as close to the South of France new shoreline as possible. You will be ferried ashore and up river to Lake Geneva by shallow draught boats and vehicles where practical.

Enough for now, there up on the screen you will see your names and the units you will be attached to. Z7 and Z8 personnel are detailed for each group. Mark my words about desertion. Wilful disobedience is not an option. Natural leadership and initiative will be rewarded. I leave you now. Expect a further briefing in a day or so's time. Do not listen to rumour. Do not spread rumour. The non-active passengers are off limits. Good day, ladies and gentlemen.'

***

Out in the corridor, Taylor was forced to move aside as a squad of four SPs tramp marched past. Either move or be moved, he thought. They seemed to have a purpose, a destination. He and Ben followed at a distance along the corridor to come to a heated debate. A large woman screeched and squalled; she stood guard over her man, a grey pallid creature on hands and knees. He was not well, the evidence lay before him on the decking. Two wide-eyed youngsters looked on. An official in normal clothes stood by. He wore a "Warden" armband upside down. He looked scared, out of his depth; would have avoided such confrontational responsibilities in his former life.

He whined, 'I told 'em. Clean it up or the kids don't eat. They ignored me. They came up here and he did it again.'

Taylor winced as the squad leader, a hard mean faced thug, kicked the kneeling man.

'Clean it up, or your family don't eat.'

The wife beat her fists on the squad leader's chest. 'He's ill you bas...' but two troopers restrained her, forcing her arms behind her back until she stood on tiptoe. She hissed and spat at them.

'Clean it up, or your family don't eat,' repeated the squad leader.

Before Taylor could stop him, Ben stepped forward.

'Leave them, I'll clean it up. The man's not well, anyone can see that. Let them eat. What difference does it make?'

'Rules,' the squad leader said.

'Fuck the rules, you want it cleaned up, I'll do it. You deaf?' said Ben.

Two SPs made to grab Ben.

Taylor moved. One trooper went down on his knees clutching his middle, winded. Taylor gripped the other in a stranglehold. He held the SP before him. The trooper writhed and struggled but could not break free without hurting himself. Taylor could feel the man's anger, his helpless fear; smelled his greasy warmth. They could not bring a Taser to bear. Ben, shouldered aside, looked on in shock.

Taylor, coming out of his instinctive mode, was conscious again of the heaving deck, the condensation streamed windows, the blatter of wind driven rain outside. The rest of the tableau was frozen, rooted to the spot. Three – Two – One. The group started to move, breathe, and look around again.

'Three seconds. Half your men down. Imagine ten seconds worth,' Taylor said. They stood, Tasers drawn, looking for an opening. They'd let the woman go; she was as stunned as anyone at the speed of the action.

An impasse. An impasse broken by the winded trooper throwing up on the deck.

'We'll clean it up,' Taylor told the leader.

A voice came from behind him. Livingstone's. Two junior ZI peered over his shoulder.

'OK, let's break this up. You men are dismissed. I saw everything. I'll not have bullying. Squad leader, report to the admin centre in fifteen minutes. You two recruits, ah, Mr Taylor, I see. I believe you needed cleaning materials? Warden, I want a report. How civilians can go off limits and why there are no channels of communication - with this family named as an example. Get this man to sickbay. Tell your colleagues this policy ends now. Tell them to draw up a roster of shifts for clean up jobs like this. No clean, no eat maybe. Any trouble, see me. Madam, back to your quarters please once you have your husband treated.'

Taylor and Ben moved away.

'Watch and learn, Ben. Natural authority. No guns, no kicking,'

Livingstone turned, called to Taylor's back. 'Thank you but remember, noble deeds can make enemies. Keep out of the way. Tell me and I'll deal with it in future. Understand?'

Taylor nodded. Jesus, he thought. I'm a trouble magnet.

'What happened then?' Ben eventually said as they returned with mop, bucket, cloths and disinfectant..

'Don't worry about it, I'll scrape, you swish and mop.'

***

Two days on a heaving swell found them in the Mediterranean. Livingstone ran a busy schedule for his new people. Lectures on future intentions. Film footage on the fast assembly and construction of bamboo dwellings. Hints at the new low tech science. Agriculture; fast early crops. Crops which grew quickly enough to eat within a season. Economics of how much seed and fodder to save. Winter crops. Seaweed and algae which thrived in sea or salty water.

Introductions only, a taster for further training. A chance to find out people's strengths and interests. Taylor soaked it up. He was already interested from before. He despised the bandwagon greens and champagne socialists – "couldn't knock a nail in, useless lot,' he said to Ben more than once.

Ben was surprised to hear Taylor knew of companion planting, crop rotation, nitrogen fixing plants to nourish the soil and other horticultural matters.

'My wife has an allotment. Must have rubbed off on me. I built the shed and put water barrels at the side fed off the roof. Used to inflate the wheelbarrow tyre, sort of thing,' he explained in his gruff manner. In return, Ben told him;

'I worked at Kew – I could have done farming but poly-tunnels and greenhouses held more appeal than wet muddy fields. Farmers are just businessmen with dirty hands. I wanted to do sustainability. Darwin caught my imagination…'

Groups formed into natural alliances in a short space of time. For Taylor and Ben, a tiny but perfectly proportioned woman, Marie, gravitated to them. She said she was training, "reading biochemistry" were her words, and "would have gone on to PhD but for all this." Sparks flew straight away. She was opinionated and Ben, maybe a bit jealous of her education, would only give so much ground. Taylor remembered children's birthday parties. Wary child strangers would circle each other, wide eyed and at the same time, pretending not to see each other. Then, something in common, a toy, a game, gave them opportunity to cooperate. He called them his "kids" from then on.

Marie stopped him on the way out at the end of one lecture. She held him with a small hand on his forearm. Firm, strong, insistent. He could break away but not without undue effort. He looked down at her. A black sensible bob of hair, it moved in an appealing way, quickly dashed out of wide brown eyes and away from flat, almost oriental cheekbones. Small in stature but by no means helpless. A determined clever young lady, he thought.

'My father says I should stick with you. He says you were born to this world of strife and rebuilding. Whether you realise it or not, you will survive and adapt.'

Taylor grinned.

'I have a fan club of precisely one. And who is this discerning father?'

'I'm Marie Livingstone.'

Taylor blinked. He wasn't good with names without faces. She looked at him askance; surely the name was supposed to mean something to me? he wondered, then felt foolish as it dawned on him.

'Ah! Sorry, er, that Livingstone, the ZI leader!'

As if he knew any others bar the man Stanley went to find.

She blushed. 'And your fan club…is more than one. There's Ben, for a start. And me of course.'

***

The Muscovy anchored off the shore north east of Monaco. The actives were ferried ashore to make the journey to Geneva.

The Actives. They had taken the reference as obvious. Handy, motivated, organised, on-the-spot people. But who were the non-actives? Where did their role become a part of it all?

Livingstone said, in one of his briefings just before they came to a halt,

'All will become active but we must start somewhere. Someone

36

must lead; most must follow. Most must know what they follow and why. Here is an organisational chart.'

Up on the large wall screen shone a box hierarchy diagram.

-ESO-
Alphas
'A' Committee – Policy. 'Z' Committee – Admin.
'A' departments – Manufacture – Science and Technology – Agriculture - Food – Energy – Housing – Transport - Planning etc.
Actives
B [management grades 1-7] allocated to A depts.
C [technical grades 1-3] allocated - as required
D – semi skilled - " "
Non actives
E - yet unclassified
ZI - Admin, policy implementation & enforcement, discipline and defence policy.
S.P. - ZI Implementation

'As I said, all will become active eventually, as much as we were before. Some will fall through the net; some will climb high. For now, non-actives we control, via food and shelter, will become a pool of manpower, and I don't want to hear the word 'slave' mentioned.'

Livingstone looked around the room to see his audience jerk at being pulled back from what they had just been thinking.

'Alphas?' someone said.

'The deep thinkers, long term strategists, the people who foresaw and planned for all this,' Livingstone said.

Taylor kept quiet but he couldn't help thinking of the non-actives who were not under ESO control; the unfortunates, the unlucky, the witless, the criminals, the drunks left behind in timed release cages, the hidden dangerous unseen part of the iceberg.

***

For Taylor, no stranger to foreign travel, the transfer inland passed without undue consequence. After first views of the changed landscape he was indifferent to the changes all around and sat, either reading anything to hand, or dozing; frowsting with arms tightly folded. Reports of what went on beyond the various transports were met with grunts and barely raised eyebrows. Eventually, Ben and Marie gave up and spoke of more general things and the future whereupon Taylor sparked alive again.

'He's trapped in the convoy – he calls it the tunnel,' Ben told her. 'He can't walk on the outside, he said. What do you think he means?'

She raised an eyebrow. 'He must be either a claustrophobe or a control freak.'

'Both, I imagine. He seems to withdraw, hibernate. But he comes alive quick enough.'

Marie looked thoughtful. 'Talking of quick enough, has he told you of that martial art thing? I can't get anything out of him. He calls it Foo Yung or Chow Mein. Faugh! As if I'd never seen a Chinese menu.'

Ben scratched his itchy half grown beard. It would have to come off, his facial hair ginger as against his mousy hair. Marie said so.

'Only thing he said was "DTM, Displaced Timor Mortis" and "Neuro Holistic Programming" but he wouldn't expand on it.'

**

Livingstone sat there in his tiny cramped cabin. They were on a river leading up to Lake Geneva, or Leman, as he called it. Taylor sat, wedged in the doorway, leaning in for the interview. He kept one eye on the Z4, who liked to crouch in dark corners, and the other outside to the river. He was free again, untrammelled, squashed in cabins and trucks a fading nightmare memory. Still, he felt ill at ease, tense, wary; not in control.

Behind them a line of large wicker-woven boats followed in line. Taylor's imagination played with the scene. He imagined them sprouting billowing sails, jolly jack tars leaping through the rigging. A convoy of wooden fighting ships; gun-smoke wafting across the water. It was mist. He quenched the vision, turned to pay Livingstone attention.

'Kettuvalam. These boats are from India. Don't tell me they were sailed here.'

'No, they were built in Switzerland. Ostensibly for tourism. No one asked why so many… Taylor, I'm promoting you C3. This means you have acting leadership. If nothing goes wrong you will be C2, authority over all Dees, and once you have a mission, C1. What do you say?'

'Thanks would be gracious for a start.'

Livingstone smiled.

'This martial art thing. Sharpe and the others want you to train them and want you in the SP. I said I doubted you'd oblige; that you wouldn't fit in with their corps. Am I right?'

'Too right. Sharpe's a good guy. Some of his lads as well I suppose, but SP's a nest of psychos otherwise…'

'Hmmm. Tell me about your thing. I heard reports but I'd like to hear your version.'

'I was living in Germany. I was drinking too much, getting unfit. Everyone did then. I went to a Ju Jitsu class taken by one of the Germans we worked with. He said, "if I was a gun, I couldn't hit the box I was kept in". All the sayings are the same really. Suppose he meant "I couldn't hit a barn door". Anyway he said there were "other ways" I might benefit from. Said he needed someone to pass on the tricks when he was gone.'

Taylor sat, thoughtful, gazing off across the years. He caught himself, returned to the present.

'I was doing quite well, I could put myself into a sort of instant trance state where everything around seemed to stand still. A great advantage if someone is attacking you. They appear in slow motion; I could almost take their wallet as they went past. You might hear me one day saying "Three-Two-One" or, "Drei, Zwei, Eins" if I'm in a group standing still – if I'm squashed in, like on a standing only train. He taught me that in case I just stopped one day – how to get out of it. Weird.'

***

He paused again. Livingstone watched as Taylor's eyes glazed and peered off into the middle distance. Livingstone began to feel uncomfortable. He'd heard what could happen. He coughed, rapped on the bamboo wall of the cabin. A flash of inspiration came.

'Three Two One,' he said.

Taylor laughed. 'Just testing eh? No, I was sent on a five week trip to Cyprus. I was to move to the next phase when I got back.'

He sighed. 'When I got back he was dead; cancer. He never said; it never showed.'

Was it grief, nostalgia, times gone by? thought Livingstone, watching Taylor wrestle with the past. Was he trying to push it, and all associated memories, away?

Taylor continued.

' I can't teach Sharpey and co. I don't know how. That was next. The "how". I've been claustrophobic ever since. Excuse me, can we continue this later?'

Livingstone nodded, watched as Taylor unfolded himself and

moved away along the deck.

**

It took several days to reach their destination during which Taylor plunged deeper and deeper into a dark depression. He avoided everybody when he could; when he had to be with people he responded in short grunts and rarely opened a conversation. He had started to wish he had gone his own way, braved the storm and the chaos on his own. Better to be fighting for his life, foraging for food and living like a hermit than be stuck here, institutionalised. He couldn't rationalise but, deep down, he realised he would come out of it. One day soon the despair would lift, he would no longer doubt his own competence and abilities; like a new dawn rising, banishing the darkness.

And it did; he awoke to greet a new day. The first day of the rest of his life, as they used to say.

**

Geneva was calmer than they expected. Many of the trees were gone, used for firewood in the crisis when the power went off. Taylor, Marie and Ben didn't stay long, but long enough to see the bamboo construction going up; here and there an opaque membrane was being spread, when the wind allowed, over a latticework roof covering the older part of the city. The temperature was climbing daily; climbing far more than the usual Spring to Summer transition.

They found themselves out of town, up high in a mountain bunker complex, built in the nuclear threat, Cold War, days. The Academy; Ararat Academy. Lectures; back to school.

**

A blur for Taylor; a blur made up of: Building, fabrication, agriculture, husbandry, processing of algae; new, high tech and low-tech ideas; mere speculation in the scientific journals a year before. They were issued their personal computer sleeves with their wi-link to the nearest hub. *Wrists* they called them.

**

The Academy, more practical than academic. An introductory brief

40

started a topic and then the students were dispatched to workshops and outdoors to train and practise the skills they would need. Taylor and company and most students there would forever refer to it as "The Ararat Phase" or "back at Ararat"; qualified by descriptions such as "the basketwork lessons".

Taylor struggled with stiff sore fingers to emulate a basketwork pannier. He gazed forlorn at his cramped curled hands, his basket a shapeless parody of the neat example sat before him.

'I've been knocking bits of wood and metal together for years. Look at me! Hands like an arthritic old man.'

The instructor, at one time Taylor would have called him a hippy, laughed. 'Here, rub this oil in at night. Before you do, immerse your hands in cold water, then hot, then cold again. Make sure they are dry. Exercise your hands on a less harsh medium like this.' He handed him a ball of plasticized dark stuff.

'Looks like bread dough,' said Taylor.

'It is,' said the instructor.

Ben and Marie, with younger more supple fingers, laughed at him. His revenge came with their turn to measure, cut, saw and bind their scaled down bamboo practise structures. Ben nearly sawed off fingers several times. Marie hissed in frustration trying, with a wooden mallet, to drive a glued wooden dowel into a hole. Taylor grinned, took the tool from her and demonstrated.

'The idea, my dear, is to hit the dowel, think of it as a nail, squarely and in the direction you want it to go, so... Let's see you - No! Here, watch. It's the mallet which does the work, so, not your arm and hand. The eye guides the arm, the hand; then the mallet drives in the dowel. Shit! Look at the bruises on your hand! Go and see Gizmo the hippy...'

'It's not Gizmo, Taylor. It's Guillaume...'

Marie turned the tables on the men when it came to teasing out the nettle fibres. Her small deft fingers spun them into a crude but near version of the thin diaphanous cloth; the accolade of a centuries old skill – not needed in these early days but to show what could be done.

'Look at this she showed me.' She nodded and smiled to the wizened old Nepalese woman over her shoulder. Marie threaded a large shawl through Taylor's wedding ring. The material slipped through unobstructed, like a snake.

'Spooky,' Ben said. Taylor held it up, spread wide between his outstretched hands.

'No insect can get through it, Ben, but you can see through it. It breathes, allows air to pass, amazing.'

41

The old lady came over with a woven bag; produced a wide mesh net. She held it up to the light.

'Look!'

Taylor had to pull back to focus. Spread out he could barely see it.

'Fish cannot see!' she chuckled through brown gapped teeth. She bunched it together, rolled it, gave one end to Ben and tugged.

'Pull, strong man!'

But it was Ben who was pulled, nearly losing his balance as she dug her heels in.

Taylor smiled at Ben's dismay and embarrassment. Scratching his chin, he said,

'I remember from old...never mind...but it's typical of the old East. Tiny old lady, applying strength where it's needed, no wasted energy, no grunt...wonder where we lost it?'

***

Then it came to more, for Marie and Ben, exciting modern technological developments; for Taylor, developments which left him uneasy. The Siddiqui Bee; "the Bee phase". A larger creature than the typical familiar honeybee, this bee resembled the bigger humble bee, but brown rather than black and yellow striped. It carried an electronic chip and a nano-camera.

The lecturer, a morose pale man barely looked at his students as he went through his introduction.

'Bees have found their way home, transmitting their findings and delivering their cargo for millions of years. Their dance, their way of transmitting the whereabouts of good foraging, is relatively recent knowledge. Siddiqui questioned how this could be turned to our advantage. His reasoning, that they served us unknowingly already; that we might rely on their searching instinct, their homing ability and their use of pheromone and signalling to communicate. This creature, ladies and gentlemen, can seek out arable ground, return and tell us where best we can concentrate our efforts.'

At last he looked up to assess their reaction.

'Arable ground and the nature of plant life on that particular ground. The chip can store the geo coordinates, the camera, visual evidence. Crops in unsafe or – er, unhealthy locations can be monitored remotely.'

'Why not use solar powered cameras with wireless capability? Taylor said.

'Maintenance, for one. What if the wild people object to their

42

presence for another. Nobody sees bees as hostile and, as I mentioned, cameras don't bring back evidence of pollen and soil type.

'Hmm, OK,' Taylor admitted but grudgingly enough to prompt Marie, Ben and a few others to give him questioning glances. They wondered if his dark mood had returned.

The lecturer, oblivious, went on.

'We use the hive principle, they carry on as normal. Return to the hive usually means the bee is checked by the soldier guards – a security checkpoint. Maybe early interrogation took place at that point before – we don't know. Now, we do. The information stored on the chip is downloaded at the hive entrance. Here…'

He opened a screen and they followed a bee's eye video clip of its return home to the hive entrance.

'How do you control the bee – give it its outward mission?' someone asked.

'A pheromone baited programming station. More of that later. This is more by way of introduction – more specific training will be given to those who are down for Dome based lab work. Those who are less likely to brave the outdoors – there are those who cannot tolerate the increased ultra violet we are experiencing, for example.

'Will the SPs have access to the bees' control?' Taylor said.

'That I cannot say but there are obvious applications, I imagine.'

Taylor was fully aware of remote surveillance camera applications, transported by whichever means, including bees.

***

Afterwards, alone with the kids, he shuddered.

'Big Bee Brother' he said and; 'Needs must when the Devil drives,' which they thought mysterious when he wouldn't expand further.

'Why not birds?' said Marie.

'Birds are stupid,' said Ben.

'And bees are clever then?' Sarcastic now.

'As long as the bees do as they are told. I hope they don't mutate and turn against us,' Taylor said. 'Now shut up the pair of you and help me with this slurry.' They were now starting "the Tube phase".

***

The slurry, the porridge like mixture that made the lightweight but strong papier-maché for the algae tubes. The means of production in

43

quantity was gone ahead to England and other parts. How to start afresh, to get the mix right and to repair the existing floating tubes was knowledge to be spread among the population; should the need arise to start again one day.

The tubes. They began to take on a life of their own, ESO people, were now servants, acolytes to these floating farm tubes. The lectures, both academic and practical, dwelled on them to an exhaustive degree.

'It's just a floating poly-tunnel for Christ's sake,' grumbled Taylor.

They stood by a full sized but cut away model. The instructor, by way of introducing himself, walked through the tube with only a slight crouch. He had a table of things to show them. Ingredients for manufacture, possible crops which would thrive within.

'The tube, papier maché – not a new idea but with some new science attached. A tube is a very strong shape – it applies the concept of the arch in all directions except along its length, where it may even be stronger.'

The instructor sifted his fingers through a grey powder in a bowl, invited them to feel the texture.

'Is this explosive in powder form like this?' Taylor said.

'Oh yes, very much so. Why do you ask?'

'I remember the flour and other powders in lorries, tankers. They were escorted and the fire services warned. If they had an accident, spilled the load, it could go up with a big bang.'

'Yes. I've never mentioned it before but you have a point, thank you. Now, the finished tube will allow some water in from the sea where we are going to float them. Once the fabric swells then the tube is sealed, water-tight. We can pour in a nutrient and sow the algae culture within The uppermost surface will establish itself naturally with the weight of water, algae and external seaweed holding the tube down in one more or less fixed orientation, which, by the way, will attract seaweed, which we will be farming for nutrient also.

So, to our uppermost surface. It will fry and be bleached white by the sun, thus reflecting away the hazardous sun energy while allowing enough light through for photosynthesis...'

Marie and Ben were impressed; Taylor not.

'Never mind the science, these things are going to be complete sods to manage. Once wet, up and running, they will weigh tonnes. Surely this handy "bleaching" hot surface and cooler, below sea bit interface will become fragile and crack ... if they don't sink that is.'

'A Doubting Thomas in our midst I hear,' said the instructor. 'Wait until you hear about the magic, the secret ingredient, before you judge.'

'What magic? What secret? How does it work?' grumbled Taylor, louder for all to hear.

'Er, well. It's a secret for now. Ha! How it works is magical, suffice to say the fabric lives, breathes and, to some extent, will repair itself.'

'Ah!' said Taylor. 'Now you're talking.'

'There are other uses Taylor. You may actually be living in one. Not on the sea of course but so.'

' Why not make a boat out of one? Use it to move the others about?'

'Good to see you're with me now. Do me a sketch, we'll discuss it.'

***

For Taylor, and many, one fascinating lecture – hydrogen – delivered by an Icelander with a twinkle in his eye.

'People, people, you know this from school, all of it. If you listened that is.'

He winked. 'Hydrogen – H - combines with oxygen to make water, a particularly useful commodity we take for granted. H stores itself under ground in oil and coal. H hides itself in foodstuffs – carbohydrates. It's everywhere around us in some form or another but it's a sneaky and potentially destructive devil! Hydrogen bombs! Hey! Wow! But we can use it.'

Taylor and his colleagues instantly warmed to this man in direct contrast to the sinister bee technician.

'In Iceland we are lucky to be able to exploit the geysers – the volcanic nature of the land. We have being using hydrogen fuel for many years. We have the free geo thermal energy to exploit it and a small enough country to make the logistics of transporting it feasible. Even now, here in Switzerland, holes are being bored to reach the hotter parts below. Enough of that but the key to hydrogen, brackets, successful exploitation, close brackets, is energy. In the oil driven world it was uneconomic. We needed electricity to make hydrogen; electricity provided by coal, gas and oil. We were making, I like to joke, water as if it were dehydrated – just add water, ha ha…blank stares eh? Need to work on that one… but, there it is again, hiding in the word "hydrated". Like water it needs to be contained, channelled, stored, dispensed, administered and, as I say, it is a tricky devil. Any idea why?'

A hand went up. Marie.

'Yes madam?'

'It is the lightest element, it will escape to atmosphere.'

'Precisely. The screw threads to join the pipes need to be engineered to fine, and therefore expensive, tolerances. The bill goes up already. Anything else?'

'You need to freeze it, compress it down into a liquid and keep it so. The compression takes away a high percentage of its energy value,' said another woman.

'Ah! Easy day for me! Yes, thirty percent or more. I am surrounded by people who listened at school! Ho ho! Exactly, you are with me, if not ahead . Now hydrogen, when it is not busy attaching itself like molecular glue to everything around it, is busy with escape plans – it likes to seek outer space. Perhaps it feels it belongs there – a busy cosmic entity indeed. In fact it fuels the suns. Which begs the question, what?'

'Are we going to run out some time?' Taylor said.

'Not in the immediate future, sir. I have come to have a strong belief, regardless of religious beliefs, that Earth is very well administered and run. By Gaia, the Earth Goddess, some like to say.

Our recent tribulations? A mere bad cold which is stabilising and getting better, with geography and climate changed somewhat. Now, some, don't groan, arithmetic…'

He went on to show how much hydrogen was needed to lift a certain weight. A lot. What about helium? Is hydrogen not dangerously explosive? Flammable? were questions.

'Flammable? Yes, but not dangerously so. You may be thinking of the airship disasters. It appeared it was the fabric paint that caused the huge flames. In fact the upward flare slowed the descent enough to allow survivors on one occasion.

Helium was mainly brought in from USA – again at huge energy cost – and, it has only ninety percent of the lift capacity of hydrogen.

Here on our screen is one of our new ESO zeppelins – a beauty and quite big, yes? It will carry cargo and twenty or more people or combinations of either to a specific load. It must bear its own weight and heavy engines and fuel. Still, a mighty workhorse. So, with such limitations what do you suggest we do to use hydrogen to carry more load?'

They sat and pondered, looked around at each other. The number of bewildered shrugs reached a point where the lecturer prepared to continue, then;

'Tow non-directional balloons behind the main one – no fuel, no crew, no engines; to lift an increased load maybe?'

'Oh sir, I am indeed in the midst of genius today. I must write down your name so I can conspire against you, vilify and betray you, if only to keep my own job.'

'Keep your job.' Taylor laughed. 'I need no enemies.'

The Icelander smiled.

'Anyone else want to relieve me of my employment today?'

Ben put up a nervous finger.

'Aha! Careful Taylor, we will both be unseated from our thrones in turn. Yes, young man?'

Ben coughed and stumbled a little.

'Well, the Zepps are made from contemporary materials, bamboo and fabric, yes? Why not build them up from, or surround the cargo they would carry? Make the load a temporary zeppelin. Dismantle them at the other end?'

The lecturer gaped in mock shock.

'My work is truly done. I must do the honourable thing and resign; retire. Hand over to the quick thinking newcomers. I am a Neanderthal who must step aside for the new Sapiens. But! Not before I lead you down the warrens of Ararat to Workshop Eight. There, after weeks of prayer, I have assembled the demon gas, donated by Gaia herself. There, you must humble yourselves in the task of containing it and directing it to your needs. On! To Workshop Eight!'

'Are you sure you're from Iceland?' Taylor asked him in the bottleneck at the door.

'Yes, but you refer to my style of English? An expensive education in one of your, sadly drowned, universities helped though.'

***

There were numerous other topics: building with bamboo, ancient ideas sadly neglected in modern times, cunning adaptations to the harsh environments of the planet; a beetle from Namibia which would perch on a sand dune, gathering and condensing water vapour from the hot desert breeze which would be directed by its fluted wing cases directly to its mouth parts. Taylor and company would come to see this and more in action in the eco domes of England.

***

A bright note, he could choose his team. He asked Marie and Ben if they would like to "stick around for the ride". Ben said he'd put it under consideration. He couldn't carry it off. Besides, Marie had a nasty mean vicious pinch.

An even brighter note, to cap it all, one day, the three of them were going to a workshop when a bright smiling face, still free of cynicism, halted them.

'You made it then. I've been waiting for you,' Taylor said.

'Did you find them?' said Jack.

***

His family, according to the admin office, were last known on a certain *SS Klondike*, a similar ship to the *Muscovy*. Safe and well as far as they could tell...

More alarming news out in the wider world; the Americans and Russians had drawn lines across the maps. In their mutual distrust, the Cold War was resumed.

'God knows what resources they are squandering on their militaries instead of recovery,' said Marie. Taylor was philosophical. 'History repeats itself; it was ever the case.'

He was less philosophical when he found that the *Muscovy* and the *Klondike* had anchored on different sides of the divide.

***

Seeking Sal and the kids' final destination, he discovered their ship, thirty six hours before his, was driven south and east before the storm – beyond the boot of Italy. His aggravations with the admin people reached a head when one impatient woman told him,

'Look Taylor, you jumped ship back in UK. You made your way on your own. You went to get them against all advice. They probably think you are dead. I have it here. She spun her screen, showed him a familiar message –

- Levington dam – mudslide. Missing: Taylor: Mark...presumed gone to seek family. Assume lost for evacuation. -'

She sighed. 'Taylor, Taylor, you're not the only one. There're colleagues whose families didn't get out of England. We are working on it but it's a never-ending mammoth task and, I hate to say, it's not a priority. We will let people...we will let you know...'

***

The mental and physical exhaustion from the time-compressed instruction was a relief to Taylor. He would lie down, dreading the lonely night, in his narrow cot in the windowless bunker room but he was usually asleep before he could consider the oppressive weight of mountain above him.

Dreams, nightmares of gruelling horrors for Sal, Rachel and Andy would bring him awake, soaked through. He applied a reverse of the mantra, *One- Two- Three*, and usually managed to regain sleep, only to dream another variation of some terrible situation they found themselves in.

***

Taylor and company completed their training. He knew many new things but the source of the information was distant, like a fading dream. In a similar way to driving on a straight road, then coming to a place with none of the last ten miles registered, he got the impression he woke up one day, bound for England on a northbound Zeppelin airship loaded with supplies for the base camp there. The storms were over, the sea levels stabilised. It was time to kick start the recovery.

Looking back from the zepp gondola, Ararat became indistinct; the mountains took up only half the view, then a quarter. Three unmanned cargo zepps strung out on long lines behind them. He pondered.

It's getting a habit; to leave a stronghold, a fortress, and head into the unknown. At least last time, back at the reservoir, I was going in the right direction.

A memory of the cage people, with their aggressive chant, came to him;

"Let us out, let us out, let us out you…'

He jumped. Jack stood behind him apace.

'Hey, Taylor. We'll help you find them, man. We need to get ourselves an army together first. Takes a bit of time, that's all.'

***

On the journey north there was little to do except peer down, clouds permitting, at the watery landscape. France appeared to be little changed further south but, at night, there were fires burning here and there out of control.

'Civil war in places,' said the helmsman. 'I wouldn't want to lose gas here,' and for luck, touched various wooden parts, including his own head, with a smile and a wink.

'Between who?' said Ben.

'The industrials and the agriculturalists we think, for food first,

49

maybe political control second. There are many refugees, from southern England, Belgium, Holland, Denmark. The Swedish were taken in by the Norwegians but neither had such huge populations.'

'What about Germany?' Taylor said.

'Eastern bloc mainly. We keep away, they've fired missiles and we see the odd aircraft below. There are no radio signals; or stations who respond, at least.'

They sailed on past Paris at dawn, the Eiffel Tower the main landmark, then the water, the sea, began. An hour north of Paris Taylor wondered where the English Channel began.

'We're over it now,' said the Zepp Master.

'Where are the White Cliffs?'

'Exactly,' came the reply and all fell silent. Below the sea sparkled its reflections through banks of mist and mottled patches of sunlight.

'There, ahead, the Kent Dome; Dome One, the first foothold of the recovery. We will drop in there to unload and load. You new people will be carrying on to the South Midlands, to Dome Three, by the new seaside.'

'South Midlands?' said someone.

'When east is driven too far west by the sea...' said the Master. No more need be said.

A little later Taylor asked quietly.

'And further north?'

'You will be briefed but...' The Master considered for a few seconds.

'The industrial areas were badly affected, food riots and so on. The ZI have not fully established diplomatic contact yet.'

'Diplomatic?...it's England for Christ...'

'It *was* England. See those buildings peeping out of the water? London.'

All were left to their own thoughts as they slid past the drowned capital.

Taylor pondered his circumstances. Where would he be now but for Sharpe? Or Livingstone? He seemed to have been saved for a purpose. He was competent at what he did or, at least, he tried his hardest. He'd given up on responsibility, corporate striving and such long ago. The new organisation here seemed to endow him with qualities he wasn't even sure he possessed; would even like in another man. How long would he last on his own resources and cunning? Down there in the madness of France or the industrial Midlands? If he chased off to the east in his quest to find Sal and the kids, how far would he get? Not far, he decided. These ESO people, his new friends,

Marie, Ben, seemed to like him and defer to his experience but he needed them too; just as much. It made him feel good, warm inside. Hope I don't screw it up, he thought to himself.

Part Two

England. The Tubes.

Chapter One

Taylor was back in England. Back more than three years now, one of the early doves sent to find dry land. He still thought of Z4 Livingstone in those terms. Now with friends - he was motivated, alive - the recovery was underway. Apart from a few awkward brushes with the autocratic and the often thuggish SP, his enduring sadness was the separation from his family. He would find them one day but for now, the luxury of chasing off on personal quests was denied him. His reward? Co-custodianship of the recovering parts of England.

He treasured a letter sent to him two years back.

We're safe and well- if you're alive, we wish we could be with you- we are behind the resurrected Iron Curtain. Don't try and find us – they shoot people from the West...I will try...

The rest was censored with savage black lines.

He heard no more and letters he sent were returned undelivered; unanswered. The ZI admin people reminded him that thousands of refugees wanted to go home; assured him that negotiations were under way but, as usual, the recovery was paramount. Taylor put his sadness and fury aside and got on with things.

***

He remembered standing on the new shore looking out to sea as the first tubes were floated out.

'We haven't enough boats and people to expand this; push it out, make it practically viable, Taylor,' said Wallis, a new colleague at the time. 'These big Zepps are so ponderous and wind prone.'

'We'd be OK if we had helicopters.'

'Most were lost in the evacuation. Where the f... are we gonna get a helicopter, you idiot?' Wallis said.

***

He now hung in the air in a flimsy heli machine of their own local design; Heli-1, their helizep.

Its beauty lay only in its functionality. He'd gathered many of its smaller parts at great risk, scavenging inland from old abandoned cars and private aircraft piled up rusting here and there. No SP help, he missed Sharpe; he would have helped but had been sent North. Sent

North armed with real bullets.

He harboured some resentment for the SPs' indifference; along with memories of some bloodcurdling escapes from savage Scallies.

Heli-1 crabbed along and needed a deft hand on windy days. Thanks to his own persistence, and what he'd learned from an electronic book by a man who knew about bamboo frameworks; a man called Cartwright, he'd built a strong lightweight four seat, five at a squeeze, structure. With similar remote help from a man in Geneva called Benson, a genius of composite materials, lightweight engines and hydrogen lift, Taylor now flew a functional workhorse machine, the helizep, the airborne tractor of the bio tubes.

They'd thought him crazy, but nice crazy and left him to it. They'd stared slack jawed on the day he flew over their heads and landed, first on the sea, on its floats, then to hover and then back to shore for their inspection. 'Where do we get a helicopter, Wallis?' he couldn't resist saying.

***

Taylor and his crew, Jack, Marie and Ben, flew over the tubes after a routine inspection trip. Reflected in the windshield he could see a similar, slightly bigger machine behind, Heli-2. His nettle weave coverall stuck to him in the heat and humidity. He looked at the thermometer. 35° C in England; and these the old winter months. Summer the year before saw over 50°. This year they would go up to Iceland during the "Scorch", as they now called it.

England lay below, now a dangerous frontier. Down through the haze, he could see the tubes, floating, linked like horizontal organ pipes on the sea. The crew were constantly alert for minor tidal waves; always on guard for the mutated biting insects which attacked from nowhere without warning.

Inland to the high areas, anarchy. Gangs of roving bandits, the aftermath of leaving so many people behind, controlled the high ground. The recovery teams were not welcomed with open arms. Scallies, as they were called, held no love in their hearts for those who deserted them for class, academic, poor organisational or whichever reasons. A vastly reduced population of only the toughest survivors, they'd learned a pragmatic self-sufficiency by force of necessity. Doubtful they appreciated the difficult decisions made before.

***

For Taylor, the day they found the young Scallie's corpse out on the tubes was the day things changed again. A tough established routine, only to be broken by a minor event.

On their way home that day, Jack held up a hand and then pointed downwards.

'There's something odd back down there; floating between the tubes.'

Taylor saw and brought the aircraft round and down to a skidding landing, the braking action of the blades throwing up a welter of spray. He hovered, backing off the power to allow the underside to settle to the tube profile. He ducked from the sudden buffeting as Heli-2 zoomed overhead and climbed to top cover height.

Marie complained bitterly.

'You're making us feel sick.'

He turned to see her rear seat companion, Ben, making mock stomach heaving motions at her. Ben winked at him and ducked to avoid her half-hearted blow. Jack was pointing ahead. They followed his pointing finger.

'Poor bastard...'

***

Airsickness, stunt flying and the weariness of the end of a day's work out in the heat were forgotten. He looked out at a severed body, only the trunk, head and arms bobbed up and down in the sea gap between the tubes...

'Out you go Marie and Ben.'

He watched them climb out and don the anti solar headgear. As the mid afternoon sun caught them, the solar panels on their reflective outdoor suits blazed white until he dropped his visor down again. They walked ahead, a well practised balancing act on the upper curve of the tube.

Looking up, he saw Heli-2 circling; a faint 'voff-voff-voff' sound from the blades in coarse pitch. They were safer with them up there. Helizep crews always went out in pairs for safety; a long walk home in the baking sun. In his experience, no one ever made it back on foot.

'What you have down there?' Hansen the Norwegian, Heli-2's chief, called over the radio. Jack thumbed the button.

'Dead body, half eaten...nasty.'

The cockpit was heating up, even with the doors wedged open to allow the breeze to blow through. They couldn't stay here much longer.

Marie beckoned. Taylor pulled up on a lever clamping hooks into the tube before he followed Jack outside. He scrambled over the netting of the forward float, instinctively ducking below the blades idling overhead. He trod carefully on the gently moving tube surface. Walking on the outside of a tunnel? His old friend didn't think it through.

He paused to regain his balance then continued, edging forwards, feet sideways.

He watched them hook the corpse further up out of the water. The sea in the curved vee between the half sunken tubes sluiced back and forth, reflecting, flickering the bright sun back into their faces, hurting their eyes. The plunk and splash reminded him of old boatyards with moored sailing boats and lakeside wooden jetties. Luckily, it was calm today. Sometimes the tubes heaved up and down like the deck of a sailing ship. Today the sea salt and algae brought back memories of warm summers, rock pools and seaside holidays.

'Shark attack this far in?' said Marie. Ben shook his head.

'Nah… maybe happened out near the edge and the tide brought him in.'

Taylor looked sidelong at the remains of a young man, maybe eighteen years old, face down on the tube. Tattoos and metal rings adorned nose, eyebrows and ears. The sun burned exposed flesh on one side was nearly black.

'Scumbag Scallie shit' said Jack. 'Let's just drag him back to the edge and let the sea finish him off.'

Taylor listened with half an ear as he tugged at the wet clothes of the corpse, trying to turn it over. Bits of blood stained T shirt, denim jacket, and cheap leather waistcoat covered the upper body. He avoided looking at the severed area. Sadly, Marie said,

'He was someone's little baby once…'

'Yeah, and his mother abandoned him because she didn't want to look after him,' said Ben.

'You don't know that,' she said, frowning at him.

He ignored them, they always bickered; he found it reassuring, normal. He turned the body over and went through the remaining pockets. A handmade shiv knife, a crucifix, stolen from some unfortunate Dome dweller perhaps and lastly, tucked into the jacket, a small container wrapped in some dark oilcloth. He wondered what to do. Nine pairs of eyes saw this. If they just dropped the body out at the sea edge who would know? He didn't know Hansen's crew well enough to know if they would keep quiet or not.

A movement down in the water caught his eye; a shark or

something big, as if to contradict Ben's verdict. Something cruising for food anyway.

'Watch yourselves, if you don't want to be on someone's menu.'

They all peered down. Where were they in the old world? Somewhere over a drowned Norfolk? Cambridgeshire? Deep below lay the lands, towns and homes of the ghosts of not so long before. He looked at his crew. Jack was back at the heli, bored with the situation, standing watch for the unexpected. The other two still grumbled at each other. He'd tell them to shut up in a minute – if only so he could think. Half heard was;

Marie to Ben, scornful; 'No sharks here then?'

Ben to Marie, shrugging; 'How would he get out here without being washed off by waves - or stung to death by the insects then? Shush – Taylor's hissing at us...'

Taylor peeled the package open to reveal a clear plastic organic container. The contents were liquid, like fluorescent oil floating on glowing water. As the sunlight fell on it the outside began to warm up, so much so that he yelped with pain. He flung it down and dunked his hands in the water.

The container started to burn into the tube surface. He kicked it in to the water where it started to bubble vigorously.

'Back to the heli!' The others were running already.

With all aboard he took off sideways. He hover-circled at a safe distance. Anything that hot burning through the skin of the tube could easily ignite the methane inside the tube. They watched the container flame and burn with angry force; even on the surface of the water. His own schoolboy chemistry was a remote memory. He would be surprised if the people they left behind were any different.

***

Hansen must have left his transmit button down. Below, in Heli-1 they could hear the conversation in the circling heli above their heads.

'Ari's got his camera out again,' one voice said.

'Leave him, does no harm.'

'They say we bring back wild tales from out on the Tubes. I like to prove them wrong,'

'Shit! Transmit button is stuck again.'

Click.

'Damn thing, ah there it goes. Did you hear that Taylor?'

'Let him film away. We're clearing up here, bringing the body home...'

***

'S-s-sss.' Hansen clicked off, shaking his head. 'Big mistake. All sorts shit now.'

***

Taylor circled the base, allowing the second heli in first. He looked over a ramshackle huddle of bamboo and tarpaulin buildings pushing out from the barren shore. Nearer the ground, he could see the dome of water spreading from the central fountain, its reflecting razor thin film a fluid umbrella encompassing and cooling the base. No luxury, he thought; it was so hot now, with no shortage of water; the new efficient solar panels and wave generators everywhere. As he let down through the umbrella the water scattered in rainbows and droplets and then reformed itself.

The base reminded Taylor of missionary hospital compounds in Africa that he'd seen in documentaries and films. Both helis settled down on the landing pad. The crews climbed out stretching stiff muscles.

Taylor sat waiting for the blades to slow to a stop before he could hand over to the hangar crew. The back of the heli shook as Jack directed the removal of the body from the cargo net. Two assistants forced into service joshed and joked at first and then went quiet. He watched one run to the waterside rails and throw up. Some of the more seasoned techs came out to help. They dealt with it with minimum fuss and then he was on his own.

Outside, the potted plants and bamboo grab rails reinforced the colonial atmosphere.

Inside, he looked round the cockpit. He smiled to himself, touched switches, stroked the texture of the various surfaces; the well worn bamboo control stick, its transmit and release buttons salvaged from an old joystick.

When he'd hit upon building their own aircraft he'd not taken himself any more seriously than the others. Filed away on one of his salvaged memory sticks were little articles and downloaded features that once interested him, stored for future reference. Browsing through one, using an old PC, he found an article on self building micro-light aircraft from plans. One inset panel proposed a home built helicopter. Technically no more difficult than making a toy model but on a larger scale. He'd smiled and closed the file. Where could he ever get the tubular aluminium, the Perspex, the engine, the blades?

60

Not much later, in the bar, he sat with one of the techs and joked about the project.

'I've got a free hand to make one. Mainly because they think it is impossible.'

The tech, what was his name? Sanjiv? Sanjay? showed him an e-book on his wrist. "Cartwright on: Alternative materials using bamboo and composites…"

Inside, flicking to a random page he saw stuff he already knew but hadn't applied to the problem:

"Bamboo, if used and treated with care can be stronger and lighter than steel. Easily bent and curved with a blow torch gun to form rigid frameworks, shredded to a mash and reconstituted with certain glues to make light boards and planks…"

***

Chapter Two

Safe back at base, with the helizep's hummings and thrummings winding down, he became drowsy. He was nudged back to the present by one of the ground techs.

'Mesmerised by the blades again, Taylor?'

Stiff from sitting tense at the controls he became aware of the slowly spinning blades running down, casting a hypnotic pattern of shadows.

'I obey, Master,' he said in a robotic tone but he spoke to thin air. Everyone else was gone, leaving him brooding alone at his controls. He climbed out and eased his sore limbs.

He limped for a few feet like an old man. His back still bothered him from his old Jeep days. He took off his helmet and visor and fingered the scar from that bump on the head in the barn at Top Farm. Then, life restored to cramped muscles, he forced himself into a sprightlier figure and made his way to check in.

One of Hansen's crew was waiting for him. The one with the camera. Was it Ari? Taylor didn't know Hansen's crew yet, sent over from Dome 2 after they lost…well, he didn't want to think about that. Heli-3 was still in pieces in the corner of the hangar; a severe reminder to the careless. Yes, Ari, there, on his name badge. Ari mumbled something about,

'…need some more visual proof when you write your report…' then handed him a memory card and left without another word.

He watched him go. What report?

He tried to sneak past the admin area but Wallis, their administrative leader, stuck his head out of his office window.

'Taylor, got a minute?'

He sauntered over the pad, stumped up three shallow steps and crunched his way along the shaded bamboo mat landing to the admin offices. The door was ajar. He knocked and entered. Wallis was rubbing his chin and looking at a chart.

'Take a seat,' he said without turning. 'Oh, you already have…'

'The old ones are the best.'

'I try to earn respect for my authority; you seem to have none. I saw you trying to get past my window. How long did you think you could avoid me?'

'The word "Report" was mentioned.'

Wallis grunted in satisfaction, turned and sat to face him.

'Thought as much; maybe something to do with the matter of a body; a Scallie? Half a Scallie, and you people bring him home for a decent burial? Why not just drop him out at sea? It's not as if dead bodies are so rare these days…'

'Scallies with incendiary devices initiated by sunlight are. Two or three of those thrown in here and we're out of business. The Tubes would go up like an inferno. Ten or twenty let off in the Dome and we're homeless. I've had enough of homeless, Wallis.'

'Well you can report it to Zero Interference, then.'

'OK, Wallis, I'll sit here and do your job. You go out with the kids and mend tubes, dodging mad bugs, sharks and who knows what else Mother Nature has lined up…'

'Taylor, it's a significant event. You made it so by bringing him in. We've seen these things before and ignored it as too difficult. Now you've highlighted it; shoved it into the public domain. Crew Captain reports it. You were there.'

'Bollocks. I've never seen them before. This is new to me and my crew...'

He paused; considered.

- Is that why Hansen hissed in disapproval over the radio? -

Wallis continued.

'They've kept a lid on it. We've heard reports from the other two Domes; burnt bodies in the sea. These people are savages, man. You told me you saw it developing yourself, before the evacuation. Who knows what weird rites they've come up with?'

Wallis's expression relaxed.

'Look, I know you don't like the ZI and the SP. I know you don't like going into the Dome beyond the accommodation area. One of these days, I'll move on and you'll be grounded because you've done too many tours out here; you ain't thirty-five anymore. Then, you'll have to deal with them. I'm warming this seat, just for you man. You're a C1; they'll make you "B" grade. Better to retire as a "B" with a grateful ESO to look after your creaking bones. Do the report. Do it before Download Night. The file will say you are preparing. Last word Taylor…'

***

Day Seven. Heli-1and Heli-2 wound themselves up. In turn, the helis took off and burst out through the water veil. Nobody out in the open would flinch as the cool misty downwash hit them, a momentary cool refreshing few seconds until the heat and humidity went back to normal.

Two Helizeps with nine people, seven men and two women, swept over the tubular landscape.   He glanced left. Jack tinkered with an

63

instrument on the dash. Marie sat behind him. He craned over his left shoulder to see Ben next to her. Jack, his number two, his electronics man tinkered on. Along with Wallis, probably his best friends in this world,

Marie was the bio expert and Ben, the botanist and horticulturalist. They were all younger than him, but all trained together for this at Ararat. Taylor looked upon himself as the one with the supervisory role with a skill for getting things done. The base team members came up with ideas but lacked the ability or wherewithal to make them happen.

Wallis once mocked him for proposing a helicopter made from local resources; now the helizeps assumed the status of always-been-there. Marie wanted a laboratory to experiment with new ideas. A bundle of boxes appeared one day. Not only that, a lean-to annexe to the existing base appeared to house the box contents. Marie came on shift to find it was Christmas morning. He hugged himself with smug glee when he saw her face. There were other things but the helis and the lab were the triumphs, the cards that would never be trumped. He was very fond of his crew and they were fond of him.

There can't be many left from the early days out here on the Agribases, he thought; only me, the crew and Wallis on Base 3. He thought of the shadowy half remembered faces of those gone home with nervous breakdowns, some wasted with the tropical diseases emigrated north in the new climate; some who never left at all; alive.

They were in the lead aircraft, the letters He-1 stencilled roughly on the side. Two sat in front, two in the back, in a cabin of bamboo struts, Plexiglas and ply. A hydrogen-filled envelope above him shaded the cabin from the fierce sun. A biofuel turbine motor thrummed somewhere behind. Below lay the new inland sea with its floating agriculture.

Already hot and sticky from the humidity, they sat with their visors down against the reflected glare from below, a surreal blinding landscape spread out before them. Anyone familiar with old time East Anglia would, at a glance, think the tubes were poly-tunnel farms, now spread over the land to a huge extent. How the purists hated them, he thought. Unnatural; a blight on the landscape, they'd said. Bored, he pushed the stick forward. They dived down and levelled out, skimming low. A bit lower and the pressure wave would throw up a fantail of water. The view forward was a world-spanning skein of white and grey corduroy lines converging on a projected misty horizon. Patches of green algae, a more pugnacious species, defying the glaring new sun of the times and burgeoning seaweed thrust up here and there;. The quieter, subtler strains were held within, brewing their bio concoctions, which would later be turned into bio fuel, plastics, food base, clothing and construction fabrics.

'Let's just get home in one piece Taylor.'

They weren't in the mood for games then.

'Yee-hah,' he said softly to himself and eased up to a safer height.

He raised his visor and looked outside and behind. Following him, close and to one side, he saw Heli-2 with Hansen and crew. He could sense the other crew, like mannequins in a flying toy but suffering the heat and fatigue just the same.

He wondered how their idle conversations went during the transit flights, strapped into their flimsy eco craft with only a few sticks, glued bamboo ply and physics holding them up in the air. The new crew kept themselves distant but Hansen sort of drifted in and out socially; on the edge of friendship.

Jack, with a box of tricks on his lap, directed them out to a zone a few miles from the sea edge. Blips, beeps and graphs told Jack a story and now he pointed down and made a spiral gesture.

Heli-1 dropped down; again Heli-2 stayed on watch up in the air. They hoped for a quiet day here, out on the edge, but this was vasp territory….

'Why do we have to risk coming out here before the harvest?' Ben said over the intercom. 'I thought these pressure transmitters were automatic?'

'They are,' Jack said. 'Until they go wrong or the tube cracks from too much flexing. We have a pressure drop somewhere here – either a tube is leaking or the transmitter is faulty.'

Taylor circled lower until he saw a light strobing on one of the tube joins.

'Try that one first?' he said and settled Heli-1down onto the tube.

The sea was livelier today, the tubes heaved up and down with the waves. Jack climbed out and over the front. He edged sideways with bent knees acting like shock absorbers as the tube rose and sank.

'People used to pay for rides like this,' he called over his wrist radio link.

'Concentrate man, don't fall in. Watch him you two.' Ben and Marie extended the long bamboo pole with the line attached to Jack's harness.

One slip and they could haul him back out of the water in seconds. Taylor leaned out and scanned the water. He remembered years ago, before, when the sharks were attracted to the beat of helicopters. The sharks were much further south in those days. Now they were here, attracted by the burgeoning fish stocks and the tropical waters. Some of the teams would catch a shark or tuna and bring it home in triumph. All would eat well at the base canteen. He was never keen on eating something he could have eye contact with. He wasn't a hunter but he would share the other's bounty easily enough.

***

Up in the air, Hansen maintained an easy circuit. His crew kept an eye out for rogue waves and anything out of the ordinary. It could be them down there next and they would want sharp eyes scanning for danger on their behalf. One of the crew, slim blonde Kristen, slid the door back and leaned out further than the others. She pushed her visor up but shaded her eyes with her free hand. She stared, fixed in one direction. She became animated and prodded Hansen hard on the shoulder. He pressed the transmit button.

'Swarm!' he yelled. 'You got a swarm!'

Down on the tube, Taylor barked orders.

'Jack! Swarm! In you come! Ben, Marie, haul him in!'

They wasted no time. Jack came scampering back on ludicrous tiptoe, semi elevated by the pole and harness. The pole was jettisoned into the sea, all were aboard, the doors slammed shut; Taylor spooled up the engine. None too soon for all of a sudden they were surrounded by hundreds of mad insects; vasps.

Taylor groaned, pulled a bored face. 'Here we go again.' They were trapped in a flimsy aircraft out here miles away from civilisation. He powered up and eased forward off the tube, gathering speed and height.

The lead insects splattered metallically as the blades sliced through them. A few were sucked in and spat out of the engine which coughed, faltered, and then picked up again. He closed the intake vents but only trapped the creatures. Jack shouted to the other two in the back.

'Keep away from metal. You know the drill.'

They all shrank back as the insects, clinging desperately to the slippery windows, arched and plunged in their long stings only to shatter against the plastic. The airflow whipped the creatures from their precarious hold, leaving behind rainbow streaks of venom.

They stared outside in fear and loathing. The crazed creatures clung to the outside grills, nets and rough protrusions of the airframe, clogging the intakes, determined in their quest to destroy this intruder

They were high enough above sea level. Taylor yelled, 'Shrink.'

Each called, 'Ready.'

He pressed a button. A misting of water vapour soaked the outer surfaces; the aircraft was shrouded in blue electric fire. Insects clinging to the hull were fried and fell away. Some died stuck in crevices of the aircraft structure.

***

Marie watched a vasp corpse on the other side of the window. One of its legs was caught on the door hinge. She nudged Ben. They stared, mesmerised as its dead body fluttered and vibrated in the airflow. The creature looked as angry dead as when it was alive, seconds before. It looked like a huge wasp but more vicious, tenacious and deadly. Its mad dance of fury carried on for another few seconds and then the wind took it, whirling it away behind them.

'Clear back here.'

The airflow whipped the last of the insects away. Taylor wasn't bored at all. He was trapped in a confined space again. Today a cloud of vasps, mad killer insects surrounded him, held him inside his cocoon of bamboo struts, hydrogen bags and aviation paraphernalia. Now most were gone he breathed freely again.

'Looks like it's time again, Jack.'

Time to suit up and go seek and destroy the hives.

***

They climbed to re-join Hansen. Experience told them 1000 feet but they never knew if a new strain might jump them one day.

'You still got a few angry ones, Taylor,' said Hansen over the radio.

Jack complained; a much worn complaint.

'I hate that prickly nettle armour shit; it's too hot as it is. Why don't those bastards in the Dome take a turn?'

'Domeys out here? Yeah, right. Not while they think the sun's gonna boil their brains,' said Ben.

Taylor coaxed the aircraft along. A fully loaded helizep could not climb vertically but must spiral up gradually. He glimpsed two or three determined chasing insects out of the corner of his eye.

'I've got the airspeed. Time for evasive action.'

They fled. The reduced swarm fell further and further behind. He jinked and swerved the aircraft; climbed high and set a course first out to sea, then north, then south and finally, once the crew were satisfied the pursuit was over, back west to base.

Jack thumbed the radio; called to their sister aircraft.

'Hansen. We clear?'

'Ya, I think so man. Just some debris; some remains. You boys coming round to check me?'

Heli-1 slowed to let Hansen past. Weaving left and right, then underneath Taylor and the others peered out at the other airframe. Marie pointed out a fluttering object on the outer netting above Hansen's left hand float.

'Hansen, got any juice left?' Jack called.

'Ya, you see one?'

'Just to be sure…we're pulling back. Now.'

Heli-2 soaked itself and then became surrounded in blue incandescence. Nothing could cling alive with that amount of voltage.

A pretty sight, Taylor thought.

'Right, we're sure we're both clear. Nobody forget what happens if a single one follows us home. It goes back and brings its friends to the party. Remember Heli-3 and Base 2. Remember how many we lost,' said Taylor over both intercom and radio.

'I'll call base now. Give them time to lock down and suit up,' Jack said.

'Who's on vasp control this week?'

'Heli-4 and 5. I got the bearings…they can investigate the leak when they come out. You know; it was almost as if the bad transmitter was bait.'

'Bait? Who wants to get us? What did we do?'

'When we stopped they attacked…'

'So…? They attack things that stop. They are obviously territorial.'

'I don't see where they lie in the scheme of things. I mean, bees do the pollination and the honey thing, wasps clean up all the debris, keep the bugs down; what bloody use are these…?'

He leaned forward, cracked his visor open and pointed ahead.

'Yo! Home sweet home. Nearly there guys.'

The two in the back craned forward to see; gave subdued cheers over the intercom and high-fived each other.

***

He sat again on the pad in the front seat of Heli-1. Outside, spacemen in nettle armour probed and checked. Long grabbing tools reached to remove dead insect remains, dunked them into buckets of fuming alkali. They were cleared. Marie, Jack and Ben climbed out once Heli-

2 was pronounced clear. Banter and explanations went back and forth. Alone again, his thoughts drifted back to the development of the machine he sat in. Bamboo. There were plantations south of the Dome. It grew like wildfire. Over a metre a week, some of it. The Dome and the base were built with really thick, long, more mature stems, brought in by airship from Europe.

Always the name Cartwright appeared. Taylor, using his book, constructed his basic cockpit frame. His colleagues visited it and admired it, then joshed him for ever thinking it would fly. He sat one evening leaning over the rail with Wallis. Simpler times then, the two men's disagreements, if any, were mainly banter. Below they watched the fish cruising around the floats of the base.

'What are the floats made of again, Wallis?'

'A bamboo frame covered in some nettle fabric. They boil out the cellulose from the bigger type leaves and make a waterproof gastight resin. Even contains hydrogen; clever stuff. Why?'

***

Tonight was Download Night and Wallis was insisting he make his report on the strange Scallie. The crew usually wasted no time stampeding away from the base at the end of a shift. Today even more so; he was in a rare bad mood. He was always shaken by the vasp attacks, they all were. He hated being confined and they knew what he thought of going to meet the Dome authorities. Marie and the others needed no prompting. They scattered.

***

He knew he was being watched. They were probably watching from a safe vantage point through a lab window. He eased his stiff frame as he left the helizep. Marie once told him he possessed a chameleon like ability to appear young and carefree one minute and then sober and grumpy the next. Ari approached him and handed over the day's memo tab. If that included the vasp attack then at least he would go armed with some moral authority.

He was not philosophical about obligatory reporting to the 'dwellers within', as he called the Dome people. He wouldn't get a warm reception at the Dome.

***

The crews dispersed to their various quarters. The semi-floating base trembled underfoot as the last departed in float cars. Taylor looked round the door of the base control office but it seemed abandoned for the day, everyone off to get ready for the monthly meeting, Download. At the comms room, he requested clearance into the administrative zone. He asked to speak to an administrator and was given a direct flight clearance to an admin helipad. He ran outside.

'Hold it. I just need to fly over to the Dome.'

'It's needed tomorrow, bring it back in one piece,' shouted the head tech.

'I always bring it back in one piece, it's my baby. What are you saying?'

'Oh it's you...one piece is good is all I'm saying.'

Taylor jumped in and ran it up. He looked over to the head tech, made an obscene gesture, winked and took off.

Chapter Three

Flying inland towards the higher ground, he crossed the ruins. The helizep cast its moving shadow over agricultural land of the more traditional type; non bio-tube culture. He flew past soya crops. More tropical food crops appeared below; mango, sweet potato, cocoa, coffee, tea, bananas, sugar cane; opium poppies for medicine. Dome 3 was self sufficient in energy now, food later, according to Cartwright's great plan. The Dome soon appeared in the haze taking on size and substance as he flew closer. Not quite a regular dome, it had a fluted beetle back shape, the idea being, Taylor was told at Ararat, was to capture moisture laden air and channel it down to the reservoirs to both capture clean water and to act as a cooling and reflective barrier. The technology was from nature, a beetle found in the raging temperatures of the Namibian desert.

He swerved left and right avoiding blowing his down draught over towers supported and braced with bamboo. Fungus for a meat substitute grew inside.

Extensive nettle fields surrounded the covered Dome area. Nettles grew much bigger now. They benefited from the climate change; for the humans, a crop for medicine, herbals, clothing and insulation.

He veered to line up with one of the cleared avenues radiating out like spokes from the covered city. These were guarded by SP, backed up by automatic Taser fences; a dangerous world out here at the new frontier.

The nettle barrier, over five or six metres tall, now thrived on the rich nitrogenous soil. He wondered, not for the first time, who it was came up with such ideas. - Let's grow a tall deadly poisonous nettle barrier – someone must have said; probably so and so, Cartwright; again.

These particular nettles, New Zealand *Ongaonga*, were extremely poisonous. They thrived on the high level of nitrogen via the city sewage system. Taylor looked them up once in Cartwright's *New World Frontier Flora*. These could kill a horse. Not that he'd seen any horses lately.

He selected the Dome frequency and called them.

"Dome, this is Heli-1, requesting a radial lane entry to land at Admin helipad,"

"Heli-1, Dome. Roger, proceed to lane 340. Pad has four greens lit awaiting you. Stay over lane. Not advised to shortcut over barrier, out."

Crash landing in the nettles meant an unpleasant wait for rescue. Hurt or not, he would have to suffer the flies and biting insects and worse, fight off the feral rats which eked out a savage existence there.

Looking down, he tried to see the shanty folk's unofficial tunnels. These contraband routes were shaded from the sun and official aircraft view, criss-crossing in irregular patterns. Nobody used them uninvited. Nobody went in without wearing armour against the stings and the rats.

Slowing down, he looked down between the Nettle Barrier and the Dome. Here and beyond, he looked over shanty areas glowing in the early sunset. The shanties were cobbled together in clearings from the ruins of the old world. The people there were either not welcome inside the protected area or did not want to enter. Not all were prone to the wicked sun and its dangerous rays. Not all needed the clinical safety of the Domes. Nevertheless they clung close to the new organisation, perhaps recognising the need for the new world order; yet not ready to commit to the dome leadership.

A motley crew set them up. Tough street entrepreneurs, the meeker Scallies and tame dropouts lived there in a thriving black market barter world that clung as much to the ways of the old as the new. He was no keener to lose engine power here than over the nettles.

***

He landed at roof level on the bamboo braced helipad platform protruding from the main dome roof. The first thing he always noticed was the smell, organic and sickly sweet from the various covered processing factories The waste system, channelled out to feed the nettle field and the land beyond, lent its unmistakeable odour to the cocktail. A fresh breeze helped today.

The claustrophobia set in, like before, when he got near to the old city centres. He flicked switches and extended the after landing checks to an exaggerated degree just to delay the inevitable entry and descent into what he perceived a possible trap.

Behind him two bored SP guards, watching him from their shaded lookout, sneered at his over pedantic checking. He disentangled some dead vasp parts from the intake filters and flung them over his shoulder. The corpses bounced over the pad, the breeze blowing the evil looking remains towards them. They stopped sneering and shuffled back, wide eyed. He strode across the platform to the door they guarded. They grunted him through. As he rode down the descender, Taylor pondered if he'd met a cheerful friendly SP since

72

Sharpe. Sharpe, the sergeant, who he'd last heard of desperately and unsuccessfully trying to establish an ESO foothold up in the north of England.

At the next level, he went through a decontamination procedure attended by young technicians, and then on to a reception desk attended by a supercilious young man.

'Reason for visit?'

'...to report to Zero Interference.'

'What report? What is its significance?'

'Are you ZI?'

'No, but I have to process you. You come wafting in out of the sky, dressed in...in...outdoor clothes. Who knows what diseases and poisons you carry?'

'I don't care if you let me in. Instead, what if I drag your little scrawny ass out to that air machine and give you a tour of the outdoors you like so much?'

'Oh, yes, I see it here. Chief Taylor. Agribase 3. Expedite entry to Dome Admin. Prior contact Z6. The descender platform is that way. P-please enter...'

He entered another descender and watched the water, displaced by his weight, rushing through the tubes pumping water into a reservoir to run the associated ascender. "More than two must descend to send one back up", the notice read. He imagined he would have to use the stairs on the way out.

At floor level, ahead lay a pearl coloured spongy surface, each step he took would pulse microvolts back into the system. He knew the young took the floor surface for granted. It made Taylor feel uneasy and he looked back in distaste at his footprints, fading gelatine puddles, the spoor of an invisible man. He came to a door marked 'Z. Admin'. He knocked.

A dapper young man opened it. He wore a nettle weave uniform, but black, tailored like a former business suit over a V neck T-shirt. The lapels were the same blue Taylor remembered from before; the Z logo was prominent.

'Ah, Mr Taylor. Good of you to come. I am Jarvis, Z6'

Taylor frowned at what seemed his false breezy welcome.

'Come, this way.' Taylor followed him to an office. The door was labelled,

"Zero Interference Team Operations - Jarvis Z6 – Z9 Assistants."

He scowled as Jarvis waved him to a hard chair while he sprawled himself in an executive recliner. Noting the scowl, he shrugged.

'I got it from high-rise forage over near London. We must recycle where we can...'

'Were you on the foraging party then?'

'You know from my radiation badge I cannot brave the outdoors like you.'

Taylor was struck by the contrast as Jarvis shuddered and gave an involuntary glance towards where he perceived outside; where the cancerous sun lay. - He loathes the outdoors like I hate the indoors. Taylor let it lie.

'How can we help you today?'

Taylor, tense with irritation, bit his tongue and got down to business.

'Two days ago, out over the tubes we found a body; a Scallie, just a lad.'

Jarvis took the proffered memo tabs. Taylor watched as he inserted one into a slot in a box on his desk and selected what he thought must be the 'Play' button. Jarvis stabbed controls to shut down a screen he, or someone, had been viewing earlier. Taylor caught a glimpse of naked young women giggling, cavorting with ... a small pony? He raised an eyebrow then shrugged. With some adjustments, Jarvis opened the first vid taken by Heli-2. The day's images were displayed on the far wall.

Jarvis stared, manipulated controls to lessen the bright glare of outdoor reality. Then his eyes narrowed at the scattering of the crew and the ensuing incendiary. He inserted the second memo tab. When the vasps' attack started, his eyes widened again and he squirmed in discomfort.

'Lucky escape for you and your colleagues...'

'It's par for the course out there.'

'What do you mean, par for the...?'

'From Golf, a game from before...'

The Dome man sat pondering, gnawing on a knuckle. He turned back to Taylor.

'What's your take on this?'

Taylor paused, reflected.

'It seems they are getting more organised; as if they had a leader. I'd have left him but for the incendiary. Last time I looked that lot didn't listen at school. I hear he's not the first to be found in the sea. Perhaps they have made contact with Europe, with the French. Maybe he is from France... tattoos and piercing were international after all. Perhaps the French authorities see them as recruits for whatever their plans are...I just don't know. I doubt these incendiaries are their invention. They must be getting them from somewhere else.'

74

Jarvis frowned back at him.

'Really... why should the French recruit scum? Outside assistance would arm them with guns as well?''

Taylor shrugged, bored now. He studied the man. Jarvis would be handsome under normal circumstances, from a good family, with a good education; with the self-confidence all those things endowed. The young man lounged there with an aura about him he couldn't place.

Unbidden, his imagination took over; the features of a huge vasp started to superimpose themselves on Jarvis's clear complexion. The wide eyebrows sprouted antenna, the eyes became compound; the supercilious mouth began to grind its mandibles.

He shook away the illusion and answered;

'Why do they do anything? They still have some nuclear power; their agriculture is not all underwater, at least not in the north. Their country is a madhouse of indiscipline and murder, or so I hear...in fact a bit like the inland countryside that you choose to ignore here...'

Jarvis sneered at him.

'I'm not sure the Administration wants idle political speculation spreading to the Dome workers, especially by fieldworkers...'

This was too much. He did not like it in here, he did not like the ZI that ran this Dome, and he did not like this pompous snotnose lecturing him. In spite of his best intentions, his tongue took over.

'Yeah, right, the poor humble simple folk who make sure you get fed; make sure you continue to take it easy in this...' he swept an arm around to encompass the furniture, the cool shady pleasant environment.

'Yes, well, we can't all be heroes...'

'No, but while the outside teams risk their lives and people inside live lives of drudgery, what are you parasites doing here? Not being able to go outdoors is not an improvement in mankind's progress. I thought we were trying to repair the situation, not build cosy little niches for ourselves.'

Jarvis swung his chair away. He pretended to consult a document but Taylor saw he was furious. As if he was counting to ten under his breath, composing himself and now he swung back, forcing calm onto his features.

'I don't like your attitude, Mr Taylor. Perhaps two weeks zero tolerance on your profile might bring you into line.'

A shadow crossed Taylor's peripheral vision as an inner door he'd not noticed swung open. Jarvis stood and shifted his languid attitude to one of respect. Taylor remained seated. The newcomer was a Z3, maybe their boss. Pretty high Z rank for the frontier.

'Good afternoon, Sir,' said Jarvis.

'I heard raised voices. I couldn't help overhear but I suspect Mr Taylor thinks you are an arrogant soft living parasite? '

'Well sir, he doesn't have the bigger picture....'

'Bigger picture? Bigger picture? Taylor is of an age with a much broader view of the world than you will ever have; yet you wonder he gets annoyed when you patronise and antagonise him. He cares nothing about the dead Scallie. He is just reporting as requested and required by his and our procedures. Isn't that so, Mr Taylor? Thank you for your report. We will look into it. We won't take up any more of your valuable time.'

Taylor stood up to leave. As he left their office he was forced to step aside while two junior ZI pushed their way in, holding him up in their arrogant way. He overheard the Z3's raised voice tell Jarvis, 'Stop showing off and attracting attention or I'll get someone else to do the dirty work. Is the next shipment ready? Try not to lose anybody next time.'

It made little sense to him and he dismissed it as he made his way back along the voltaic walkway. He was in luck. The ascender was free. He stepped in and looked back. He could see into Jarvis's office window. He could see the senior man looking at the Z6's screen console. He watched him turn Jarvis a cold glare, say something harsh, judging by Jarvis's recoiling expression, as he pointed a wagging finger of negation at the screen. - Shouldn't humiliate your juniors in front of others; Jarvis won't forget that and now he'll blame me. I hate this shitty Dome. One of these days I'll find a way out of here....

***

The ascender rose giving Taylor time to watch the Z3, now some way below, leave the ZI office and move off along the walkway. He noticed the slight man with the domed intellectual forehead did not seem to activate the PV floor much. His own trail was still there, fading gradually after his passage. Z3's footsteps barely made a trace puddle before reforming to the flat pearly grey floor surface.

76

Chapter Four

He flew back to the agribase. At least he could get back in time for a shower and still make Download time. After that, a few beers, a cigar, a new batch smuggled in someone said, so some illicit smoking and take it easy. They worked one day on, one day off so maybe a lie-in tomorrow, then over to his workshop; to his "shed", as he called it.

Back at the base, he checked to see if anyone stayed behind working in the laboratory; if there were any findings from the incendiary. One woman in a protective smock was peering into a microscope. She acknowledged him with a nod. He wasn't hopeful but he asked anyway.

'Anything on the stuff we brought in earlier in the week?'

She gestured to a full rack of requests. He turned to go. The Tech relented and called after him.

'SPs took the torso away half hour ago…glad to have the freezer space back.'

'Already?'

'Have you upset the ZI? They asked about you, the SPs. Asked what you were like.'

'And?'

'I told 'em.'

He grunted, laughed and made his way to his float car. Checking the power gauge, he jumped in and headed back to the city.

***

Tonight was the monthly symposium; like a village meeting only bigger. They called it Download Night. The screens would display production quotas, news and announcements. The community leaders would announce the result of solar panel downloads after each of the outside crews drained their solar suit saved electricity into the central power bank. Then the beer would flow.

Taylor and his crew were bored by the first bit; loved the later bit. The outside crews had little time for the agoraphobic Dome dwellers. In turn, the insiders seemed to barely acknowledge those who went outside; those who maintained the apparatus of their survival and sent in the material justification of their existence. The Dome dwellers, the "Domeys", huddled inside frightened but, at the same time, haughtily defending their cave like existence.

Docking the car in a recharge booth, he rode another ascender to his sleeping quarters.

According to his rank, he qualified for a tiny tubular three-room module with bedroom, lounge area and bathroom. In fact, it was a large Tube; made from the same sort of material as the ones he tended out over the new sea.

In a bed-sit at my time of life! How sad, he often thought.

He thought it daft but, along with the room came a woman, a girl, to clean and tidy, to make sure he had clean clothes. No unemployment in the Dome. His appointed girl was Da-Netz, 'Da' for female, 'Dee' for male. Unskilled status. Netz, a strange name; eastern European? He shrugged. He was formally Cee Taylor. She looked after several similar modules but always seemed to be there at his of an evening. She greeted him shyly and made him tea. She laid out fresh evening relax clothes while he showered.

When he emerged from the shower, he smiled his gratitude and, wrapped in towels, waited for her to leave the room. Used to his ways she normally left him to carry on. This time she waited, demanded attention, as a woman partner greeting her man might.

She stood there, a slight wistful creature in a one-piece slip loosely tied but accentuating her female figure. She was not unattractive with her dark hair done up into a pony tail, almost so tight it seemed to make her eyes pull up at the corners, he thought.

'What's up?'

'You're nice; you have a vigorous way about you. Unlike the men here; either brain dead or police bullies. You ignore me. Am I so ugly? Where is your woman from before? Why not find a new one?' she said. She paused.

'You want sex?'

He stopped his towelling.

'You are not under any pressure to do anything other than your work, nothing you are not doing already…'

'OK. I'd like sex with you.'

He was taken aback. It didn't seem right. Shouldn't I make the first move? No, I can't…

'I'm flattered but I'm old enough to be your father. Look, I'm sorry, you're a lovely girl but I promised myself…'

He watched her race away down the landing. He hissed between his teeth.

Woman scorned, shit, could have handled that better. He slid the door to.

***

He headed out to the Civic Centre for Download. He was still disturbed by the girl's behaviour; she was his for the taking, a companion on the lonely nights. He wouldn't get a second offer he imagined. Now he swung his energy store pack over his shoulder. The pack indicated near full, enough credits to keep him going until the next Download in a month's time. In the dark, the path lay before him marked in glowing algae lights. He patted his belt; checked his Taser was there.

Due to a quirk in the Dome construction, he claimed his own outer door; he could disable the Dome integrity alarm. Now he slipped outside to walk at least part of the way without being monitored by cameras or watched by SP.

He silenced his wrist alarm to subdue any vocal warnings of straying off route. The wrist computer, a large wristwatch, holo-phone and link to the Dome system, was programmed as a rudimentary guard and guide. He'd seen them before the storms. Then they were expensive wrist PCs for gadget nerds. All personnel now wore one. The Wrists. They gave unwanted irritating patronising advice most of the time. He liked to turn the volume control low; or off.

The air was thick with humidity and organic odours. To his left lay the edge of the nettle forest. He imagined the nearby nettle plants were silently contemplating him, as if daring him to come closer; daring him and his kind to take some responsibility, some punishment for the changed world.

He brushed aside the feeling. What nonsense! They never proved human activity was the real cause of climate change. To him, the problem lay not so much in what caused the disaster but mankind's lack of readiness for it.

In that strange way of plant-life, the nettles nearest him suddenly shivered and shook, making him jump. No doubt they were settling with the change in light and temperature. Uneasy now, he quickened his pace, hugging the nettle-fabric Dome wall. Rats scurried across his path; rodent eyes reflecting eerie green from the algae lamps.

He mulled over his day, his life both before and afterwards. Before, he drifted from job to job after leaving the military. He could never stay one place too long before it got on his nerves. In Taylor's opinion the Jarvis type should have been erased in the catastrophe, but now somehow fitted into this world like a natural. Meanwhile Taylor was somehow stranded in the present between the past and the future. He was homesick; homesick for an idea; a life which was long beneath the waves. He often wondered what life would be like now if he hadn't been a week late; if he'd been home in time to join them.

The path widened, he was nearing the edge of the shanty area. As he turned a corner, he noted a movement out of the corner of his eye. Four shadows slipped into the green light.

'Where you goin' big boy?' said the lead silhouette. 'Someone upstairs wants you taught a lesson.'

'Here we go again,' Taylor growled to himself after poleaxing the first man to the ground with his energy pack. Three to go. The next raised a metal bar to strike down at him. Taylor was inside his guard already and kneed him in the groin, almost casually relieving him of his weapon as the Scallie collapsed wheezing to his knees. Two down, two left. The violence and sudden dispatch of the first two of their group made them hesitate. Their advantage was lost.

Taylor, keeping his momentum and twisting sideways, smashed Number Three on the knee with the heavy bar. He heard a nasty crack and the man howled in pain. The bar flew out of his sweating grasp.

Number One recovered and came roaring up from behind to walk straight into Taylor's Taser. Blue sparks flashed, dazzling both of them. Number One slid to the ground with small spirals of smoke coming from his chest.

He cast around but there were no more assailants. Did he imagine a fourth? *Three-Two-One* He found himself gasping, the adrenalin coursing through him with nowhere to go.

They were taught their own lesson. He carried on his way, leaving the three figures on the ground. He was upset about the dead one. He'd forgotten to turn the dial down to a lower level before he set out. Still, he was away from the cameras here in the dark. One of these shanty Scallies would not be missed. Not for the first time he breathed

80

thanks to old Kurt, his Judo teacher.

***

Number Four ran for his life. Numbed by near tragedy he burst into a nearby SP perimeter watch station. Gasping, he told the bored desk officer with three stripes on his arm:

'A madman! An animal! It's not safe on the streets any more!'

'What did he look like?'

'Huge! Mean! Hungry! We were jus' walkin' along and the weirdo attacked us!'

The deskman consulted a screen, pressed keys; a screen on the wall sprang to life and a thermal image video of the attack ran for a minute. Taylor would be interested to know that ZI had put a spy bee on him, thought the deskman. Number Four was now horrified to find the bee's stored information sent back in time to prove him a liar. He now stared, crestfallen. The desk officer sneered.

'Sorry man, unjustified complaint. Looks like self defence to me. You got away. I would celebrate if I were you.'

He consulted a chart. He pressed a button. The outer doors clamped shut.

'Anti-social behaviour…waste of public service time…phew! Let me see… ah! Yes. In you go, into my little punishment room.'

Number Four trembled.

'No way man! I was just doing my public duty!'

'In you go; thirteen kilovolts comin' up.'

'You muthafukka! You power mad sumvabitch!'

'Oh I see! Not polite. Your manners need brushing up. Pain coming to you my lad.' His smile was fading now.

'No! You can't do this!'

'Really? In you go or it'll be twenty five thousand volts!'

'Bastard!'

'Sorry Pal, that's thirty seven thousand lovely volts. All I can give you. Now, if you don't like my little room, I can always oblige manually.'

A Riot Taser appeared in his hand on top of the desk. He squeezed the trigger. The two barbs struck Number Four in the belly. Wicked voltages flung him savagely across the room grounding themselves through his body. The thrashing figure bit through his own tongue, finally soiling himself before he fainted. Strands of St Elmo's fire from stray methane flickered around the corners then extinguished themselves.

81

Two SP guards, annoyed at being summoned from their vid show, grimaced in distaste at the foul smell. They dragged the limp Number Four outside and round the back to come round in his own time. Out of earshot, they muttered and grumbled.

'Surprised he didn't give him fifty, that Collins. He ain't right in the head,' said one.

'The other day, he made us throw that body in the nettles.'

'Ugh! Gives me nightmares when the rats come for the bodies. Glad they can't get in here…'

'Never know if the sonics are working. Only the rats can hear them.'

'Believe me, they're working. We wouldn't be out here if they weren't.'

* * *

Taylor, thought Collins, the new desk sergeant, looking at his screen.

"Two weeks zero tolerance; observe."

He didn't know anyone who respected the local ZI. He didn't. He wondered why they were interested in Taylor. He'd find out. Whatever, they could take their turn. Sharpe wasn't coming back from Cumbria. Now he'd found the next on his list. He hadn't decided how he could reproduce the terror Taylor managed to subject him to that last day on the reservoir. He'd been classed as traumatised for months afterwards. Forced to employ great cunning to work his way back to apparent sanity. Once the medics had you down as psychologically suspect; hard to escape their attentions. But he had. One side of him spoke in his head. Told him if only they had a few more troopers who could look after themselves like this guy, then the SPs could wrap up the Scallie problem in quick time and go home. He could report that Taylor killed the man in self-defence. Which was true.

He pressed buttons and sent a spy bee out again to survey the area. It came straight back. He ran the recording. He shuddered with half glee, half fear as he watched the two wounded guys fighting with the rats. If they survived tonight, they would still have the tetanus and Weil's disease. Another writhing sea of rats dragged the corpse away deep into the nettles. There went the evidence. That could have been Taylor's fate out there. But not chosen personally by Collins.

His other voice spoke, resuming control. He would have to do better than sending some tame Scallie knuckleheads. He'd been on the receiving end. The man was a blur; Sharpe had said he couldn't control it himself. He wouldn't dare face Taylor without having him

82

completely disabled and at his mercy. He closed the file.

ZI were his lords and masters and gave him this easy life. Free to plan his little games he called "Missing Persons". He erased certain parts of Taylor's evening from the video and zipped it to the Z6 Office. Little shit Z6 will be disappointed in the morning, he thought.

Chapter Five

Download Night.

Download. Everyone looked forward to Download. A public holiday when everyone got together. Every means possible was employed to make electricity. The outside workers stored solar energy wearing the Protec suits. Devices like windmills, wave generators and cofferdam hydro-electrics; solar panels on the rooftops, even shantytowns roof surfaces, sent their product to the grid. Technology, simple good husbandry, the wind, the sun and the sea, all went into the common pot. Unused power was stored in power cells in a range of standard sizes.

Taylor and his crew, colleagues and friends met in their usual corner of the main square. As usual, they greeted each other with affection. Marie appraised him.

'What happened to you Taylor? You look like you've been in a fight. Your energy pack is covered in mud and...what's this? Looks like blood...'

'Yeah, I had a run in with some Scallies. A disagreement over energy pack ownership. Lucky, I had Mr T with me.' He patted his Taser.

Something told them not to pursue it and they turned to the matter in hand. Being scientists and engineers, as one they were sceptical that their outside suit cell contribution amounted to any real difference. They admitted the community feeling, the get together were positives and, if nothing else, the celebratory drinking session was a good thing.

One by one, they trooped past the download units and drained their energy packs into the system. Their wrists were interrogated at the same time and their contribution recorded. The lines petered out, a few latecomers rushing in out of breath to plug their packs in, jeered and joshed by friends and colleagues; jostled by the less well wishers.

A gong sounded over the public address. The mayor and two assistants appeared and made for the central dais. The Z3 and Wallis joined them. Wallis, the local ESO recovery chief, the only one they really knew. The Mayor, voted in every year by the Domeys. The Z3, an ESO civil servant; a quiet government man, but in uniform.

The various self interest groups gathered in their traditional areas. Here, the Weaver's Guild, the Electricians, and the Builders. There, the Watermen, the Caterers and the Chemists. Teachers and office workers held aloof on the upper levels, those that did not directly contribute to the energy or fabric pool.

The labourers, the Dees, jostled together in one corner, often as antagonistic to each other as to the more formal groups. All were welcome. All were expected to show up. All were equal under the cruel sun. All wore nettle-cloth fabric which was hardwearing, soft and comfortable in spite of its origin. Some wore different styles with motifs and belts. Some were clean and pressed; some dirty, worn and torn.

Taylor saw the Z6, Jarvis, aloof with his assistants up on a balcony, the admin area where he reported his news earlier on. He saw the Z3's upward look of contempt and admonition; saw the effect as Jarvis ducked back and reappeared on the floor a few minutes later. He wanted a word with Jarvis but he was holding off while he decided what form the word should take.

Back at civilisation, the Zero Interference Teams were just public servants; there to help and allocate resources. He thought of his first meeting with them during the Storm – he'd thought them sinister but conceded they saved a lot of lives during those days when they directed the evacuations with chilling efficiency. Here at Dome 3, they were like some sort of dark cult. Taylor remembered "1984", and other evil fictional dark lords. The younger ones would just give him blank looks; another one of his "stories". The term "Orwellian", a mystery to some, they could not imagine that not all were on the same side; pulling in the same direction. Shipping in to Dome 3 soon revised their opinions.

Taylor didn't supply a label but they soon understood the concept.

The mayor held up his hands for quiet.

'Everyone!'

For a politician he was a man of few words. He turned to indicate the broadcast screen on the wall.

'Download results for last month!'

A column of luminous green filled up and stopped. All were silent. The mayor swept his gaze around the crowd. He was enjoying the drama; his moment of stardom.

'How much did we use?' He turned again to indicate the screen.

A red column crept up, adding to the drama. It stopped at two thirds of the height of the green column. Cheers and applause from the floor but this was not the news they came to see. Last month's figures. The two columns faded to grey and a third column, again green, started to rise.

It moved up to the same level as the previous, faltered, then edged up to stop a little higher. More cheers, followed by hissing and shushing as the majority waited to see the consumption column. It did not matter what height the level was if the consumption was too high.

Silence again as the new red column rose. Much to everyone's enthusiasm, it stopped at two units lower than last time. A net gain! The mayor congratulated everyone, rattled off statistics and implored all to keep up the good work. But the interest was gone and most started moving towards the beer halls. The meeting lights high up in the ceiling faded as the groups dispersed. Taylor and the other agris headed off to their favourite bar; Joe's.

**

Taylor stumbled, bleary-eyed, from his overnight cell at the Civil Correction Centre. Well outside the Dome in the shanty area, the authorities saw it as a punishment in itself to be sent outside the safe confines. He'd spent twelve hours in a hypnotherapy cell.

Not allowed to sleep he was forced to listen to and view hours of 'reasonable' lectures; video lectures on the dangers of tobacco and the hideous consequences to his and other's bodies of his antisocial habit.

Caught smoking his first cigar in a year. Caught in public by a street warden and arrested. He could have escaped with a caution but for Jarvis. A zero tolerance code on his profile, too many nettle beers and residual grumpiness from both the day and life in general added up to Taylor delivering a vile tirade of his opinion of such worthless occupations as "smoking warden".

The man protested he was a public health official. Taylor called him an old before word for female anatomy and enquired if he was the "ink monitor" at school. The warden's wrist computer alerted its owner to the fact that he was being insulted. Two SPs nearby were watching the exchange. Bored and half amused, they were "obliged" by the warden to fire a Narco dart at Taylor.

**

Today a young Chinese attendant sneered at him. He spoke like he'd just arrived from far away.

'No expect you back in hurry nex' ti' eh?'

He wore a green pseudo combat uniform with shoulder bars which, in the twentieth century, would have had the power to unleash nuclear weapons. He wore five shiny stars and some medals on his breast pocket. Taylor stared at them.

'Where you get the stars, MacDonald's?'

The attendant scowled at him and keyed a number into his comsole. A trap door opened and a drawer extended to Taylor. His belongings included an energy unit, his Taser gun, the contents of half a dozen pockets: credit swipe, his wrist computer bracelet, pocket rice paper tissues, an assortment of electronic and electrical connectors, tiny nuts and bolts, a multi tool, folded faded bits of paper, a clear plastic wallet holding two faded photographs and a note starting "Gone to shelter…" a scratched and battered fob watch, a worn well used penknife with corkscrew and various blades of mysterious purpose, and last, his bundle of old USB memory sticks wrapped in a waterproof cloth. The attendant looked on.

'What's all that shit you keep?'

Taylor looked at the collection, his face, half smile, half sad.

'It's a life. You should get one.'

He could not collect them until he inserted his middle finger into a hollow recess. His fingerprint was read, his current citizenship file appended with his offence: SmokePol directive XX490DTaylor15:- demerits 8 points. His enforced lack of sleep meant his float car was disabled for eight hours. He was issued a credit card sized chip. It started a holograph count down – 7:59, 7:58, 7:57, 7:56...

The attendant snickered.

'PubTrans for you. Enjoy!' He pressed another key and Taylor's wrist energised, ran through a self test and murmured "Ready" in its competent matter of fact artificial voice.

Taylor ignored him and checked his Taser power level. No knowing how many Scallies awaited him between here and the PubTrans stop. The charge was down in the red. Again, he reflected on how he'd been over zealous with the Scallie the evening before.

'Any chance of a recharge, Brigadier…?'

'No chance for you Polluter man. You no deserve protection. I still smell your filthy tobacco twelve hours later. I put you back twelve hours more but a big storm's on the way and I close here!'

Taylor paused, formulating racial obscenities. The attendant read his mind and pointed to the wall poster which gave stern warnings and penalties regarding hurting people's feelings, racial abuse and the use of obscenities in heated debate.

Taylor shrugged. His smoking materials confiscated, he'd heard enough bullshit for the last thirteen hours to last him several days. He donned a dirty public issue Protec suit, the photovoltaic material crackling to his movements as he adjusted the UV visor.

The automatic door slid aside. The usual bright sunny hot humid day greeted him but the door electronics gave warnings of heavy rain and an occluded front, whatever that was. It reminded him the barometer was dropping to danger levels and advised him to check the charge on his Taser before he ventured forth. Behind him, the attendant's voice warned.

'Remember. Hand back Protec at Dome store!'

Taylor growled and made for the PubTrans RV station

'....blerr! Bus stop in my day,' he muttered to himself. He shook himself alert, stared around in a mean no nonsense fashion, brandished his Taser for all to see and strode off.

His wrist shone a small holographic screen only he could read. He could select menus by touch screen. To the uninitiated, it looked like he was prodding at thin air. He selected "PubTrans: Nearest". A row of small holo lights dotted away superimposed on the ground before him. Following the light path, he came to an electric gate. This scanned him for citizenship and allowed him to pass. If he had not passed challenge, he would have experienced a 10kV jolt - 10,000 volts, the gate would emit a warning siren and send a wi-call summoning the SP patrol.

He was outside of the Dome in a run down area of ruins. Nettles grew everywhere. They were encouraged, almost sacred now. Nearby a workcrew gathered the tallest. They trailed a hydrocart, a sort of large bamboo trolley floating on a hydrogen bag. They did not pull them up he noticed; they cut them, leaving a leaf or two to help the plants recover.

An armed SP guard supervised them. He scanned all around for Scallies. His charges ignored him as if he were not there. Taylor would bet the guard wished he wasn't there either but at least the man could feel content he was outside capable and not fighting for his life suppressing some Scallie stronghold up in Yorkshire or the Midlands.

The work crew were Scale 'D' People. Dees. Manual labourers. The Dees considered themselves luckier than most. At least they could go outside in daytime. Some bore the scars of careless nettle handling. Welts like burst sausages and broken veins disfigured several of them. The powerful sun and the humidity had turned the old temperate zones into jungle extremes. Plants grew bigger, defended themselves harder. Insects were twice the size, four times as mean.

The old classification of people for advertising and sociological purposes still ran true. Throughout history, people were super conscious of their differential status.

Scale A the top people.

Scale B the clever, the well educated and well to do.

Scale C the practical engineers and technicians. People like Taylor and Jack who, nevertheless, must start with ESO at the bottom as 'Dees'.

Scale A people were not found anywhere near agriculture. With no more ownership of land this was unlikely. The 'Z' people kept to their own rank system and pecking order.

Taylor was conscious that there were people somewhere coordinating and pulling strings to rebuild the world. He was sceptical of any higher status being due to these invisible high priests of recovery. He must admit respect for the man who cropped up everywhere; Cartwright. There seemed to be no pie Cartwright did not have a finger in.

Scale D was generally either a lifestyle choice, a refusal to take responsibility beyond the basic level, or an indication of natural selection at work. Students and people in training were also classified Scale D. Not a dead end but stupid or shiftless people did not cyanide vasp nests, fly aircraft or manage a biofuel nutrient agricultural system. Taylor smiled to himself. Jack and some of his kids would be quite happy for the Dees to do some of the unpleasant work.

Which left Scale E. The hopeless, the derelicts, those who fell through society's net, hence the "Scalies"; or Scallies, a term from before. As Taylor was to discover, this classification was not necessarily an indicator of lack of intelligence, poor character, lack of organisational ability or inability to belong. In history, so called savages were a classic example. Around the Domes though, the Scallies were hated and feared.

Chapter Six

Mesh screens and a roof protected the RV station from UV, rain, pollution and rock throwing Scallies. Inside, Taylor sat on a bench and drew his discharged weapon. Tasers were designed before as a non-lethal means of subduing hostile street assailants. Guns were outlawed, issued only to SP and sometimes to citizens if under high threat conditions. The Taser resembled a handgun. Its handle held the power pack and capacitor. A dial on the side could select a range of unpleasant consequences from a low tingling warning to a sharp crack of lightning.

Taylor aimed his at an imaginary assailant. He could almost smell the body odour and metallic ozone of the fried Scallie who'd walked into it the night before.

Official Tasers were linked to the wrist computer. The direction of aim would project a light, green for safe area, red for danger – eyes, head, heart, and genitals. Red lit up for more than a second would occasion the wrist to announce a verbal warning.

He pondered his brush with his attackers. Old Kurt, long dead Kurt from before, with him on such occasions as last evening.

'You have zero reactions, Junge.'- a German, he pronounced it "Younger"

'Your head is cut off from your body like all modern humans are now. But you have reflexes and fear on your side. A snake does not strike out of spite or anger; a cat does not pounce out of evil or contemplation. It is fear; fear of death, timor mortis. They are afraid of dying from starvation, from attack. It is not a reaction, it is a reflex. If a man raises a stick to hit you, you have a choice. Run or fight. Do not stop to think of the consequences. If you cannot run then you must strike like the snake; pounce like the cat. If you want, I will show you how…but you must learn to control it.'

***

After ten minutes or so, the PubTrans vehicle appeared; another bamboo contrived capsule with shining metal effect chassis and glossy black windows. The door hissed open to admit him. His wrist linked with the vehicle onboard computer. It requested he sit quietly and enjoy the trip; not to engage other passengers in unwilling conversation; not to make eye contact; that smoking would have dire consequences and thanked him for using PubTrans and therefore reducing his Global Footprint. Credits deducted from his account – 4.

'Horseshit!' Taylor said. The constant contrast with hi tech and low tech unsettled him; the indoor people's insistence on maintaining correct public behaviour an irritation because it survived at all.

"Profanity is neither encouraged nor polite", his wrist said as he went to his seat.

'Centre 4 East 15,' he declared his destination.

His wrist hummed as if in thought and spoke:

"Centre 4 East 15 is outside the Dome - not in the advisory zone – while Scallie free there is evidence of Vigilante behaviour; illegal smoking clubs and other non PC activity. Bad weather is imminent. PubTrans will not be responsible for your safety but will transmit its concern to the authorities who may or may not take action if you do not come back into the Dome."

The PTV system was quite new. Self sufficient in energy, it allowed the ZI and the Dome dwellers to move about outside the Domes and between outlying work centres.. A PTV weighed little but could transport thirty people safely through the nettle fields and the ruins.

It ran, clickety ratch, clickety ratch for a while over the surface, and then linked into a surprisingly strong nettle stem and bamboo monorail crossing the nettle field before returning to ground level. The note changed. Dot dot, dot dot. It reminded him of the London Underground. He shivered. A tunnel. He looked up. No escape hatch.

***

The girl saw the PubTrans stop for the tall rangy man. She took note of his stance, his droll expression. He didn't look like one of the Dome drones. Something stirred in her. For a moment she hoped he wouldn't get hurt, she could easily…No! He was one of them! They left us behind to fend! Now they wanted to come back, take over, order our lives until they screwed it up again!

She spat her emotion away on to the ground, alerted the rest of the gang with her whistle. Their scavenging and nuisance raid. A PTV, a coveted capture. To take one would mean hostages and access into the security comms system for a short period until ZI closed them out. Their leader, Raoul de Klayven, greatly desired the Taser Dazer system. PubTrans vehicles were harder to get at now. They were armoured, armed and monitored continually; their occupants were safer than ever.

Last year he lost several of their boldest when a targeted PTV, apparently disabled by their roadblock, had spewed forth an SP SWAT team. No Tasers and narcogas that time but real ceramic bullets and grenades. Those who survived, the ones who were captured, were never seen again.

***

The vehicle speakers beeped an alarm.

"...please sit tight! Scale E alert – do not look or gesture out of the vehicle windows!"

Outside the vehicle slowed to bulldoze aside debris piled up on its route. A gang of hooting screaming apparitions appeared. Wild haired, covered in tattoos, they brandished metal bars and stones. The leader discharged a stolen Taser, the coiled wires and barbs extending only to bounce harmlessly off the sides. His colleagues followed up with a barrage of stones; imaginable filth and refuse were hurled at the windows.

Taylor lost sight of them as the windows blacked out to protect the nerves and sensibilities of the occupants. The obstacle now cleared, the PTV gathered speed. Unseen by the occupants it discharged Dazers at the mob. A spider web of wires trapped and stunned them with 50,000 volts.

Simultaneously, a cloud of fast acting Benzo-diazepam surrounded them and a message was zipped to the SPs. In minutes an SP helizep would appear; the dazed mob rounded up and taken captive to be sent on somewhere no doubt unpleasant.

He imagined the scene outside must have resembled a cross between American Indians attacking a wagon train and a 1980's apocalyptic movie. He had no illusions of what could happen if the Scallies were ever successful.

***

Today de Klayven was testing the younger ones. He knew they would not listen the first time, would only learn by real experience. The girl watched as the PTV slowed for the debris roadblock and the first five launched their attack. They went down in seconds as the electroweb enveloped them. 50,000 volts; 50kV.

50 kV meant little if you hadn't gone to a conventional school. Today they were on 'intimate terms with 50kV', as de Klayven would put it.

She thought of De Klayven who, in his thirties, was old for the organised Scallie gangs. You didn't reach thirty outside the Domes if you weren't something a bit different, a bit special. The older ones were bandits, or crazed, mad, adrift in the wilderness. De Klayven was a leader, if she'd known the term, a messiah. He'd come out of nowhere, and somehow taken over.

She watched the backup spring from concealment, seven or eight of them with heads wrapped in wet improvised balaclavas to filter the remaining dazer gas. They used bamboo poles to twitch the sparking electroweb aside, clear of the downed youths. The PTV retreated further into the distance. The five, dazed and stupid, were scooped up and hurried away into the ruins. She followed, circling wide, stopping at a safe distance to see what else de Klayven planned. He always had a backup for the backup; a deeper plan.

As expected, two SP helis appeared; a light attack and a transporter. The light attack circled, enveloped the air with a white noise field and pounded the area with stun shots. At her safe distance, she was still numbed. Her eyes and teeth jangled and throbbed with the stun waves. The transport landed and a platoon of SP disembarked. They stopped, stared and became instantly aware. From the ruins, a cloud of arrows swept in.

Some found weakness in the nettle armour. Down went troopers. Some arrows had fire tips and penetrated the floats of the heli - "Boomff", as the hydrogen escaped and flared briefly. Weapons blazing, the top cover light attack craft arrowed towards the ruins to be met by a new variation on the arrow theme. Used inactive electroweb mesh flew up to entangle the heliblades. The pilot was quick and veered off, his craft taking a volley of flame arrows in the belly floats. They did not ignite but valuable lifting gas was lost. The craft dipped before the self sealant repaired the leaks and headed, limping away towards the Dome, leaving its partner craft grounded and burning. Two troopers running away raised their fists at their escaping colleagues.

Did de Klayven want them to escape? Maybe, whatever, the game was changing. She made her way back to the gang, melting into the ruins to report to de Klayven.

***

Shortly before Taylor's stop, his wrist advised him it had taken the precaution of partially recharging his Taser by induction and reiterated PubTrans concern over his choice of destination.

Taylor's immediate goal was nicotine and cholesterol; Joe's, the venue.

The people who gathered at Joe's were of a type. Like Taylor, they didn't like the ZI or the status quo. Like Taylor, they were at a loss what to do about it.

Joe's was not a bar as far as the officials of the Dome recognised. A waiting room for people visiting for Joe's Therapy, this fooled no one. SP turned a blind eye. Joe kept the objects of their interest under one roof. The SPs liked a bit of therapy too.

Like many local watering holes of old, the bar was decorated with souvenirs and trophies. The floors were of a wood simulation, stained and smeared artificially to look dirty and beer soaked. A redundant prior effect, Taylor thought.. The floor was a donation from some agri crew from the past, probably when Joe first got the bar up and running.

To him, Joe's was just a pub. He burst through the door making people, and Joe, jump in fright.

'Hey Joe. Steak, coffee, the works. Anything bad for me, double portion.'

'No pleasantries today then!' said Joe. 'Like, "Hey Joe, where you goin' with that gun in your hand…?" which, by the way, you still haven't explained…'

'Just got out of twelve hour Hypno, Joe.'

Joe pointed an old digi-cam at him. He kept it as a memo recorder of his customers. A rogue's gallery decorated one wall. The camera was attached by cable to a solar cell, the batteries long given up their charge. It flashed and strobed in one of those anti red eye flickering ways while he pressed a button and a book case door popped open to reveal stairs leading down. Today the camera had other uses. He coughed to attract Taylor's attention and motioned with his eyes to the temporarily blinded spy bee hovering up near the ceiling. Taylor nodded.

'Came in five minutes before you arrived…on your way back up don't forget – if….'

'..yeah yeah… if the red light is on don't come up, make for the other exit. I know.'

Nobody ever used the other exit. It was practically rusted shut.

The stairs led down to an old cellar whose walls oozed times and memories long gone by. A remote signal from Joe upstairs made a false wall slide to one side to reveal a comfortable room. Complete with chairs, a bar complete with bar stools and empty optics, cooled by extractor fans and dry. The usual crowd, no strangers and, in their usual corner, three favourite familiar faces.

'Taylor!' said Jack.

Cigars appeared. Real factory made ones, stolen, looted, smuggled in from France, no one knew. Candles doubled as lighters. Taylor took a cigar and lit up. The first intake sent him dizzy.

'Don't know why I do this,' he grimaced. 'Ideal opportunity to stop and what happens? Bloody French.'

His crew, now in relax gear, looked different out of the nettle weave uniforms.

Away from the tubes, here at Joe's, maybe to dispel her scientific status, maybe to make herself attractive to a certain person, Marie wore a revealing black dress. She wriggled sensuously over to him, went up on tiptoe up to barely reach and plant a big sloppy kiss on his cheek.

'If only I wasn't promised to another,' he schmoozed.

"Food in five", came over Joe's speaker.

'Have you invented his new self cleaning, self deodorising floor yet Ben?'

Ben looked gloomy.

'Just because I was pissed he never lets me forget. He still doesn't realise the material does not exist. What sort of guy runs a bar and sneezes at the smell of beer?'

'Better than the Weaving Shop or worse, the Tube works,' Jack said.

'He was promising Hansen free beer if he took him on a vasp hunt!' Marie said.

They laughed at the thought of Joe's reaction to a vasp attack.

'Pub landlords before were known for their opinions, a bit like London cabbies,' Taylor said.

They all looked at him; looked meaningfully up to the sign on the wall.

NO 'BEFORE' IN THE BAR –THIS MEANS YOU TAYLOR!

'Sorry…sorry…'

He drank his beer, stared gloomily into the swirl and wondered for the thousandth time, What's the point of surviving with nobody to enjoy all the old nonsense, the old clichés with?

Marie touched his arm. He smiled ruefully at her. Her grip on his arm tightened. He looked down at her hand. One final squeeze and then she let it drop.

They made their way to the stairs. Upstairs they sat and ate together, a scene from anytime in history.

Now and again, one or other or all visited the downstairs hideaway. No one knew why the authorities hated tobacco so much. It seemed disproportionate compared to the chaos after the storm. They just did and the propaganda machine rolled on out of habit. The world was in ruins and still old arguments clung like old habits. Some said that growing the tobacco plants stole the food from the mouths of the hungry and innocent.

They sat and ate as he told them of some of the therapy he'd failed to absorb.

'If you didn't absorb it, how come you're telling us?' said Ben.

Taylor just curled his lip and ignored him.

Outside the wind increased to a moan with occasional buffeting of doors and windows, as if testing which bits it could break first.

Marie and Ben gave their report on the exploding device.

'It was made out of tube skin. Whatever the contents were they must have come from a lab. It is not simple chemistry to be set going by sunlight. Perhaps some photo electric diodes in the mix. Not as if anyone can just pop into an electronics shop for those. The mix was too diluted by the water and oxidation to determine the chemical but it could have been a peroxide and acetone combination. The tube was bleached white where you dropped it. Plain as day on Ari's vid.'

'Terrorists used that before,' Taylor said. They looked curious but obeyed Joe's rule.

'Are the Scallies trying to burn out the methane? If so why? They steal the electricity they don't make themselves anyway, so why not let us carry on laying it on for them?'

'What was the Scallie doing out that far anyway?'

'Was he carried out? Or in?'

Taylor's wrist alarm flashed. He took out the timer chip.

'I can drive again in six hours!'

Marie eyed him.

' Where you gonna take me Taylor?'

'Oh, maybe a romantic drift along the Seine. Follow the Moon until we find where it meets the World. Then who knows?'

'Never mind the drive, just keep that up all night and I'll know!'

'Maybe later Missy. Anyway, I'm outa here. Storm on the way and we'll be needed tomorrow if this coming blow does any damage.'

He got up and made his way through small groups of customers. As he hauled open the door, a puther of rain and wind blew in causing a minor crisis among the guests in the immediate vicinity. Jack and the others laughed at their ruffled feathers. Joe shook his fist at Taylor's back but when he turned back, they saw he was laughing too.

Joe's was about as far away from the Dome as some of his bold visitors were prepared to go.

Marie watched Taylor go with a sad expression. Ben put his arm around her.

'Don't try too hard kid!'

***

An uneventful PTV ride to the Dome. He made his way around the perimeter, dodged aside behind a tumbledown wall and watched the spy bee accelerate to search and reacquire him. Not that clever then, he thought. Back at his lonely apartment, he threw his clothes off and collapsed on his bed. He was thankful the girl was not there. He didn't feel up to any emotion tonight, like his guilt as Marie's eyes and female intuition bored into his retreating back on the way out of Joe's. Bah! Nonsense!

Here he was in the safe part where the dull ones lived; those who ate Pronto Grub, the fast but ZI controlled healthy food. Where they sat and watched old ViDs until their wrists told them they should retire and be ready for the next dull day. Taylor followed suit. He dozed through Apocalypse Now – showered to freshen up, sketched an idea for his robot tube inspection crawler, then ran out of ideas for staying awake.

In the morning, I'll collect the car and drive to the heli base. Back to routine, although routine we've got used to over the last few years is coming to an end, he mused. His eyelids were heavy, then closed. Much to his relief, the next thing he knew it was morning.

***

Chapter Seven

The storms which tore apart mankind's fragile hold on the surface of the planet were long gone but their next generation could come along and strike with equal ferocity. Lately the Dome people and the Agris were prepared. In the worst of the weather all simply huddled in the lower inner reaches of the Dome.

The new architecture took a leaf from nature's book, a plan which the people of the far south east knew for centuries. A straightforward idea, rather than irresistible force meets immovable object, to build a natural inner structure, in the Dome's case a bamboo overlapping interweaving domed framework. Everything else outside, repairable or replaceable in quick time. A sacrificial area to satisfy the angry storm.

He still marvelled at the bamboo, both lighter and, if used scientifically, stronger than steel. The Dome inner frame was a series of interwoven arch shapes. They linked together to form a natural pattern and were covered with a special transparent membrane. In wet weather, the rain would pour down into the underground wells. This cascade in itself provided a beautiful display. The rainwater internally reflected the light and moved it about like a transparent green lava flow. It reminded Taylor of activity seen under a microscope.

If the wind blew too hard, the membranes were designed to give way, allowing the wind to pass through the framework to vent its spleen elsewhere.

Taylor, albeit with his loathing of being too long inside the Dome, was forced to take shelter against the storm. No one who survived the storms took the weather lightly. The big storms were a series of weather disturbances never seen before. The reference to Noah and his Ark still rang true from his brief conversation with Livingstone. The lightning was still indiscriminate and deadly but some feature of the design of the bamboo framework kept most of it at bay.

Back at the Academy they learnt the heat of a lightning bolt was nearly five times hotter than the sun. The interest being to harness such brute power, sadly impossible in the early days of recovery; but one day perhaps. Not an option to stay outside or in the fragile agribase. The agribase itself, another sacrificial design designed to float and move with the forces of nature. Upon receiving warning of a storm, the helizeps would lift all seedlings, tools and valuable equipment to the Dome. Taylor's workshop took its chances. Typically, he'd taken steps and anything he could not carry was shoved into an old steel cargo container forming the backdrop to his area. The container had not been moved there by man, the flood must have carried it there and he simply got it upright and arranged his workshop around it.

There were very few roads. There were few lorries or trucks. Whenever a storm loomed Taylor experienced a line of people beating a path to his door with: 'look after this, Taylor', or 'please stow that for me'.

He held quite a collection of other people's stuff from many storms. Not being the tidiest person himself, every so often he would curse and swear and announce,

'...have to sort out of all this shite! Come and get your stuff or it's going in the Oggin!'

'What's the Oggin, Taylor?'

'It's where your stuff will go and never be seen again.'

'Yes, but what is it?'

'We're floating on it...'

***

The storm threatened, bullied and annoyed all the next day. The helizeps were grounded. He went with the others over to the agri base where they made sure everything was stowed safely away. Wallis was there. Today he paced up and down on the creaky landing by the control room. He caught sight of Taylor.

'Taylor! A word if you will...' and ducked inside his office.

Taylor grit his teeth. Headmaster's time. He sauntered into the office and sat down.

Wallis wore his hangdog expression. He watched Taylor adopt his.

'What happened with the ZI then? All you had to do was make your report. I hear there were harsh words and then trouble and then you spent a night in Hypno?'

'From who?'

'Come on Taylor, someone who thinks I should know what the hell's going on around here.'

'I reported the body to a certain Jarvis, a Z6. He didn't like my interpretation of new Scallie activity. Man's an arsehole. He set some of his bully boys on me, because I told him what I thought of ...well, he knows my opinion now anyway.'

'And what happened to these "bully boys"?'

'Was a time I learnt how to take care of myself. In the old days we'd have said I sent them packing.'

'Packing into the nettles? You know Taylor, there's still such a thing as the crime of murder.'

'Who says murder?'

'Nobody says. They suspect. A Dee was given electro on the spot by the SPs and two of his friends are in the hospital with grievous wounding and rat attack. A fourth hasn't been found yet. Who helped you Taylor? All your team were accounted for on the security system.'

'They were not Dees; they were pure shanty losers, Scallies. Get to the point Wallis and then you can listen to me...'

***

Wallis recoiled. He wasn't confrontational. He knew and liked Taylor and he knew he didn't go around causing trouble. He'd told Z3 if it weren't for Taylor's steadying hand here, they would lose more people to the Tubes. If it weren't for the insects, he'd have no casualties to report barring accidents from clumsiness. The Z3 reassured him, told him not to worry. Jarvis struck sparks off a lot of people, he said. But the veiled threat was there. He was supposed to be in charge and be seen to be so.

"Perhaps he would like to oversee some less pleasant little operation in the much warmer south?" went the between the lines warning.

'The point is Taylor, they don't want any loose cannons rolling on this heaving deck...please keep your head down and let's not have any more trouble.'

***

Taylor inspected his nails for a minute then narrowed his eyes at Wallis. Wallis blinked at him and began to look nervous. Taylor stood up, gave him a final stare and said;

'OK, Wallis. No more trouble,' and left the office.

***

Wallis breathed a sigh of relief. Too bloody easy, he thought.

'Too bloody easy,' he said aloud.

One of the clerks walking by popped his head in.

'You sat with Taylor in your office and now you are talking to yourself?'

'No work to do?' said Wallis.

100

That evening Taylor let himself into his room. The agribase was battened down and abandoned. The buffeting wind was just a warm up exercise and now a full storm was on its way to do the job properly.

The girl was not there although he peered half hopefully round his few small corners to make sure. The Domeys went deep inside when storms threatened. Taylor usually kept to his room. He looked about. The room was a pleasant light enough place. The tubular walls allowed some light through the opaque material. The room was basic, functional and the ubiquitous bamboo and tube material creaked pleasantly like a rattan or wicker chair. He would have preferred to stay out at the base but, after one particularly violent blow a year or two back, the whole base needed rebuilding. He saw the sense in self-preservation.

It wasn't the building that oppressed him. The Dome was light and airy enough as long as the wind blew the factory smells away. A sort of claustrophobia of the soul, he thought. People like Jarvis and all the others who feared the outside huddled here. Their small lives with their details, which no doubt mattered to them, cloyed at Taylor's senses like sticky elastic bonds. His feeling of being trapped, of being locked indoors, was at its strongest on storm days and nights.

He decided to explore the Dome and try again to overcome his groundless phobia. There wouldn't be many about. He would be able to roam about relatively unmolested. For fun, perhaps he could confuse the spy bee and get the other side of a membrane from it; dunk it in a nettle vat maybe. He wondered if it would stop after the two weeks was up. Where does Da Netz live? Perhaps I should try and make it up to her? ...no, it's too complicated. Don't go there. Or?

He erected his screen but thought better of putting her name in directly - who knows what that little shit Jarvis is up to! He called up an overview of the accommodation areas. They were arranged around the edge for outside workers, like him, the Agris and the SP troops. There were longer wider dormitories for single Dees and Da. Dotted here and there were the inner accommodations near the factory zones where the weavers and tube exploiters lived.

He got ready, turned his taser to a low charge and set off.

The Dome was the refuge. The safe place. In the old cities, some were more secure surrounded by their own kind. The country folk were oppressed by cities. The country folk who relished the open air, the horizon, the proximity to nature. In the new times the outside workers did not consider themselves country people; Taylor's teams and colleagues, the SP, the nettle and tropical crop tenders. Not forgetting the criminal and non institutional types and, through circumstance, the Scallie bands.

Apart from the latter, whenever a storm drew near, most headed for the Dome sanctuary. Only a scattering of the brave, the foolhardy or those who made precautionary preparations in the underground areas of the ruins, stayed out.

This evening Taylor moved along corridors and down steps, leaving rapidly fading blobs of his footprints behind him. The steps were sponge-like and acted in a similar way to the corridor floors; they generated small amounts of electricity, enough on a busy work day to run the lighting for the whole Dome, or so they were told.

It was quiet. The combined effect of the gathering dark sky and the afterglow from the Dome roof cast eerie shadows and a surreal light. His wrist shone direction indicating holo arrows ahead. He reached the bottom level. His apartment was on the blue floor. He'd transited down yellow and red. Now, at floor level he followed a green series of arrows.

He saw people as vague shadows going about their own business, mostly heading for a protected inner area. Whoever they were, they ignored him and each other as if in a daze. Taylor tried to compare the people of now with those of before but he still struggled with the Domeys, with their indifference; their shallow disinterested existences. They seemed neither happy nor unhappy apart from the few, like Da Netz and other younger girls. While shy and reserved, they had some life in them; some vibrancy. Some life force which strived to surface in spite of the oppressiveness of the Dome. Taylor often wondered if the Dome exaggerated his claustrophobia but his colleagues and friends said not. The difference being, they took it for granted as part of their outdoor superiority.

He reached a factory area. Signs warned of the dangers of machinery, high-pitched sound and the risk of falling weights from height – that he needed to be escorted through the area until such time as he was inducted into the work environment. No children were allowed here under any circumstances.

Children? When did I last see one? he thought. They are about, people were encouraged to have them. He supposed his avoiding the Dome and the fact of the strong sun kept them tucked away. How sad, not to grow up in the fresh air and explore their new world without fear...

No machinery ran, there seemed nobody about so he carried on.

While Taylor was out and about exploring, his crew met up elsewhere in the Dome. They brought beer in sample flasks and installed themselves at a public seating area one floor up from the shelters. A pleasant place with its bamboo to the roof. The rain started and streamed across the roof membranes. Chasing the shortest route to the ground, it sluiced down hollow bamboos into the underground reservoirs with a satisfactory hissing sound. If the sky became too black and angry they would retire downwards but for now, they had the place to themselves.

'New crew member - pilot coming in soon. Harry something or other. No doubt he will be as green as a baby...' Ben said.

'...remember when we were new here, Ben?' Marie said, eyebrow raised.

'I blush at the thought of it. The first time we were hit by vasps I nearly shat myself!'

Jack laughed. 'What do you mean the first time? You still do, judging by the way you smell in the heli!'

'...wonder what Taylor is up to?' Marie peered around as if he might appear any minute.

'Oh, inventing a new something or other. It's as if he was running out of time and he wants to get everything done before something happens...' Ben said.

'It's an older thing, Wallis says one day you'll regret every minute you spent in bed...well, sleeping anyway...' Jack sounded unconvinced.

They paused as a file of rescue children crossed the open area at the trot. They were escorted and chivvied by two older girls. They seemed fearful, glancing sidelong, huge eyed at the three outsiders. Their teachers, or nannies, did not look in their direction.

'What did we do wrong I wonder?' Marie said, frowning. Ben said, 'It's just part of the xenophobia they are brought up on, poor little bastards.'

'Their teachers didn't look at us, I mean, what are we? Rapists? Murderers?'

Jack stared after them, bunching his fists in irritation. Would any kids of mine have stared in fear and loathing at strangers? I'll never know probably. He brushed away dismal thoughts.

A flash of lightning, followed quickly by a big crack of thunder, made them pause. The storm was overhead. They collected their things and headed down to the next level. The whole Dome reverberated and shuddered as the wind moaned and buffeted the roof membranes above.

***

Taylor winced at the thunderbolt and raised his eyes to the ceiling. He blinked away shivers and trickles of dust misted down between the floor supports above. He found his way into a large hall where conveyor sluices carried the shredded tube material in from outside. The big shredding machines in the outer Dome fed this place. For what? Presumably inspection and then diversion on to further processing. The smell was unique, half wood shavings aroma, half cloying combination of solvents and paint. The sort of aroma which is OK in small doses but sickening in close proximity, like cheap perfume on unwashed bodies. Taylor reflected that one must be a certain age to use that as a comparison. He had a choice. Follow his holo lights to where he thought he might find Da Netz, or explore more. He selected 'pause' on his wrist itinerary and followed his curiosity. Through a curtain wall and around a corner he came across a group struggling with a large flask of liquid. A ZI was giving instructions to a handful of Dee labourers, urging them to be careful as they pushed their wheeled trolley up a ramp leading away from the conveyors to the food processing area. Behind came two bored and disinterested SPs.

The ZI took note of Taylor. She shouted over the wind above.

'What are you doing here? Who are you?'

'Going for a walk during the storm; Taylor, but you have a wrist do you not?'

The wrists interrogated each other. A diplomat's dream with never any awkward forgetting of names.

'You cannot just wander around…!' she said. She flinched as another thunderclap overhead pressurised the inner air. Taylor stared at her.

'I have never read anything to the contrary. I have as much right to ask what you are doing here, under cover of the storm as it were, doing something which could be done during normal conditions during work hours.'

'It is none of your business what the ZI do, or not do, or when or where.'

'I claim the same conditions for myself…'

She consulted her wrist, tapped her holo screen. A grim smile of triumph appeared at the corners of her sour mouth.

104

'Show me your factory safety induction profile. I don't see any record on your wrist.'

Taylor shrugged and held out open hands.

The woman, a Z9, motioned the SPs forward. Heavy lidded they swung their dazers down and pointed them loosely in Taylor's direction. Taylor raised his hands in surrender and turned away.

'Take shelter or return to your accommodation is the general advice when a storm blows!' the Z9 called after him.

'Yeah, yeah, OK, I get the message…' He retraced his steps. Once he was out of sight, he reactivated his wrist and set off for the dormitory area.

Soon he came to the area his wrist indicated as his general destination. A holo directory and signpost with arrows stood to one side. A useful device, it held an electronic phonebook with directory enquiry facility. A map showed him where he was and may want to go.

He typed in Netz. There they were; the Netz family. Should he call ahead and announce his arrival? He decided to just turn up. He pressed for tracer light and set off.

***

Down in the shelter, Jack surveyed their storm companions. Attempts to strike up a conversation were rebuffed immediately. These people were pale skinned and physically slight in comparison with himself, Marie and Ben. They all had a healthy outdoor tan; a robust enthusiasm, the three "Outdoors" people appeared larger than life. The "Indoors" people viewed their rude health and vigour with dread suspicion. One balding grey haired man came within hailing distance and addressed Jack. He barely acknowledged Marie or Ben.

'Why do you come here?'

'Shelter. There is a storm…' Jack gestured overhead as if the man needed reminding of the cracks of thunder, flashing lightning and the shuddering Dome around them. The irony was wasted as the man rolled his eyes up to the heavens. He mentally assessed the storm.

'It has yet to reach full force – I – we - hope you will leave as soon as it is safe.'

'Why do you say this? Are we not the same?'

'We don't want you to bring the Cancer in here…'

'The Cancer? Cancer is a situation from within the body where the cells become rogue and out of control. Not an infection like a virus…!'

'My wife worked outdoors. She said much the same but it took her from us…' Here he indicated a pair of teenagers on the other side of the room, playing a game, some 3-D holo adventure, on their wrists.

'…whatever you say. There are many here who think as I do. We'll be happier when you have gone.'

***

Marie looked around. The others in the shelter were as far away as physically possible. The barrier was palpable. They were not welcome.

The storm raged above. A sudden bang and a buffet of air came into the shelter. One of the membranes gave way and water cascaded down the steps leading into the shelter. It drained away in no time but all were left uneasy.

***

Taylor found himself at a door. Not numbered, no family name but his holo tracer arrow blinked on and off in the centre. He knocked twice. Overhead the wind still sought entry through the Dome's roof surfaces.

The door opened a crack. An eye inspected him, scanned left and right before the door opened wider. A sulky suspicious pallid Dee grunted at him. He reminded Taylor of the type he'd ran into the night previously.

'What you want?' Abrupt; unwelcoming.

'Da Netz, please.'

'Which one?'

'The Domestic assistant on Blue level accommodation.'

This was all Taylor could think of to describe her. He wondered if he was becoming cold, callous and reserved, not thinking to ask her first name.

'Wait …Ginny! Ginny! Fellah here for you – what you done wrong?'

Then she was there, eyes wide with fear and distrust. On seeing him, she dragged him inside and shut the door.

'You must not come here!'

'Why ever not?'

'Because … you do not understand! Go! I will come to you when the storm subsides!'

An old man with a nettle stick came through. Backlit as he was

106

Taylor thought he looked like a supernatural, a gnome or some such fantasy figure. Close up in the light he wasn't as old as he first seemed. He had obviously been struck down by some tropical disease, he was wasted and grey and didn't look as if he had long to live.

'A Cee! What brings a Cee here? We do not entertain Cees without preparation. It is not good to call in off the street! It is not Liverpool or Manchester or Portsmouth any more you know…!'

A middle-aged hard-faced woman followed him. She sniffed at Taylor in a disparaging way.

'Come on John, won't do to have you all excited!' She took his elbow to lead him back into the inner rooms. She turned to Taylor;

'Gentleman come a courtin' eh?' and aside to Ginny,

'What you about bringing his sort here? I ain't afraid of his cancer but a lot are round here. Why d'you think we drove the nettle boys away?'

'It's OK Mum. He won't come again…' With this the woman withdrew, her last act a warning finger of admonition to Taylor.

Taylor was astonished. He was not ready for this, this Victorian, this caste-ridden state of affairs. The ignorance! Cancer an infectious disease! Who let this nonsense proliferate?

But then he realised he knew.

Ginny hugged him and gave him a brief kiss.

'I'm sorry; I'll come and see you. You should have never come here. It is…' she looked over her shoulder to check she was not overheard.

'…it is evil here. You should not have seen.' She urged him out of the door, his last view a flutter of her fingers as she pushed the door to. As he walked away, he heard the inevitable altercation break out. He was livid.

He paused, ready to return and kick in the door if he heard any violence.

It is not my business, it is not! It is! It is everybody's business! The ZI have so much to answer for! What can I do? One day these wrongs will be put right! One day!

Angry, he made his way back to the public areas. A group of citizens attempted to erect a big nettle tarpaulin sluice to direct pouring water away from the steps leading down into Jack, Marie and Ben's erstwhile bolthole. Taylor ran forward to lend his weight, greeted by his friends, cold-shouldered by the others, with much heaving and grunting, they succeeded in routing the water into a nearby drain.

Nearby, half a dozen Dees watched and muttered amongst each

107

other.

'Why did you not help?' shouted Taylor in disgust.

'That is our job. Now we lose work credits for a nice repair job restoring the flood damage!'

'You wankers! What is the matter with you? Do you have no community spirit? No humanity?'

'Don't know what you are talking about pal – and who're you cussing? We got rights!'

Taylor was dragged away by his team mates. He muttered imprecations and profanities.

'I was never a lefty; never a socialist but people fought for a century to stop this nonsense and now! – after a disaster when everyone…oh bollocks! What's the use?'

'Come on Taylor. The storm's dying out. Let's see if Joe's is open! Come on man!' Ben said.

Chapter Eight

A few days of routine followed. Taylor flew his team and parties of hydroponics workers out over the tubes and back. Under normal circumstances, the work would be fairly easy, inspecting for wear and tear on the tubes and accumulators. All pitched in on the maintenance. Only then did the specialist work get done. The biomass, the clean water and energy were sacred. Out near the edge however, the reality could be high-octane danger and life expectancy less than cosy.

The storm was relatively kind. A helizep went out to survey the areas.

'It only ripped up three hectares of tubes,' Wallis said.

Being organic, the tubes were usually repairable. Taylor and Hansen flew the work crews out and delivered new tubes where necessary, tow floated under the helis to be slotted into place and bio welded together.

The storm – kind? Only three hectares?

Heli-4 and 5 went out and cyanided the vasp hive; the one that swarmed on Taylor. The two crews were welcomed back at the base, their helizeps decorated with vasp corpses, some still twitching from the poison. Taylor helped get the armour and breathing gear off one of the crew. A vasp had found its way into a fold in the girl's armour before it died. Its sting was still extended; a smear of venom glistening around where it had made a last ditch attempt at killing its adversary. The young woman emerged from the suit looked beaten down and haggard.

'Thanks Taylor,' she said and made her way to sit, head in hands, on one of the walkway steps. The other crewmembers were much the same. That haunted, "I'm still alive" look.

It'll be rowdy in Joe's tonight, he thought.

***

A few days later he limped into a medical station suffering the trivial but agonizing complaint of an in growing toenail.

Notices exhorting healthy regimes were all over the walls. 'You smoke! You pay!' caught his eye and prompted him to sneer.

The medic looked about fifteen years old. He examined the toe. Glancing at his screen he noted Taylor's most recent offence. He scowled and handled the sore area causing Taylor to hiss and inhale.

'It's a wonder you can feel it smoker man. Have you heard of late onset diabetes? Gangrene? Arterial constriction?

'Yeah yeah and we're all working our way through to a happy retirement in the sun by the sea!' grumbled Taylor. Well the sun's here and we're all by the sea so, what's the point?'

'The point is you are wasting the time of the medical services. We pour the fuel in the top, you let it drain out of a hole you've put in the bottom!'

'The point is, 'medical man', that you are supposed to repair the machines which feed you and allow you to live in this soft environment of filtered air. So get on and do what you are here to do.'

'Good management then would argue I look after my machine and, if it was breaking down, getting old, procure a younger more efficient model!'

Taylor scowled, but conceded the point.

A bit more humility would have attracted more anaesthetic and less of the stinging nettle antiseptic but the medic worked quickly enough with scalpel and forceps. A green nettle weave bandage of excessive proportions crowned his efforts. Noting Taylor's expression the medic smiled.

'Rest there with your foot high for an hour. I will check for bleeding and any complications before you go. If it's OK, I'll put a smaller dressing on. The treatment will cost you twenty-five credits. Ten of that a levy for your personal abuse habit.'

'Twenty Five?!!! Jeez! I'd be better off going to the Street Nurses! A week's beer!'

'Go there and you may never need medical aid again. Those witches do more harm than good. Now if you'll excuse me...'

While he waited, smarting at both ends, the news holo streamed filtered news, some of it days old.

'SP heroes ambushed – 4 killed, one transporter lost, damaged Litak limps home with survivors!'

French fishing boats intercepted and sent away.

Norwegian fish factory ship held for 12 hours after failing to heed warnings.

Protests of missing shipments received from the Scottish and Welsh governments.

Are Dome Chiefs losing it? What are they doing about Scallie activity? Are the wild folk getting organized?

Increased Shark activity in the Thetford Forest Zone.'

This last caught Taylor's interest. Flying out over water as he did he often looked down, still amazed to see the slinky outlines of the sharks and dolphins cruising down what were old East Anglia streets. The warm waters and the fish husbandry areas attracted them. No pilots or hydroponics workers relished ditching away from the tubes. The Navy were busy, no time for Search and Rescue.

No mention was made of the sharks' latest victim. Or his strange sabotage device.

***

He wished he had a stick as he hobbled away from the medical station. He waited at the ascender for somebody to come down. Irritable enough already, he fumed at his disability. An exhausting ascent hopping up the stairs. A crimson stain was already appearing on the outside of the bandage and he imagined his sock awash; slimy with warm blood.

The platform creaked and water bubbled as somebody walked onto the pad above. At last! he thought. He watched the platform come down. His feeling of relief dissipated when he saw the occupants; Jarvis the Z6 and a pair of Z9 assistants.

One of them was the woman he'd met deep inside the Dome during the storm.

'Mr Taylor I believe,' said Jarvis. 'How convenient, we wanted a little chat with you. Come with us please.'

'Maybe some other time. I need to get this foot up before it bleeds any more,' said Taylor. Jarvis snapped his fingers and the other assistant walked past Taylor towards the medical station. They stood silently in a group until she returned with a wheelchair.

'Please, let ZI take the strain,' smiled Jarvis. Taylor, seething, sat down in the proffered chair. The Z9 produced a key and inserted it in the ascender control. They pushed the wheelchair onto the pad. She turned the key and the pad ascended.

So much for two must descend, thought Taylor. He was worried now. They had him at a disadvantage. He tried to manoeuvre his wrist so he could send a discreet signal to Jack. He received a sharp rap on his knuckle from Z9's baton. Jarvis turned with his odious smile.

'Oho! Taylor. Who do you think we are?' Turning his eyes to the Z9, he made a cutting motion with his flat hand. The woman seized Taylor's wrist and tapped in a code.

'You can communicate again when *we* are ready,' she said. The ascender stopped at the next floor and they carried on to the office.

Jarvis sat in his recliner and waited as they manoeuvred Taylor into a suitable angle to see the screen wall. The lights dimmed and a vid ran.

Taylor saw himself circling the outside of the Dome on his way to Download. The green algae lamps, the rats with their glowing eyes and then the picture turned to mush and crackle. It picked up again at the watch station with the Scallie screaming his complaints to the desk sergeant. The picture went dark and flashes of lightning could be seen escaping from the cracks in the building fabric. Two SP dragged a limp figure round the back. A new shot in the hospital showed two heavily bandaged men lying comatose with tubes leading in and out of their beds. Monitors beeped and displayed life signs. Very low life signs indeed.

A new shot showed Taylor out of bounds in the factory area. Another where the spy bee searches for him in mad haste to recapture its target. The scene faded and the office lights came on again.

'Well, Taylor what do you think of that?' he said.

'We live in dangerous times,' said Taylor.

'You like killing Scallies don't you Taylor? You killed that one on the tubes and tried to blame it on an accident for a start, and now this. Several have gone missing, unexplained, lately. What do you think the Mayor's Court would think of all this, especially if we told them you liked evading surveillance bees and have clever people who can destroy video evidence remotely – your little friend Jack, for instance?'

He beamed at Taylor.

'I have no exact proof but it doesn't look good does it? ESO doesn't want psychopaths out here. Here, where we have to watch each other's backs. We are at the frontier, accidents happen but to lose the rule of law is to lose everything.'

Taylor decided to say nothing. The psychopath was there on the other side of the desk. He daren't make him snap. He raised his eyebrows in question.

Jarvis stared for a moment and then giggled unpleasantly.

'I see we understand each other. You're mine now Mr Taylor. You may go. You two take Taylor home so he can rest his foot. And help him to repair his wrist – we may need to contact him at any time.'

He swivelled away in dismissal.

***

Back in his room, Taylor reviewed his situation. What had he done? How had this state of affairs come about? At a loss, he lay back, keeping his sore foot elevated.

He drifted to a much earlier time. Outside, sat gloomily surveying his helizep framework. It squatted on tubular floats, inspired by the base floats. No engine, no propeller blades. Yes, he could float it on the water but all he stared at was a complicated boat.

Wallis had called him. What now? I'm not in the mood, he'd thought. He'd trudged wearily around to the base. Off to the south he saw the airship leaving. It came in once a week or so. They were buoyed by hydrogen. To use hydrogen on his design he still needed motor assistance to provide lift as well as propulsion. A hydrogen canopy required a huge gasbag such as would make his design unwieldy. Cartwright's notes indicated the amount of gas required to lift a framework, engine and crew. Hard to get, hard to contain, hard to store, hydrogen was one of those wonder promises for the green age that needed more energy to make use of it than it delivered. Unless used in the form of the airships; the Zepps as they were known.

His crew and Wallis were gathered around some long packages and a large wooden crate. They were grinning at him in anticipation.

'What?' he growled.

Wallis handed him a letter.

ESO. Advanced Organic Material Development Laboratory

Geneva

Dear Mark,

Your colleague, Mr Wallis, has taken the liberty of contacting us at Advanced Materials and sent us images and no doubt copied data of your project. On first reading, I think I would be annoyed if this had happened to me but, as I looked through your designs and photographs, his reason for writing became apparent. You are no doubt stalled for a sufficiently lightweight but powerful engine running on locally available biofuel. How you proposed to engineer suitable blades in the event you actually found an engine I would dearly like to hear. Our ubiquitous bamboo can do many things but I'm afraid there are times we must rely on good old metal and composites from times gone by.

We salute such innovation and are regularly dismayed that our own proposals are often greeted with lack of imagination. I am very excited for you and am delighted to send you some items you may find useful.

I hope to send two of our engineers up to you soon to assist and advise. They will have some suggestions regarding using hydrogen lift, which, you may know, we process from the geo thermal energy up in Iceland. You may have discounted the use of hot air from the engines as a lifting gas or indeed the use of blade propulsion for vectored thrust. I attach some sketch diagrams and some volume lift calculations you may find useful.

I can see an ESO-wide use for your application. Regular helicopters are worn out and reserved for limited emergency use with limited spares. Due to other pressing projects, for now, I must leave you to soldier on with the project. Please keep me updated and I hope we can meet one day

Yours,

Clive Benson.

Taylor looked up to see the group much increased; that he was the focus of a sea of grinning faces.

'Aren't you going to open your presents?' said Marie.

Inside the box was a bio diesel engine. He recognised the make from before.

Inside the long packages were sets of propeller blades from the same source.

'Thanks Wallis, thanks guys,' the only intelligible words he could say.

***

Now, back in his room, such triumphs and highlights were fading. Murder! Attacked by thugs, persecuted by power mad bureaucrats. He needed to get out of here but to where? He was not the hermit type. He had good friends and, if it weren't for the ultimate goal of finding his family, he was happy here.

***

They were downstairs in Joe's Smokey after a long hot day out repairing tubes. Only Taylor's team was there. They sat quietly, easy in each other's company, discussing what to do when their turn came for rest and recuperation. Work outside, if only every other day, the stress of the sun, the dangers and regularly pure physical labour could not be sustained indefinitely. They'd completed four of six months, most for the second or third time at this Dome Complex and they were lucky enough to reassign together.

Taylor was offered lab or admin jobs. Many interviews with the well wishing Wallis came to naught. Taylor wanted the sharp end as he called it. The outdoors. Nearly four years out on the tubes now.

'Come on Taylor, you've done your bit,' said Wallis.

But Taylor stayed. He'd die before he sat at a desk, sat in the cool claustrophobic Domes or caves of the UN or ESO. A hostile surface world held fewer fears for him than the cloistered cramped safety of the sheltered places. Besides, he'd lost everything from before. He dreamed of building a small farm one day. He fantasised he would complete it and then fly off in Heli-1and go and get them from behind the Iron Curtain.

Now he was under threat. He thought long and hard how he could turn the tables on Jarvis. Every avenue seemed closed to him. What if he ambushed him and his two bitches and dropped them out on the tubes at night…damn, they kept a file on him. He would be behaving as they predicted.

He thought of the other crews. Not all the heli crews were happy go lucky. Some were quite unhappy, hating the job and hating their colleagues. Not guaranteed to survive, they plodded through on minimum exertion, never volunteering, never adding to the fund of knowledge or the esprit de corps. Suicide was rare, maybe an effect of the survival instinct – like wanting sex after a close brush with death.

Fights would break out. Joe installed furniture that was either unbreakable or bio repairable from tube skin –

"YOU BREAK IT - YOU REPAIR IT"

This evening the low sun shone in through ceiling level windows no doubt placed originally to illuminate the cellar from street level. Curls of tobacco smoke wreathed about in the sun's rays reminding Taylor of times long ago when people smoked in cinemas; the projector light an interesting light show in itself. He stopped. Funny I've never noticed that – it would have triggered the cine-projector memory before today… A sixth sense alerted him. He held up a hand. They all froze; they respected his antennae for trouble.

A blinding flash and a bang! The escape door fell in, detached from its hinges. A cloud of dust cleared to reveal the cellar bar now also contained three burly SPs in full amour. They weren't Dome 3 troopers. They wore green, not black and they seemed better equipped, more gritty, more determined.

They stood deferentially aside to allow access for someone. A petite woman; cocky, brunette, sure of herself, she looked around the cellar. She wore a close fitting one-piece coverall in the same dark green as the troopers. Her eyes met Taylor's.

'Ah! Mr Taylor! I've heard of your ability and now I can say I've seen it for myself!'

Part Three

Quiet government men

Chapter One

Taylor, on sensing the attack, did his trick subconsciously. Down to floor level in a ball and then sideways to wherever his subconscious planned his escape. Part of old German Kurt's training come to his aid again.

Looking round he saw Jack and the other two unconscious on the floor. Marie looking over her shoulder at Ben, equally frozen with his characteristic pout.

'It's OK. Only temporary. It's a new stun device they...' she acknowledged the SPs, and not in a friendly way. '... use on the Scallies. They wake up wondering what happened to them.'

Taylor grunted. The SPs scowled.

'My name is Zill, come, there is someone waiting to consult with you.'

'So why the drama? You can get me on my 'wrist' anytime, and why do these people have to get hit?'

'They won't suffer at all; they saw nothing after the door blew in. You should normally be like this,' she indicated Ben.

'I didn't think your reflexes were quite so fast. They'll come round in five or ten minutes and wonder what happened, as you would have. I brought the muscle in case you weren't feeling cooperative.'

She looked around at the dusty bar paraphernalia, the sign over the door - Smokey – 'Smokey! How funny. Anyway, it's your habit. Here's a gesture of good will.'

Zill, supposedly Zill, threw two cartons of cigars down on the now dusty bar.

'Compensation for inconvenience for your friends. Now, come with me please.'

Zill turned and retreated through the broken door. Her eagle eyed troopers stared, daring him to try any tricks. They didn't like the public being agile enough to dodge Tasers and stasis stunners. They'd be dodging bullets next.

'Move it scumbag!' said the one with most medals. 'We ain't so nice.'

Taylor ducked through the door. Now what?

***

Taylor's eyes followed Zill's appealing rear aspect as they trudged along a brick lined arched tunnel. Their feet splashed through puddles and slippery green slime. An old service passageway? The troopers' earlier inbound footprints heading back the other way marked their path. Now, up some steps and out into the open to a previously overgrown but now cleared courtyard - hence the sunlight coming through the window! - an area where the ghosts of Victorian nannies and perambulators hinted at the corner of Taylor's mind's eye. Beyond, over the rooftops, the sinister nettle forest loomed its dark green, leaves the size of dinner plates, stems like oars.

Two helizeps appeared over the nettle canopy, dropping below roof level to land. One was a green and white SP troop carrier, the colours of Dome 1 down in Kent. The other, a silver and white machine. This was more like a proper factory machine from before. Zill led Taylor to the silver model. A hatch swung down with built in steps.

'In we go Mr Taylor.'

He seated himself and a padded arm swung down and around him - same for the woman. The door closed.

'Go,' she said.

The unfamiliar machine landing with its escort attracted a crowd of curious nettle gatherers. Outside the troopers formed a barrier to hold them back. An altercation broke out. The troopers levelled Dazers and the Dees moved away casting curious glances over their shoulders.

The craft lifted and swung away in what Taylor thought a North East direction. He looked out of either side window. To the left was the old town with its rippled Dome in the background. Where the safe people subsisted.

Home? I suppose it is now, thought Taylor. Out to the right were the waters and their white floating poly tunnel hydroponics farm tubes as far as the eye could see. Climbing out they went past a machine Zill had not seen before. A float with arms reaching up to strange floating balloon shapes. She looked askance at Taylor. He shrugged.

'A new idea. The floats lift up and down with the heat. They generate electricity.'

'And at night when it's colder?'

'They gradually sink down and wait for the next day.... they are the brain child of one of my crew, Ben. Ben saw a problem and devised a simple solution.'

'You have clever friends,' Zill said. 'I wondered what they were. Why aren't they legion across Europe? Why are these people here so...cagey with development ideas?'

Taylor had his own ideas.

'Not invented here. Would never work,' he said bitterly. 'But when multiplied across, what? One every hectare? Across all the acres of hydroponics farms, they provide a significant energy source. Wallis put him forward for a commendation…'

They were interrupted by the monitor holo-comsole. A handsome 3D face peered at them. It inspected Taylor then turned to Zill.

'OK Zill?' No probs?'

'None at all, be there in twenty minutes.'

Handsome smiled at both of them. His head withdrew into the projector screen as if by suction, then winked out.

The tubes were soon left behind and they flew into an area unfamiliar to Taylor. Some high ground islands appeared. Completely white from a white flower crop and the white buildings of a small bubble wrap city on the bigger island. Noting the direction of Taylor's gaze Zill looked out.

'God folk. See, they've preserved the steeple of the church.'

Down below they could see a bamboo framework of scaffolding surrounding an old church.

'Looks like Lincoln maybe. Is it?'

She shrugged.

'I didn't know where Lincoln was before.'

'God folk?'

'They behave like Amish or Mormons and cling to traditional before values. Hard work, no luxuries, fear, superstition and guilt. They send their missionaries and we lose a few of the weak minded and gullible to them every year. A lot don't make the trip. Scallies, sharks, vasps. That sort of thing.'

'That sort of thing. Dull everyday reality then'

'You and your chums are not the only outside crews.'

Taylor stared, waiting for her explanation. She smiled.

'We are sort of sociologists and psychologists. We monitor the different ways the people are dealing with all this.'

'We?' Who are we? The ZI?'

'You will hear more soon Taylor but no, we are not ZI.' She gave an involuntary half shiver. 'We have influence; they cooperate'

Taylor probed.

'So why me?'

'We need a capable practical outside engineer type with …. qualities.'

She eyed Taylor as if to see if he fitted the requirement.

'Qualities? Such as?'

'We need someone who knows the land, with leadership experience, creative initiative; who the ZI didn't care about losing - whether or not you returned. They don't like you Taylor. You are too unpredictable. You saw something best left out at sea. There's more, but not now.'

The machine flew on for a time then slowed. The engine throbbed in a deeper note as the disc whirling over their heads coarsened pitch in preparation for hover.

Zill keyed her intercom.

'Turn please, so we can see ahead.'

The heli swivelled 45°. Ahead, interrupting the smooth sea surface was the top of a ruined tower and a small hump of green hill.

'Watch this, not many get to see it…'

From the top of the tower, a red strobe light pulsed, interrogating the heli. A pencil beam of laser energy shot out hugging the sea surface then, radar-like, swept full circle clockwise.

The heli pilot must have satisfied the challenge; the strobe changed to green, flickered for a few seconds then stopped.

Taylor, never easily impressed, gaped in disbelief at what came next. Out of the water rose more towers similar to the first, then roof gables, then walls. A tiny stately home emerging from the sea.

'We call it Sandringham, what do you think?'

He didn't know whether to laugh or be angry. Such folly, such waste of energy, such a grandiose statement of symbolic regal power, he was half reassured that the world was on the mend; half fearful it had gone mad.

'I don't get it,' he said at last.

'You will. We're going in….'

The heli slanted down to land on a platform; marked Z, Taylor saw with suspicion.

'Z? The platform is Z, not H?'

'Paranoia, Taylor. Z is for Zepp.' She smiled properly for the first time. A lovely warm creature rather than the previously rather serious acolyte sat before him.

Stop it! he told himself.

The disc ran down to a safe speed, the door hissed open and the padded restraints swung clear. Zill jumped down and turned to offer Taylor her arm, an oddly solicitous gesture. He paused as if unwilling to leave the safety of the cabin. Instinctively he looked east for tidal waves, then around for other hazards.

'Don't worry; we are safe from vasps here.'

'How?'

'We have an electronic field of some sort. Besides, we are some way from the tubes.'

He was hurried down some steps then onto a descender platform.

They waited a minute during which time Taylor had chance to see much of the house was a façade of bamboo and painted nettle fabric. Below the façade was a concrete or stone jetty, only partly submerged. A fortification? It couldn't be a sea wall; that would be much further below.

Two young men wearing one-piece coveralls waved off the heli and joined them, their weight finally forcing the descender down.

The next level was not false.

***

Chapter Two

Taylor being taken away caused consternation at the agribase. A meeting was called in the heli hangar around and among six parked helizeps; one apparently undergoing maintenance, another, damaged, in pieces at the back.

Taylor was a cornerstone of their efforts; one of the older generation who remembered old world tricks. Taylor who developed the helizep to the point it became a necessity; nowadays their work could not be carried out without them.

Always the pressure to farm the algae, collect the methane, the ethanol for fuel. Always the manpower limitation - to those who could go outside - to those, when outside, who were of any practical use.

In fact the outside world was something of a mystery; Taylor being a link to it, if a link to a disappeared world. So, in somewhat of a clan gathering; Wallis addressed them.

'People, People, please remain calm. Taylor is acting in a consultative capacity to a research organization. Why he was taken in such bizarre circumstances, I do not know.'

From the crowd: 'He was snatched by an SP squad! The Dees saw it!'

Wallis identified Taylor's closest teammates.

'The woman was from a research group; you were all away from Dome security. They were merely escorting her.'

'They froze us man! They blew in the back wall of the club and snatched him away!'

Wallis knew he wasn't going to be able to bullshit them and changed tack.

'So you are in a, what? A sleazy bar, off duty, a bar not approved by the ZI, I might add, and a woman comes in and says, "Come with me please".....

They howled him down. Wallis relented.

'Look! I don't know. Let me talk to the ZI again and I'll let you all know! Taylor's team, two of you, meet me in my office in an hour. The rest of you, please, back to work!'

A silence fell. They were going nowhere. Wallis pushed through them and made his way back to his office unit. He was followed by three team members. About to wave them back, he noted their expressions, shrugged his shoulders and climbed the steps to his admin area.

Taylor was riding down a descender platform with three new friends. The two young men smiled, their name badges announced them as Steve and Mick. Taylor laughed. They smiled back, perplexed.

'I thought you would be 'Zeb' and 'Zod' or something.'

They frowned. Zill intervened:

'Mr Taylor is not sure whose side we are on.'

'Side?' Steve frowned. 'Are we not all on the same side?'

Steve was the handsome face on the holo-screen while they were airborne.

The platform stopped. Zill led the way, Mick gestured in a strange old-fashioned courteous way for Taylor to follow her. These days normally people barged and jostled, a constant irritation to Taylor's before manners.

Then all was revealed. They were standing on a metal non-slip deck, the conning tower of a submarine before them.

What else?

He pinched himself, closed his eyes and opened them. The sub was still there.

The hatch door was open. A friendly face leaned out and beckoned.

'You'll be Taylor; welcome! I'm Armstrong, number two here. Any good with ladders?'

Taylor had no problem with ladders but he did with a submarine. Feelings of claustrophobia and near panic rose up.

'It's OK Taylor, we are not submerging.'

Pale, he allowed himself to be led into the hatchway and down the ladder. To his surprise, at the bottom, it opened out into an airy space. Corridors led off and pipe work ran along the walls and decks as expected but his imagined cramped space with sonar arrays, light walls and charts was missing.

'Hmmm!' he eventually announced. 'Nuclear?'

'Sure, but only the engine, this is not a full warship now, but redesigned for the government in the event of a disaster.'

'Where are they now; still on the ship?'

'They never got here.' Looking round, Taylor saw the closest not meeting each other's eyes; the furthest watching the interplay with close interest.

'Taylor, we have much to tell you, plenty of time for questions later. You have had a busy day, time for refreshment, a night's sleep and tomorrow, meet the boss. He flies in tomorrow. This elaborate construction above? We cannot dock this boat anymore, at least not around here, and we need to go ashore in peace. We'd go crazy otherwise. It is one of our homes if you like. We are quite proud of it and we like to feel there is still a sense of humour, a sense of doing something creative…sometimes it moves about and we have to find it, pop up underneath and bring it back here. Once we had to start it all over again. We tried tethering it but it survives better if it goes with the storms. Our people like repairing it, adding to it. It is therapeutic.'

Armstrong was Taylor's type. His humour went with the situation at hand. Taylor hoped they were on the same side.

"They never got here," he'd said.

***

Marie and Ben sat on the bamboo jetty looking down into the water. Dappled reflections like smoke rings shimmered across their faces. The canopy overhead seemed alive with larger versions of the reflections. Taylor would have grunted and said something like "Mysterons."

Below, medium sized fish gathered expectantly in case any food appeared from the sky

'What are they?' asked Marie.

'Fish. Cold blooded vertebrates; they can extract oxygen from water.'

This remark cost him a sharp elbow in the ribs.

'What sort of fish? Taylor would know. Can't we go looking for him?'

'You heard Wallis. Stay calm.'

She blew out and hissed in frustration and worry.

'Do you think he's dead? I mean, his wrist is down, off the system….'

'Why? If they wanted him gone they could have reassigned him, arranged an accident…the Scallies, helizep crash, I dunno.'

'He ran into some Scallies recently, at the last download. That training in self defence he did, from before…'

In these times, mention of before always brought pause in any conversation; the subject more often than not swiftly changed.

'Where were you Ben? When…you know?'

Ben's eyes lost focus. 'We were on a trip to Cornwall, the Eden project. The weather got worse and worse. Most of the activities were cancelled. We kept going to the little local airport and then being sent back to the hotel. Back and forth, back and forth like yoyos. The roads were jammed solid, see. No way out there. I remember the sky was

126

dark black, angry. The wind was blowing out windows. An inbound jet crashed on the runway. They took us to one of the shelters, the ones prepared for nuclear war. There were busloads of people, tourists, business types, and school kids. There were rows and rows of beds, bunk beds, kitchens, mess halls. We were safe but we really wanted to be home. We watched the news from around the world. It got so bad they started restricting it. Then, no news, no phones, and no internet.'

He paused, reliving the terrible experience.

'We were lucky; we had food enough for months. The ZI made sure of it. They knew it was going to happen. They stopped people coming in after a few days. Soldiers guarded a volunteer group who took soup and bread outside to the refugees we had no room for. Then the storms got worse and nobody was allowed out. After three days, the soldiers went out to look. We heard gunfire, not all the soldiers came back. Outside the mobs tried to break in. They were starving. They lit fires, tried to smoke us out. The shelters were equipped with filters, positive pressure, heating….'

'When we eventually came out there were bodies everywhere. Legs and body parts missing….' He fell silent. After a pause he went on.

'They asked for volunteers. 'Actives' they said. People who wanted to do something about the situation. Well, you know the rest…'

An alarm sounded; loss of pressure out on one of the tubes again triggering a relay beacon. The spell broken, the two of them leapt up and went quickly up to the control room. A grid on a screen flashed a red circle; a numerical grid reference and plot printed out from a small printer in the corner. Jack was there already. He pressed keys and an overlay showed the location in map terms. The information was sent to their wrists. Hearing a helizep start up, they donned Protec gear and joined the rest of the crew.

The new guy Harry was standing by Heli-1, ignored by the tech crew. Jack jumped into the left hand seat.

'You'll be Harry the new pilot, I take it. I'm Jack, this is Marie, Ben…'

They shook hands all round.

'In you get, Harry.'

' Done this before?' Marie said.

'You'll have to show me the ropes,' Harry said, strapping in and flicking switches.

Jack watched him at the controls. Seemed competent so far.

'You'll be OK. This is a routine job. We've had a bit of bother, the usual guy, who sits where you are, had to go away away suddenly. He would have given you some time; showed you around. No time today. Don't worry; you'll soon get the idea...'

Lifting off, they hovered, waiting for radio confirmation from their usual backup heli team, Hansen and his crew.

***

The two helis converged on the alarm area. A faint misting of gas blew vertical from a tube join.

Jack radioed Hansen.

'Hansen, we got a new pilot. We'll drop down and do the fix. Give him some idea of what we do, OK?'

'OK, We'll be up at 1000 feet out of reach of you know who. Keep an eye out for you. You still owe Kristen for last spotting.'

The job was routine. Thanks to Jack's signalling alarms, the number of hours patrolling was cut down. Time out over the tubes in the blazing sun was wear and tear on the crews, wear and tear on the helis and equipment.

Today a loss of pressure was leaking methane out into atmosphere. The problem with leaks was that the gases could ignite, burn and kill off the algae; eventually burning away the tube fabric for miles. Genetic engineering had not overcome the problem of the flammability of organic materials.

***

The relief pilot, Harry, was young and unsure but, not to be seen as green, he went straight down for landing.

'Whoa! Easy tiger! Go back up!' yelled Jack. The heli climbed to fifty feet. Ben and Marie threw smoke sticks down.

'Watch for the wind and land cross wind from the leak! If we land up or downwind we can set the gas alight with our engine exhaust!'

Harry, red faced, swore. 'Shit, sorry! I forgot!' He went back down and executed a careful landing across from the tube join. Jack pointed the damage to him.

'See the rip in the bio-weld? Probably caused by the surge of a larger than normal wave. The tubes are flexible to a point but, baking in the sun and UV as they were, they become brittle with time.'

Today was routine; they laid out their mixing gear, clamped a cofferdam over the split and poured the bio-mix slurry. They were finishing off when Hansen swept low overhead. They had missed a radio call. Jack leaned into his seat.

'Whassup Hansen?'

'Tidal! Incoming!'

The other three heard that OK. They were back on the heli in seconds.

Looking out to sea Jack could see a slight shimmer on the horizon. They would never see a tidal wave coming in time without warning from above. He'd been slack not monitoring the radio.

'Lift off! Go! Go! Go!'

In his panic, Harry forgot to retract the tube hooks that held the heli stable while parked on the tube profile. By lifting off hard with them stuck into the tube, they jammed and bent, burying themselves deeper. They were stuck. Stuck with a destructive wave bearing tons of water and debris down on them.

Jack and Ben jumped out with axes to hack away the tube skin around the hooks. Out to sea the tidal was coming in lifting tubes like straws, snapping and scattering some like matchwood. The other heli angled down to take them off.

'No time!' screamed Jack. 'Back aboard! Jettison the frame!'

Harry was frozen, white with fear. Marie climbed across into the jump seat; snatched the safety cover from the jettison switch and punched hard.

Explosive bolts fired razor knives through lashings and dowels. The heli lifted off like a rocket but tilted sideways shedding framework and tube skin. Jack clung to the outside. 'Go! Go!'

Ben reached out to hold Jack secure while he wrapped a rope around his waist and through his belt.

'I have control!' Marie shouted and fought the controls to get the machine level. They lost some height, dropping, skittering close to the surface then regained straight and level. The forward breaker clawed at their tail as if trying to snatch them from the air. Ben was sure a piece of broken tube hit them on the rear float. Gradually the gap got wider and they fled the tidal with its close following wind until they found calmer air. She handed back control. In the back, Ben hauled Jack in across his knee and dragged the door panel shut.

In the front, Marie told Harry quietly, 'It's not your fault. Taylor would have put you through some hard training before you were allowed out. We were lazy. He'd go ape-shit if he knew.'

They flew home. Sometimes the cool safety of the Dome and dull repetitive factory work seemed attractive especially when rookie new guys were sent out without training.

Where was Taylor? He wouldn't let this shit happen!

Chapter Three

After being fed and watered on similar fare to the meals back at base, Taylor sat with Steve in Armstrong's cabin. Armstrong poured a tot of rum for the three of them.

'Are you a rum man Taylor?' he asked.

'Some say a rum cove but I was more a whisky man once. It's been so long I'd probably drink petrol and think it was a treat now.'

Steve's smile was beginning to waiver. The two older men had naturally lapsed into before language. Armstrong looked at him and back to Taylor.

'The youngsters think we carry our emotional baggage across the years, don't you Steve?'

'I wouldn't go that far but you do come out with some riddles and fanciful ideas...' Steve said, drinking a little too large a slug, spluttering and going cross-eyed. Armstrong eyed him.

'Nelson's navy fought most of its battles off their heads on this stuff.'

'Ah, yes, Nelson. He was the one with the one eye and the parrot...' said Steve.

This tickled Taylor. Rarer now but he could be consumed with the giggles at times.

'England expects every man – harr Jim Lad!' he said, tears starting to run down his cheeks. Armstrong was not far behind him.

'Load the carronades with pieces of eight...'

'Signal Squire Trelawney to cut the enemy line in half...no...stop...' The two older men were bent almost double with glee.

Steve looked at the pair in disgust.

'OK, OK, you win...'

'Sorry man, that was unfair,' said Taylor. Armstrong agreed.

'You should read Patrick O'Brian and Hornblower for a start,' said Taylor, recovering, wiping his eyes.

'Oh, sorry, where the hell would you get hold of such books,' he said sadly.

'Write the names down – they'll be on file on the boat somewhere,' said Steve.

It was Taylor's turn to look askance.

'You have a library on board?'

'An e-library. If we do not have it I can get it sent...'

Armstrong gave him a gentle kick; narrowed his brow. Taylor saw the gesture but let it pass. I got the technical manuals when I was designing the helizep. Why not?

To break the sudden awkwardness he asked them both,

'Well, what can you tell me? What happened to America for a start?'

'We've been over. Mainly martial law over on the east coast. Many fled north to the Canadian border. They still have massive storms, huge forest fires; they always dealt with extremes if you remember,' said Armstrong.

'...and the contrails up in the stratosphere? Is that them?'

'We think so,' said Steve. 'Weather ships, scientists trying to figure out what happened and what will happen...'

'And? What happened? What is going to happen?'

'Save it for Shams, the Boss. He likes to expound his theories. He generally thinks mankind is far too arrogant; too self important; that Earth neither knows nor cares we are here, like we don't notice bacteria or tiny insects.' The sailor seemed doubtful.

'He says that Earth is a spaceship; a biosphere that is going through a shake down, spring cleaning itself.'

'What about the sea levels?'

'We were much further underwater once, he says. In the last ice age, England was half a mile under ice. A few hundred feet of water here and there is not significant globally but it cleans up the carbon dioxide imbalance; the marine life increases in the warmer waters. We are down below 300 parts per million; nearly back at eighteenth century levels...he tells us.'

'Do you have reason to mistrust his figures?' said Taylor.

Steve looked at Armstrong. Armstrong nodded.

'On other days he talks about the Milankovitch Cycle. The Earth has moved a bit closer in to the sun,' said Steve.

'I'll be interested to meet this boss of yours. What about Europe, to the east, Russia and so on...?'

'Russia became Soviet again. The Wall is back up. If you think it was hard to cross over before in the Cold War, well, you can imagine. They and the Americans are still at fisticuffs,' said Armstrong.

Again, Steve thought he was being left out. Armstrong and Taylor sketched out the Cold War for him. Steve sat, eyebrows raised in amazement. The severance of communication made more sense to him now. He would have pursued them mercilessly for more details but Mick and Zill joined them. They let the conversation lighten up for a while before a natural pause heralded bedtime.

He was shown his cabin. Not much bigger than a cupboard,

nonetheless it held a shower cubicle; two narrow bunk beds, a narrow desk and chair with a screen which first welcomed his wrist electronically and then Taylor vocally by announcing:

'This is temporary accommodation – considered adequate for rest and bathroom facilities. Any extended stay here will attract more space and comfort. The ship is below sea level; we apologize but your communicator is not visible on the Dome system; this maybe either for a technical or a security reason or both. You will be briefed in the morning by the crew.'

Taylor imagined the screen entity pausing to assess the reaction to this announcement then, hearing no more, going off elsewhere to do things. He was tempted to call out 'Screen' to see how far it went before he called it back. Nonsense! He scolded himself for being over imaginative. He stripped his coverall off and used the shower. Cloth towels reminded him of old Italy – nobody's yet managed to work out how to simulate fluffy towelling from nettle weave, he thought.

Amusingly, a false porthole lit up and ran a simvid of a changing view as if seen through a real window. All the more unrealistic because it showed views as if from a ship hugging a coast of little fishing villages and coves; an unlikely sight these days.

Taylor fought off the temptation to peer closer, to look left and right as one would with a real porthole. He shuddered at the thought of opening the catch of a real one and turned away. All the same, it served a reassuring purpose and distracted him from this claustrophobic tomb he found himself in.

He climbed a creaking aluminium ladder and lay down on the top bunk. He mulled over his day and eventually fell asleep.

In the morning, he woke naturally to the porthole video displaying a sunrise over a marshland wreathed in fog and flickering green methane fire.

Fresh linen and a clean coverall lay on the bottom bunk. The clothing fitted as if tailored and he wondered briefly how long this meeting was planned. He shoehorned his boots back on in that lazy way of not undoing them sufficiently then struggling to force his feet in. A shoehorn! He'd picked up a shoehorn from the table with other complimentary toiletries without pausing to consider such an incongruity. Either a sense of humour or simply weird! Things you will need at the end of the world; encyclopaedias on physics, biology, agriculture, hunting and survival gear –fire lighting materials, axe, knife, fishing line, hooks, tarpaulins, ropes, first aid kit – shoehorn....

Then he considered his predicament

"We are not submerging" Armstrong had said. How could I stop them? Where would we go?

As if prompted by this thought a knock sounded on the bulkhead door. He waited; the knocker waited too so he opened it, somehow surprised that it was not locked.

Steve leant easily against the corridor wall. 'Ready?' He winked and led the way through several bulkheads. To the sides were laboratories, storerooms, small meeting rooms, and workshops. Some doors were closed tight guarded by radiation trefoil and skull and crossbones posters.

He heard a heli landing above, a minor hubbub as, presumably, the boss was reinstalled on his throne and then, quiet again.

They carried on to the mess hall where they ate breakfast. Nothing out of the ordinary; selecting a tray and then choosing from a row of bain-marie under hot lamps. He smelled coffee though, a nice change from nettle tea, the staple of the Dome areas. He looked around, found nothing amiss. The crewmembers were happy enough, joking and teasing like any people thrust together in a common environment.

After breakfast, Steve led him on through bulkheads past an exercise area and more cabins similar to the one in which Taylor spent the night. Eventually they came to a less stark, less functional carpeted area in a well-lit corridor. At the end was a conventional wooden door. Steve knocked and thrust the door open; gestured Taylor through before him.

The room was dark; an expensive desk filled the middle of the room. At the far end a screen flickered, some mathematical symbols and equations scrolled down the wall. The operator was hidden behind a high backed office chair turned away from him. It swung round.

'Taylor! Come in! Take a seat, stand, or wander about, whatever you want.'

A tall light skinned Asian Indian stood up, came round from behind his desk, a handsome man in his fifties with a bright smile and a warm dry handshake.

'My name is Shams. Shams Siddiqui. I am...' He laughed. 'I am the... they call me The Boss!' He looked around the room as if to confirm this for himself, turned back to Taylor.

Taylor waited, shrugged; gestured to indicate that the man's authority and status were not in question. *At least not at this stage.* The man's faint accent was from India or Pakistan. He did not move his head about though.

Siddiqui's eyes twinkled.

'You are not a fan of authority Mr Taylor. You don't suffer fools gladly!'

Taylor smiled. I'll take that as a compliment for now.

'I'd be exhausted for a start – not really into suffering either.'

'Yes, quite, we've all taken too much of that. So why are you here? It will take more than this cosy informal first chat to answer but for now, we want you to do something for us, something that might appeal to your sense of adventure. You will have many questions that I will try and anticipate. Look upon this as a first date – yes? No leaping into bed together yet? Ah-yes, Armstrong said you would understand that; would not take it literally… We have to move soon so I will not trouble you for long.

One question is: Who are we? A philosophical, separate branch of ESO, if you like. You may have heard of the Alphas; Cartwright and so on. We are a part of the Old World who was set up to deal with such a world as we see now. We thought to descend into savagery and barbarism would be a pity. It would be intolerable to lose all the knowledge: the Music, the Art, the Culture and the Science, everything that Mankind achieved. We earmarked certain people to be taken to safety in such an event. Quietly, the sum of all knowledge was stored centrally with copies in safe electronic and paper form. Quietly, a core of 'rebuilders' was trained to assemble, post holocaust, and help rebuild the world. Overtly, ESO and the Zero Interference System. Covertly; people such as myself. Resources were set aside…'

Here he indicated the vessel in which they now sat. As much to himself as to Taylor he continued, almost absent-mindedly…

'…many of the chosen did not make it, the catastrophe came so fast. We need new people but not the type we are seeing in the Domes. They seem to have picked up where they left off; the old house with a different roof and a different garden….'

More directly now he continued:

'How would you like to undergo some education, further education, some training, join our socio research group, visit the island peoples, report back – that sort of thing.'

'And if I don't?'

'You are free to go…'

'Now?'

'Of course, you are not a prisoner, although I would advise you that you are on a ZI watch list. You may find yourself moved away from your friends, your team, against your wishes. Our interest in you will forestall some of the unpleasantness. Do you know something they would…do you have information of any sort which could lead them to want you out of the way?' He already knew, thought Taylor. Zill knew.

Taylor told him of the body out on the tubes; the incendiary and the Z6's rather patronising indifference, instantly replaced by barely concealed anger when Taylor became forthright with him. Shams nodded. He looked inward somehow, as if it were no surprise.

'Yes, they don't take kindly to criticism. Zero Interference is a very competitive branch. A young one could very easily feel threatened.'

'They seem to interfere in direct proportion to their remit to not... interfere,' said Taylor.

'I might explain that they are to prevent outside interference from other organisations...' said Shams.

'Such as...?'

'Remember Americanisation? Coca Cola and so on...the general idea is to rebuild without foreign interference and cultural pressures from...well, not necessarily beneficial influences...'

Shams looked a little owlish, as if he relayed a message he did not particularly agree with.

'To some extent, ZI, such as you see at your Dome 3, are intolerant of "interference" from "Head Office", as it were.'

'And that's a good thing?'

Shams smiled but did not answer. Taylor drummed his fingers on a desk surface. He looked at the picture of the Royal Family. He would ask when the time came. He turned to Shams.

'I'd like to work with your organisation. It seems I am under pressure from various directions to move on. Always the same before. But now there are some loose ends and I'd like the opportunity to sleep on it, ask a few questions; get an overview. Also it is near harvest time and I do not want to completely withdraw from my agri post completely yet. Zill said you had influence. Can you keep them off my back for a while?'

'A sensible enough request. I can threaten to delay some resources but let's not highlight our mutual interest too much. The one who is causing you trouble is not in England for a while. A breathing space, where we need do nothing. As long as you keep a low profile. OK?'

Shams slapped the desktop; the deal was done.

'So, do you want to look around here? Get to know the crew?'

'Plenty of time for that and, if the truth be told, I am a little claustrophobic. To submerge...I'm not sure of my reaction, and I wouldn't want to make a fuss...do you have, I mean, where else do you go? Your crew must rest; there must be maintenance to carry out.

Armstrong said the crew used this, this elaborate construction, as a shore base. It all seems a bit Jules Verne to me. You must need fresh water, food and so on...'

'All in good time; yes, we do have other facilities. You will come to find out these things. For now we are interested in Dome 3; your zone, your specialisation if you like...'

A knock at the door; Steve poked his head through.

'There's a SP heli in the zone, Boss. Says do we want anything?'

Shams looked at Taylor.

'Our heli is away for a few hours. Shall I get you a lift home with our gallant custodians of the peace?'

Taylor nodded. Shams prodded a button on his desk.

– 'Mr Taylor is leaving – please make sure no part of the boat is visible.' To Steve;

'Yes, please arrange the transport.'

Shams turned back to Taylor who was shifting his weight from one leg to another; having second thoughts.

'What now? I get dropped to the sharks? We aren't on the best of terms back there.'

Shams shook his head.

'You are burdened with clichés! I'm not a villain. I'm a VIP Scientist who they gave this nice boat to ride around in. One of the grey men – the quiet government men. These SP are under central command. The ones you see back in your zone are similar in many ways to your agri teams. They act in support of the Dome bureaucracy, on loan if you like. Away from their command, well, they are the mice that play when the cat's away.

Remember you are like frontiersmen out here; it is not so long since it was a watery, barren wilderness. You well know yourself the struggle fighting with nature on a daily basis. Your local SP consider Dome 3 and its environs a backwater, a punishment. As do your junior local ZI personnel.'

Taylor went along with this assessment. It was only too true when viewed from the benefit of perspective. Quiet government men? Where was that from? Siddiqui? He was useless with names but it rang a bell.

'Taylor. I know it was you that designed most of the helicopter zeppelin concept. The central shaft drive – who would have thought of using Benson's ideas? Now your helizep is standard issue. The old capitalists would be spitting feathers because they could not sell such good ideas. I also know about the accumulators, that young man...' he consulted a sheet of paper, '...Ben, who is credited with the invention.

137

One of your crew. ESO have a file on you both.'

Taylor blew out his lips.

'...and Spy bees no doubt. You have me at a disadvantage. You know all about me, I know so little about you!'

'Go home Taylor. Think about us. If you decide against, you are little the wiser. We will fade like the ghosts we are.'

'I must admit to a sense of unreality. The...' he jabbed his thumb upwards, '...house takes some getting used to...'

'Did you know Sandringham before?'

'Saw it once. On a trip to the Norfolk coast'

Shams produced a worn and tattered pamphlet. Queen Elizabeth and her family were on the cover. He turned the pages. Saw a much bigger, much grander home. He passed it to Taylor. The modern above-water version was pale, skinny and rickety; its only credibility a trompe l'oeil, a trick on the unsuspecting eye in a heat-haze shimmering mirage.

'We hold on to the past. We know it, we like what we know. Mother Nature has decided against. We must learn to like the future.'

'We should learn to like what we have. '

'I think you will like being with us ... for a time anyway Taylor. I believe your team break for R&R soon. Don't leave it too long. This boat has...errands.

Steve will leave a code on your communicator. On your 'wrist'. I love simplicity. 'Wrist,' he said. He tried it out for size in a pompous accent:

'Excuse me I must consult my wrist...oh dear!' his delight faded to a frown.

'I would love to get back among the ordinary humans, the gossip, the jokes, the simple things. What would you call a communicator which resided on your elbow?'

Taylor raised an eyebrow. Siddiqui laughed his delighted self-deprecating laugh. The chair swung away. The screen on the wall scrolled. Taylor would come to recognize the end of interviews by the swinging chair. What was it about the name, Siddiqui? He couldn't remember.

He let himself out. This time Mick was waiting for him. Instead of retracing their steps, presumably intended as part of a guided tour, they climbed a ladder straight up to a hatchway on the deck behind the conning tower. The crew scurried about with an air of urgency.

'We were hoping for a bit of fresh air with the shade from Sandringham and the sea breeze...' He indicated the false towers and bamboo platforms. Tables and chairs, the trappings of outdoor garden activity folded and struck down a nearby hatch. The tidal had done some damage and part of a canvas wall flapped in the breeze.

'You have a storm coming,' Taylor interrupted. He pointed to the swell of the sea, held a wet finger up. 'No apparent wind direction. Pressure is dropping.'

Mick looked closely at him.

'You a walking weather station? We rely on electronics and equipment here.'

Taylor gestured inland.

'You need to be, working out there. Sometimes a minute's warning can save lives.'

They climbed up to the helipad in time to see an SP heli letting down to land. A Light Attack.

'Where's the fancy machine?'

'Dunno, maybe Zill's off again.'

'Busy girl our Zill.'

***

Chapter Four

Taylor squashed in with two grumpy SPs. He strapped in and looked out. Mick waved and turned to leave the deck when something hit him on the shoulder and clattered to the platform.

Mick picked up the object. A shoehorn.

***

The Litak closed hatches, took off and swept away southwest.

The heli was an ex Army model. It held extra comms and gun racks with panniers strapped to the outsides and Dazer racks slung below. The pilot sat ahead, shoulders in a determined set. He did not acknowledge his passenger. His two silent escorts stared moodily out of the windows. They paused once at the tube edge. A canister the size of an old fashioned vacuum flask was dropped into the sea.

'Beacon for the boffins back there,' mumbled the SP. The only words spoken for the rest of the twenty-five minute ride back inland. Taylor noted the pilot's competent but crude handling, no mechanical sympathy, he kept it flat out all the way; something he and his crew may regret one day out in the unreclaimed territories.

He looked around. Compared it to the elementary design of a helizep. One of these would use huge quantities of fuel, frowned on in these times.

The sun was climbing in the sky, already baking England for the day. A haze blurred the horizon. Coming in over the shantytown, they rapidly lost height and came in to land near Joe's. A metre from the ground, one of the SPs slapped Taylor's harness release open and gestured for him to get out.

A cloud of dust blown up from the rotors enveloped the area. Taylor closed his eyes against the gritty air. Jumping clear, he landed, staggering to regain his balance. Without waiting to see if their passenger arrived in one piece, the Litak was up, spiralling away.

Attracted by the landing and dust cloud a small crowd gathered. Familiar faces pushed through to the front. Jack and Marie. The dust cleared to reveal Taylor dusting himself off, and then he was surrounded and borne inside by a cheering throng. Cheered by complete strangers. The Dees, who normally held themselves aloof from the other groups, were caught up in the excitement of the hero's return.

Marie and Jack took inventory.

'We got a message, "Be outside Joe's", it said.'

***

One Dee nudged his comrade, indicating the reunion:
'Who's that?
'Feck knows; they're happy. Beer flows when people are happy. Let's stick around.'

***

A semblance of routine followed. This was a lull in the storm seasons. Although no seasonal cycle was established, or at least not in Northern Europe, the Northern Hemisphere was still in what could be termed Winter. Maybe the storms were in the south. There were no worldwide weather bulletins. No global village now, merely villages around the globe.

For the next few days, Taylor's base carried out repairs and fixed leaks. Old tubes were evacuated of their gases, which in turn were sucked into a compression plant for further processing at the Dome factories. Taylor and the heli crews cut out tube sections into manageable lengths and heli'd or towed them into the sea basin down the sea canals left open for the purpose. There, Dees removed the sludge and put the empty tubes through a mincing machine. Manageable sized cubes were sent to a processing plant inside the Dome.

Taylor divided his time between one of his experiments, general coordination planning and training new personnel. His ESO group was due for rest and advance teams were coming in to provide continuity. His tired people would be given two months in the cooler higher parts of the world. This year it would be Iceland, a name that remained in spite of conditions.

***

All did not greet his return with the same joy. The new pilot, Harry, who'd nearly brought the crew to grief, was summoned to Taylor's workshop cum office. He stepped through the cooling veil, hovering nervously at the door. Enough sunlight passed through the thin water film to burn his shoulders. Under cover in the relative cool, Taylor was busy at a bench. If he noticed the young man, he did not show it so, when he eventually turned around, the poor guy was in a sweat

141

from both the baking sun and nervous terror.

He smiled at the woebegone face of the new boy.

'Best unhook before take off is my advice; especially when there's a big wave coming. When I started flying I made so many mistakes, it's a wonder I survived. They had wings then, wings and propellers. You had to race down a runway until you had enough speed to lift off. Helicopters, choppers, were for the military, police, rich men and big companies. Come.'

He led Harry round the back of the workshop. Two peculiar miniature versions of the tubes, apparently made from the same material as tube skin lay under a waterproof sheet. He flung the sheet aside. The bottom front edges had the bows of a boat. They were held apart by a stout bamboo framework weld, grown into the tube skin. The device looked like a raft.

'Floats,' said Taylor smugly.

'…Floats for my floatplane.' A little further on, he drew back another cover.

'Know what it is, Harry?'

Harry looked dumb.

'Internal Combustion Engine. Air cooled, horizontally opposed, this fan here, that's the prop, the propeller. Sucks air in and pushes it backwards if you like.'

He lovingly covered them over. 'Happy days that one but this…' he unlatched the lid of a wooden crate next to the engine. He beamed in triumph.

'I found this in an old warehouse on a drowned airfield. Gods were smiling that day…this is an aviation diesel. Two litres capacity, water cooled. Runs on diesel or Jet A1.'

Harry looked askance.

'It runs on biofuel!' explained Taylor in triumph.

'Does it work?'

'Oh yes but it uses fuel at a rate, well, I'd have the mayor down on me like a ton of bricks! This would use ten times a helizep would. No hydrogen lift, no efficient disc effect'

'A ton of…?'

'…sort of square or oblong rocks for building with.'

'They had strange concepts before.'

'Yes, I suppose we did!'

Harry blushed.

'I-I-I didn't…'

'Yes you did but it don't matter a shit now does it? Come; let's see if you can fly. I might show you some bricks…so, where's your heli?

142

We won't fly far without one!'

And so Harry joined the rest of the crew. Taylor made Harry do things with the heli, which once would have had Harry grounded, with the book thrown at him. Now there was no book other than the one you threw at yourself, for taking off 'hooks-in', for running out of fuel over the sea or nettle fields or for landing downwind of a gas leak.

Flying inland, Taylor showed him an old chimneystack and got Harry to hover over the top while Taylor climbed out on the frame and removed a loose brick from the rim. Harry nearly died from stress. How could he go back if Taylor fell? Inside or outside…? Jack, Marie, they would fly him back and drop him down the black hole as well.

Taylor climbed back on board. Harry, so busy keeping the heli stationary, hadn't seen his safety line.

'That's a brick, young man.'

Harry was beside himself. 'Are you crazy? I know what bricks are! What if you fell then? What if I'd not kept it steady while you were reaching? What would I do back at base if…?

'Lot of ifs there; mainly concern for what happens to you if *I* fall off. You gotta think like a team man. I'm on the edge of a broken tube, pulling Jack up out of the water, the sharks are circling, one false step from you and I'm down, Jack's down, under the tube, drowning, sharks…if you don't fly right.'

Taylor took control and they shot down to the surface, Harry's stomach heaving. Taylor knew none of his flight training included such drastic manoeuvres. Harry would've been taught to fly straight and level, to pick up weights under directions of a crewman on the ground.

Navigation over water would mean following a direction finding needle back to base. Now Taylor flung them across the sky into regions they were told never to go, inland to the ruined areas. The areas the ZI indicated as not recovered. Danger lurked here where the Scallie gangs and anarchy ruled. Mad survivors inhabited the ruins; with talk of cannibalism, escaped wild animals from the zoos, disease, mosquitoes in clouds and every child's nightmare – the vasps. The vasps were every parent's nightmare, transmitted to the kids.

'What about these vasps, Taylor?'

'Only over the tubes, vasps. Never seen inland for a long time now.'

'But they said we were never to go inland…'

'They? Did "they"? You'll soon find out what "they" say is true or not,' said Taylor.

The speed Taylor was going was not going to occasion Vasp

exposure at any rate. Until they slowed to a hover over a derelict road. As a road, it was useless. It was littered with abandoned vehicles. Smoke drifted up from some, the larger ones.

Taylor held off.

'That's a bus; someone lives in it by the look of the smoke…'

'A bus…?'

'Yeah -like a PTV on wheels.' Like most, Harry hated being patronized. He knew about cars and buses.

'Why the interest in a bus with wild people living on it?'

They continued circling the bus out of range of improvised missiles. He swung away and headed further down the road. It was a wide road, two distinct grey ribbons led away to some high water in the distance.

'This was the M6 I think, here, you have it.' Harry took control.

Taylor opened a paper map, unfolded it with great care and found their position. 'Yes – the M6. If we follow it west, we reach Birmingham…'

He looked over at Harry.

'Sorry; those people on the bus…'

He considered, wondering how "on side" Harry was. He shrugged. What the hell?

'The ZI are supposed to get to these people, reintroduce them to society; help them.'

'I thought they were not to interfere?'

'Quite; not allow interference with rebuilding societies. Let them grow naturally under healthy conditions. But these wild people, look, they are surviving in a harsh world. Back to primitive almost. The ZI should offer rewards for reclaiming the metal and resources on that road. Instead, they send squads of Resource Recovery Teams. The locals don't like it so SPs arm up for a big fight and end up alienating the survivors further. Driving them further into….'

He stopped, on the verge of rant.

'The Domeys? I hear you thinking. The Domeys don't give a flying toss. Follow the road. Keep to the north side so we can look down.'

Below lay the motorway, a junkyard of rusting abandoned machinery. The odd surviving windscreen flashed back the sunlight, momentarily dazzling them. Harry didn't have his sun visor down; the heli banked left and right, weaving about.

'Don't stare! Shut your eyes and look away!'

Taylor took control while Harry rubbed his eyes, after images of black and orange orbs faded slowly as his vision returned.

He sensed the lad beside him gazing at him in wonder. What mistakes did I make and get away with? He probably thinks I have a trick or a tip for every occasion! Bet they told him the old were sent to the weaving and algae factories.

Looking down at the human disaster on the road below Taylor's thoughts, as usual, went back to before. The Basra road out of Kuwait to Baghdad; burnt out trucks and jeeps with their charred skeletons. The road to the sea at Dunkirk; packed with refugees in their overloaded cars, vans, horses and carts; Stuka dive-bombers with wailing sirens hounding the fleeing families; Messerschmitt fighters strafing the people in the ditches at the roadside with their cannon.

How many roads of refugees littered history? Why did mankind flee from adversity along roads? Surely, survival would be more likely if they scattered in all directions but no, mankind liked to bunch together; liked to flee desperately from known danger to the unknown ahead.

Where were all these people fleeing to? Surely they were safer in the buildings of the city?

But then he remembered the million ampere lightning striking like invader's rays from outer space. The panic, the confusion; a blitz from nowhere…

Up ahead an urban area shimmered. The heat haze obscured it up until now; the hot bricks, stone, metal buildings and tarmac heating the air relatively more than the land. Mirror like layers of floating mirages danced before them.

As they got closer Taylor tensed, chopped his hand to signal 'slow to hover.'

'Down we go!'

Below they saw a remarkable sight, across some parched former open grassland, a human ran like the wind. He was pursued by a pack of wild dogs. Big nasty loping brutes. Surely, they must soon run him down? But no, the figure, a youth, maintained the gap with ease, performing prodigious leaps and bounds over obstacles.

'Look at him go!' cheered on Taylor.

'Right, Harry, man down on the tubes – tidal incoming – snatch him off!'

'Oh shit!'

With clenched teeth, Harry took the heli down and levelled off parallel with the ground, pulling level with the dogs. Taylor was out of his seat pulling open the door. Leaning out he emptied his Taser into the pack. Several went down squealing and yelping in a web of crackling sparks. Then he hurled a cargo net out in front of the lead dogs. This tripped and bowled over four more of them. Still three dogs bounded ahead. Nothing but their quarry mattered.

Taylor swung out the cargo loader gantry; clipped another cargo net into place.

'Down, close. Closer! Ahead! Get the boy!'

The runner seemed to think there were now two enemies; he changed course away but Harry was ready. Taylor had a second to be surprised with admiration for Harry's deft piloting then had to hang on as the heli's catch net scooped the runner neatly off the ground. Taylor bellowed and signalled 'Up! Up! Up!' - with the boy powerless; gravity from the fast lifting aircraft pinned him to the mesh.

The lead dog's teeth snapped closed short of the youth's dangling leg.

The heli made distance, up and away. The dogs snarled and bayed at their disappearing dinner.

A hundred feet up in the air, Taylor beckoned the lad aboard. As wild as the dogs he snarled and spat his refusal. Some freak of aerodynamics flung the spittle back in his face. Briefly, his vicious countenance was gone, replaced by such a look of innocent surprise that Taylor laughed.

'Find us somewhere safe to drop "Grateful" off!'

They dropped down to a flat roofed building. Before landing, he waited as Harry spun round 360°, looking for trouble.

'Bravo! We're getting there!'

Taylor clapped Harry on the back.

They touched down, the boy jumping clear, down into a crouch looking for exits and adversaries. He ran towards the edge. Taylor followed him, hand ready on his Taser. It was empty but the boy didn't know that. Harry switched off the engine; it went quiet. The boy looked around, looked at Taylor and pointed.

'Nem? You?

Taylor pointed to his name badge stencilled on his overalls.

The boy shook his head and then, to their surprise, took out an old cell phone, aimed the camera, first at Taylor, then Harry, then closer at Taylor's badge. He put it away then tapped two fingers to his head, and then to his wrist, presumably in salute. A half smile played on his lips and then he was gone, over the side of the roof and down.

'Shit!' Taylor ran to the edge and looked down, expecting a body. But no, the boy hit the ground running. He was off and away. Peering over the edge Taylor saw a drain pipe. He rejoined Harry, climbed back into his seat.

'Is he dead?'

146

'No he scrambled down a pipe, hell of a drop though, and ran off!'

'Jeez! But again, he was motoring when we came alongside.'

'How fast...?'

'...must have been nearly thirty kph.'

'Thirty? In old money that's...over twenty miles an hour! You sure...?'

'Yep.'

They circled around the area, recording grid references, photo-imaged the dog pack that had recovered and reassembled, barking and snarling at the helizep.

Taylor shook his fist at them, sending them into a comical fury as they jumped and bit at the air.

'Look at those bastards. They won't be fetching your slippers! Don't drop in here for a picnic, Harry.'

'Picnic?' he ventured. 'Slippers?'

'Take us home via the chimney.'

He laughed at Harry's face as his heart visibly sank.

'The chimney? What are you gonna do?'

'Give them their brick back of course. Forgot we had it. Could have taken out another dog... if it's a nice day tomorrow we'll have a picnic.'

'Taylor ... can I ask a favour?'

'Fire away.'

'C-can I have the brick?'

Taylor clapped him on the back for the second time in an hour.

'No. Get your own. Imagine how much I was shitting myself as you wavered all over the sky...'

The lad would never dare ask where exactly the chimney was. He was too proud and flushed with his day to spoil it. He would find it himself; if it killed him.

Which was exactly what Taylor wanted.

It was not until later that Taylor wondered about the strange salute. He tapped his head then his forearm. Had he ever worn a wrist? I will remember this – it is stored in my memory.

***

Unknown to them both their little adventure did not go unrecorded. A high flying Litak trailed them home.

Two SPs muttered.

'...fokking good pilot down there, what they doin' out here?'

'Can't be training, flying like that...why not let the Scallie feed the dogs?'

'Hmm, pilot's on the watch list,' noted Number Two.

A screen scrolled…

Taylor, Two weeks Zero…report all significances to Z6.

'What are signifi…snifi...snagances?'

'…rescuing Scallies from dog packs…' mused Number One.

'Scallies that run like…like…' stuck for comparison he gave up, 'like fast things.'

SPs were not chosen for their literacy or imagination. Taylor would have provided words like Greyhound or Cheetah, but they would have been little wiser…

Chapter Five

Next shift day, first thing, Taylor was called in again. He sprawled easily across from Wallis who fidgeted, sighed and thumped the desk in a half-hearted way.

Wallis spun his screen, indicated a memo. 'Signal from ZI here.'

Taylor went heavy lidded.

'You failed to report an SSE – a Significant Sociological Event!'

'What...a smiling SP?... a ZI with dirty hands... sunburn?'

Wallis rubbed his eyes wearily.

'Why can't you rub along with them? Keep the peace? Christ, we all rotate out of here in...' he consulted a wall chart. 'Sixty days.'

He blew out a sigh.

'...give me the details, I'll file it.'

Taylor gave him a brief outline. Wallis jerked up in interest.

'How fast...?'

Taylor knew Wallis. Like many intelligent men, he would only listen to what he wanted to hear. He would sooner claim the dogs were slow, debilitated and sickly than accept the idea of an Olympic sprinting, hurdling Scallie.

'...fast as dogs.'

'What sort of dogs?'

'Well I think I saw a King Charles spaniel, a Dachshund, couple of Corgis...'

'Stop taking the piss. What do I report?'

'Hungry, mean, wild, fast dogs.'

'What was that new boy doing? Didn't he record the event?'

'He was doing a good job of flying but his pen ran out...against flight rules to operate his wrist while flying, is it not?'

Wallis glared at him but transmitted the report anyway.

'Keep your head down Taylor. I still don't know what your little outing on weird helis was about yet,'

His eyes pleaded for information. Getting no response, he slapped both palms down on the desk. Taylor was already out of the door.

'How do you know I've finished with you?'

'You always finish like that, palms face down, face like a disappointed troll!'

Taylor was back in his workshop before he remembered the Scallie's camera phone. He paused. No; Wallis would throw him out for real; a Scallie with a mobile phone? How would he recharge it? How would he display any worthwhile images? Shit, what if they had

149

a GSM cell network back in action? The mobile phone network died with the storms. No, such information would never be received gladly by the likes of Wallis. He would treat it as a spoof, a further erosion of his fragile authority. He thought of the Z6; "Thank you, we'll deal with it. You're mine…"

Later, back in his rooms, Taylor discovered a new terminal in addition to the issue version. This was neater, smaller, a glass orb with a fibre optic solar array reaching to daylight. The keyboard was virtual and shone onto the desk. He wondered how, and on whose authority, it was installed there.

His wrist interrogated it and the screen came to life. A spinning 3-D image slowed; a picture of a shoe horn on a steel deck plate.

The message, from Shams, read:

"You have a choice, Taylor. Be one of our quiet government men, or remain accused of murder."

And;

"Best you lie low with us for a spell. Ten days while we bring pressure to bear on ZI. Cleared with Wallis. Pick up usual place. 4 pm. Workday 4. Mick."

Day Four? The day after tomorrow.

He sent a message to Wallis and Jack to rearrange the crew shift. – Harry OK – he added.

He heard a footfall behind him. He whirled round ready to fight.

'Ginny…Hi! '

'Do you like your new toy? It was in my basket with a note to put it in your room.'

'Oh, thanks. Sorry to have caused you any…'

'It's OK. A surprise though. Kept Mum and Dad going for an hour or two.'

He watched her move around the room, straightening and tidying. She came near and he resisted the temptation to grab her round the waist. He stood up and she pretended to stumble and fall against him. Taylor's nerves were on fire. It had been a long time. He put his arms round her. She looked up and smiled. This was it.

A knock at his door and it slid open. Marie stood there. Ginny broke away and made for the door.

The two women greeted each other with frosty smiles and nods. Entering, Marie slammed the door on the retreating figure. Marie sniffed the air and, as if confirming her suspicions, said,

'Screwing the help are we?'

Taylor eyed her. 'Your concern being…?'

'You know very well, is it not obvious? You've always made out

150

you were waiting for Sally. You're a fucking hypocrite, and that little Dee girl is barely an adult!'

Taylor manoeuvred himself to protect fragile objects. He'd been here before, seen that look in a woman's eyes.

'If you don't like it…I'm just a bloke…I promised nothing…my family probably think I'm dead! Fuck off! Get off my back!'

'I will not reassign! I stay with you!' she hissed.

She hurled a vase at him. She forgot Taylor was not an easy target. She saw the new terminal. 'What's that?'

'A present from my new friends…' He reached down to pick up the vase, unbroken, adding to Marie's fury.

'So! You reassign! You want to leave us!'

'It's not like that…'

Bursting into tears, she fled the room, leaving Taylor half reaching after her.

He turned to the new screen. A second message – N E 1 u want from your crew? He cursed; Thought that shorthand texting went away with the phones! He answered in the negative. It's not their problem. If they join me they'll have Jarvis after them.

He threw a cloth over the fibre optic. The screen holo faded away to a glass ball on the desktop. The projected keyboard disappeared.

Checking his Taser charge he headed off out for beer, not Joe's, away from the crew. He rode the PTV around the Dome and got off at a small public plaza three quarters around the perimeter. There were chairs, tables and a central water feature. A veil of water fell, leaving a pleasant cool breeze. A young woman came out from a small convenience café; Da-Gill on her badge. She dropped a composite cup on the table; pressed a button and a holo menu shone on the table surface.

'Like a Pronto burger? Any Pronto Pasta for the outdoors gentleman?'

He shook his head. He couldn't believe anyone actually enjoyed the horrible meat substitute food served in the Dome. He might try some seafood.

He helped himself to water from the veil. He watched the play of water for a while. It gave the impression of both falling and rising. Inserting his hand into the stream he experienced a tingle of static and his hand was gently nudged upwards.

He pondered the phenomenon – it goes both ways! Nothing is ever wasted or poured away –nothing is drained away for frivolity here!

Seeing no outside use for such an application, he gave up. Da-Gill took his order, a pitcher of beer and a prawn sandwich. She wriggled more than necessary, fluttered eyelashes. Some Dee girls were students waiting for full status. Scale D did not necessarily mean one was stupid or illiterate. Da-Gill looked bright enough.

Wish I was younger – the young lads use 'em and toss 'em aside – think nothing of it.

He considered Marie. She was a lovely, clever girl. Mankind was better off because of her. Her lab experiments significantly cut wastage of algae due to disease and sun attack. Work, which before would have gained her a Nobel Prize.

She always made her feelings obvious. The more he feigned indifference the more she pursued him. Months back, he had stipulated he couldn't have a relationship – a thing – with someone he worked so closely with. He suggested she reassign to another crew. Only then could he entertain such an idea. Bad for morale, causing resentment, accusations of favouritism were failed arguments. He had the last word:

'What if we get into trouble out there? What if you and the others are in the water? Who do I choose to save first?'

He knew he sounded pompous but he'd lost dear ones – many people had – and he didn't want a repeat. Nevertheless, he felt like a coward, unable to commit. He knew she wouldn't move.

The water. Always the bloody water. The water changed all their lives. The single most crucial element to man after oxygen. Now, too much of it. It teemed with tropical predators; its invisible water vapour controlled the whole planet's weather system. That, and the boiling sun, made the differential pressures and maelstroms of nature constantly trying to put itself in equilibrium; constantly failing.

Now, with not enough of the right sort of land in safe areas to sustain the food requirements; the water supported the tube system, cooled it and presented it to the life giving sun.

Interrupting his reverie, up strode Hansen. Hansen the Norwegian.

'No hiding places for you Taylor!'

Taylor corrected him. He usually did.

'Hiding place – not places. I believe in coincidence but not all the time! What do you want?'

Hansen made no pretence of dissembling. He'd sought Taylor out.

'Those ZI bastars came to see me. A Z6 and cronies, Jervaise…'

'Jarvis…'

'Yeah, Jervis. He said things could go better for me, being a Noggie, if I kept them informed of your – er – activities'

'Not surprised. Your Noggie pals are always after our fish…'

'Ya, fuck you Taylor by the way. You know I have not been in home for…since before…'

Taylor considered.

'I am to help set up a new tube system up north. The SPs have finally cleared the Scallies and bandits. Special project; pure bio-ethanol.'

Hansen feasted on this. It sounded good, Taylor was known to have been away for a meeting; the ZI had announced SP successes in the North…

'Taking your crew with…?'

'Dunno yet'

'Can I have them?'

'They aren't mine to give. Ask them. Besides, what's wrong with your gang? Seem competent to me…?'

Hansen gazed away, troubled. 'Out there they are fine. Back here – night horses. As soon as the pressure's off, they turn back to before. Shit, I've got an Israeli and a Palestinian, an Irishman and a French lesbian…they fight like cats and dogs, Taylor. They do my mind in.'

'Head…'

'What?'

'They do your head in.'

'So you know already – why do you ask?'

Taylor gave up, tried again.

'I'd have thought a modern Scandinavian would be ideal to stand between the warring tribes of the world.'

'That French bitch, I'd give it to her one, and she knows it. What a body. She makes up to Flynn, to drive me wild.'

'What does Flynn say?'

'Feck off ye feckin' cow!'

A passable imitation, thought Taylor. He imagined Kristen changing places with Marie. Hansen got up to leave. He noticed a spy bee hovering nearby in a decorative orchid, an oxygen plant.

'Shee-it! they gain nothing from me... looks like we are typed!'

'Taped.'

'Eh? Oh yeah – must listen to your Norwegian one day!'

Droop shouldered he wandered off.

Chapter Six

On Day Four, Taylor went to Joe's and made his way down to the Cellar bar. He let himself out of the escape door. It was repaired and left to open and close; now the not so secret was known.

He squelched along the corridor. He saw the old footprints there and back. It reminded him of his last sortie; reminded him it was real.

Outside, the Dees had been and gone, done their work and cleared the nettles away. Already, young shoots sprang forth. As he brushed past them, they smeared their poison on his boots. He remembered nettles as a young boy. One sting and a whole patch would be laid waste with a temper driven stick. That such a weed should be a saviour, a valuable crop, was not new. Armies, including Napoleon's and the Kaiser's Germany, had marched to war clothed in nettle fabric.

Out in the clearing, he heard a faint 'voff-voff-voff' and down came the silver machine. The hatch swung down. The pilot beckoned him forward. He was the only passenger.

***

Marie wandered into Taylor's workshop; his shed. A clutter of unfinished experiments and projects lay about. A miniature version of a tube-straddling robot he hoped to introduce next season. His airplane – "aeroplane" - he would correct them fiercely - he was still unwilling to proceed on that one unless they promised him fuel for his engine. He was distracted now. The ZI had annoyed him and then this mysterious project.

She regretted the harsh words with him before he left.

An old desk from recovery sat in the corner. On the corner, Taylor's Red Button – it was a joke of his – labelled "Press the Red Button to End the World". It was a wooden box with an old, what looked like an emergency machine stop button, which it was. Only half joking, he said he could tell a person's character from their reaction to it. The superstitious would shy away, roll their eyes, maybe pick it up to check it was attached to nothing. They would not press it. Now, Marie pressed it to see if he would come back to her. She paused, looked around. Apparently its power was diminished for today.

The day before, Taylor called a crew meet to discuss changing around a bit while he was away. Not for long, he'd said – "we rotate soon" - before Hansen's crew joined them. They trooped in and arranged themselves wherever suited their personal ways. The girl Kristen sat down in a lewd way directly on the button, leering at Hansen who scowled and blushed and folded his arms. Flynn, the Irish guy who acted tough but secretly read poetry and practised a mournful violin with a sound deadener switched high in his room. Flynn, who jabbed fiercely at the button in defiance, tilted his head, held a cupped hand to his ear. 'Bollocks!' he'd announced with satisfaction.

'Ah, but the world has changed – yesterday's world has ended,' ventured Taylor.

'How so…?

'Yesterday everyone thought you were a Schmegegge!* Today it is a certainty!' chortled Ari, enjoying the game. But he would not press it himself.

'Oi'll fokkin' Schmegegge you, you bastard!' growled Flynn.

'Gai kakhen afenyam!'**

*Schmegegge - A petty person, an untalented person. **-go shit in the ocean

In agreement, Hamid the Palestinian poised a hand over the button. He and Ari were best of friends but they liked to play a game:

'Tomorrow Allah will drown the infidels and the Zionists – I press so!' He made deliberate press, held it down for a second and then a more deliberate release. Taylor's crew stared, glanced at each other and settled their gazes around the room at objects less confrontational.

'You're a fekkin' eejit,' said Flynn. 'Maybe you should keep up with recent history! If Israel is gone so is Palestine!'

'Allah will provide! Allah Akhbar! God is great!'

Flynn jeered, 'So how come Saudi and Dubai kept all the money while you bastards were grovelling in the dust with the Israeli army's boots in your necks?'

'It is Allah's wish. It may be Allah's wish you do not return from the Tubes one day.'

'Enough!' roared Taylor 'Keep your witch doctors to yourselves! Jesus!' He looked towards Hansen as if to say - 'I see what you mean!'

Jack, Ben, Marie and Harry sat in dread. Taylor looked at them; decided.

'Hamid, change crews. Hansen, run short until we get some advance crews in.'

Meeting over they trooped out, Kristen drawing a finger lightly over Marie's chest as she left. Marie ignored her; she cared nothing about lesbians or religious minded either way but she knew a psycho when she saw one. She fingered her Tube knife meaningfully. Kristen shrugged and ducked out through the veil.

Taylor called, 'Hamid!' The Palestinian turned.

'Your religion and politics is your own business. Keep it that way on Crew One.'

Hamid nodded his acceptance and left. Taylor's crew breathed out.

Jack said: 'I'd drop them all out on the tubes'

Ben agreed: 'Take the ZI with you when you do,'

Marie, not to be left out, said: 'Not fair on the ZI....'

Tension broken, they'd made for Joe's.

***

Out past the tube extreme edge they flew past the tower. Taylor, looking down, could see the framework beneath the surface. Where now?

As if on cue, the holo screen came to life. Mick's 3-D face leered at him; withdrew, to be replaced by Steve.

'How's it going Taylor?'

'Bit informal aren't we? We hardly know each other. But, as you are asking, I am very well thank you in spite of being manipulated, spied on, fed on shit and kept in the dark.'

'Tasered any dogs lately?'

This, from Mick, whose face squeezed into view, the two faces merging into a weird conjunction, as if trapped in a glass sphere. Taylor was queasy.

'You're freaking' me out. Don't do that..!' Steve withdrew his face, growling at Mick who ignored him.

'Oho Taylor. You are top of the charts on the boat. Intrepid rescues and wild exploits, never a dull moment. That chimney? Do you have a death wish? Harry must have been shitting his suit!'

'How the f...?'

'The weather didn't blow the satellites away Taylor – no floods in orbit!'

-Of course! How could I forget?-

'So you must know what's going on worldwide? More than you told me, Steve?'

Steve replaced Mick. It would seem Mick was premature.

'There's a lot to take in. Best you get here and we'll brief you.'

'Here being? Where are you now? Disneyland?'

Steve consulted a screen.

'We have you on radar now. You land in about fifteen minutes or so.' He closed the link.

He thought, *where now?* as they flew over the seemingly endless North Sea. All would be revealed, no doubt. He made himself comfortable and closed his eyes.

The change in engine note woke him. The wind buffeted the craft as it began a circling descent. Taylor peered out of the window. Below lay an old North Sea oil platform with an 'H' symbol on the heli deck. Taylor found this strangely reassuring. The pilot spoke for the first time.

'It's a tension leg platform. Floating but tethered, built to take high seas. A good base if you want away from that madhouse you live in...'

He attended to his flying. Taylor could see Mick and Steve sheltering in the lee of a deck cabin. The heli, flaring down into a stiff breeze, was caught by a strong gust and skidded sideways. The pilot fought it back under control and took them up and round for another go.

'Want a hand there in front?'

In response, the pilot brought them back down for a perfect landing dead centre on the 'H'.

He turned to Taylor and grinned,

'Maybe I let you try her out on a calm day first.'

This small banter put Taylor in a good mood to greet his hosts. He swung the hatch open and down manually. The two young men stood to mock attention and saluted him.

'Zeb and Zod at your service, oh great confounder of dogs!'

'Get the kettle on you tossers!'

'The pot is warming as we speak. Earl Grey? Or Liptons?'

Chapter Seven

This time his accommodation was a big improvement on his transit bunk in the sub. There were real windows. Taylor looked out over the North Sea. The sea was a mighty beast, he reflected; water, salt and debris from the millennia but on a scale the human mind struggled with. No wonder it was such a beguiling thing, of such continuing interest to men of the ages. What impelled the early humans to set out across the unknown wastes to seek their food and fortunes? He turned back to the room; a suite with separate bathroom and sleeping area. Who lived here before? A burly oilman with wife and kids back on shore? Where? Aberdeen? Dundee? His wrist struck up a connection with the local system. Again, he was informed he was not in contact with the Dome – not to take alarm, merely a matter of range – that he would be able to connect with friends and colleagues once he was briefed by the crew. Again, he got the impression the voice was of an entity, a little bored with dealing with domestic trivia, under utilized, waiting for a challenge. Zill's holo image came to life in one corner.

'The Boss would like a minute of your time if you are ready.'

He looked around for no reason other than, perhaps subconsciously, wanting to give the impression he had something else to do. Turning back he nodded. The holo winked out. He was not sure he liked these hologram visits. What if he was naked or sat on the loo at the time? He would establish a protocol early on, he thought.

***

He found his own way to the meeting. Navy people moved here and there and pointed him in the right direction. Shams greeted him at the door this time.

'Taylor, come and sit down,' and led him to comfortable sofas around a glass coffee table. In place of magazines was a sheaf of notes. The Boss was as old fashioned as he was. Paper was frowned upon back at the Dome but Taylor still found a list, sketches, drawings which could be scribbled on, highlighted, made for better communication, better explanations face to face.

He paused while Zill poured tea; real tea on a tray, with a teapot, spoons, sugar lumps; cups and saucers. Polite conversation while the ritual was observed. Biscuits, home made apparently, were arranged in a fan on a plate.

'Taylor, we have a hectic schedule. I think this little...'

Here he indicated the tea set and surroundings with a sweep of his hand...'these little observances of old cannot but help slow down our frantic plunge towards death. Why are you back with us so soon? We intercepted your Mr Jarvis pushing hard to have you arrested for murder. His Chief is down in Kent and will curb his venom when he returns. We can't have our quiet capable people arrested, can we?

This aside, you were not comfortable with the submarine for one, and I know you want to wrap up your crew's work detail. Two, you are going to be busy so I suggest you do that and take your break with your colleagues. In the meantime, I want you to go away with some things to think about. We will talk over the next few days.

What's that, Zill? Mick? Oh yes. I hear Mick was premature in telling you of our surveillance. As pirate captain, I should give orders that he be walking the plank but he is quite useful. Maybe you could show him how to eradicate a vasp nest or do some brick collection inland.' He smiled.

He keyed a remote. A screen filled the end wall, a satellite map of Europe showing the drowned areas. Belgium, Holland, Denmark gone, great bites out of the European countries. Paris was still there, just. France and Spain, except for the south and the coastal areas were relatively unscathed.

'There is no census but we reckon on fifty per cent casualties as a direct result of the catastrophe. Another twenty five per cent maybe as a result of anarchy, disease and starvation. A dismal picture. I will arrange for a synopsis to be available in your room for your private viewing. Some find it a closure; most find it distressing. We do not have time. It would take as long to tell the story as the history itself.'

He looked at Zill.

'The young are fortunate; they do not have such constant adult comparison between before and now. However...' in an attempt to raise the mood he went on.

'We old soldiers have our own bag of tools, our own armoury of weapons, do we not?'

He picked up the sheaf of notes, shuffled them and slid them towards Taylor.

'Have a look through.'

Taylor leafed through the notes. As he read his eyebrows began to rise...

...: The predictions of global chaos had come true but for different reasons than the Greenhouse effect. Planet Earth now runs slightly closer in orbit around the sun than normal. It is a phenomenon known as the Milankovitch Cycle. Solar radiation melted the Arctic ice cap and Greenland and raised the sea level to such an extent that parts of UK and Europe were abandoned. The sea level is not fully explained by melting icecaps. An ice cube melting does not significantly alter the volume of a glass of water. Some tilt or relationship with the moon is suspected as possible.

The rich and influential got out in good time to meet uncertain but mostly dire outcomes but the less fortunate static masses came under socialist martial law. The economics of the times were ruined. Cooperative societies under the direction of the newly announced ESO sprang up on the high ground of Europe to house their remaining people and allocate necessary resources. One good spin off was that the scientists and engineers were under no economic constraint and were actively encouraged and free 'to do something about it'

Examples of note were natural solar cells – with energy resources depleted, coal mines flooded, oil rigs submerged, oil wells rendered useless by flood, - mankind needed energy and the increased solar radiation was free in more quantity than ever. Synthesised photosynthesis. Where the flat lands of the East Anglia fens once fed a nation now tubular white organic plastic tunnels criss-crossed the waters in sectors. White to reflect the sun as the ice once had. Tubular to hold the synthesis plants, the algae, which provided the base food material, the methane and, one day the hydrogen. The methane to burn and fuel the boilers; the hydrogen for the future hydro-motors...

***

To Taylor this all seemed to be written from a historical perspective; as if from the future addressed to a future further ahead. On the other side of the big room, Shams and Zill were busying themselves at a screen. Static crackled as they jabbed fingers with emphasis at the holo images. He read on and began to lose focus. There were many more pages with scientific data and statistics. He decided they could be absorbed later if required. Deeper in the pile he found an essay with the heading, "Ten Steps to Fascism".

It listed, with discussion and references, the following:
'Ten Steps to Fascism'

160

1. Invoke a terrifying internal and external enemy
2. Create a gulag
3. Develop a thug caste
4. Set up an internal surveillance system
5. Harass citizens' groups
6. Engage in arbitrary detention and release
7. Target key individuals
8. Control the press
9. Dissent equals treason
10. Suspend the rule of law

He paused, looked up to find both Zill and Shams watching him closely.

'Well, well, I know this place. I work there. Did you write this?'

Shams looked to Zill and back again.

'Have you heard of Raoul de Klayven?'

Taylor considered. 'Isn't he some Scallie bandit? A sort of warlord as was?'

'Yes, he wrote that, and now he is the leader of the Scale Es and is turning them into a guerrilla army.'

'You do have a lot of information.'

'Yes Taylor. He used to be my assistant.'

Chapter Eight

The two helizeps flew in loose formation. Hansen was leader in Heli-1 with Ari, Kristen and Flynn on board. Away from base, they were a tight team, scanning their sectors with close scrutiny – not a harsh word between them. Harry flew the larger heli-2 as number two with Marie in the co-pilot seat; Jack, Ben and Hamid at their stations in the back. Both crews were suited up in full protective clothing; air tanks and masks at the ready.

They were on a vasp hunt. At least four pairs of heli teams were geared up to sweep the area clean. In two weeks time the agris would start the harvest, bringing in the ripe seeded tubes for exploitation. At the water's edge near the Dome, the nearest tubes were already on their way into the factory to be processed. This left a natural harbour to float in the next level of tubes to be grappled and hauled inshore for processing. Many Dees would help, the groups, led by Wallis' teams, bolstered by the advance parties coming in to gain their own experience before their six months stint. Other helizep teams were coming up from a Dome further south. It was a big coordinated effort and they were under pressure to get the old tubes in and processed before the scorch and its storms season started.

They didn't need the attention of the predatory vasps so this was a concerted effort. Three nests had been sighted and now Helis 1 and 2 were tasked with their destruction. Vasps seemed to have uncanny hive intelligence. On detecting the approach of a helizep they would send up their guards in a suicidal storm wave to batter themselves against the helis, poison stings armed, always seeking murderous access to their sealed enemies. With an element of desperation, many more would react than a normal swarm like the one that hit Heli-1 recently. The helis could electrify their hulls with high voltage, draining their power cells to no avail, but there were too many of them. The vasps defended the hive; their queen.

***

Today Hansen and Harry would release dazer gas from their forward probes. The soporific would blow back across them, dazing any creature trying to gain access to the interior. This was dangerous work, any weakness in the pilots' mask seals would send them into a drunken doze. The dazer gas would subdue the attacking vasps. They would fly around aimlessly and eventually fall down to the water and drown. One weakness of their frenzied attack was that the attacking stream led back to their nest like a homing trail.

Hansen went in first; the nest could be seen as a slight bulge in the side of a tube. Clever creatures, they chewed the tube fabric and built their watertight hive down and round, the bulk underneath the tube, into the cooling seawater.

Landing a few feet away from the nest, Hansen signalled Flynn to open the side sliding door. Flynn reached out with his cyanide tube, a curved lance designed to reach down and round underneath the tubes. Behind him Ari swatted away drunken vasps and prepared to open the valve. Flynn probed deep into the nest skin and signalled Ari.

'Go!' he screamed, a muffled shout. Ari opened his valve and the deadly poison gushed forth into the nest. Bubbles appeared as desperate hive vasps fought their way out from under water and tried to flee, only to drown. Flynn plunged the probe in again and again, using it as a crude scraper, until the nest started to pucker and wither, to fall away into the salt water.

Ari closed the valve while Flynn probed and sorted amongst the debris until he found what he was looking for. He raised the lance end with a huge vasp queen wriggling, impaled on the sharp hypodermic end. She still struggled, trails of semi transparent ovipositor sac hanging from her abdomen. Ari opened the valve again briefly; the queen's struggles ceased.

For good measure Flynn held the corpse under water then wiped the wand end clean against the tube surface. Hansen took off backwards to survey their work. Pulling clear, he watched as Harry's team dropped a parachute canister; it floated down and exploded more cyanide above the nest area encompassing an area of fifty metres around. They didn't want a return bout.

Harry, up in Heli-2, was wide eyed. His first vasp trip, he was amazed that the dysfunctional crew down below worked so seamlessly, so efficiently together. Hamid, an old hand, watched critically but he nodded approval at his former teammates' efforts.

Both helis circled around. A few odd vasps struggled on the water and tube surfaces, their venom and fury spent, their home, their raison d'etre now history. Marie was almost sorry for them but shook herself free of sentiment remembering the deaths of Heli-3's crew a year back. They were sealing a leak when the heli engine failed. Baking in the sun without coolant from the heli system, they were surrounded by a swarm. Low on breathing air and unable to bear the heat they broke out to die horribly five minutes before a rescue heli with gas reached them. Heli-3 still sat unused with its curse at the back of the hangar

She also remembered the school children who played truant in the ruins near the shore, only to die horribly when vasps chased them into the sea to the waiting predators.

***

One down, two to go. 'We're next Harry! Stay cool, you'll be OK – Taylor said so!'

Why am I scared senseless then? he thought to himself.

Chapter Nine

Zill hung back as Taylor questioned Shams endlessly. The Boss bore the brunt well as usual. Newcomers to their band were always stunned to hear that their work was part of…what? Taylor spluttered with surprise and anger.

'I've been part of an experiment for …how long? The implications… you are conducting some sort of political experiment from, from this armchair here…'

Shams shook his head.

'Experiment? We have been instrumental in establishing peaceful strongholds on the new shores of England. Food and fuel are abundant, if a little basic. You export your surplus and support a paramilitary defence force. All under attack from the elements, wild creatures and half crazed people with barely a veneer of civilization. To bring these wild people together we need a common cause. How about fighting the SPs? Pitch them against typically lazy bullies and psychopaths who otherwise would be forming criminal syndicates and gangs of thugs.

The SPs would never sow seeds and put down roots. They would never work together with the Dees. Unfortunately, in influencing the Scallies to combine against a common enemy we neglected to tell them that the Domeys and the Agris were not part of the same enemy.'

'You are not telling me your man upped and left with no other resources than his own personality? You don't walk into the Scallie camp and say, "Excuse me, but I've come to take over your gang!"'

'It depends what gifts you bring with you,' declared Shams mysteriously. 'It depends what support you have and who supports you while you approach. Mankind thrives and prospers, makes huge advances in war, Taylor. Your Domeys are moribund; it is as though nothing happened. They plod on recycling their bit of time until retirement. If they are not told everything, life is more peaceful, they have routine, which some folk crave. Even you established a routine Taylor. An adventurous and exciting version but, nonetheless, a routine.'

Pausing he considered Taylor sitting there. Here was a straightforward man, a practical person; a kind man, it could be said. Taylor had that gene, that fast moving ability, the sort of ability that the Scallies would admire, would follow. But first he would need convincing. He watched Taylor's expression. Taylor seemed to be casting about for purchase. Life was less complicated in the new world, sometimes fraught with danger and frustration but something to endure with a philosophical bent. He'd survived the catastrophe, maybe he mourned the world of before. Taylor uttered his characteristic 'harrumph' and asked:

'What do you want with me? I've seen this movie: good guy goes in deep with a mission, goes off track, becomes an embarrassment to his lords and masters…'

Shams hooted. 'Your imagination Taylor! I too have seen this film…' he looked to Zill for affirmation; received a blank look, frowned in realisation, turned back. 'No, I do not want Raoul, killed, oh no! We want the Scallies to prosper; but nor do we want the Domes raped and pillaged; the delicate eco system you and your organization have helped to build, destroyed. Not at all, we want to set the Scallies up as an alternative society; a strong new race of men and women. Our problem is twofold; one, we want them to prosper elsewhere, in other words, to not destroy the Dome system; two; we want to stop the ZI overreaching their remit. The more they attack the Scallies, the more the Scallies focus upon the Domeys. Humans seem to need enemies as much if not more than friends, it is sad to say.'

Taylor was bewildered.

'So where do I come in?'

Shams considered again, nodded to Zill. She operated a remote. A vid screen appeared on the wall. A high bird's eye view zoomed in to a bamboo platform built out from the water's edge. Inland was a small Dome. Taylor was not familiar with the location. At the end of the platform a small ship, the size of an ocean going fishing boat, was tied up. The view changed to almost horizontal. A single file of manacled Scallies driven on board by SP guards.

They were seated in rows under a tarpaulin awning out of the sun. Taylor could see cooling fans blasting cold air over them; nothing untoward or inhumane so far. Shams made a circling motion with his forefinger; Zill fast forwarded to the ship departing, heading east out to sea. A superimposed compass rose showed Taylor the direction. East to where, Sweden? Fast forward again and Taylor could see two trooper helis following at a distance. Fast forward again.

'Elapsed time is about two hours,' said Zill. On deck something was afoot. Two SPs were doing something with small packages, unwrapping them and throwing them down amongst the captives. The helizeps drew close; hovered alongside taking off SPs. One lifted away. Two remaining guards whisked aside the roof tarpaulin and jumped aboard the last heli.

Realisation dawned on Taylor. Horrified he watched the canisters

166

explode and burn. Some prisoners managed to burn through or saw through their bonds and leapt for the side. Some stayed and tried to put out the flames using anything at hand to shovel the incendiaries overboard; some tried to free their companions. Most dived overboard to escape the heat and flames. In the sea around the ship characteristic triangular fins gathered.

The nightmare scene faded.

He was cold, pale. He now knew the fate of that half Scallie out on the tube edge that day, a brave lad who tried to bring the evidence of atrocity home. The sharks did not know they were allies of the ZI; He thought of Jarvis, the Z6 and his chief.

Thank you – we'll deal with it. Try not to lose anyone…

Taylor turned back to Shams.

'What do you want me to do? '

***

Harry flew number one for the next nest. He was nervous. Better now with Taylor's crew but still, he must make up for his first, in his mind, disastrous outing.

Marie, as if she read his mind, told him,

'Forget the first time we came out here, we survived didn't we? Taylor has given you his Thumbs Up – I thought he was being vulgar the first time he said that!' she giggled. Harry didn't respond; he was watching the course track too intently.

'Here they come! Mask up! Doors check!' All scrambled to comply. They themselves looked as much like insects as the vasps did, with their armour, helmets and breathing equipment. Marie deployed the front tube and in seconds the canopy darkened with the cloud of crazed insects. Splat! Blat! on the windscreen – the engine ingested a few, Harry closed the intakes as much as he dared, the engine note chugged, then cleared. She punched the spray release and a spray of benzo-diazepam, dazer gas, engulfed both heli and insect cloud. Hansen's machine followed suit and now the way down to the nest was clear, a minor swirl of late upcoming reinforcement vasps showing the way.

Harry manoeuvred in with instructions from Ben in the back. He landed on the tube and the right hand door slid open. Jack held the lance today; Hamid controlled the valve. Jack plunged the cyanide gas tube in deep, down, down and round. Hamid turned the valve. It was a smooth operation to echo Hansen's crew's earlier performance. Jack displayed the queen as a trophy and again she was dispatched. Taking off and pulling back clear, Hansen's heli dropped their cyanide canister.

Harry's first vasp op; they thumped him on the back in congratulation and relief that all went well. Harry, flushed with pride, joined formation with Hansen for the last one of the day.

***

This one was back nearer home near the harbour. The infested tube was floated in unnoticed during some bad visibility. The nest was on a loose drifting tube. This meant they could not land on the tube for fear of it rolling over and dunking them in the water. It was an awkward job and Harry was secretly glad to let the more experienced Hansen do this one.

This time they were not met by the same blind fury of defenders. A few flew up in a halfhearted way and were quickly dosed to fly off in drunken circles.

Ben looked all round. 'This is different! Where are they?'

Over the intercom Hamid voice sounded bloodcurdling.

'They have swarmed; someone else is on the receiving end today.'

Up in Harry's machine all eyes were scanning the sky in all directions. Hansen let down to hover over the loose floating tube. The tube, bottom heavy with sludge did not roll over much but the downdraught pushed it away. Using the downwash of the blades Hansen tried to blow it towards a group of tubes in order to wedge it still. After some manoeuvring he was successful. Harry, watching from above, saw Flynn emerge with the lance.

Afterwards he would remember what happened in slow motion. He saw the big shark launch itself out of the water at the heli float on the opposite side to Flynn. Hansen's crew was concentrating on the job in hand. They failed to see the predator's attack. The creature bit deep, first into the float, then into the rigging. Its teeth became entangled and it fell back. A ton of meat and gristle dragged the heli down and sideways into the sea. Now quarter submerged the heli rolled and ejected Flynn overboard. Its engine screamed in protest at the demands Hansen put on it. The tortured engine, intake now dangerously close to the water level, pushed the heli in a mad anticlockwise swirl, a desperate dance with the frantic shark fighting to disengage itself. Then the heli blades bit into the water. The racket attracted other interested predators. Flynn, burdened by his armour, swam for his life. For him it was like a bad dream, he swam in maddening slow motion for the nearest tube.

Harry heard a voice in his head. *Man down on the tubes!*

Before Harry knew he was down at water level, flying sideways toward Flynn keeping the heli between him and the incoming sharks. Marie, jumping from the front seat, seized the cyanide lance and shoved it under the surface of the water. Hamid, catching on quick, turned the valve. The sharks beat a hasty retreat but, too late, some absorbed the cyanide through their gills and rolled over dead, white bellies to the sky. On the other side Ben and Jack hooked into Flynn's harness. Marie signalled Harry to lift and they hovered over to some stable tubes and dropped him off, Ben to administer to Flynn while they returned to help Hansen.

The big shark broke free and retreated in disgust but Hansen's heli was beyond help. The engine ingested water and stopped; the hydrogen float on one side punctured beyond the capability of the self sealant. The crew climbed out to sit on the now horizontal side surface, Ari first helping Kristen out and then both hauling Hansen from the pilot's seat. Jack, leaning out of Heli-2's door, flung a rope and, with Marie relaying instructions to Harry, they towed the downed heli to the edge of the tubes where Ben and Flynn waited. They were all still suited up against the vasps.

Hamid's voice came over the radio: 'We must land the remaining heli! All must take shelter! We do not know where the swarm is and we have not killed the nest!'

In the drama, the threat of vasps was quite forgotten.

Chapter Ten

Taylor spent a morose second day on the rig. Back in his quarters, he opened the file detailing the extent of the catastrophe. It made sickening reading and viewing. The death and destruction was one thing but the savagery of starving dispossessed humanity was worse. He turned it off without looking at three quarters of it. Zill said she could give him the good news, the survivors, the efforts to rebuild, anytime, if he didn't want to continue.

Typically the story conflicted with the ZI version. It seemed that, between Russia and USA, France and Switzerland were the power now; international cooperation was still in a new infancy. The USA, a once mighty conglomerate, still fragmented and prone to civil war, still rattled its sabre at the East, but the nation, always prone to more damage from Nature, now lay low indeed. Many nations licked their wounds in relative silence. Trade, due to the parallel destruction of infrastructure, communications and economic foundations, was yet to reach a fraction of before levels.

'The Boss has not, hopes he has not, inserted a key in your back to go gunning for the SPs and the ZI,' Zill said that evening.

'It is hard to know who to trust, impossible to bring a European in, someone who knows nothing of the Dome World. We know that ESO, like the old United Nations, tends to turn a blind eye when the truth does not suit them. The Boss says it was ever the case. Do you know what he means? These before references, I cannot keep up, our world seems to have as much history in sixty years as the rest of history put together. How did we live then? So confusing.'

Taylor made a sour face.

'Most didn't bother. News was sensation – a cat stuck up a tree would excite more interest than 50,000 Bangladeshis drowning in a flood,' said Taylor. 'Tell me about Raoul…'

'He was Shams's assistant. I sort of took over from him. I didn't know him long. He was some sort of anthropologist, been with Shams forever. The Scallies excited him, he knew all about them…'

***

The subject of their discussion sat watching a practical lesson in a hastily contrived classroom in the corner of a warehouse. The instructor was teaching first aid, pointing out the priorities – airway, breathing, circulation…

Raoul was proud of his efforts but what a struggle!

His thoughts went back to the beginning, four years ago when he convinced Shams he was wasting his time on the sub and the rigs and wanted to go "out on the ground."

Teaching savage kids to read what they were using for firelighters. He got them to drag old cars in under cover of night. Foraging found tools and other garage equipment. He was followed by blank looks most of the time but eventually he got them to follow him out of curiosity, then interest and, at long last, the brighter ones held their hands up –"No! You stay! We will do…things… ourselves!"

Highlights were getting a car engine to run, a petrol engine; and then a diesel engine. A big truck engine with a power take off, a generator – electricity!

He showed them how to siphon fuel from old fuel tanks and eventually to drill in and tap the underground tanks from garages and depots here and there.

He demonstrated the dangers of not storing fuel away from the domestic area by causing an inferno with an old battery, some petrol soaked cloths and a handful of wire wool thrown over the terminals.

He unearthed service manuals. He referred the drawings and diagrams to the real things. They were labelled, these were words to know- little packages of knowledge which could be sent without shouted relays, or saved for later reference.

The civilising process went on.

Bullied at school with his odd name and maybe because he was slow reaching full stature, he should have been good at sport, light on his feet and quick. His classmates seemed to put so much effort into tripping and barging him out of the way that he wondered whether they grasped the point of the game at all. His normally absent or drunken father clipped his ear and told him not to be a baby. His mother, when she was not with some "uncle", would go to the school and complain but he got the feeling she chatted up the teachers and left them in no doubt why her little boy was bullied.

Affiliated to school was a cadet group – you could do army, air force or navy. Living some way from the sea made the navy seem – well, odd. However, the army cadets encouraged fitness, self reliance, discipline and self defence.

Many years later the silver heli would drop him, with his rucksack full of survival and civilisation, miles away from where the Scallies seemed to favour. He trekked his way towards them, avoiding larger groups until he found what he was looking for. To either side of his track were the lost labels of before. Dry Cleaners, a kebab shop, newsagents, a petrol station, a library. Pharmacies, bookshops, a doctor's surgery. He broke into some of those and chose various items that he could carry easily. He found it odd that there was anything left to loot. He didn't know Taylor or Livingstone but he would have been interested in their conversation about looters; all those years before at the reservoir rescue base.

The first three Scallies he allowed to attack him went down in a whirl of arms and legs. A sharp blade held to their leader's throat and the menacing beam of a dazer playing green and red over the rest of the group were convincing arguments. He had more but he wanted to convince not dominate. They took him in. They were lodging in a more or less weather tight old building. They could light a fire, safe from the sight of SPs. Rough beds and tables were scattered about. A woman was dying in childbirth; the leader's woman. Blood curdling screams rent the air. They were helpless.

He looked at their anguished faces. These were not sub humans. They were hurting, preparing to grieve! The leader looked at him – looked to him. Raoul asked for cloths or towels and water, indicated he would have to cut her. The leader's expression said, "anything, do anything!" Raoul saw a light. He opened medical files on his wrist display. He'd done advanced first aid with ESO. Dare he? Not a caesarean, no, but he read where to cut to widen the birth canal. Out of this group something may come! If he tried and she died – they were expecting it. If he succeeded he would save one, no, two human beings! He could make his play and start to undo some of the damage from the catastrophe.

The screams were appalling. Some sat with hands clapped to their ears. Some girls came and went, wiped the woman's brow, sagged, walked away helpless. He'd brought a few "things" with him, including his acquisitions from the doctor's and pharmacy. He went to work.

Chapter Eleven

Taylor was ill at ease and out of sorts. He wondered how the kids were managing without him. Two days away? Only two days, it didn't take long for the red button to act.

He got drunk with Zill and the two lads that night in the bar, a converted canteen from the old "no alcohol allowed" days of an oil rig. Taylor adopted the role of, first; a supercilious barman from an expensive hotel lounge, wiping glasses with care, squinting through them at the light. He would impart no gossip he gathered in the course of his duties.

Next, he was the garrulous village pub landlord, first feasting on and then, as repayment, freely distributing all gossip as if it were a currency. It took them a while - the stories of Mrs So and so from Number 38 who was 'having it off' with Mr Whatsit from round the corner, now unemployed after falling off his window cleaner's ladder. 'He's employed on another ladder now' he winked – 'climbing the ladder in her tights I'll bet!'

Were these people fact or fiction? Whatever, Taylor brought them alive to the extent that they followed the direction of his winks nods and innuendo to an imaginary place - down the street next to the post office - which, in reality, lay a hundred metres out in the sea from the side of the rig. Other rig members came and went but for them they were yet to be joined to the Taylor umbilicus and they wandered away, shaking their heads, bewildered.

Bored with his role he made Mick barman while he regaled them with all sort of funny tales from before, like the Darwin awards, where people who died accidentally in the most unfortunate but laughable circumstances were posthumously awarded a "Darwin".

Tales of the tubes were a serious note – they listened rapt to the problems of the floating bio farms. They were there for the first time. Disconnected from reality at their satellite-linked screens they could watch the tidals sweep in. They'd kept a record of Harry's little brush with Mother Nature but now, to hear it from one who actually worked day to day out there, their blood ran cold at the timing, the second's difference between life and death.

Jokes were difficult with these kids; they accepted his stories as gospel and, as the beer flowed, they, and eventually he, struggled to differentiate between truth and fiction.

Becoming drunk it didn't seem to matter. He doubted they would remember everything. At the end he called "Last Orders" in a stentorian voice. He helped Zill put the giggling boys to bed, the boys who loved him, their best mate, their lost Dad.

Zill, ever solicitous, saw him to his door. He looked at her. She really was a stunner. Hansen would be a fidgeting hormonal mess in her presence. She made him think of his daughter...what happened to her? Is she alive somewhere? If not, did she die quickly? His son? In some Dee gang somewhere? And she who I don't dare think of – she who I keep alive in here. He wasn't sure if Zill was coming on to him. He was too drunk, too old today and too confused to work out the difference between friendship, affection and physical attraction.

A vision of Marie, hands on hips, pouting with jealousy, came to him. In the shadows of his mind, the sad little face of Da-Netz turning away, her slim boyish figure retreating into the darkness.

'Goodnight Zill, thanks for tonight.' He turned and slipped through his door before matters reached a point he did not want to reach, not with a skinful of ale anyway.

***

Back at the crash site, the two crews huddled, baking and sweating in their armoured suits. Heli-1 drifted and bobbed with the slight tide and, as night fell, they worried a wind or rough sea could start up and topple them into the water. They could see fins circling some distance away. A tinge of poison or maybe the biofuel from Hansen's wreck leaking out into the water kept them at bay for now. Inland they could see the tubes drifting about in the temporary harbour. A spit of land loomed in the fading embers of the day. Nobody on foot would be about at nightfall.

All friendly outside workers retreated indoors, surrendering the night to the new nature and the wild people who fished or foraged in the cool and dark. If they tried to escape inland, who knew? There may be more water to cross with who knew what dangers? Vasps didn't fly at night; or so they thought. Good news was they were close enough for a radio link. Help was on its way.

'Has my hair gone white?' Flynn pleaded with them.

'No but you smell disgusting,' Jack told him. 'I'd put my mask on but we need to save the air.'

'Remind me how tight your sphincter is next time you go swimming with those bastards!' growled Flynn.

Harry was silent, his thoughts whirled. His parents did not want him out here. Scientists both, they'd pleaded with him to carry on his education and work on their team at the labs down in Kent. "Boys go

174

out there and come home different, changed, if they come home at all," his mother said. "Let him try it for a season," said his father. "He'll soon be back with his tail between his legs."

Now, after today's events, Harry had gone past the dabbling existentialist curiosity stage. Here, you didn't dip your toe in the world's waters and run back away in fearful glee, like a small child on his first beach.

Marie interrupted his train of thought.

'You did OK, Harry.'

'Yeah, man, that was quick thinking. Shame this ungrateful bastard didn't notice,' Jack said.

' I noticed, Jack; I noticed. You're OK Harry, I owe you,' said Flynn, all the time glaring his defiance at Jack.

'Do the same for me?' Harry said.

'Yes, but I don't want to do this anymore. That was too close. This is not a fucking game. Never forget Harry. Never.'

The spell was broken as rescue zeps, Heli-4, Heli-5 and even an SP heli turned up. Apparently the missing swarm were absent for a reason. Heli-4 and 5 had already caught them swarming to relocate and dealt with them before they could consolidate their new nest.

The survivors were none the worse for wear; still suited up they destroyed the nest on the loose tube. It was still a mystery how spare pregnant queens survived though.

One thing for sure, the day conspired to bring them all closer together. It was a weary pair of crews who struggled into Joe's that evening. Rescue had come quickly with no further drama. No drama apart from the terror the vasps would return.

Kristen said to Marie,

'Sorry I was such a bitch. That stroking thing – I'm still interested though.'

'That's OK. Maybe when the world runs out of men eh?' said Marie.

When the world runs out of Taylor men, thought Kristen, congratulating herself on keeping her thoughts to herself. What happened out there today? she wondered.

Flynn told Hamid, 'I was a shit – maybe your Allah was feeling generous.'

Hamid raised an eyebrow.

'Allah...' he stopped himself. 'Maybe we should never press the red button.'

Turning to Ari, Flynn held out his hand. 'We were too close to the water today to wish any more on anyone... I'm thinking...'

Ari took the offered hand, 'Yes, we should all be friends now. Before is before; before it is too late.'

The others, listening, pausing briefly to digest three "befores" in the same sentence. At last it seemed to make sense and they cheered, bought beer all round and toasted Harry's first vasp hunt. He was a fully fledged crew member now. The silent thought - I wish Taylor was here to see this - was on everyone's mind.

Chapter Twelve

Taylor's head ached. His bleary, bloodshot eyed mind was very much on his "kids", Jack, Marie and Ben. Without any shocks to his status quo, he still suffered from that hung over paranoia brought on by alcohol, never mind unknown residual poisons in nettle beer. He imagined Harry showing off to Marie, dropping her down chimney stacks; he thought of Ben fighting a last stand against drunken SPs. He groaned. Stop it! he told himself.

Zill, with the benefit of youth on her side, looked frisky and dapper until Taylor noticed her massaging her temples and simulating vomiting whenever Shams's back was turned away for a second.

Shams carried on as normal, expecting all to fall in behind him in whatever was his crusade of the day. Strong on motivation, as long as he remembered to do the motivation, Shams seemed tireless. Taylor didn't like Shams today and rehearsed insults like "smug sober bastard" to himself. Taylor reserved the right, if he didn't like himself today, what chance did anyone else have?

'Your new education starts then; an appetizer,' said Shams. He patted his pockets and scratched his silver head, wondering where to begin.

'You're a weatherman, Taylor. What do you know of the composition of the atmosphere?'

'It's mainly nitrogen and oxygen with a few trace gases,' mumbled Taylor.

'Good start; 78% Nitrogen, 21% Oxygen, which leaves…?

'One percent I guess.'

Get on with it. Write it down on some paper I'll look at it later!

'And of the one percent remaining…?'

'CO_2, Kryptonite, agricultural smells…'

Shams looked closely at him. 'I'm sorry Taylor, I meant the dry atmosphere minus water vapour and pollutants, but you are right, CO_2 and Krypton but…' in triumph now – 'of the remaining 1%, 93% is Argon, from the old…'

'Electric light bulbs,' yawned Taylor.

'See Zill, people of an age, from before, have such depth of knowledge; of no use 99% of the time but dredged up on call; at a seconds notice,' he beamed.

Zill stared in full mock admiration; Shams was low on irony detection today and she was going to take advantage of it:

'You are so clever Taylor. You bring knowledge from before!

177

What are electric light bulbs?'

Taylor gave Zill a look of pure evil.

Shams again failed to detect any irony, or if he did, he ignored it and carried on.

'What was the population of Earth at the beginning of 1750, the start of the Industrial Revolution?'

'Dunno, billion maybe?' Did it start on New Years Day- on a Friday? He remembered tables that could tell you what date certain days in certain years were. What a waste of mental effort we were guilty of.

'OK, close enough, and who's to argue? A nice round number for now – but what was the population at the time of the catastrophe?'

'Six billion give or take a half billion.'

Where is this leading?

'CO_2. Did you follow the arguments of the time? And what did you think?'

'Horseshit mainly, struck me it was political crap by people who were too lazy to do the maths, knew jack shit about chemistry. Bunch of bandwagon jumping useless bastards.'

'So you did not succumb to the zeitgeist, the spirit of the times?'

'I remember them all weeping and wailing, gnashing their teeth about 375 parts per million CO_2. Some yank tosser, banging on, after a Nobel Prize for talking utter crap, moaning about polar bears drowning when really they could swim 60 miles without getting out of breath.'

'Precisely so. You have a rich turn of phrase Taylor. It must be hard for some to keep up.'

He went on. 'Did you know that the human race was exhaling ten times more CO_2 than all the whole of industry, agriculture and transport put together?'

'Suspected as much. Most, the silent majority, thought it was tosh, why?'

'In round figures then, humanity multiplied six fold, 600% in two hundred and fifty odd years. We were allegedly polluting the world with a gas, a regulatory gas which makes up a mere .04% of the whole and yet this gas, this poison gas we got along with fine and dandy for thousands of years? Think man! CO_2 levels only increased by 40%!'

Taylor was sure this was all good stuff but - please, not today.

Shams desk lit up with Armstrong's holo call; a pleasant chime requested a connection. 'Ah! Excuse me Taylor, for one moment!'

Armstrong shimmered in the room, bands of him flickering in and out until he stabilized to almost solid. 'We are 20 miles out. Are we docking permanently or do you need to go somewhere?' Shams turned, following the direction of Armstrong's gaze over his shoulder, in time to see Zill's back retreating down the corridor. Taylor was nowhere to be seen.

Later, feeling guilty for his truancy, Taylor sought out Shams.

'I was overtaken with the different water here,' he explained. Partially true.

'Are you feeling better now?'

'Yeah, fine, carry on if you like. The CO_2 thing was a load of bunkum seemed the point.'

'The point I wished to make, which by the way you summarized so succinctly, was that people did not question what they were told, even those with the capacity or the education.'

'Exactly.'

'We are not sure of the cause of the disaster. Did an asteroid hit the Moon? Or perhaps maybe somewhere on Earth? The sun's heat has increased is for sure. Whether a function of distance or a change in our axis we are not sure.'

'We being who...?'

'The scientific community. Always a fragmented group, as prone to politics and human weaknesses as everyone else.'

Shams dropped the subject and continued.

'Religion then; what will be your individual view on religion Taylor?' Taylor paused. He had unpleasant memories of conversations starting like this.

One reaction, the result of over heated debate could have gone like, "Superstitious mumbo jumbo."

But Shams was not a fellow drunk in a bar. He would have a point to make or would ask such a question - to establish a basis for further discussion.

More careful now, Taylor feigned deep thought. He scratched his head and appeared to prepare to weigh out the various arguments.

'I've always been interested in what other people do and why. Long ago, I decided religion was nonsense. For me, but if that was what they liked to do or think then fine, OK, as long as they didn't try to include or indoctrinate me...'

Shams gave him full attention, raised an eyebrow slightly to encourage Taylor to develop his point.

'... I was always surprised that quite eminent scientists could fall into the religious ranks. Had they discovered some proof? Surely they would publish? Was there some secret knowledge? I remember listening to the radio once. I was in the car on some motorway or other and they interviewed this guy, Professor Boffin Quark or something. He was quite adamant there existed some superior force, otherwise how come the maths and physics was so perfect; so well laid out, so apparently designed...chaos being what it was would surely not allow such structures and laws to remain?'

He paused but it seemed Shams was keeping up, nodding a cautious acceptance.

'...and then this guy, Quark McPhoton, or whatever, said he was lucky enough to meet with theologians, theosophists and found common ground. They had proof on such an intellectual level that the existence of a super being was surely obvious. His next bit annoyed me though. He said the big God boys, the larger thinkers said that God's part in the universe, like Einstein's maths, was beyond most average people; that the watered down, filtered version was all they needed; patronizing parables using agricultural analogies...' Taylor gazed across the years, across the planet of before.

'...I met an old Bedouin once. He was in the Gulf, I forget where but he couldn't understand a computer. Not only the file handling, the actual keys and buttons. He seemed to struggle with the concept of cause and effect. I wondered if he thought electricity was something provided by God or Allah and therefore no more need be said.'

Shams was still, fixed on every word. Taylor's train of thought returned to this room. He continued:

'We live in what they would have called godless times. It suits me, saves a lot of pointless philosophical debate. I can't accept things without some sort of proof. It sounds terrible coming from me, who hates being patronized more than anything in the world but...'

Shams waited. The two seemed frozen in time; no outside routine activity to be heard, no wind, no dropped tools, no shouts or laughter from outside on the rig.

'...I can't help thinking we've thrown the baby out with the bath water. I read once that Voltaire said he was an atheist but he preferred it if his cook and butler were not. Or something along those lines.'

He looked at Shams; he'd gone on a bit too long.

Shams polished his glasses and replaced them.

'Odd how our perceptions change with time and experience but I concur with your views in as much as I don't believe in a magical being and we have both seen the damage that blind faith can wreak across our world...'

He hoped Zill had set the recording to catch all this. He would like to go over this quietly by himself later. It would seem Taylor was not some existentialist barbarian action man.

'…your conclusion, at least so far then?'

'I think I'm probably a Bedouin at heart. Folly to be wise and all that'

'A Bedouin of the soul, of the mind. Still Taylor, we cannot put the tooth paste back in the tube. We are victims of our own success. Or is that too many mixed metaphors for one day?'

'Toothpaste? I remember that!' They laughed. Shams's chair began to swivel. Taylor was heading for the door but Shams called after him. Taylor paused in the door. Honour was satisfied; Taylor avoided dismissal; Shams may still have the last word.

'Interesting then that I thought your first – er – sortie with us could be to visit the God Folk Island.' Taylor came back in, poised ready for escape in the event that chair began to turn away.

Shams went on to describe what seemed to be an experimental cult, what would have been an experiment if it weren't for the fact the experiment was involuntary – thrust upon them. This particular group were mainly Christians but, respecting others' conclusions that some sort of heavenly power or influence existed, they absorbed a smattering of Islamics, Buddhists and other worshippers.

The point of the visit, a reconnaissance to check on any change of heart. To see if there were any normals held against their will and always to check on disease and, as with all his teams visits, to check out any genetic effects the new sun may be having; for better or worse.

Chapter Thirteen

The raft boat, contrived from drums and life buoys lashed together with rope and bamboo, was dropped off out of earshot and sight of the island by a squat heli lifter, a type Taylor had never seen before. Steve and Zill had chosen a foggy day for the visit.

'These people are very superstitious; they think the high tech stuff is devil's work. We go in as fishermen adrift in the fog, our compass overboard. Mick has stunned a catch of fish here...'

He threw back a plastic sheet to reveal a creel of home woven mesh with a few dozen fish suspended in a sea water bath.

'We can trade the unfortunate ones. Maybe have a nice grilled dinner ourselves and let the rest go.'

'You're all heart.'

Taylor, like the others, had not washed or shaved. They all wore old before-style homespun clothes and Zill, in spite of paying no attention to her appearance whatsoever, looked like a sea goddess. Hansen would be venting body fluids if he were here. His other boys would struggle with the job in hand! he thought.

Taylor suspected he was transferring the guilt for his own lust onto others. It was obvious Zill wore no underwear of any sort. Her loose fitting clothes shifted here and there, allowing tantalizing glimpses and hints of what lay beneath. He forced delicious images away and subjected the two younger mens' outfits to some critical appraisal.

'Did you raid the BBC costume department?' he joshed with Steve.

'We watched an old movie, Waterworld with Kevin Costner; thought it was appropriate.'

'Cost a fortune to make and lost a lot of money, that one, but I liked it. Do you think you should resort to fiction for authenticity? Hollywood was not renowned for that you know, and don't forget it was in a future world – it was not real.'

'Are you sure it was not real Taylor?'

'Hmmm touché!' He chuckled to himself at the thought; of Steve and Mick; even with the benefit of old movie footage, foraging in the wrong clothing warehouse. Coming back with the brown suits favoured by older Pakistanis - flower power shirts – platform soled shoes. More rarely now but he still got the giggles of his youth. A stray thought of Mick up ahead in the bow, wearing a bowler hat, a wing collar, armed with a bow and arrow convulsed him into helplessness. The others looked on in concern.

'What is it Taylor? Are you sick?'

***

With Shams again, they discussed the new world. It occurred to Taylor that Shams did a lot of listening and prompting; as if he was taking a tutorial and patiently had to bear the ramblings of a gawky student.

To Taylor, to be patronised was, along with forcing claustrophobia and hypocrisy, one of the ninth, tenth and eleventh deadly sins. He would get grumpy, irritable and aggressive at the slightest hint.

'So, Professor Brainstorm, what do you actually do sitting here in your court with your lackeys running to and fro for you?

'Oho! Wrong side of the bed this morning, is it?' chortled Shams.

'Right! I can't help thinking this is so remote from reality you are losing touch. The worst is you seem to think you are some conductor, waving his baton and expecting things to happen. I can't help thinking you are a little redundant. Maybe it's time you got your hands dirty, joined in, and invented something. The dreaming spires and the centres of academic excellence are under water. Seems to me you have merely uprooted, climbed up the steps to keep your feet dry!'

Shams was a little taken aback.

'I'm sorry you feel that way. On reflection it is not the first time I have heard these sentiments. My boy Raoul said much the same, the difference being he included himself in the accusation.'

He cast about for some means with which to force back the flow of Taylor's antipathy. He daren't change the subject.

'We are, I am, watching what unfolds. The food supply is under control we think. There is some semblance of civilisation, some international cooperation. Communications are opening up but they are restricted to stop them being swamped, overloaded with people seeking their lost families, uprooting to where they think the grass is greener.

We must avoid a race of migrant travellers never laying down roots, never rebuilding while others erect citadels of local common interest where we have the surfacing of the foolish chauvinism of religion and group self interest. Do you remember the eternal debate between 'laissez faire' and state control? Of course, you must. We…the human race are in a state of flux. New balances must appear. We are not sure where we are going. To move back into a consumer orientated, nuclear family based society that suffered so in the face of Mother Nature; to move too soon, another weather quake is not

183

impossible – could be a step backwards. A thousand years backwards '

He indicated Taylor might want to comment at this stage. Taylor sniffed.

'Your précis -what I suspected. Too much, too fast, you are saying. So what's being done to stop corruption, murder, illegal distribution of resources? Your Police force is a militia. As far as my Dome is concerned, it is almost under martial law. The tube system is almost feudal; the agris are villeins to the big castle, the workers inside, the serfs. We only feel superior in our role of what? Scouts?

You do remember "Big Brother" Of course you must...' he couldn't help himself... 'For Thought Police read - The ZI; Imperial Storm troopers? – SPs, and so on.

'Imperial Storm troopers in 1984...?'

'No, 1977 I think, but you get my meaning...' he paused, waited – Shams did not get it. These academics have no sense of humour, he thought to himself.

'I'd like you to settle in next season Taylor – this is an appetiser – a look round. When you return from your R&R I'd like you to work with Raoul and, as we discussed, defuse the inevitable confrontation.

'How do you know the inevitable will wait for me to have my holiday? Events, in my experience, tend to have a force of their own.'

'Raoul is on hold for a while. There will be no "events" as you call them. Excuse me; you have reminded me I have not attended to something...'

***

Inch by inch, little by little, Raoul grew his little band. First in numbers, then in a code of behaviour, a code of loyalty to the group, a system of rewards, a family court for punishment. He introduced sports. This took some effort at first – natural competitiveness would often resort to bloodshed. He was philosophical about this – the arena of old and the stadium of more recent times were classic examples.

The long-range satellites' cameras failed to show these Scallies were barely more than children running wild. The shanty scallies were older, wilier, more cowardly, preferring the safety of darkness and numbers.

He had not accounted for the wild men. These deranged people could well be survivors of before, driven by the circumstances of the times or simply unpleasant scum who never fitted, whatever the society. Before he arrived, his group killed any small half organised band on sight. They avoided the city bandits. He found himself learning the hard way.

He was strangely attracted to one particular girl. She had a quiet intelligence; self respect. She had not recoiled when he delivered the baby that night. She had known to pass clean cloths, prepare needle and thread, reassure the mother. The mother and baby survived and, along with her man, the original leader he usurped, were part of his nucleus of rock solid supporters.

He taught Alys many things, she became "his woman" His nights were no longer feverish dark periods of waiting, of mixed anxiety and boredom, waiting for the relief of morning and ghost free daylight.

On the run from a SP raid, he and Alys became separated from the rest. Taking cover in an overgrown park, he became aware they were surrounded by hostile faces. Too many hostile faces. They ran, became separated and he made his way back alone to their temporary base. She did not return. He took a team back to look for her. They held a vagrant down over his own brazier until he screamed his information. Raoul recoiled at the savagery but when the wild traveller told his news of Alys's demise, Raoul drove the stakes in himself – four of them and tied the man in place; in his place of torture. Tied the ropes to hold him there burning alive, his screams a warning to others. The scum had used his girl and then thrust her out into the open when they heard a SP's heli. They had laughed as the heli's guns straddled the road where she ran.

Raoul turned out all of his people. He showed them how to make petrol bombs – Molotov cocktails. He got them to make long poles with V forks. The next night they surrounded the overgrown park. He directed them to throw the bottles so they broke on hard surfaces. They hurled dozens of firebombs into the park. As the inferno built, the wild people ran out burning and screaming only to be pushed back and be held in the flames. In his mind's eye, they seemed to bear the faces of his school tormentors.

After this, he was a cold person for quite some time. It was in this time he became ruthless. In turn, he taught them to be ruthless and quick, and clever, and light on their feet. He taught them tactics, self defence and discipline. He'd already taught them to belong. He was already scavenging in the ruins of the old towns looking for tools, equipment, weapons.

He found an old hunting, fishing tackle and gun shop, surprisingly unexploited. Shotguns were no good without ammunition but they were taken in case of future usefulness. Catapults had a use and could be reproduced. What he did seize on with gusto were hunting bows and arrows. For close work, he found a treasure – a crossbow. His people were learning to be mechanics – they could arm themselves. And then he started to take the fight to the enemy; and Shams began to wonder what to do about it.

Chapter Fourteen

Taylor's moisture laden eyelashes made him blink as he Steve, Mick and Zill coasted in through a ghostly sea mist. A makeshift jetty loomed out of the gloom. forcing him to swerve the tiller to one side. He manoeuvred to join other moored boats; ramshackle devices like their own; dinghies, oars long replaced with crude paddles; an old cabin cruiser bobbed up and down at its mooring as they bounce-walked along the jetty to the shore. Men and women attended to various duties, cooking, smoking fish and mending boats here and there on the shore. They all looked on with suspicious darting glances, never meeting the visitors' eyes.

All turned to watch a small welcoming committee, down from the white town. Sunlight struggled through the fog. The white glare of the painted town dazzled them.

The leader wore robes. He walked with the aid of a shepherd's crook. One had to visit the hillsides of Scotland and Wales to see a sheep now Taylor thought.

'This is different,' muttered Steve in an aside. 'Looks like a new gang in town. Keep your guard up!'

The two parties met halfway up the beach.

'Welcome! I am the Pastor. Do you bring the devil's devices with you? What is the purpose of your visit?'

Taylor, conscious of the paleness of his arm where his wrist normally shielded it from the sun, surreptitiously slid his sleeve cuff down; moved his arm from open view.

'We are fishermen. What are these devil devices you speak of?' said Steve.

'Why does not the older man step forward as senior? All eyes were on Taylor.

'He was punished by the chopper men; punished with too many volts. He has not recovered his wits. The sea and the fishing we hope will mend him.'

-You wait Zeb – I'll recover your wits -

The Pastor and his group nodded sagely. 'We have experience of those men of Satan.' He spat to the side, an act repeated by his followers.

'They came here recently but we sent them on their way.'

- A likely story! The SPs probably couldn't be bothered to land! - Taylor hid his sneer behind a gormless vacant expression.

'You have not said your purpose here though.'

'We ride the fog. Our pointer is lost. We wish to rest safe until it clears. We will pay with fish; maybe trade for a pointer.'

'We may have a compass young one. It is a compass you need.'

Aside to his group he laughed, 'a pointer indeed! Satan has stolen the words of old.' Turning he said, 'Come! Take refreshment with us. We will tell you of our work here. It is the work of God the Almighty!'

'Does God live here?' enquired Steve, casting about for this superman they referred to.

'He is everywhere. He is in you; he is in all things, including your crude boat'

Their boat seemed to amuse them. Some of the group at the rear of the party pointed rudely and critically at their rigging and float bags; muttered and sniggered behind their hands. The Pastor frowned them into silence and continued.

'He was angry but we work to console him...' He waved his crook to include a whole damaged world.

'We fight the Devil where we can. We are quietly confident we are getting somewhere. The storms are bad but are getting no worse and we live like God's children, as you do, before they knew of God!'

- A fruitcake, thought Taylor. -

They were led into the township, stopping first at the Church. The four of them stood in a rehearsed bewildered huddle while the Pastor gave thanks at the altar, 'for leading the poor innocent fishers from the sea into the safety of his chosen people's harbour.'

Taylor shuddered in distaste. Churches made him claustrophobic as well, claustrophobia of the psyche. He would love to see this hypocrite dancing at the end of a few kilovolts. Taylor could introduce him to mercy and humility – if you stop talking shit and join in with the rest of us I will turn off this devil's dance machine,- you scrounging, work shy charlatan, he thought.

Mick was strangely quiet but played bewildered well enough. Taylor wondered if Mick was enjoined to keep quiet as well. Zill contrived to wrap herself up well. Not knowing where women fell in the pecking order it seemed wise to make herself as invisible as possible. It was Steve's project – he was welcome to it.

Worship over, they were led through dirty streets under cover of a rudimentary Dome. The beetle technology was partly working but it wasted its water in dribbles and small cascades here and there, spattering into the mud of the streets. The Pastor pointed out various items of interest: a bakery, weaving shop, carpenters, nothing out of the norm, until they came to an improvised bamboo cage with three prisoners.

Two of them, gripping the bars, knuckles white in rage, hurled obscenities at them. The third hung back disdainfully in the shadows; he didn't dignify the newcomers with any reaction at all.

Scallies!

'What is their crime, these painted ones?' enquired Steve.

'They are devil spawn. We cannot convert them; we will soon send them back to the land, dry land, soon.'

The Pastor dismissed them with a gesture and they moved on.

Next, a public meeting hall decorated with icons of Jesus, rescued from the flood no doubt, with strange woven or carved driftwood crucifixes here and there.

Water pitchers, dried fish and unleavened bread appeared, crockery plates were dumped down. Taylor turned one over. It was marked, Made in China. He mock marvelled at the art, rotated its shiny ceramic surface; he smiled at the play of light. The Pastor noticed.

'Look! His wits return! He enjoys the beauty of God's gifts again! We make these ourselves here in our humble workshops!' Taylor could not help but stare slack jawed at this gross untruth.

Steve dug him sharply in the ribs and grimaced to put the plate down. The Pastor nodded approval at the young leader's display of respect. They all ate and drank. The Pastor excused himself, claiming urgent business. He indicated rough benches around the hall where they could spend the night and wait out the fog.

Taylor was never a fan of drinking water. He seemed to derive his liquid from the air, tea and beer. In an imaginary tea drinking competition, he could leave the table a normal person; behind would sit folk with contracted pupils, high blood pressure; their nerves jangling them towards a sleepless night.

Something odd about the water, he thought from the taste of a few polite sips.

The others all drank with gusto. The Pastor beamed and exclaimed the benefits of "Adam's Ale," as he called it.

Night fell.

They settled for the night under blankets that were none too clean, thrust at them by a surly acolyte. The others dropped quickly into deep sleep.

Like innocent babes, thought Taylor. He was not ready for sleep and slipped quietly from under his blanket. He scratched at imagined fleas and stole on light feet over to the door. Opening it a crack, the night sea breeze blew in, pushing him back, forcing him to lean his weight against it. The airflow made his eyes water. He shut it again.

Muttered voices were outside; coming closer. Some sixth sense warned him he should not be found at large wandering about away from his blanket. He looked about frantically for a hiding place. He was too far from his blanket. Quick! Under the big meeting table!

The door opened slowly. The Pastor and two men halted in the doorway.

'They sleep the sleep of the Devil juice!' whispered one. From Taylor's hiding place, he could see that, luckily, his blanket stayed on the bench and did not appear unoccupied in the dark

'Let them go deeper for another hour or so – then we take them! Heh! We get their fish, their boat and they join the Scallie in our sacred offerings - Glory to Jehovah!'

'Glory to Jehovah!' they echoed in quiet pious tones.

The door closed. Taylor crawled out from his hiding place and stood erect. He was alive! Exultant, he crossed the room to his friends, shook them; shook them hard. They did not wake.

What to do?

***

           ***

Taylor had an armoury of similes, metaphors and mottoes to go with his library of clichés and anecdotal references. Whenever the young were about their business; beating their chests and testing their weight in their soon-to-inherit world, he liked to remind them; Youth and speed will never overcome old age and treachery!

While they made preparations for the trip, Taylor, at a loose end, wandered the rig, exploring here and there. To his delight, he came across a workshop with tools, stores, electrical parts and other items. To him, incredibly useful items abandoned by the oil workers and ignored by the Navy boys.

Quietly keeping his inspirations to himself, he introduced a few modifications to the raft boat.

What devil devices do you bring?

Oh yes! - he'd thought.

Oh yes! - he thought now.

Naturally suspicious, he installed safeguards on the boat.

           ***

As they disembarked at the jetty, he'd activated a hidden switch. In his pocket, a remote control disguised in a piece of bamboo.

Steal the boat now! he thought, as he trailed the others along the

190

bouncing jetty.

***

In the church, he fretted. Steve was adamant they should carry no tech, no weapons, apart from their knives and fish gaffes, onto the boat.

What if some curious innocent were to stumble on board? He'd worried as he gazed like an imbecile at the shiny plate.

Sometimes he wished his personal guardian angel had a name. Whoever he was, he was on form today but, as usual, left a few loose ends for him to tie up.

Three unconscious dead weights to haul on board a rickety boat, across half a nosy village, in silence, along a creaking bouncing jetty.

He opened his pouch and took out three thick bamboo sections each the size of a fizzy drinks can. If tasked he would have said they were floats for the fishing net, in his pouch to keep dry. A twist here, a thumbnail there, a slide and a click and he had the green light of a fully charged Taser. He was armed. This was a 100% improvement on a minute before. Now, Think!

Loping on tiptoe to the door, he slipped out into the night by a roundabout route until he came up behind the Scallie's cage. They stirred and stared with malevolent distrust. Finger to his lips he whispered,

'You want to escape?'

One came forward close to the bars.

'Why you do this for us?'

'My friends, drugged, asleep. Crazy Pastor – later you!' he hissed, drawing a blade hand across his throat in emphasis, all the time scanning for God Folk.

'We go to my boat, escape. Drop you off some place!'

The one at the rear, a different breed, came forward. He had an air of authority. He sported no tattoos or body piercing but he had that same expression of barely concealed hatred Taylor always saw on Scallie faces.

'Desperate man. Once we are free, what's to stop us leaving without you?'

'Two things.'

Taylor revealed the green light of his Taser.

'One reason is here.'

'And the other…?'

'More painful than the gun…'

191

Clearly, they had respect for high voltages. Two looked to the articulate one. He looked at Taylor, made his decision; nodded. Taylor cut through the lashings of the bars and in a minute, they were free. They dropped down in an agile springy way that Taylor found amazing. Trussed up in there and out they come – like cats! Big, strong young men, waiting on his directions.

Like cagey tigers – an old song came into his head.

He led the way to the hall. The three snatched up the sleeping trio like weightless dolls; flung them over their shoulders. They made for the beach.

***

They reached the jetty without incident, made their way to Taylor's boat at the end. Then, from the beach came an explosion. A signal flare arced high in the sky.

"The Devil works his best in the dark of the night!" boomed an amplified voice.

Taylor, taking up the rear, turned, shading his eyes from the dying flare. A semicircle of cloaked acolytes ignited oil soaked torches. At the front, the focal point of the circle, stood the Pastor. He cast aside his speaking trumpet, came forward.

'So! Not an imbecile but one possessed!'

Taylor looked over his shoulder towards the boat and the Scallies with their limp baggage. He groped in his pouch for the remote control. Not there! He must have dropped it! They had not quite reached the boat, Taylor saw to his relief. Instead, three acolytes confronted them, sharp blades flashing in the light, balancing easily on the jetty end. The Scallies dumped their loads and crouched snarling, fingers like claws.

Taylor noticed theirs was the only boat. The Pastor called to his three men.

'Cut loose their boat! Bring it round! We have them! It will cost us a jetty but they will burn or drown!' He signalled for torches to be brought to the beach end of the jetty.

The Scallies moved.

'Wait!' roared Taylor, some natural authority freezing them to the spot.

The three acolytes made jabbing motions towards the Scallies with their blades and jumped down into the raft boat. The first to touch the deck set off Taylor's little surprise.

A huge blue zigzag spark lanced across to envelope the man in blue fire. His robe caught alight. Almost simultaneously two more lightning bolts seized the other two, thrashing them back and forth, screaming, burning, until they plunged overboard, sizzling and hissing as the sea extinguished the flames. Smaller, almost gentle electric arcs, played across the floating bodies as if to confirm their demise, then flickered out.

In the following seconds, all were frozen in surprise. Taylor ran to the Pastor. 'Your turn you bastard! Try this!' He fired his Taser on a low kV. The barbs sprang forth, burying themselves into the Pastor's skin. He pressed the trigger button again and, holding it down, flew the Pastor like a kite in a convulsive jig on the sand. He turned up the power and the wires burnt out with the deadly current. The Pastor crumpled and fell smoking to the sand. The two torch bearing acolytes fled.

Turning, he joined the others; they were loading Steve, Zill and Mick aboard, preparing to cast off, waiting for Taylor. With him safely aboard they set off into the night leaving the flickering torches of the stunned, now leaderless, God Folk behind.

Chapter Fifteen

With the dawn, he saw his three were still asleep, peacefully unaware of where they were or indeed, why they were here at all. He tended to them, trickled water onto their lips. They were pale but alive. The Scallies watched like owls – did they ever sleep?

Their eyes gleamed somewhat as Taylor propped up Zill in a more comfortable position, rearranged her clothing for modesty. Nothing amiss there! noted Taylor.

Taylor and the Scallies saw land at the same time. They steered into a suitable beaching place. The two associates shoved the bows up a piece to allow their leader to disembark with dry feet. Perversely, he jumped over the side into the same depth of water and waded ashore. He sniffed the air, looked inland, and turned to Taylor.

'So, Devil or Imbecile, we are in your debt.'

Taylor offered them water and rations which they took without comment. He offered a compass, another item from his emergency stash, but the leader shook his head. He tapped his head with two fingers. For some reason, Taylor tapped his wrist in the same way. The Scallie frowned, then followed suit. He motioned the other two to push the boat off the shingle to float free and then they were gone, running fast inland.

Taylor set back out to sea and, after half an hour; with the Scallies long clear, he triggered the rescue beacon; something else he'd hidden away against Steve's instructions.

They only started to come round as the heli lifter was dropping down to get them.

'What the..? Where..? How did we get here? Where are we Taylor?'

'All at sea me dears, all at sea...' and then he collapsed.

***

Back at the rig the boat was in. Armstrong and his sailors moved about in an efficient business like manner. The raft was stowed. The navy techies chuckled at Taylor's modifications, marvelled at the scorch marks across the deck and gingerly removed the fused power cell and capacitors for later analysis. Meanwhile the medics ushered the groggy trio to sick bay.

Zill, Steve and Mick were blood pressured, tapped, probed, examined, blood taken and eventually allowed to go and see how

194

Taylor fared. A curtain surrounded his bed, silhouettes moved with grave concern. They were given a clean bill of health and told to rest but they waited, anxious to hear news of their colleague.

The Doctor came out from behind the curtain, walked over to them. With a worried expression he announced:

'His system has shut down. It is a medical condition which has interested the medical community for centuries. We were lucky – we got him into shelter and into a sickbed in time.'

'A coma – is he in a coma?' worried Zill.

'No, not at all but he has been under a great deal of mental and nervous stress and strain. His body is exhausted, tired out. Quite simply, are you ready for this?' Now they shouted;

'Doc!!!!'

'Quite simply our man there, your buddy, is asleep.'

***

The next morning Shams addressed his bright young protégés.

'You young people are our future. I am very attached to you but at some time in that future my generation must stand aside, hand over to you, secure in the knowledge we can rest easy in our rocking chairs in our twilight years with you at the helm. I make no apology for any mixed metaphors. Consider then, with your recent escapade, had it gone worse for you, how sad but how annoyed I would be if I had to start again with a new bunch; my rocking chair –' he waved to an empty corner of the room – 'standing cold, unoccupied, unused.'

Zill, Steve and Mick shuffled their feet uncomfortably. They remained silent.

'...under cover of fog indeed! Have you been brainwashed by old war films? Must I close down the movie file access if so?'

He counted on his fingers.

'No emergency comms! No weapons; no offshore support; no satellite cover – the most sophisticated optics struggle to see through fog! N'est pas?'

He fumbled with a remote. 'I hate these things!' The lights dimmed; the windows blacked out; a bird's eye view, a thermal image vid started up on the screen wall.

They watched themselves and the lifter separate; four glows seen from above mysteriously crossing the water. They watched their walk along the jetty. One figure remaining behind a few seconds then hurrying to rejoin them followed by a meeting with another group of glowing figures.

'The Pastor and his men on the beach!' breathed Zill.

Fast forward now, their movements played out in comic staccato steps. Normal speed again - less distinct blurs in the meeting hall – Yes it was a thatched roof

Fast again until three motionless blurs shimmering in horizontal – us asleep! The last we remember! A fourth figure moving to the door; – in the street outside three more figures converging. The moving figure inside retreating to become even less distinct – Under the refectory table. He hid under the table!

And on it went. The single figure leaving the building to rendezvous with three more; the flare on the beach whiting out the image, then fading to a semicircle of wavering lights.

More white outs at the end of the jetty...

Shams stopped the show, fumbled with the remote, the room becoming light again.

'A drunken short sighted nettle gatherer could probably make a stab at interpreting that footage!'

Shams consulted his screen.

'The medics found residual diazepam in your blood! How did that get there, I wonder? Taylor apparently evaded being drugged. Later, unable to move you himself, he recruited assistance. Three others carried you to the boat. I would like to hear your ideas on that tomorrow!

It would seem our resourceful Mr Taylor took the trouble to look into the possible futures; to extrapolate a future where things went awry and took steps to remain in some semblance of control!'

'Darwin,' muttered Steve.

'Quite. Natural selection would seem to have placed a survivor in our midst. I suggest you take steps to learn from this *before* man. Aside from his cynical sense of humour I think you may find a rich vein of contra Darwinian advantages.' He paused for effect, and then headed for his high back chair.

'The next time we meet, consider this forgotten. You may go.'

His chair swivelled to face away from them.

***

Walking down the gangway towards sick bay they breathed out, a sense of their own mortality, a new sensation to them, dogging their thoughts.

'A bollocking then, 'said Mick.

'What?'

'That's what Taylor would say we experienced,' explained Steve.

'I'm not sure I like bollockings,' said Zill.

***

Taylor woke early and escaped the sick bay. Pursued by two anxious male nurses he made vile threats – they must sleep sometime; he would visit them in the deep of night; he hinted at unpleasant consequences. They retreated and could be seen at the windows affecting a casual interest in the weather.

He leaned over the rail, the sea breeze fluttering his bathrobe, his cigar end glowing bright.

'Bloody sea! Bloody water! Not a drop to drink!' he muttered.

Sensing company he turned to face his three co adventurers. He smiled.

'Will you tell us one day Taylor?'

'How about tonight? In the bar? Let's see, yes, I'll get old George, the President of the local Angler's Club on the job.'

***

A week passed. The sub had been and gone; Shams, Steve and Mick with it and they took it easy. Not that Shams was a harsh master but with him went terrible purpose, urgent missions, higher projects and his absence made for a more relaxed atmosphere. A skeleton crew stayed on the rig. Although the rig survived the foulest weather, normally all crew would go with the sub but some daylight, vitamin D and general rest from pressure were necessary factors. Taylor called it *holiday*.

Shams left some lectures for Zill to go through. Taylor and Zill sat together in Sham's room and looked at some statistics and Dome agritubes dispositions; some details of which he could enlighten Zill; some her him. The central base nearest the continent was in Kent, not far outside the submerged London, a dispatch and receipt point for power cells and excess biomass going out; specialist stuff such as electronics, frozen meat, fresh vegetables, medicines and other coming in. Their relief crews would assemble there, some to get training and updates, some hopping in to be posted out to where they were needed. Most transport was by Zeppelin lifters.

There were a few traditional floating, diesel engined ships plying back and forth to Europe – some direct to Paris -but they were vulnerable to the storms which either swept them miles off course, stranded them like Noah's Ark on high ground or sank them completely. R&R would begin at the Kent dome and the tired crews coming off their stint would climb aboard a big Zepp to be flown, usually north, to their rest place. The big Zepps shouldered aside the weather, riding high to wait for conditions to be favourable to resume their journeys. No timetables for Zepp rides – Taylor always found his sojourns quite restful.

Fuel was not so much in short supply as poorly distributed, hard to get at within the range of the vehicles of the day. It was a bit like the early treks to the South Pole. Fuel and supplies were dropped ahead of the route in staged locations. Each drop crew returning from one leg, to collect enough fuel to drive the next – a sort of long range bucket chain. Sham's rig was one such a drop but recent disagreement over the fish allocations with Norway cut down all but diplomatic visits across the North Sea. Taylor thought it nonsense – let them fish here in return for their wood and steel – he thought. Not having a full grasp of the situation he'd kept his peace, all the time suspicious of ZI politics and motives.

He'd experienced a hectic few weeks. This pause allowed him to consolidate a little. He would soon be itching to be off. First, came the dreams; mixed up conglomerations of before and now. His lost family would start to figure more and more and he would begin to fall into a depressed state. The numb existence he saw so often in the Dome dwellers. On the other hand the rest allowed his subconscious mind to percolate and plan; to compare notes; to, as Shams put it, exercise his contra Darwinian advantages.

On the third night after their return from the God Folk Island, he dreamed he was pursued by huge dogs ridden by mad monks with curved sabres. He managed to keep ahead but their blades sliced more and more of his clothing away, an affront to his modesty. As he ran, Scallies looked on from the side – their arms folded in non participation, idly curious of the contest. They tapped their bare wrists in concert but remained indifferent

He sat up bolt upright in a sweat.

The dogs! The mean hungry dogs he and Harry thwarted!

No, it could not be, but the more this flash of alternative possibilities grew, the more he wondered. They, the dogs, now he came to analyse it, were not putting any supreme effort into catching the boy – yes, he stayed ahead, at an incredible pace by normal human standards but now on reflection, the boy seemed to be running without panic or fear, hurdling obstacles, now Taylor came to think of it, with almost exuberance. Taylor fell back on his pillow and ran the day over in his mind.

Where was he been running from? Where was he heading? There were buildings around, why not head straight for somewhere to leap up and climb to safety? The boy was obviously athletic enough. Taylor groaned – pieces of jigsaw dropping faster and faster into place - mocking him. No!

The boy leapt from the roof, an incredible feat, and headed – Shit! – back to where they had left the dogs! His dogs!

Further, Taylor remembered remarking to Harry about those boys not fetching slippers. Idiot he was, he was so busy playing big man from before, showing off his *before* shibboleths to Harry, he'd never considered the dogs could be either, one; Looking for their master - or was it pack leader? –taken by them in the heli. Or two; that the boy was in hiding in the foliage below and they were protecting him.

He would ask Zill for a heli ride tomorrow. He wanted to see them back at base anyway. He was not imprisoned here was he?

***

Zill agreed to a trip to the agribase. Furthermore she told him of some surviving strongholds further west that they could drop in on; people he would find stimulating; of interest. She made some arrangements and they met up at the heli-lifter hangar. They were joined by the usual taciturn pilot; he was to fly them. Seamen loaded packages and equipment, lashed them down, retreated, waving them off.

They scudded low over the waves until they reached the tubes edge. They went up to the 1000 feet height guaranteed to avoid vasp attention and soon arrived at the agri base.

All came out to inspect the new machine.

'Why ain't we got one o' these? – we could shift tubes in a jiffy with this mutha!'

Taylor, reunited with his crew, introduced Zill and the pilot who turned out to be called Blair. Marie came forward to greet Zill in a matter of fact professional sort of way but Taylor could see she writhed with curiosity at this new cohort of Taylor's; ever ready to strike with poison jealousy. Jack and Harry were pleased to see them in a 'friend of Taylor's is a friend of mine...' way. Ben came shyly forward, Taylor allowing him a brief embrace which for once Ben did not overdo. Puzzled, Taylor followed Ben's gaze. Blair! The pair had locked onto each other as if no one else existed.

Taylor made a courtesy call on Wallis

'Fifty days to go Taylor. What's your programme?'

'Back in ten days maybe. Finish off my stint – R& R with the gang – can't see much further ahead for now.'

'Kids are getting on fine without you; you'll be pleased to hear.'

'Is that a guilt trip you're putting me on?'

Wallis grinned. 'Half one maybe, they had a close call out on a vasp hunt the other day, could have been nasty. They pulled together and came through. Heli-1 and Heli-2 are like a mini family now, like your Heli-1 gang extended. Oddly enough, without their chief catalyst around; which means I have twice the discipline problem'

'Catalyst am I now?'

'Not sure that's the right word. You know what I mean though.'

Jack and Marie showed him Hansen's wounded heli. Taylor measured the bite in the float, whistled.

'...must have been a Great White! A big bastard like that - this far north!'

Hansen's head popped out; Kristen looked over his shoulder.

'Hoy! Look what that fikker did to my flute!'

Taylor looked on; Marie handing Kristen a tool; his kids bantering.

-That's what you wanted – what they needed! Kids – they're not kids – it's you getting older! -

He turned to see Zill watching from a discreet distance, hanging back, not a part of all this. He knew how she must be feeling.

They had a party down at Joe's. They made Zill feel welcome; they made Blair welcome, but not as welcome as Ben made Blair feel welcome. Into the evening it became apparent Ben and Blair had slipped away. Marie kept her peace but clung to Taylor at every opportunity Zill was close by. Taylor had dug out some music from archive at the rig that now he zipped to Joe's system. Jimi Hendrix. 'Hey Joe' He watched Joe pottering about his bar, wiping, checking, grumbling, barking food orders to the kitchen, yelling advice to the people on the other side of the bar, constantly on the move. The song played and Taylor thought Joe was not listening, then, at the second Hey Joe, Joe looked up in consternation, as if seeking the whereabouts of the caller. Realisation dawned and he sought Taylor out with a look of coy pleasure.

Hey Joe – where you goin' with that gun in your hand?

Chapter Sixteen

The next day Zill made the reason for their cargo apparent. Justification for the trip, as usual was progress and recovery research. As part of Taylor's induction they were to fly west over the wild lands to Wales. Blair elected to stay; 'to learn more of the agricultural work done here,' he stammered.

'Think he can fly the lifter OK?' teased Zill, sparing Blair no blushes.

They lifted off amid waves and cheers from their friends, curses from the admin staff, whose desks and offices became minor earthquake disaster zones from the lifter's extra thrust.

Heading inland they flew via the dog pack area, Taylor explaining his suspicions to Zill.

'I think we can expect more surprises from the Scallies,' she said mysteriously but would not be drawn further. Today, with nothing untoward to be seen, they continued on their way.

'What's the cargo anyway?' Taylor nodded towards the back. Zill had said she wanted to drop off some necessities to a small farm Taylor would find interesting. From the agri base stores they had added some bolts of cloth – nettle weave; some tube photo-microbes; tube bio-weld; rope, netting and other items of trade.

'If we have any adventures here, I will start to wonder about you – they showed me the red button…'

'Did you press it?'

'Not bloody likely! The Jewish guy, Ari and his friend…Hamid?... got quite anxious when I went near it!' They laughed.

They flew over more high ground. Recent fires had scoured much of the midland areas – a sharp tang in the nostrils even up at this height. They crossed motorways similarly arrayed with their abandoned cars, trucks, coaches and buses. A greener land appeared covering higher, much higher, ground.

'She pointed to two big hills in the distance. 'Over there! Between them!'

He corrected their course wound the trim wheel to gain height.

'Why are you climbing? We want to drop down the other side!'

He pointed out a lens shaped cloud. 'See that cloud – a lenticular, it will be dumping cold air down into the valley on the south side – could push us down too close for comfort!'

'Cold air in these days?'

'…relatively cold air. Hot air rises, cooler air takes its place'

Taylor concentrated on gaining height, he also approached at a 45° angle. 'If we are pushed down by the wave we can turn away and try again.' She wasn't sure what he meant but he sounded confident.

They came close to the gap and he increased power to climb again – pointed to a dial winding down indicating rapid loss of height. They skimmed a ridge with 50 feet to spare. Zill remained silent; wondered if Blair knew such tricks.

Clear of the ridge they descended, now under control, into a green valley. It reminded Taylor of southern Asia. Neat paddy fields followed the valley contour. Workers knee deep in the field water – workers with coolie hats could be seen dotted here and there.

'Over there!'

Buried in the side of the hill was a concrete structure. Taylor would not have noticed it flying by routinely. Its harsh corners were broken up with exotic foliage and other planting. They slowed; a flat area presenting itself as the obvious place to land.

As the engine ran down a tall distinguished man in a white – was it a dish dash? or a cassock? - came out to meet them. A crowd of others held back peering from a covered balcony, Chinese and, yes, a European standing apart as if in disdain.

The man's shock of white hair billowed about in the residual wind of the aircraft's displaced air. Taylor stopped in his tracks – the man wore a dog collar!

'Meet the vicar!' smiled Zill.

Taylor gave her a long look before he jumped out to be greeted by their host.

'Zill, my dear!' They embraced. The vicar looked over at Taylor turned back to her.

'So you have brought – what? a lamb to the slaughter? - or the Prodigal Son? Is that a dilemma? – or a conundrum? Without one you cannot welcome the other!'

In spite of his reservations Taylor suspected he was going to like this man. The vicar led them, now chattering inconsequentially to Zill, now enquiring about the flight to Taylor.

'Did the katabatic get you on the ridge? SPs have lost a couple there. What have you brought to our humble acreage this time young lady?'

Zill looked back at Taylor. 'He climbed miles up. I wondered what he was doing – and still we scraped by!'

'Aha! a man of before then!'

'We are not completely stupid, we of the new world!' she protested. 'Sometimes the old knowledge can be useful though...' she admitted, giving Taylor a thoughtful look.

She turned to greet a smiling Chinese lady of indeterminate middle age. Taylor was surprised to hear them exchange compliments in Chinese. They both looked at him and laughed. Zill continued in English.

'Meet Madam Betty. My Chinese repertoire is exhausted. '

Taylor took the proffered hand. Betty smiled her examination. 'Come inside Mr Taylor, it is time for our midday meal. My husband delayed it when he thought we would be picking pieces of you off the hill side.'

Taylor said aside to Zill, 'Did you tell him we were coming?' She shook her head.

Husband?

They were seated in a weave tent at a long refectory table next to the vicar and Betty, his wife. The sides were open to allow a cooling breeze to blow through. The European, an Englishman with a northern accent came in to greet them.

'Davis, Rob Davis er…you tuck in, I'll chat later. ' He eyed the rest of the table with a resigned expression and left them. A dozen or more Chinese; men, women, youths and girls appeared. A turmoil of laughing squealing little ones climbed in and out of the bamboo table supports, peeping at Taylor and Zill as if they were aliens on show. One bold one got close to Taylor and peered at him through the folds of the table cloth.

'Boo!' said Taylor. Big mistake - for nothing now would do but all must be boo-ed in turn and repeated endlessly until the grown ups, exasperated, shoo-ed them out with barks of, what would it be? - Cantonese or Mandarin?

Dishes of rice were thumped down, thin brittle bread – Papadoms? – confirmed when the group members periodically reached out to chop, karate style, the round wafers into shards and pieces. All ate.

Taylor could not contain himself; enquired of the vicar.

'Were you a missionary? A wandering vicar?

The vicar laughed.

'You see a stereotype here, oh lovely, amah, but so it must seem. Betty used to pole a junk down the Yangtze until I rescued her from slavery. Eh? Old girl?'

Betty batted at him half-heartedly.

'We used to eat the missionary men. This one? He too stringy, smell bad – pf'oah! No, Mr Taylor, I was a librarian in Wrexham.'

She pointed her chopstick over her shoulder in the approximate direction.

'Susan here...' A pretty woman had appeared over Taylor's shoulder. She offered steaming hot vegetables, bamboo shoots, water chestnuts and some sort of dock leaves.

'...has a degree in history from Manchester.' She went down the table identifying various members of the commune: garage mechanic, stockbroker, hairdresser, dentist.

'I only marry him to save the other girls from his wandering hands, the old goat here...'

'Married before? – or since?'

'Before? No! Only in these desperate times would he marry me. He had a la-di-dah BBC wife before...'

Taylor waited while she exchanged pleasantries with Susan and answered some question in Chinese further along the table. Zill, chatting to the others further down the table was obviously quite at home here in this secret valley, this...it took Taylor some time to recollect the word, a rare one in these times...this Paradise?

The vicar, clearly enjoying fresh company, a new audience, explained.

'Now I had a dilemma, to rescue this book cataloguing heathen from sin, but how? She was not a Christian and I had no Bishop from whom I could seek dispensation. Who would conduct the ceremony? Dear, dear, dear, what to do? And then I seized on the answer. I decided, in the absence of guidance, that I would delegate the authority of head of the Church of England to myself. Ho ho! I could find no references which might contradict this, admittedly they had mostly been washed away, and so, I conducted the ceremony myself' – he wheezed with laughter...intoned in a solemn:

'Will I, the Reverend John Smollett take Betty ....and so on... I will! And, to cut a short story shorter, here we are, man and wife these last years...!'

***

Lunch over, all the Chinese helped to clear the table. Apparently no washing up was required. Scraps went to the chickens and the cats and dogs here and there or into a wicker basket for compost. Each had chopsticks and a knife and spoon which they licked and wiped clean on the papadom plates, the ones they hadn't eaten that is. What a novel idea! He examined one. It had a firm but rubbery consistency. The vicar noticed his interest.

'Yesterday's ...they were baked yesterday or the day before; left out in the humidity they set like this.'

'Who discovered this? Is it an ancient Chinese thing?'

'No – no Taylor it is my discovery! Once, before, we had a barbecue party with an Indian theme. In the morning, we came down to the usual post party mess and I discovered that, with the damp night air the papadom had turned into a wonder building material. You can make slippers out of them! I wouldn't go so far as shoes! In fact I am surprised you don't recognize the theory where you work!'

'Where I ....? The tubes!'

'The Lord works in mysterious and amusing ways Taylor. All the answers are there already provided, but we have to work out the clues ourselves...'

***

Later, Zill directed the unloading of the heli. No shortage of willing helpers from the men. No shortage of scowls from their wives and women either, Taylor saw with amusement. He walked with the vicar who pointed out the paddy fields and other more western produce, grown under dense nets to filter the scorching sun. There were interesting irrigation solutions which Taylor mentally stored away for later contemplation.

They halted in the shade of a huge boulder protruding from the side of the valley. Away in the distance Taylor saw Davis swing a golf club, shade his eyes to establish where the ball had gone, and then go striding after it.

'A sad man, Davis,' said the vicar. 'Without him we would not be here.'

He went on to tell how he was not always a man of the church. He had studied as a meteorologist.

'I find the weather of great interest. It is the constant striving of the atmosphere to balance itself out; to zero itself. The sun's heat warms the ground with microwave radiation, the heat carries the air up, taking the water vapour up with it. Once the dew point height is reached the water condenses from its gaseous state into visibility – clouds – which get heavy and drop the water somewhere else. Very frustrating for a neat and orderly atmosphere god; no wonder it loses its temper so often. Recently must have been a nervous breakdown.'

He went on. 'I joined the Church; they in their wisdom gave me a parish and my own shop, the biggest, most ornate one in the village. Davis was one of my customers. I offered to save his soul. He was a common sort. He loved the back pages of the cheapest newspapers, an unlikely worshipper. He had a pretty but vapid little wife...'

They walked on; a cloud had obscured the sun, bringing some relief.

'I was watching the weather closely. It was more out of balance than ever. Snow in May, heat waves in October. I wondered how long such an odd cycle would last. Abnormal became the norm. Everyone, as you know, was getting jittery about the global warming thing. The government paid lip service but really did nothing.'

They reached the shade of another outcrop. Someone had fashioned a bamboo bench and table; a thoughtful respite. The vicar sat. Davis swiped in apparent temper at a bush on the other side of the valley.

'Do you know the story of Noah and his Ark, Taylor?'

Taylor nodded.

'God spoke to me…' Here the vicar held up a hand to ward off Taylor's dismay. He pointed back to the concrete bunker, swept an inclusive hand across the valley.

'I found this for sale. I fell in love with it. Where would I, a church mouse, get the money? I prayed for guidance; for a sign. God gave me Davis.'

Taylor frowned. He could tolerate this tongue in cheek clergyman. He had a twinkle in his eye and he didn't take his God fearing very seriously. But where was he taking him?

'Thank you for keeping your atheism in check as it were…' said John.

'Who said I was an atheist?'

'It takes one to know one, Taylor.'

The vicar smiled at memories. 'Davis won the lottery. He shared a sixth of a £42 million pound Euro Lotto.'

Ah! thought Taylor.

'I brought him up here. I showed him the possibilities, explained he could survive hurricanes, nuclear wars in this bunker. If nothing happened, look at the view. He bought it, the idea, the house, the whole valley. We made plans to provision it. Whenever his enthusiasm wavered I showed him my weather charts, sunspot activity and so on. Davis was far too ignorant to query them. He wanted his own golf course. A start was made; see how he mourns it. How he resents the water crop which maintains us; the rice.'

He stood up and gestured for Taylor to come back with him. As they walked, he described the terrible trick played on Davis.

'Within four months we had spent so much time on our project our obsession had its consequences. My wife ran off with the curate; yes, my la-di-dah BBC wife. I forgave her; Betty has not, though she never met her. Davis's wife ran off with one of his co-winners – hah! A Belgian! They met at the cheque presentation ceremony. Hell of a one way ticket to Brussels! Did Shams show you the satellite images Taylor?' Taking Taylor's silence as a "yes" he continued.

'If there's a God then it follows there's a Devil. I sometimes think, when I came here before, this was my wilderness. Here I was offered, where the Devil offered, escape from the little people, the annoying, selfish hypocrites, who I was set to watch over. In turn, I was the devil who tempted Davis. Davis saved my life by paying two, no, nearly three million for this piece of real estate. There were other houses but wind and flood took them away.'

The vicar went on to describe the 'build up' as he called it.

'I bought seeds from cheap discount stores. I bought garden tools, chicken wire, plastic netting. Davis bought power tools and a petrol generator. I bought books; I learnt to make a simple radio and bought some second hand amateur radio kit. Davis bought the DVD of every film made; he recorded sports programmes. I found an old tractor going for a few quid and got it going again. I went to all the chip shops and restaurants and took their old cooking oil. Davis bought crates of beer, wine and spirits. I bought the brewers kits and demijohns. I bought shotguns and got us a licence. He bought an air rifle. When it came we made our way here; he brought along a few drinking friends and his tart of a girlfriend. What could I say? I couldn't send them away. I hated them. Anyway, the big storms came and we were thankful for our preparations. Enough said. Then the Chinese turned up. Davis wanted to send them away but I had my way.'

He trudged on, pointing out this and that with his sweeping arm.

'We built a dam to keep the soggy ground wet for the rice…'

He had to finish getting Davis off his chest to this newcomer.

'In turn, my dream saved his life but ruined it at the same time. He enjoyed his wealth for seven months and then the big storms came.'

Shaking his head, he pushed his way into the cool interior of the bunker.

'Now he thinks he is the unluckiest man in the world.'

***

Later, Taylor, with the help of Zill, showed the vicar and the Chinese how to seed a small tube and seal it; let them make another one themselves.

'In a day or two put a small hole through the skin; light it. Tube 1 will burn green. You have methane…natural gas'

Later, after the evening meal, Taylor went outside, lit a cheroot and gazed out into the night.

He was joined by Davis.

'What did John say about me?'

'He said you saved his life with your money; that you didn't get chance to enjoy it for long.'

'I am the unluckiest man in the world…'

Taylor regarded him a moment. Before him stood a weak man with a weak mouth; his spark, his aura, one of mean uncharitable disappointment. He spoke, trying to temper his dislike.

'Many many people lost everything. You live here, I don't understand how but, you go unmolested by wild men, outlaws and Scallies. You live here in a relative Paradise; I think you are incredibly lucky…'

'Stuck here with the Chinks, clever Chinks, who despise me? Stuck here with "I told you so" Reverend John? These people read books, play musical instruments, talk about philosophy, plan crops, rotation, that sort of boring shit. I can barely read and write. I might get to shag one of the chink girls on occasion but one of these days I'm gonna get my throat cut…I brought some mates and their girls with me. We got pissed every night. I laid in enough booze and DVDs to last a century.

My mates, we had some parties; never mind the outside world. Sometimes we played re-runs of the football all day. I had enough microwave TV dinners to last forever. Then the Chinks turned up like bad pennies. They brought rice, fucking rice, and convinced John the conditions were right for paddy farming. Fucking Stone Age farming! I didn't even water the garden in my day! When John turned round and announced it was time some work got done, my boys decided they had some foreigners to boss about. Big mistake! Anyway, they took the piss and we had the Rev with his packets of seeds, his survival stuff and his ham radio.

We called him "the nerdy vicar". He waited his chance and then one day, when we were arseholed, he showed the SPs in. They rounded up my mates and the girls; took most of them away. "We're short of Dees and Da's," they said. John said he'd had them "press ganged", whatever that meant. They left a couple of blokes, no room on their choppers. They didn't last long … the Chinks were already fed up with them…they disappeared, no goodbyes, nothing'

Taylor wasn't sure how to react. What to say. As he flicked his cigar butt over the rail all he could think of was:

'It seems to me that the Vicar saved your life. You're not a nice man are you? I would be grateful.'

'Nice doesn't get me into Ping Pong here's shorts does it? I try to be "nice" to that Zill. She looks at me like I'm a piece of shit.'

"Ping Pong" was Susan, come to ask if Taylor needed anything. She barely contained her contempt for Davis.

'Good evening Robert. I thought I heard you whining. Telling Mr Taylor what you have achieved today?'

She turned to Taylor.

'You really shouldn't smoke you know; give them to Robert. He doesn't enjoy his life.'

Taylor was uncomfortable. He made his excuses and went to bed. He had been shown his room earlier – a simple enough windowless bunk which reminded him of the submarine.

Lying there, he went over his day. No doubt Shams's people led an interesting life. So, John the Vicar knew Shams; he had known of their visit beforehand. How? Amateur radio? This place; they did not need this fortress any longer; the valley seemed a safe enough haven. The produce; the rice, far more than this small group of people needed. What did they do with the surplus? SPs came here. His eyelids were starting to get heavy. He decided to leave it with his sleeping subconscious. Perhaps Zill would fill in the gaps...he shut his eyes, made his mouth comfortable.

He heard a tap on the door. Something told him to ignore it. Whoever it was went away.

***

In the morning, they had a late breakfast. The Chinese always started early, to take advantage of the relative cool of the morning, so only four sat down around the table; himself, Zill, the vicar and his wife. No sign of Davis.

'He will keep to his bed until at least midday,' said John. Susan passed through, fluttered her fingers at Taylor. He raised his eyebrows briefly in reply. The brief exchange didn't go unnoticed by Zill; she wouldn't meet his gaze and excused herself to go and stand outside. The vicar watched her through the window.

'A man like you could be happy here, I think. Some fresh blood for us; fresh ideas, a new point of view. I'm not getting any younger, am I old girl?'

Betty smiled fondly at him, got up from the table and busied herself with trivia.

'Get yourself a nice little wife; steal yourself a heli...stroll in one day...'

'I had a nice little wife. I'd like to find her before I settle down...'

'Years on, stories of joyous reunions rank with the fairy tales. Resign yourself; it is kinder in the long run. Leave happy memories behind in "the before".'

'So I get myself a wifey. Who?'

The vicar nodded outdoors towards the trim figure outside, gazing down the valley. She cut a lonely figure.

'Zill? She is one of Shams's acolytes. Independent type. Besides, I'm twice her age.'

Betty turned to look out of the window at Zill.

'Those...she has no such reservations, I think you may find.'

Shit.

They all walked down to the lifter. In the cargo hold, there were two brimming sacks of rice and a small parcel. Betty pressed plant cuttings and small glass bottles on to Zill.

'I will share these with Marie,' she said, for Taylor's benefit.

The vicar shook his hand and pressed an oblong of cigars on Taylor.

'Better enjoy them now; the humidity has been kind but things don't last forever. Davis won't miss them.'

Chapter Seventeen

'Head west; follow the valley,' said Zill over the intercom. She stayed in the back for a time, ostensibly sorting out packages but he sensed a cold shoulder nonetheless.

Bloody women! he thought.

Eventually she ran out of things to pretend to do and came through to the front seat. Taylor had been casting about for an icebreaker.

'Zill; what nationality has a name like that?'

'It is Gillian. I couldn't say soft 'G' when I was little. Then I lost my baby teeth which didn't help. It stuck.'

Where have I heard someone call her Gill?

***

They stayed low over the paddy fields as they petered out to become scrub. The dam went by – quite a feat of engineering for such a small group, thought Taylor. He was sure Davis and his friends had not lifted a finger and pondered on where the manpower came from. He could see no heavy machinery. There were some cattle type animals rooting about in the scrub and the mud but they were past and gone before he could identify them.

They left the valley and flew over an open plain rising up to the mountains of Wales, the tops of which were shrouded in cloud. Lower down, mist blew across the ground as the sun warmed it, causing eddies of mixed hot air from the valley and falling cool air from the mountain.

Taylor moved over to the other side to keep away from any downdraught. The visibility was getting worse and worse.

Zill consulted her wrist and transferred information to the heli's navscreen. Taylor donned virtual goggles and the mist disappeared. He now viewed an eerie video game landscape but now he could see all the high ground ahead.

'Follow the mountains right, left and right. Look out for a lake the shape of a footprint. Our stop should show up soon after,' she said in a matter of fact tone.

'Roger, Wilco,' he muttered.

Zill scowled at the "before" phrase but did not pursue it.

'We are visiting another country; Wales. Forget any "before" associations. They guard their borders with zeal. They suffered badly from early Scallie and refugee depredations. Many Midlanders tried to escape here and there were not enough resources to sustain all. Bad, bloody times; now the Welsh do not welcome strangers gladly. We are OK in this heli – we are known from previous visits and carry a positive association. I should leave your weapon in the cockpit or at least keep it out of sight.'

Taylor's head inclined towards her; he looked like a space alien.

'Are you reading this from a data sheet?' He could not see her with the virtual goggles and dared not raise them. Outside, for her, the world was a white blur.

'I am not.'

'Sounds like the Rough Guide to Much Bloodshed'

She smiled in spite of herself. After all, how long could she keep this up? The man did not know she tapped on his door last night. He did not know that last night she had waited until the place was quiet, tantalised with a schoolgirl crush waging an internal battle inside, waging a war with a simple need not to be lonely, to be held, warm, safe in this vicious world.

Taylor, oblivious to these thoughts, tapped a finger to some music in his head. He sensed a relaxation in the atmosphere. He weaved the stick about. She yelped in alarm.

He had height to spare but she couldn't see that.

***

He saw the lake ahead. The radio altimeter superimposed on his vision indicated the ground was falling away to a plateau of flatter ground. He slowed and started to descend. The virtual screen flashed a beacon pulse ahead.

'Taylor! We are in visual!'

He raised the visor and glanced at Zill. She was smiling at him.

'I've been enjoying the view for minutes now!' she laughed.

'You're not too big I can't put you over my knee!'

'No,' she murmured. 'Look, across the lake!' A strobe laser, similar to the one at the Sandringham tower pulsed its red "Friend or Foe " signal; changed to green and winked out.

'*Ddihingol Clythrea*,' she said. '*Safe place…*'

Spread out before them was a big house and grounds. Not a house but a small castle, built out of the hillside and of an age to have taken on the shades and tones of the area as if it were a natural feature of the landscape. The remains of ornate gardens were now given over to garden crops. A solitary figure ran forward and marshalled them into a gravelled parking area more suited to horse and carriage than the

212

incongruous bulk of the lifter.

Shutting down, Taylor looked out to the marshaller who, after waiting for the engines to spool down, ran in low to meet him. He was dressed in uniform. "British Army Disruptive Pattern; Tropical; Man's", Taylor would have guessed. He saluted.

'Sir! Welcome to Ddihangol Clythrea! Please follow me!'

They climbed out and Zill ran ahead to greet a silver haired man, also in uniform, stumping, aided by a stick, down the entrance steps.

Taylor followed, walking alongside the soldier, a lad of perhaps nineteen or twenty.

'What news sir?'

'Oh, you know.' The lad clearly did not.

'Let's get the stories out when everyone's together, eh?' He winked.

Zill had done with her personal greetings. She waited, more formally now, for Taylor to catch up.

'This is Colonel Owen Edwards of the Welsh Guards,' she announced. 'Owen, meet Taylor of the East Anglia Tubes.'

'Good to meet you Taylor!' He pronounced it "Tay-lah!" 'Been looking after my little Gill then?'

'I like to watch out for the kids in these times, Colonel.'

'That's the spirit! Ah! Here's the sergeant major now!'

Taylor turned to meet a stereotype; a rigid, regimented, wiry martinet of a man with a polished cane under his arm.

'Sar'nt Major Jones. At your service sah!'

Taylor nodded, smiled, and indicated his name badge.

'Taylor! - if you like.'

Jones, stiffly at attention, winked.

***

The Colonel led the way inside, Taylor and Jones taking up the rear. The youngster tried to come with them only to be stared into a nervous retreat by Jones.

Taylor held back long enough to mutter an aside to Jones:

'Am I stuck in a BBC drama?'

'Oh yes. No commercials now are there sir? After you...' he waved towards the door and, for Taylor's ears only;

'...fly boy!'

***

213

'Television drama...?' laughed Owen. 'What are dramas but real life from a different viewpoint? I know what you are thinking Taylor. I have a private army like some millionaire eccentric. No, sadly, no, this is real. This is the border control HQ for the Welsh Defence Force. We have a few thousand men up and down the border. This particular place is peaceful now so we use it as a training and rest base. We keep an eye out for trouble, mainly sheep rustlers, but we don't get the gangs coming down from Lancashire these days; maybe the SPs sorted them out; maybe they've formed some sort of local government.

The Welsh have a proud tradition in the British Army, which, whatever your politics, has quite a good record of proficiency. The British Army, what was left of it, was integrated into the UN and ESO during the emergency. Unless you call those thugs in SPs the Army.

SPs attracted a lot of our young men into their ranks. What else were they going to do? They needed food, employment to look after what was left of their families; why go wandering overseas thanklessly to leave bits of your body and soul behind?

No Taylor, the British Army is gone; only a shadow remains here; effectively in another country. We live in a barter world. You trade your agri, bio, whatever skills, for a bed and food. We keep the Scallies and other undesirables at bay. The Welsh hill farmers now live secure and carry on much as they always did...'

Two lads brought in steaming plates, placed a large joint of meat in the central place of honour on the table. Lamb! Taylor had to stop himself visibly drooling.

Owen smiled at Taylor's loss of concentration.

'The Welsh send us their slaughtered lambs; early on they sent us their youngsters, like lambs to the slaughter. We lost many of them. Now we are as likely to lose a lad in training as in a fight with the wild people.'

Slaughtered lambs; the old Bible hangs on everywhere, thought Taylor.

'Wild people? You mean Scallies?'

'Bandits, thugs, travellers. "Scallies" was a derogatory term to generalise feral city street kids. During the worst of the anarchy, the people turned to savagery. They formed into gangs of bandits and stole whatever they needed or wanted; food, villages, young women, slaves. Our little army takes pride in ending that; a few scores were settled.

The Scallies are a different proposition now. If the new organised type we see lately really wanted to start trouble, I think we would be fighting a rearguard action. We keep an uneasy truce, we both respect boundaries. Whether they are biding their time, I don't know. We do have some intelligence and surveillance advantages...'

Here he acknowledged Zill.

'...and we can place maximum firepower in the right place at the right time. He nodded out of the window where the bulk of the lifter shaded the room.

'For some reason we can't get hold of a few of those.'

Taylor was about to say that they were not that hard to put together when he noticed Zill signing in the negative. Jones, at the other end of the table, watched the interplay with interest. Owen seemed not to notice. Taylor changed tack.

'If you lost one, captured say; they can be repaired and turned against you maybe?'

Owen agreed but countered: 'But who is making such strategic decisions, I would like to know. The old Ministry of Defence used to make such god like policies until we found the government had short changed their pocket money to send people on the dole on holiday...'

He slapped his leg and rolled the trouser up to show an artificial limb.

'I was a Lieutenant in Afghanistan when I lost this. Jones here had to keep the tourniquet on so long, from lack of a medevac chopper, they had no choice but to amputate.'

***

Taylor walked with Jones. He led him through the barracks making up the east wing, past an assault course with teenage boys and some girls enduring shouts yells and curses from instructors; past stables used as classrooms, stores and rest rooms. Then on, up a rise overlooking the crops to eventually stop at a stout rock table to peer down a sheer face with a waterfall. Hidden in the spray Taylor noted a hydroelectric generator. He'd wondered what they did for electric power. Jones began to answer Taylor's other unasked questions:

'We came out of the Army after that Afghan tour. The Boss had to; he wouldn't have been able to sit at a desk after trips like Basra, Helmand or Sierra Leone. He had some compensation money for his leg. Not enough but he scrounged and borrowed to buy this place. He got one big backer I never met.

I'd lost a few mates by then. Still, what was there back at home? The lefties were starting to call us murderers; not much call for a trained killer especially one without a degree in media studies,

215

sociology or some other useless shite. The Boss took me with him. He was a good officer but he should have been in the European wars. They wouldn't have sent him on to Staff College. He had the answers they couldn't present to Parliament. "If we couldn't win their hearts and minds then put them in concentration camps and then nuke 'em – hah!"

The Yanks wouldn't have had to be told twice with that shit hole...they were losing more men than we were; poor bastards.

So we came home; ran survival courses for people who wanted to play but not commit. We offered blood, sweat and tears but with fake blood.'

He pointed out camouflaged guard sangars, guard posts cleverly concealed until one was on top of them; occupancy only apparent by pairs of gleaming eyes. They walked up a further slope and stopped to look back.

'Whoever built this old place was a military man.' He pointed out the lake, the mountain behind. From this height, one could see an enemy coming for miles.

Below, a platoon of young men, led by an NCO, ran in formation. Jones watched them critically but, Taylor noticed, with pride. Jones's stick pointed east towards England.

'You must have driven to Germany and back before. What did you notice?'

'It was easy for an army to drive across west and north; difficult to fight back the other way; an ambush every few miles.'

'Not bad for a fly boy! Yes! The D Day landings nearly went badly for us. Look, we are in Germany here!'

'Have the Welsh made him a Colonel?'

'Lieutenant Colonel actually. No, he was a Lieutenant, I was a Corporal. We promoted ourselves to what we considered we would have been if we'd stayed in. The amount of blokes we've got don't qualify us for any further promotion; you can't have a general in charge of a few platoons...'

Taylor stopped to admire the lake.

'I could land my seaplane there.' he said.

'Always thinking about flying, like fucking birds you are...'

'Up there you have an altitude problem; you can look down on people...'

Jones led the way back.

'It was all turning to a load of bollocks before anyway really...at least now men can be men again...'

Taylor turned a last time to look across the approach from England.

He imagined Jones would not let anyone approach this place; he would make it his last stand.

***

The old building reeked of history; history oozing from the thick stone walls. In spite of the prevailing heat wave conditions, Taylor could feel the cold stone drawing the heat from his body. What was it about cold stone? Did it have an inbuilt balancing mechanism which sought heat to draw in? He thought he must look into a Physics text when he had a minute.

He mused along these lines as Owen led him into a large cool hall. He looked up to the ceiling. It reached away overhead. His breath rasped in his throat; uncomfortable to both breathe and look up at the same time. Walls, hung with tapestries and medieval weapons. Fake decoration? Or real? Rude to ask, they were probably genuine but quite frankly he didn't care. The objects of the Colonel's interest today were in a more modern corner.

Favouring his good leg, Owen leaned over glass cabinets containing an assortment of hand grenades, Ghurkha knives, machetes, a revolver, some automatic pistols along with bits of military paraphernalia; webbing, water bottles, cap badges and bits of brass and canvas straps of unknown purpose. Taylor scanned framed photographs of men clustered around jeeps, helicopters and armoured vehicles. Labels read: Gulf 2 – Basra, Helmand Province, Afghanistan. A framed part of Flecker's *The Golden Road to Samarkand*.

We travel not for trafficking alone;
By hotter winds our fiery hearts are fanned:...

You had to be there! thought Taylor. Others' memories and life detritus, some of the things were familiar to him, the weapons and articles of uniform, for example. Gas masks, respirators to the purist, from different wars, hung mournfully from wooden pegs. Never one for the army in the past; brave boys messed about by governments; they seemed to celebrate as many defeats as victories, he thought.

Do not yawn! he urged himself.

Owen remarked on this and that, as much to himself as to anyone in the room. Read from the poem:

'.....For lust of knowing what should not be known
We take the Golden Road to Samarkand... '

217

Taylor read it again. Familiar from some regiment but he couldn't remember. The Colonel tugged his sleeve.

'You will appreciate these things but they meant nothing to a whole generation. I still feel bitter about the betrayers, the trendy liberal know-nothings. Men didn't come home from those foreign places; nor women. What happened at home? Louts and scrubbers drunk in the streets, rapists, paedophiles, anti-social illiterates, chavs, football fans disgracing us in Europe...'

***

Jones appeared, he had a way of 'being there' all of a sudden in counterpoint to Taylor, who could somehow 'not be there'. He nodded to Taylor. 'Now then Boss, not getting on yer soapbox again?'

Owen sighed. 'You're right as usual. Y'know Taylor, these last years after the...' He snapped his fingers twice to avoid the inverted commas of it all. '...I've been glad I was in a position to hunt down, wipe out the post disaster scum. They couldn't hide behind human rights acts, ineffectual police procedures, magistrates, social workers...' He drew a bead with thumb and forefinger, closed one eye, "boof" - his hand recoiled – another imaginary scumbag dispatched.

'War changes a man. He can't come home and pick up where he left off; home in time for tea, eh Jonesy?'

'Home in time for tea it is, sir!'

'You saved my life. Maybe in more ways than one...' he slapped his leg. 'How many times have I ordered you that 'sir' is not necessary between two old chums.'

'Lost count, s..., lost count Boss. Come away from here now; come away from before...I was going to take Taylor into the village for a beer. Come on, cheer you up, you know you fancy that Megan...'

'Are we all secure Jonesy, all tucked up for the night?'

Jones tilted his head, askance, raised an eyebrow. Owen realised his error...

'Of course we are. We always are, always were...' He picked up a photo frame. 'Oh to turn the clock back, knowing what we know now.' He put it down, stumped to the door with Jones poised, ready to turn off the lights. Taylor stared at the photo. Stared too long to remain casual. Owen looked back.

'Happy days, the world was rosy for a few years after university; Aberystwyth. There's me; that's Shamsy and his wife, she didn't make the shelters. Shams read Biochemistry with Entomology as a

218

hobby; he loved insects, especially bees, they fascinated him. Their little girl, recognise her? Just losing her baby teeth, bless. John the Met-man before he took Orders, you have met him? Yes of course you have. The other guy, I forget his name; read political science, friend of Shams, didn't like him much. Let's go eh?'

Taylor joined them. He didn't do jigsaws, however, this one seemed to be being done for him, there were still a lot of gaps, he was still in the dark but the general picture was taking shape.

Shamsy! Owen's friend –Shams. Shams friend - the Z3? - a little girl with her grown up teeth peeping through; who couldn't say "Gill".

"For lust of knowing what should not be known…"

Chapter Eighteen

Jones led them to a garage in the stables, swung open a tall door to reveal an ancient Land Rover in drab green. They climbed in and headed out into the night. With enough moonlight to see by, he kept the lights off. Taylor jerked his head in query and Jones drew close to a hedge and slid the window open.

'All clear?' he called into the night.

'All clear sir,' said a voice from the hedge.

Winding up a narrow lane, they came to a village of low cottages with slate roofs reflecting the moonlight. They drove into a narrow courtyard. Through a door, pushing past a blackout curtain Taylor found they were in, a pub bar!

'Army's in. Stand by yer beds!' said an older Welsh voice. Taylor's eyes adjusted to see a narrow bar with tables and chairs, candle lit with figures hunched over glasses here and there. A buxom girl heaved on a beer pump handle. Judging by the Colonel's bashful silence, this must be Megan, but she was pouring a light brown frothy, delicious... Taylor's mouth watered for the second time that day...cool, sparkling, amber, with hints of candle light and a light creamy head of froth pouring....oh! A pint. A pub pint!

Tears came to his eyes. Jones nudged him.

'Come on fly boy blue job. Chin up, can't weaken. You're in the army now!'

***

Zill wandered the cold stone corridors. She found a huge bathroom with an indeterminate ceiling height. She tried the taps and was overjoyed to find that hot water ran. She opened a cupboard – towels! A bit crispy and hard, washed by men no doubt but she twisted and flapped them, folded and refolded them and they became less starched. The boys had gone for a beer. Boys will be boys she thought, a before term floating into her head. From where?

She put the bath plug in and ran a mixer tap to a bearable temperature. While it filled up memories of warm quiet safety sprang up; before bed, the security of two grown ups watching over her, sensed as much as seen; plastic floating toys, bubble bath from a blue container with the face of a laughing sailor, white lid like a sailor's hat...

She examined herself in a faded mirror, decided she liked what she saw, and, if she liked it... she flung her one piece overall away from her and climbed in. Aah!

***

The pub was livening up as more came in, maybe alerted to a newcomer in town, escorted by friends; a new sensation. Taylor was plied for information. Trying desperately to play down the life out on the edge of the flooded lands he nevertheless attracted some admiring glances, not least from Megan. For the first time he realised how much he was in the claws of the mysterious Cartwright, ESO; how strange his life story, how him and his friends' lives had turned out, must be to these people. Here, they recycled the time of the ages. He fought a daily battle on an alien landscape.

Megan! He stayed well away from her while prompting Owen into bolder advances. Beer was never in short supply. Not once did he have to take his glass to the bar with a mouthful left for passing the waiting time to get served.

Songs broke out in Welsh. Taylor recoiled a little, never one for folk or pub music and stood back in an "I'll sit this one out" sort of way.

***

Zill, clean, rosy from the heat of the bath, sauntered along the corridor to her room. Nobody about so she let her towel slip. Feeling a strange delicious naughtiness she went first into her room, brushed her hair, sparingly applied some rose water Betty had given her, patting some here, some there, in strategic positions. She took out the two candles Betty had also pressed on her, that time with a wink and a nudge, and made her way naked to Taylor's room. She lit the candles with a match from a matchbox she found earlier in a drawer. Everything is so convenient tonight! She left the curtains open to let silvery moonlight flood the room, got into bed and settled down to wait.

***

She woke. The moon had moved round away from the window. It must be late! Where were the boys? What had awoken her?

She heard singing, noisy slurred banter, hushed with hissing shushes that were louder than the singing that it was meant to subdue; laughter. Sounds carried far on the still night.

221

Going to the window, she saw the Land Rover had left the road and was stuck in a ditch.

Helpless with laughter, the three men were extricating themselves. They were singing.

'Shabby dooh! Shabby dah! – indeterminate owner.

'Show me the way-ah – ter go home…!' Taylor?

'I'm Jake – ther – Peg – deedle deedle dum…' - no prize for guessing…

Slurred; 'Fucking army! All tough shit and boot laces! Tough shit and mess tins…come on Jonesy, get the leg out from under the pedals unless you want to carry him! Told you, never let an officer drive!'

She could see Owen on the ground holding up his empty trouser leg and flapping it about.

'It's OK this time Jonesy, the chopper's already here!' He lapsed into wheezing gasping giggles. He was reunited with his leg and the three hobbled towards the house.

'… the final leg, Colonel,' Taylor said.

'Oh yes Taylor, very good, the final leg! Hear that Jones, you great stiff fanny fart?'

'Shabbah dooh…fuck off lootenant! - I love you Taylor – you're a nonce and a flyboy, can't take yer ale, yer shit stinks but I still lerv you…'

They were back in the house.

'To the den! Got some whisky I was keeping…!' Owen's voice boomed through the house.

Zill put the room to rights. She blew out the candles, dropped them in a waste bin and made her way back to her own room.

Chapter Nineteen

Taylor didn't get up too early the next day. He woke early but, for the first time in ages rolled over again for an hour or two more. After all, he was under no pressure to do anything. He was safer here in this rambling old place, this haven, than he had been for – well, he could remember, but he shied away from the memory. He made his way downstairs and had a late breakfast in the dining hall. The steward was a little stiff with him at first but when Taylor glared at him; stated to no one in particular that he was thinking of giving a briefing and a flight round the area in the lifter… 'but not to any miserable mardifuckers,' then matters continued on a friendlier basis.

He strolled outside in time to meet Jones coming back from a run, sweat streaming off him, staining his combat fatigues. Behind him, by several hundred yards, staggered an exhausted group of his men. Jones turned to wait for them. Out of the corner of his mouth, he told Taylor,

'Big mistake, taking the piss out of a hung-over Sergeant Major. Good job you weren't around blue job, I'd have embarrassed you into joining the funny guys out there.'

The dozen stragglers struggled in. 'Last one does it again!' roared Jones but he didn't carry out his threat.

'If I can do it at my age…! I suggest you gentlemen don't let me have to show you what is expected again! Get changed and meet us at the Taylor machine in ten minutes!'

He turned to Taylor. 'We haven't done a night patrol beyond our cleared area for a while. How do you fancy helping out? I'll get the Boss to keep Miss Brainy Boots out of the way.'

He winked, paused, changed colour, clutched Taylor's arm.

'Can you entertain 'em for me? Think I'm going to throw up…'

Jones was gone. Taylor walked over to the lifter and checked here and there. The lads reappeared in eight minutes. They peered around for Jones, cheated to find they'd had to rush back for a mere civilian.

Taylor was pleased to see his marshaller in the group. He got them to take him to a classroom in the stable yard and, after some fiddling with the old fashioned classroom aids, linking his wrist to an old wifi router he managed to give them a video slideshow. They sat, slack jawed; devastated to discover they weren't the only "sharp end."

He showed them the tubes and explained their history and purpose.

'It started with plastic bottles in Africa. Put any old crap ditch water in them and leave them in the sun; leave for a few hours and strain the water through a clean cloth. Drinking water. Especially for the locals who have a stronger resistance to the local bugs...

Then they seeded clear plastic water pipes with algae...food, fuel - far more productive and quicker than biofuel crops...'

He explained the algae which changed from giving off oxygen to giving off hydrogen with some simple schoolboy chemistry.

'Ever lit a fart?' caused some mirth. 'Methane or... natural gas. Well cattle, not us apparently.'

He showed them a few more things and finished up with the vid from the dead Scallie out on the tubes; then the next trip's vasp swarm. They sat, stunned. Taylor raised an eyebrow; Was I showing off too much?

One of the lads, a corporal with a particularly strong Welsh accent that oddly reminded Taylor of an Indian or Pakistani, spoke up;

'We had a guy...' sounded like *Wi-yadagai*... 'here,' He pronounced "here" like "year" - *wi-yaddagai-year* once – kept bees he did. We had honey - *add-un'nee* - for ages. He went away for months and, when he came back, they'd all gone. They'd flown away somewhere. Scary stuff, they flew like that in a cloud like those birds and fish that all move together as one, like...they're on parade somehow...like Jonesy was commanding them. He said he'd come back with some queens in a...can't remember now...basically the queen was in a wax container which she had to eat her way out of. If they didn't do this, the other bees would attack her. During the time she was getting out they would get used to her...smell, I suppose.'

'...Pheromones?'

'Wouldn't know about them sir!'

***

He took the first six of the morning's eighteen for a ride over the lake and up the mountainside. They buzzed the village. Megan came outside. Looking up, shading her eyes, she waved. The lads were quiet, each imagining she waved to them individually. Flying directly above her one of them, looking down her cleavage, said, 'Sure I saw her ankles – from inside her jumper...'

'Not many girls about here...' Taylor probed.

'Bloody right sir, it's a man's life in the army! We have our own girls but half the time they've got a fellah waiting at home. They only do six months every two years, see.'

'Taff don't mind sir, there's sheep and, if you let him, he'll paint tits on your back!'

A minor scuffle broke out which soon subsided when Taylor

demonstrated negative G over a nearby ridge.

Returning to Ddihingol Clythrea. he skimmed low over the lake; the ground effect whipping up a plume of spray behind and around them. Taylor daydreamed of the day he would be able to do the same with his floatplane.

He slowed to land back on the original gravel parking spot. On the front steps stood an apparently fully recovered sergeant major; jaw thrust out with moustache bristling. Why do they always have moustaches? wondered Taylor. He had six converts to the Taylor lifestyle – time to nip it in the bud, he thought.

'Corporal!'

'Sir?'

'You know what to do!'

They did, and, exuberant, they filed out of the lifter in an orderly fashion and fell in to attention in two neat rows.

'Welsh airborne recce detachment back on Terra Firma. Ready for duty Sergeant Major!'

'Thank you Mr Taylor!'

***

Jones inspected his men, formulating some remark or other about coming back down to earth with a bang but he saw their excitement; their shining eyes. He hadn't lost them to Taylor and his joy riding but the umbilical was stretched quite thin at this moment.

'Well done men. Good job, someone's got to keep an eye on these flyboys! Get them fed Corporal. Get them rested, night patrol at midnight. We're going a bit further afield this time!' He nodded towards the lifter and winked. 'Fall out!'

Taylor, leaning on a balustrade, lit a cigar. Jones joined him and they went to seek shade.

'I'll have to go back to the Dome for fuel if you want to go far.'

'Not far, ten miles back toward the vicar's.'

***

From an upstairs window, Owen and Zill watched the landing, the impromptu parade, and the two older men moving off in a companionable way.

'Fits in wherever he goes I imagine, that Taylor'

'Unless he doesn't,' she remarked bitterly, a lewd double entendre rising up against her will.

225

'Explain!'

'Well, any sort of pomposity, any attempt to control him against his wishes and it's fireworks – the local ZI put a watch on him, tried to rein him in... He proved uncooperative, they accused him of murdering Scallies.'

'Murder?'

'He didn't. Someone did but it was convenient to point the finger at him...we had to get him out, put pressure on Z3, ostensibly on a pretext of wanting a pilot with local knowledge. Shams liked him and became further interested in his catalytic leadership style,'

'Catalytic...?'

'He doesn't bark orders; he sort of makes things happen. People follow out of curiosity almost. If they don't they soon realise their mistake.'

She told him about the Pastor and the weird God Folk. She still didn't know how he persuaded the Scallie prisoners to help.

She looked down at the men outside. Are men a different species? she thought They bark, shout, thump, wrestle, punch, jeer, argue, bully, fart, piss, get drunk, help each other – things that could disappear in seconds if women appeared amongst them. Were men naturally gay? Not sexually but did they prefer each other's company to that of women?

She was frustrated that she couldn't join in. But there were women back on his Heli teams back there? Had they turned into men? The way that Marie looked at him; surely not? Kristen, little doubt of her inclinations while the men drooled at her curves behind her back. The other crew chief, the Norwegian, Taylor had introduced them, yes, Hansen. He had shaken hands with her politely, stared at Taylor, shook his head and walked off throwing a spanner or something across the hangar floor. What was that about?

Her two colleagues; Steve and Mick; they had their sniggering moments, times when she was excluded. She sighed – Hell hath no fury than a woman scorned – that was another thing. Where did these old sayings keep cropping up from? She was sure Taylor never actually said them but since he turned up, they started rising to the surface. She must have stored them from childhood; kept them in a dusty file ready for use at a later date. She should not be furious. She had no right; he had not scorned her. She had made no advances. He had been a perfect companion; in this day and age he still behaved like a gentleman. He'd gone out for beers with the lads. She never said she would be waiting there with romantic candles.

Owen sensed her internal conversation batting back and forth. He had known her for...?

Forever it seemed. She would tell him if she wanted to. For now some internal strife gnawed at her.

'I'll get some of the lads to drag the boat out. We'll have a scull round the lake; see if we can't catch a fish or two. That's if they aren't all on the bottom after your man's little demo. The boys have got guns and helicopters to play with; no sense out of them until it's out of their system.'

'I'd love that Owen, like before...' she turned and darted off down the corridor, but he'd seen the tears welling up...

***

Mid afternoon came. With all the eighteen soldiers Jones had detailed for airborne familiarisation firmly under his spell, Taylor had a snooze under some trees. It was cooler here higher up with the Vicar's katabatic breeze flowing down the mountain. He watched Owen and Zill out on the lake fishing; laughing, casting their rods, the odd flash of silver proclaiming their success. Taylor was not a great fish fan although it made a nice change from the processed food back at the base canteen. He dozed.

Chapter Twenty

Jack was scratching his head. On a workbench in Taylor's shed, he was making a crude transmitter and receiver. Taylor had taken him on one side and asked him if he could track a submarine! Anyone else and he would have doubted their sanity. Jack said he thought he would need a very low frequency transmitter with a very long antenna wire trailing behind; but where to get the diagram?

'Google, Yahoo, Wikipedia. There must be something similar. I got all sorts from Cartwright and Benson straight to my wrist. I don't think it came direct from Geneva,' Taylor said.

'How am I going to get access to Google?'

'Dome has a library, does it not?'

'Yes, but there's no Internet4!'

'Where does your wrist get all its info from then? Is there some ZI call centre waiting for questions? Who does the weather forecasts?'

'Hmmm – I can have a look.'

'Sign in as someone else if you do.'

'Why?'

'What did you think when I asked you to track a submarine? If there is the Internet then what happened to the links we know? They must have been renamed, rerouted or something. Why? Be careful – be ready with an answer.'

'Such as?'

'For Christ's sake Jack, use your imagination! You want to monitor great white sharks under the tubes; something like that!'

'Brilliant! Why can't I think like that?'

'Old age and treachery – how many times do I have to tell you?'

'Taylor, when are you coming back?'

'Maybe when you lot start thinking for yourselves!'

'Thinking for ourselves? ...who thinks about tracking submarines?'

'...people who think for themselves maybe!'

And he was gone and here he was, Jack, with an old set of headphones, a box of electronic wigglies and an old laptop listening to whale sounds and other beeps and cheeps of the deep. All he needed now was a strong magnet. What would Taylor do?

Harry came in.

'Yo! Jack!' Harry wasn't the coolest of dudes but he tried.

'Where's we gonna get a magnet on a Three day Harry?'

'Out on the old roads man, the old cars had dynamos,

alternators…'

'How you know that shit Harry?'

'The Taylor man – he told me.'

'Shit Harry, that man's a ghost! He's everywhere you look!'

Marie came in. '…talking about Taylor again are we?'

***

Taylor and Jones were rooting about in the stores. There were all sorts of old equipment lying on the shelves. They would be gathering dust if dust were not included in Jones's vocabulary of blasphemies. Taylor picked up an odd looking pair of binoculars, thrust a querying chin at Jones.

'Remote listening device. Works off a laser; don't ask me how.'

'I heard of them. Why don't you use it?'

'Batteries are all dead. We can't recharge them.'

'Hang on.' Taylor disappeared, returned carrying a power module. It looked like a big vacuum flask but with connectors and LED lights.

Taylor stripped the ends off some wire. He fiddled and twisted here and there and attached the other ends to the module connectors. A slight but keen whistling sound started up and a cherry red lamp lit.

'Let's leave it and see if it holds a charge.'

'You some nerdy tech wizard then Taylor?' whistled Jones, impressed in spite of himself.

'That's nothing …' Taylor routed about here and there on the shelves. He came back with a small item.

'A remote demolition firing device.'

'Wiggly amps. Why not use a cable?' Jones sneered.

'Can I take it for some trials? We could trigger things from up in the air.'

Jones made a dismissive gesture.

'Help yourself. I don't use gadgets,'

***

Some of the barracks were up in the roof of the stables. The lads were excited. What was in store tonight? Since the arrival of Taylor it seemed routine had gone out of the window. The Colonel pissed up, leaving his leg in the Land Rover, that gorgeous bit of totty wandering naked at night, Jones singing! What next?

They had their own intelligence network. Bad form not to know where Jones would spring from next; a lack of information which

229

could lead to unpleasant consequences.

'How come they always know what we're thinkin'?' said one.

'It's like yer Mum – she always knew what you were going to do before you thought about it!' said another.

Corporal Evans scratched his head. 'When my first was born, well, once he was walkin' anyway I'd hover around sharp corners ready with my hand – he'd bump into my hand all the time! Back of my 'and covered in bruises! When he got to tree climbin' I'd be there below ready to catch 'im. Showing 'im things, flyin' a kite, kickin' a ball. It was grand; like livin' it all again through a new set of eyes!' His eyes prickled, he got up and went over to look out of the gable window.

Such depth of emotion was not a regular thing in a barrack room and would normally have inspired a pillow fight or water being hurled. Today was different. They fell quiet, each in a contemplative mood.

Evans saw Taylor and Jones come out of the workshop with a pair of camera tripods and some equipment. They arranged a tangle of wires and taped them together. Jones aimed some binoculars, mounted on a tripod, in their direction.

'Taylor and Jonesy are up to something!'

***

The two men huddled together. They were having a bonding moment. Jones almost sniggered with glee. Taylor nudged him with his elbow; put a finger to his lips.

'Switch it on – we don't need the headphones yet – the laptop speakers will do – I'll put it on record.'

'Let's see if those scallywags are snoring or wanking up there! – oops - they're awake and talking...'

***

The lads gathered at the windows, peering over their noses like cats, as if no one could see them. As it happened the light was reflecting the wrong way so they were safe.

***

Down below Jones and Taylor picked up the lads' voices on Taylor's repaired laser listening device. He twisted it here and there, making fine adjustments. He handed the headphones to Jones. Jones listened, holding the earpieces close, his eyes flicking up left, then right, in that ridiculous way humans have of listening to recordings...he heard...

<< Nice to see Jonesy's got a little pal>>

<<It's nice to see them playing together – someone his own age! >>

<<Watch it. He's coming! – and fast! – something's got up his nose! >>

***

Jack wasn't that keen on going into the Dome either. He scouted around until he found the library and entered through a double door. There were books crowding the shelves and tables with old fashioned flat plasma screens. They shone a light pattern onto the desk with an old fashioned QWERTY keyboard. A young woman sat at a desk watched him wander around. He seemed at a loss where to start. He approached her. Her name tag read Da- Jane.

'You don't come here much then?' she said.

'Never – I'm out on the tubes or in the bar mostly.'

'Sounds exciting!'

'Yeah, well the bar's OK I suppose...'

'Can I help?'

'Well – it's a bit boring but I was looking for some technical information.'

'Such as?'

'A wiring diagram...'

***

'How do you know about all this stuff?' said Jones.

'What stuff...?' said Taylor.

'Well...everything!'

'It was a sort of hobby, bits and pieces of work, bits and pieces of before really...'

They had streamlined the laser listener, as Taylor called it, into a workable, portable device. Jones had plans for it this very night.

'Listen, the laser hits something hard and bounces back and gets picked up here in a photocell. If you shine light on a photocell it makes electricity, yes?'

'If you say so...'

231

'When people talk – or make a noise - the surfaces near them vibrate. This vibrates the laser light which in turn vibrates or changes the frequency of the light hitting the photocell. It's a bit like signalling with lights; a code if you like…the rest you know – the laptop and the headphones amplify the vibration like the first telephones.'

'You're a clever fucker Taylor…'

'Nah – Marconi and his mates were clever – these are just bits of theirs I picked up - off a shelf in Wales.'

***

Jack and Jane were getting on very well. She showed him where to look but there seemed to be a lifetime of research to wade through.

'It's nice to have someone come in and ask for something different. All I get is requests for nettle fibre knitting patterns and 'fashions of the noughties.'

'Naughties…? You can get porn on the wrist system…er…so I hear!'

'No, dummy - the n-o-u-g-h-t-i-e-s; - the early years of the 21st Century!'

'What happened to the internet?' he asked, once the time was right.

'Oh it's here but…' and she looked around; nervous now.

'…it's here but I have to be careful. There are so many restrictions… so many people want to track down their relatives; find out things they are not supposed to know.'

'What's wrong with tracking down your family for Christ's sake?'

'They say it upsets people when they find them on the casualty lists. I think it's because they don't want people shooting off to find them. It's quiet now; the Dome people are…so indifferent to what goes on outside. It's as if they don't care!'

Jack thanked the mind of Taylor for the umpteenth time in his life.

'Well, I only want to find out how to make a tracker for shark migrations, not family migrations. Surely that's not restricted information?'

She entered a code and a password. The screen came to life. The camera on top of the screen flashed and recorded the operator's validity. She keyed in a request: Shark tracking equipment. Several pages with harnesses and transponders came up. Encouraged she pressed on.

'Wait , how about the receivers or the other end of the signal?' said Jack.

A warning dialogue box appeared.

232

Is this enquiry related to underwater craft, submarines and other military applications? If so please enter your Z code now

Da Jane looked at him. 'Is it?'

Jack went cold. What was Taylor getting him into?

'No, ask for info on very low frequency applications, wiring diagrams and frequencies.'

She carried on, a series of pages scrolled. One showed an amateur device for listening for sea creatures. It gave pictorial descriptions on a simple device and the length of antenna needed, power levels, anticipated ranges and so on. Other pages she showed him, schematic wiring diagrams, graphs, antenna lengths, propagation, and others he affected no interest in.

Hoping she had not noticed he had set his wrist camera to record.

She was called away. 'Don't get me into trouble now!' but she patted his arm, letting her hand linger and slide away.

Jack thought if he took nothing else away, he would be taking her away at the end of her shift.

He bookmarked the page they had found and then browsed around. Found an old news item headed: Skin Cancer – the findings. He scrolled down.

It has been discovered that the skin cancer scare is a false alarm. As long as suitable skin barrier cream is used and naked skin is covered up during the midday and 2 pm period there is no evidence of skin cancer connected with the recent temperatures post disaster...

He made sure he had that one in focus. He wondered what Taylor would say to this. Lying ZI bastards! he imagined, or something along those lines.

Jane was coming back. Hurriedly he went back to the original page on fish tracking.

'Can I have a copy of that please?' Once he had the theory he could go off and experiment from his own knowledge. She sent it to his wrist. A new box appeared.

Information sent to Agribase 3 crew member - please memo Z6 to this effect

Jack looked at her; she smiled.

'Z6 is a nasty little creep. I will just...' she signed off and closed the screen...'forget!' she said with finality. 'This is not a linked terminal. It is a manual request as far as I know!'

She turned her sweet smile on him. He stopped himself moaning out loud. She wasn't like the other D girls he'd known.

'It'll cost you though!'

She had such a sweet smile, thought Jack.

Chapter Twenty One

Taylor and Jones in the front seats and four longest straw winners among the soldiers in the back hovered over a hilltop not far from the vicar's valley. He set it to quiet running when they saw a light some distance away that didn't belong. The temperature gauge was rising with the weight of four burly Welsh boys. He let down to some flat ground and ran at low rpm. He told Jones what he was doing. Jones snapped out orders and established a guard perimeter. Two scouts came back after fifteen minutes. The light was a campfire. Campfires were not a leisure feature in these times. They were not in the wild west of the USA either. Fires warned of abnormal activity warranting cautious investigation.

'Patrols have reported a gang around here. Whenever we investigate there's no sign so maybe this time we have the initiative,' Jones told him.

'Break out the Sorcerer's Apprentice box you lot!' he hissed.

They set up the laser so it peeked over the hill but could still be aimed at the campfire. They heard mutterings and grunting but no voices. Taylor fiddled with the aim, adjusted the gain on the laptop; only hissing and putt-putt noises. He scratched his head.

'Sir!' whispered one of the lads. They looked at him.

'...The fire! You are aiming at the fire! That's what you can hear!' Taylor moved the aim to a nearby rock flickering in the light. Eureka!

<<He said they'd all be tanked up, legless on that rice wine – Chinese New Year he said.>>

<<...think Davis will be able to get us in? >>

<<..fokkin better – I'm havin that chink Susan – that's after I've slit that vicar's throat from ear to ear – 'e caused me pain 'e did. Took years to desert from them SP bastards! – still I can wait one more day.>>

<<yeah! I'm lookin' forward to holdin' those chink blokes under the water – fokkin' rice botherers.>>

<<worrabout the kids? >>

<< keep the older girls- the rest can fend for 'emselves for all I care. Unless Zak fancies a bit of...ssss>>

One of the men had walked in line with the rock.

***

'I think we've heard enough Taylor eh?'

'Take 'em now?'

'I'm not losin' one of my boys to this scum. These pigs haven't survived out here by letting people sneak up on them. Let's warn the vicar and arrange a reception for our brave visitors. Bit of liaison with the community; hearts and minds eh? Which was the one who wanted Susan...?'

Davis will find out what unlucky really means at last, thought Taylor.

***

Harry was letting down to land at the base. After a routine day shifting tubes about, Heli-1's crew were tired. During the harvest they were out from sun up to sundown in the heat and humidity. They worked six days out of seven, instead of their day on, day off, routine.

Harry came, half asleep, into the base landing area on his own recently developed autopilot. Since Taylor had worked his spells he could do this now, even in such a short space of time. The others sat back, sprawled with eyes closed. Hansen was not far behind them. He had been flashed by a work crew near the basin to assist in some lifting or similar task.

Harry settled to the pad, flicked switches; carried out his shutdown. A figure approached his side window. Harry barely acknowledged him until the door was snatched open.

'Hang on! Let me get on the ground for Christ's sake!'

He turned to stare into the muzzle of an SP Dazer; behind the weapon stood a tattooed man. Looking beyond, Harry saw all was not as it should be.

***

The Chinese were pleased but surprised to see Taylor ambling around the corner as if he was out for a stroll. Chattering and laughing they brought him to the vicar.

'Ah! I see no little wife, no helicopter. Did you lose them to the katabatic? Or do I sense urgency about our Prodigal Taylor...?'

Taylor conveyed his news. The vicar handed out the shotguns and twenty rounds each of small game cartridges to the men and the more stalwart women, Susan included. The rest of the women carried on preparing the New Year celebration. Davis was off up the valley, they said, with his golf club and tube of balls.

'I thought it was too quiet,' John the vicar sighed. 'I wondered

236

when the worm would turn. Shams must be away on one of his jaunts. We usually get a signal that the bad ones are about. I leave it to the men. They go out in the night and come home covered in blood, sometimes wounded themselves. Nothing is said and we go on our little way as if nothing had happened. Where are the army?'

'They're about somewhere. We left the lifter hidden so as not to draw attention. What are those cattle down in the bog there?'

'Water buffalo! They are perfect, they keep the scrub down. We can harness them. They were instrumental in building the dam. Now and again, they donate to our table on special occasions.'

'Not native to the Welsh borders though…?'

'The Chinese got them from somewhere near Machynlleth.'

'Where?'

'Who knows where the Chinese get things. Where did they get prawn crackers and that gloopy sweet and sour sauce? They appeared one day and that was that!'

Chapter Twenty Two

Chinese New Year's Eve. Taylor sat with the vicar in the dark. Jones said he didn't want any blue job stumbling about in the dark shooting at the wrong target and, besides, he was fed up with walking home whenever he went out with Taylor and wanted someone in one piece to fly him home. In time for tea, he'd added.

Davis had not returned.

Outside, overalls stuffed with straw, topped with bamboo weave coolie hats, celebrated the early partying. The sides of the dining tent were let down and an evening breeze shivered the material and flickered the candlelight so the effect of apparent activity seen from a distance was incredibly accurate.

Those who hadn't gone out with Jones were locked in safe against hurricane and nuclear strike. Outside the paper lanterns were lit, candles flickered; lucky red symbols and folded paper decorations adorned the outdoor dining area. Paper lanterns floated shimmering on the surface of the waters lower down. Chinese music drifted on the night air; a scene from millennia from the other side of the world.

All the children were tucked up but none slept. Taylor and the vicar kept their shotguns close and Taylor double checked his own weapon– "that fucking sparkler – that Dan Dare ray gun" - as Jones called it.

'Fifty cal or, if you can't get it, 7.62 ammo. None of that 5.56 shite! People are known to die of lead poisoning Taylor! he said.

***

Jones sat in a circle with his men.

'Any single one of you in any doubt about what happens tonight?'

He looked round the circle meeting each one's gaze. Good, he thought. If they look away, I have my answer.

'Listen, my lovely lads, these men coming tonight have planned to kill, rape, steal and do other atrocious deeds. It's not as if they are barbarian savages, some are SP deserters. They know the rules of civilised behaviour; they choose to break them. Worse, they laugh and enjoy the prospect. Tonight it's no prisoners. Some of you have done this before. They will tell it's not fun, not glorious, you may doubt yourself for a while afterwards. Remember, it's you or them. Hesitate for a second of mercy; they will have none. The world will not rebuild itself with these people running loose. We cannot spend a whole lifetime looking over our shoulders for people like this creeping up on us. Imagine it is your family they are attacking. Enough, let's take up positions.'

They moved off into the night.

***

Taylor sat with John the vicar. They looked out through a concrete slot, presumably a guard window at some time. Rusty stains were left behind where the original blast proof windows were bolted in.

'I should be with them, I feel like the little lame boy sat here, can't go out with the big boys hunting,' Taylor said.

'You're not a soldier. You'd get in the way. Jones knows his stuff.'
John sat in thought for a while then announced.

'He came to me before, Jones; called me "Padre". "Have I sinned in your eyes, John?" he asked me. I told him I thought not, in the eyes of the community but, in his own mind, what was he asking? He said the dead men reached away in a queue in his dreams. Some were friends he'd lost; most were enemies he'd killed. They came to him and went past, he said, but he couldn't turn to follow where they went; to see if his friends went to the same place, wherever that was. He said he wanted his friends to turn off – to a "nicer place" – hah! What could I tell him?'

'What did you tell him?'

'I told him he was a good man; that he should try and imagine the queue of alive people, good people, and what a relatively huge queue that must be. He said, "but where is the queue heading?"

'The tunnel,' Taylor said. ' I must tell him of the tunnel.' He went on to describe his old friend's "tunnel" where some escaped through the hatch but must still follow the direction. 'Jones is walking backwards along the tunnel roof and fears he will fall.'

'Interesting. Those tubes of yours must be like that.'

'Only recently I noticed that again, I noticed how precarious they were. The metaphorical tunnel was a solid unmoving stable thing. My tubes wobble and heave. The penalty of falling off doesn't bear thinking of. Perhaps I shouldn't mention tunnels and tubes to Jones at all. May I ask you a direct question?'

'You are going to anyway…'

'You are one of the quiet government men aren't you? All that about the lottery win and all – bollocks. The Chinese didn't "just turn up" one day, did they?'

'Which story do you like best?' John laughed quietly.

239

'The first obviously, but it falls down with all the rice and food surplus here. You feed the scallies don't you – and it's not a soup kitchen church style operation is it? It's the reason you remain safe, unmolested, until today anyway.'

'Quiet government men, Taylor. Takes one to know one. The lottery and Davis are true. ESO relied a lot on lottery funds. Who knows, Davis may not have even chosen those numbers.'

The vicar's eyes wrinkled in a smile. 'So, with your suspicions confirmed, what then?'

'Nothing, I suppose. I've been here years now and never wondered how they fed themselves. I feel like a naïve fool. Like a child who finds out, all of a sudden, that stuff doesn't just wonderfully turn up out of the blue.'

'Precious thing, childhood. A vulnerable time. The time the Church pounces and sows the seeds of doubt; makes us wonder who we are. You've heard of Cartwright?'

'Who hasn't?'

'Quite. I hope you meet him one day. The ZI and the senior administration accuse him even now of being god-like. He saw that the survivors would revert to the old ways. The scallies, to Cartwright, are the new order. You can see from your dome how the rot of the old ways is maintained. Fear, ignorance, and therefore, control.'

'And what does he intend to do about it?'

'Precisely nothing. He will have taken certain steps no doubt. He was always several jumps ahead but, god-like as he is, he does nothing. Why should he? God does nothing; let's things alone; sees what happens, shrugs, looks away.'

'Pretty scathing for a man of the cloth?'

'A landowner doesn't leave his sheep out for the wolves; he employs a shepherd.'

***

Jones looked through night binoculars. Damp seeped up from the paddy field, water soaking up from his elbows. It reminded him of his own early training as a callow private. Never mind the discomfort, keep still. Not one of his lads dared move. They dreaded his wrath and his flinty stares more than any scallie stumbling through the swampy ground ahead.

They were coming! Ghoulish green and black figures loomed up from the valley floor and filled his lens. Chinese music wafted through the night. Jones's men could have made as much noise as they liked.

The corporal got Jones's signal. He raised the sniper rifle. One by one the soldiers reported they had a target in their sights. A little closer, just a little closer…

***

At the bunker Taylor and John continued their conversation.

'This is terrible, waiting, wondering,' agonised Taylor.

'It'll be a flurry of bodies, a few shots followed by a few more. The odd distant scream and then, over.'

'How do you know?'

'Jones told me.' John looked as if he was waiting to deliver a sermon or open a church fete.

'I tend to believe him,' he said.

Two shots rang out in the night.

***

The corporal saw his man go down. He took out the one at the back. He smiled grimly as he traversed to cover the others. They had turned in shock and surprise and failed completely to think of dropping low. Behind them he saw one of the Chinese men rise up behind. His night sight winked out and glared as the shotgun blast flared it out. Two more attackers went down to Jones's men and then it was a rout.

'Hold your fire!' barked Jones. They sat up and watched as the Chinese pursued the remainder, their shotguns flashing and booming in the night. Slowly they followed, in case of any the Chinese missed.

***

Taylor looked at his wrist. Some time after two in the morning the shots and screams rang out. Something less than a battle cut short, and then quiet. Forty minutes later, the Chinese came in with their shotguns, handed over unused cartridges and showed the vicar clean barrels and firing pins. Jones and his men followed. The men were seated and given beer and rice wine by attentive women who left as softly as they appeared. The vicar brought in two bottles of brandy; Betty, a tray with real brandy glasses for all.

'Do you think Davis will mind?' he asked Jones.

'No, Padre, he won't mind at all…' he motioned for Taylor and the vicar to follow him. His boys were settling down, nervously watching their manners, still struck by their brush with dire action.

Outside in the dining tent the dummies were thrown aside in a pile to one side.

Arranged around the sides were fifteen corpses. In the middle was Davis's body, his face still mean, disgruntled in death. Each had neat bullet holes central in the forehead except that of Davis and one other who each had two. Double tap, thought Taylor.

'You'll be claiming these two then, Jonesy? It's not that far from Hereford here is it? The Golden Road to Samarkand?'

Jones raised an eyebrow a hair's breadth. 'How do you know about that, Taylor?'

'Oh, you know, it was in the Colonel's museum. I put two and two together once I remembered it was an SAS thing – Flecker's poem.'

We travel not for trafficking alone;
By hotter winds our fiery hearts are fanned
For lust of knowing what should not be known
We take the Golden Road to Samarkand…

***

In the morning, Taylor brought the lifter round to the more regular pad. Of the grisly diners of the night; no sign.

'They will be mounted strategically for Admiral Byng purposes,' said the Reverend John. 'Pour enc…'

'Yes, yes – pour encourager les autres! To encourage the others! Don't do a Shams on me!' grumbled Taylor.

They packed up to go. It was a deeper more thoughtful farewell; some bonds formed as a result of the night's activities. One of Jones's lads clutched a set of golf clubs and a tube of balls.

'There are more when you come again. Here, they have unpleasant associations.'

***

Back at Ddihingol, Zill ran out to meet them.

'Your agribase has been attacked! A raid. Scallies. Captives taken! You will want to go back straight away! I am ready…'

Jones looked concerned. 'Can we help? Unofficially of course…'

'It may come to that. Let me go and find out. Can we contact you?'

'Yes Taylor, but we still need you to come and pick us up!'

'You always did, you brown jobs…'

Jones would never admit it out loud but, recently, life had become interesting again.

The base was not too badly damaged. Nothing that could not be repaired anyway. The heli hangar had been the target. The water veil was damaged and spurted an eccentric fan of water all over - like grass sprinklers of old, Taylor thought. There had been a fight. Strands of Taser wire criss-crossed the area. They must have taken a few down. Whoever had gone down on the attacking side had been hauled away.

A few dazed figures sat here and there. Victims of Dazer gas. Some had Taser burns. Nobody turned or came to greet them, so far under was their social awareness.

A groan came from Wallis' office. Taylor and Zill rushed up his steps to find him half sitting up against the wall, a steel crossbow bolt pinning his bleeding leg to the floor.

'Aren't you going to ask me what happened, Taylor?'

'Got eyes haven't I? We'll soon get you sorted out...only a scratch...you'll live.'

He inspected the entry hole of the arrow shaft, high up on Wallis' inner thigh. He daren't pull it out; the femoral artery was around there. He took his pulse; it was strong. Wallis passed out. Taylor ran outside and peered down below the floor to the underside of the office; luckily over ground, not sea. The crossbow shaft head could be seen protruding a hands width, barbed beyond removal by pulling.

He would have to go under into the dark dank underside, where the rats and snakes and other creatures of the dark crawled, and cut the head off with a saw. He shuddered. Waves of claustrophobia threatened to overcome him. He turned to Zill to find her looking at him, wondering what he was going to do.

'Ever used any hand tools, like a saw or an angle grinder?'

'Never. A what grinder?'

He headed for his shed. He called over his shoulder; 'Try and get the Dome to send a medic! Keep an eye on Wallis!'

He looked up. The sun was at its zenith. The Domeys wouldn't come until it was well down in the sky. Two relatively undazed techs showed up asking for instructions.

'Get the umbrella, the water shield running again; it's an oven here!'

***

The young SP commander burst into Jarvis's office.

243

'The agri base has been attacked. Two helis taken; hostages! Wounded people all over. Why haven't you called us?'

Jarvis smiled sleepily at him through the green haze of his screen. He slid aside the phial and hypo needle.

'Who gives a shit?'

The young new commander, Robert Sharpe, still young enough to feel he could make a difference, appalled at the thuggish corrupt ways of some of his troops, looked on in disdain.

'Is there any disciplinary action for thinking?'

'Think what you like…'

'I think you're a useless twatt!'

'Yes, but I'm a Z6…' smiled Jarvis - as if that made all the difference

Sharpe stormed out to be met by a bored looking sergeant.

'Send for reinforcements from Dome 1! I want every Litak in the air in ten minutes! Get the troops on board the carriers!'

He rushed off, taking a handful of troopers with him.

The sergeant huffed, 'Yeah, whatever…' He would need Z authority. He walked into the Z6 office. This little shit! Look at him! Can't even wait for the dark of night! He slapped Jarvis a few times and gave up. He grasped the drugged man's hand and, by covering it with his own hand and intertwining his fingers so they stuck out - used Jarvis' encoded fingerprints to poke the holo screen buttons. Jarvis had been watching a porn channel. He had been playing with himself, his now limp penis nestled, crinkled in his open fly flap. The SP man selected the official channel, opened a line to HQ at Dome 1 and sent the message. Grinning with mischief he linked the unofficial channel of Jarvis' recent choice of research to the HQ one. Only then did he look down at Jarvis' crotch and dropped the sweaty limp hand in disgust. On an impulse he picked up the hypo and jabbed it in where he thought it would hurt most. As he left he saw Jarvis was not smiling anymore - his dopey expression turning slowly to look at his lap.

***

Taylor came hurrying back with tools and a rope. He tied the rope round one of his ankles.

'When I yell, pull me out. The louder I yell, pull harder!' he ordered between gritted teeth and dived under the building.

Zill recoiled from Taylor's litany of profane defence against the only thing in the world he feared and dreaded. Being trapped headfirst

244

in a confined space. He wasn't that keen on the dark either and getting wet and dirty added insult to the injury. He wriggled and crawled, invoking all the gods and devils in the universe and threatening buggery with a red hot poker to whoever had put him in this situation. Whoever caused him such discomfort, terror and pain.

He tried to relax; he sank back into the slimy undergrowth. A trickle of cold stinking water trickled into and under his collar. Something ran over his face – a rat? Ugh! He would catch Weil's disease as well now. Zill called. 'Do you want me to pull?'

'Neurghh! Not yet!' he groaned.

He reached his goal and had to wriggle and squirm himself into an advantageous position to attack the arrow head. The grinder showered sparks into his eyes, he moved to a better angle, tried again. The grinder now made short work of three quarters of it then baulked as the safety guard butted up against the underside of Wallis' floor. He applied the hacksaw. It took an age; he imagined Wallis coming round inches above him as the arrow wiggled back and forth. Sweat streamed into Taylor's eyes. The awkward angle made his shoulders ache. He had to pause to allow blood to return. He could not see how far he had to go.

He hated Wallis with all his heart – why hadn't the bastard died? Wait till I get hold of the Scallie bastard who did this – if only for not shooting Wallis square between the eyes instead of this grotesque joke he was having played on him.

Then he was through!

'Pull! he screamed. 'Pull you fucking bitch! Get me the fuck out of here before I come out myself and…'

He was out in the open air, the sky above him; Zill looking down at him, scared. Recovering her composure she glared.

'Which gutter were you brought up in? I thought you were…'

But Taylor was up and back in Wallis' door. The man was awake, looking pale. He gripped the top of the shaft. Taylor quickly bound it in place and, reaching under the leg, placed a wad of folded cloth. His fingers found the shaft where it exited the leg and entered the floor. Wallis started to groan in pain. Taylor grasped the top of the shaft and leg together; jerked sharply upwards. Wallis screamed as if he was in childbirth - Shaft and leg came free! Taylor gasped with the effort, more sweat running into eyes, salt stinging, he fell back in relief. A shadow. In the doorway stood an anxious Hansen. Hamid, who had not been with Heli-I for some reason, looked over his shoulder.

'What's up with Willis? Jesus! Don't pull it out! You'll kill him!'

Chapter Twenty Three

Hansen and two of his people in Heli-2 took off.. The base jarred, bobbed and thudded, water sprayed everywhere as he opened the throttles wide. With Wallis on a stretcher they had no room for more. The worst dazered techs would have to wait. They headed for the Dome. Comms were back in action and the Dome medics were, by all accounts, standing by waiting for them.

***

Zill sat on the steps of Wallis's office looking down at some blood drops already drying in the heat. This is reality then? Real blood, real hurt people, terrible occurrences – I have been playing all my grown up life as well as my childhood. That man with an arrow in his leg! If it had been my problem he would have died! Taylor didn't even seem to like him from what he was saying while he was down underneath. Still he goes into a personal nightmare. Nothing I ever learnt would have prepared me for that.

Does Shams – do Steve and Mick – think these remote people are dolls? Actors on a stage? What was it Owen and Jones always laughed at with that bitter tone? - when they shared an old memory – home in time for tea. Like children having a fantasy adventure, letting their imaginations roam free and then – pouff! – turning it off like a switch. Certainly not the case here. I feel like a useless piece of…

***

Taylor was giving instructions to Kristen.

'Load Heli-2 with flares, smoke and dazer canisters. Later, I want to seek out a vasp nest inland; big new vasps. Tell Hansen it's a Cyanide run. Tell him you've loaded the dispensers and all he has to do is fly the heli. I'll get a message to you, OK?'

She nodded, repeated back his instructions and ran off. Two techs, abruptly summoned, followed her to a stores building well away from the rest.

Turning, he questioned a couple of lab girls who'd hidden away during the attack. They were on the verge of hysteria. Perhaps they should be treated for shock but he didn't have time to spare. Did the Dome medics know about shock, he wondered.

'They came from nowhere! Some of our techs tried to defend the place but, no warning, they were all over the place!' said one of them, a teenage D lab assistant.

The other, a somewhat older chemist added her version.

'Our people fired their Taser guns but these Scallies had big, sort of soldier-like guns, like the ones the SP carry. They shot a cloud of gas and down the boys went. There were a couple of theirs I saw go down but their buddies just scooped them up and took them off. Then it went quiet and we thought it was over. But then the zeps were due back and we heard one coming in. They took them by surprise. They weren't expecting it!'

'Which 'zep?'

'Heli-1. They wanted Heli-2 as well but it didn't come. They dragged another out of the hangar and forced one of the Heli-1 crew to fly it.'

'Did you see which way they went?'

'No, we didn't dare come out until you came. Sorry!'

'That's OK – I wouldn't have had the story without you keeping your heads and staying low. Well done.'

Zill watched the questioning. He didn't bully them; he let them tell their story, interrupting only when necessary. He was looking at her now, thoughtful. He came over.

'Why did you take me to Wales?'

'Show you around, a break for me, see Owen. Why?'

'Why didn't a single soul say you were Shams's daughter? Did the whole crew forget?'

She said nothing, met his gaze, shrugged.

'I want to go to the rig. Now!' he said.

He guided her to the lifter, sat her in the co pilot seat; watched her strap in.

'You are behaving oddly Taylor'

'My base has been attacked by Scallies, attacked within the Dome security province. You can't shit, can't smoke a cigar outside without an SP patrol dropping down to check you out. Now two helizeps and one particular crew are whisked away in minutes and I'm behaving oddly am I?'

He was interrupted by a Litak voffing down towards them. Taylor waited with a grim expression as the commander jumped out and approached him.

'...name's Sharpe. I'm new here, Mr...' he read Taylor's badge, '...Taylor.'

He didn't seem like the normal swaggering SP. He seemed familiar. Yes. Sergeant Sharpe? Too young this one.

'Do you have family in SP?' he asked the young man.

'A brother, Nick; dead now. Did you know him?'

'Yes, he got me into all this but, no time now.'

Younger Sharpe looked sad for a second then braced himself. Taylor filled him in, indicated the two witnesses sitting huddled together on the steps by Wallis' office. He voiced concern on the failure of security. Sharpe surprised him by coming straight out with:

'That shit Z6 had disabled this sector from his comsole. He has the Z codes; we didn't even get consulted. He was high on something, off his head. In the day as well!'

Overhead a flight of transporters and Litaks swept by heading North West.

'Where are they off?'

'Hoping to catch them - get the helis back.'

'You're the local commander but...' Sharpe seemed receptive to suggestions.

'...I'd secure the area. Stay close. Having all your air support away from here may be a part of a plan...' he stared at Zill who sat uncomfortably in her seat.

Sharpe whistled back to his own Litak crew whose blades were still running down further across the pad. He called out a request. One of his men ran forward with a communicator.

'Our frequency, match it to your wrist. I'm SP minor!'

Taylor played with the hand size device. His wrist squawked and a cascade of minor holo lights lit up momentarily.

'Thanks, I'm going out east to get some information that may help us get them back. What's the range of this?'

'Maybe ten miles at a decent height...'

***

Taylor went into the control room, called up aerial maps, nothing useful there. He headed back out to the lifter. Litaks were coming back in. Sharpe seemed to be deploying them around, waving his arms in self explanation while he spoke into his radio. He gave Taylor the thumbs up sign without stopping his broadcast.

On a second thought, Taylor veered away to his workshop. He rooted about on a workbench and filled a nettle canvas sack with things. He saw a note from Jack. He glanced at it then folded it and put it in a pocket. As a result of what he'd read he looked for a box on the bench. He saw it, peered in, smiled and added the device inside to his swag. He left and made for the lifter. Zill hadn't moved. She seemed to be sitting in her seat as if he had got out of the car and popped into a shop.

Taylor jumped in. He waved Sharpe away and lifted off.

***

He flew the lifter at full speed out to the rig. With no challenge beacon, he went straight in. Steve and Mick came forward.

'Where's the fire? Why are you covered in...' their noses wrinkled, '...shit?'

He looked at them hard. If they were part of anything then they were consummate actors. Thespian skills and confidence tricks were not in the new world syllabus.

'My friends and two helizeps have been taken by a Scallie raid – I need your peeping tom system...'

They looked to Zill. Why was she not in control all of a sudden. Taylor had taken over. He looked grim, determined. She nodded her go ahead. They led the way.

***

Steve brought up an image. He zoomed into the Dome area and around. Taylor gestured to pan west. Nothing obvious.

'Do you still have Google Earth?'

Shams had told him once they had stored all human knowledge safe. Surely they had access to such things here?

'Jeez! Stone Age or what? It was never up to date before. I remember us kids using it as a flight sim...' said Mick, but he rooted about pushing icons in the air until the old, old program shone out on the screen.

'It's from before, like I said!'

'Before is useful sometimes, Mick! Let's go!'

Down from space, UK, England with no tubes, no Dome; no floods.

Old England spread out before them. Taylor walked closer to the wall where the image shone. He traced faint lines connecting on the surface in the area as was, long before the Dome. He asked for the real time satellite picture again. He sought out the Harry chimney, the motorway, the dog pack area. They had been running in which direction? Not to a safe tree or building! He was a boy with all the lack of cunning and treachery of youth. He was acting as decoy. They would have sacrificed him. They didn't know we weren't SPs.

He drew a line of the approximate direction of travel of the chase and then extended it backwards to a small hill and some ruined factory

249

buildings. He remembered the smoke coming from the old bus on the motorway. Was that smoke coming out of the old factory?

A thought struck him.

'Is there an ordnance survey overlay?'

'Never heard of it...' said Mick. Steve looked bewildered. Zill seemed lost and indifferent.

What on earth had possessed him to grab those USB sticks all those years ago?

He fumbled in his pocket, took out the waterproof pouch.

'Can you still access these?'

After a few minutes of searching, they found the ordnance survey files. They were fine; uncorrupted. Steve and Mick looked at him as if he were some kind of wizard.

'You amaze me Taylor,' Steve said.

'I amaze myself, never throw anything away; ever.'

Mick was bent down concentrating on the unfamiliar keys and icons of the old PC.

'How about that?' he said, as surprised as they all were.

Now Taylor bent in close to the screen. He beckoned Steve and Mick to look. 'Hah! Tunnels, canals, old pathways even before the metal roads!' He seemed pleased. He looked back at the factory ruin. It was not a factory; it was a cunningly disguised railway station or depot. He drew an approximate Dome and agribase on the wall. They covered the lines which appeared and disappeared on the map leading directly to...

'That's how they come and go! They use the old tunnels.'

Another thought struck him. He looked back at the wall screen.

'Can you tell when this Google program was last accessed?'

Steve tapped and entered a query into the system console, the holocom.

'Well, well, well! – R de K.   Four years ago.'

'Three years ago he left for the Scallies...' murmured Zill.

Taylor looked at them hard. 'Do you have access to explosives?'

Chapter Twenty Four

Harry, Jack, Marie and Ben came round within minutes of each other. Once they were clear of the base and flying straight and level the controls had been taken away from Harry and Ben and they had been flown west, blindfolded. They had no idea how far they had gone. Harry had tried to count the time as he would on a navigation exercise.

< we have flown at   X knots for Y minutes on a heading of 280° – the wind is from due North at Z knots -how far have we gone?> but he didn't have the capacity under pressure to do such mental acrobatics. The helis came to a hover, the blindfold was whisked away and he was given a terse order – 'Land!'

They landed, were hauled out of the heli and smelled a whiff of.....

***

They were in a dark place, underground. A guard looked round a door at them and called to his fellows. A man came in. He had an aura of command about him. He was not tattooed but he bore the no nonsense expression of his colleagues.

'I am de Klayven.' he announced.

'Who?'

He seemed a little taken aback that his name alone did not strike fear into them.

'Raoul de Klayven.'

They looked apologetic, shrugged, glancing at each other for confirmation. No, it was unanimous, they did not know him.

Somewhat deflated he continued. 'You are colleagues and friends of Taylor are you not?'

They nodded.

'He has not discussed with you...? ...apparently not. Annoying to find him missing from your group. Well your friend seems to have a few tricks of his own which make me want some leverage – hence your presence here.

Tomorrow we take the Dome and all the things that go with it, such as your base. You will not suffer if you behave. We will need you for the first period at least. It is time to end the ZI and their lackeys. Enough is enough!'

***

Raoul went out into the tunnel. He let them follow the direction he took and when out of sight he doubled back to eavesdrop on his captives.

< …must be their leader but he doesn't look or sound like one of them…

<…no tattooing for a start and he had a…sort of educated voice…

<…not what Taylor would call a posh voice – remember when he had us in stitches that time with one of his voice characters? Air hellair- aim vair pleased to meet yew – rah (snort) No, it's a voice used to talking with, well, civilised people, about concepts, thoughtful stuff – you know…

***

Raoul had to smile to himself. In turn this made him wonder when he last smiled, or laughed; when he last talked about concepts, thoughtful stuff. He didn't want to frighten and intimidate these people. They were brave, honourable, busy, useful, healthy humans. They were the pinnacle of his aspirations for his Scallies. They had been dealt a good hand these agris – yes they had a few scrapes, more than enough to be character forming but they weren't hunted down like vermin and gassed, burnt, made to scurry from one dark hole to another… he would come back and talk with them. A thought occurred to him. He walked away, retracing his circular route and re-approached their door.

'You are under my protection. I have an upbringing you can relate to. These…' indicating the Scallies around and the guard on the door; '…are wild people. They are not stupid Dees who can be bribed, cajoled or reasoned with. It would be like a small child trying to befriend a vasp, a cobra or a scorpion. Please do not try to escape.'

He turned and left. His boys weren't as bad as all that but they had no love for outsiders, no cause to view any people not of their band with affection or tolerance.

***

<…was he listening to us?
<… he walked in from where he went off to…
< …he doesn't look the forgetful type …"oh by the way – I forgot…don't try to escape."

***

252

Steve, Mick and some of the sailors, some who were left behind to do run of the mill duties, helped Taylor load the lifter with explosive charges. These were seismic sound generators for establishing the depth of oil and gas. They would have been set off in the water and the return signals used to build up a picture of the seabed and below. Not military style but they had a charge and the means to set them off remotely, which was what Taylor wanted. He'd tasked Zill with condensing the maps and overlays into wrist and heli screen manageable size. He'd asked her to mark the points above the tunnels.

'Can you do that?'

'Of course...'

'I don't mean are you capable. I mean will you help me, can you help me, it is part of your agenda, rather than your capacity?'

'Yes – yes but why are you like this, what have I done?'

'Apart from using me, keeping me in the dark you mean? Your father, he is not from the sub continent at all. He is born and bred Welsh!'

'Is that a secret?'

'His college, his university friend is the Z3; the same Z3 who authorises your one way Scallie trips. He is either head of, or high up in UK ZI!'

He put up his screen. He called up the "Happy years after university" image.

She stared, lingered over her missing mother.

'This is your family, before?'

'Yes – yes!'

Taylor stabbed his finger at the domed intellectual forehead man 'You must know him!'

She looked dumb. '...Z3? ...no! Uncle Mark? He would never...!'

Her cheeks burnt red, her eyes went wide in shock and realisation. She held her hands up, held her face, turned away, realised more, turned back to Taylor.

He looked at her. 'I've been led by the nose down some path which leads back here. It almost seems too easy. I can't work out the catch!'

...maybe it's time you got your hands dirty – joined in, invented something, he remembered the Shams conversation.

'Perhaps there is none. Perhaps my father...perhaps he just pressed a red button...'

'What other buttons has he been pressing? I've been lucky not to lose dear friends out on those tubes; some of the crews I didn't know never got to go on R & R!'

Something seemed to occur to Zill. Something he'd said – out on

253

those tubes.

'Oh my God…!'

'What?'

'The transmitters. The ones he has dropped off on the edge of the tubes. Come with me!'

She led him along gangways, down ladders to a lab. There were a dozen of the flask like tubes on a rack. Strewn about were transmitter like shapes ready for encapsulation in watertight waxy tubes.

'I wondered why the temperature in here was controlled; for something he had dropped in the sea!'

She hoisted one up. 'Come! Let's go to sickbay!'

In the sickbay they were joined by Steve and Mick who, it seemed, had sensed some excitement and come to find them.

She set up the X Ray kit, placed the flask between the beam and receiver plate. They retired to a shielded area where the control console was kept. Zill clicked here and there. She was ready at last and checked all of them were behind the shield.

The X ray generator ticked in rapid staccato. On the screen an image appeared.

At one end of the flask was an electronic apparatus. presumably the transmitter; at the other end, the outline of a queen vasp….

Maybe it's time you got your hands dirty – joined in, invented something! And then Taylor groaned. Back at the Academy, Ararat.

The Siddiqui Bee! We had a guy year, kept bees… I'm going senile!

***

Taylor was convinced this was new information to them. He wanted desperately for this to be so. He was sure he was a good enough judge of character.

'Your Boss is an evil man, boys. What are you going to do? You can help me mend some of this; or? '

They noticed the green light of his Taser playing on their middle sections

'…Zill? Do I lock you up?'

From the two young men, not a second's hesitation; from Zill, she seemed in shock, the last twenty four hours had dealt blows she could barely contain.

'We're with you.' They turned to Zill. Mick and Steve prompting her with their expressions.

She nodded weakly and followed them.

'Where does the sub dock, underneath?' Taylor said.

'Depends on the sea. Normally down from the tidal flow but there is a central tube down the middle of the rig. This weather it should stop there.'

He fetched his bag from the lifter. They took an elevator cage part of the way down to a docking platform similar to the one at Sandringham. He looked over the side, climbed down a ladder to where the sea sluiced up alarmingly to meet him, then fell away, giving him a strange feeling of vertigo. Using some thread and an improvised cradle of stiff wire, he arranged Jack's magnetic low frequency tracker so it should swing onto the hull of the sub, hopefully out of sight of its crew when it came in. He paid out the long antenna to wave in the current, invisible in the eddies and flows around the rig leg floats. Steve and Mick watched in silence. Zill, further up seemed oblivious and sat biting her lip, twisting a lock of hair round and round and round...

They all climbed back up. On deck, a navy pilot stood with open palms and a questioning shrug. Taylor asked him:

'Bring the silver heli. We're short of transport back there.'

They got on board the lifter. A seaman peered into the cockpit.

'I flushed out the junk. You're full of bio now mate!'

'Thanks; it's not true what they say about matelots...' He smiled and pressed the starter.

'What's a matelot?' said Mick.

'A sailor – it's French for sailor...'

Mick looked at Steve. It was never ending. The older they got the less they found they knew.

Chapter Twenty Five

Back at the agribase, Taylor set to work. He sent some techs to fetch raw tube powder material. They returned towing several canvas sacks on hydro trolleys. He carried out experiments behind a nearby hummock of ground. Flame and smoke could be seen whooshing into the air.

***

He came running back as Steve and Mick watched from a safe distance. The sharp crack of an explosion followed.

'Tube powder! Deadly stuff. Good job the scallies never knew!' he gasped to their astonished faces.

***

He sent the two off in the silver helizep to tell the vicar to be on his guard. After that they were to fly to the Dome 2 complex and see what they could find out. Find out if there was a chance of reinforcements.

He transferred the photo image of the friends at Aberystwyth to Mick's wrist. He pointed out the Z3.

'See what the vicar and Dome 2 know about this man. Discreetly though mind...'

He got Zill to transfer the map overlays of the Scallie tunnel approaches. He called in Sharpe to discuss tactics. All the time he wondered why the ZI remained quiet. Sharpe seemed to think they were under some sort of investigation by the HQ down in Kent.

'There's a woman Z8 who seems to be in charge. I get everything I ask for; seems to run smoother without the other two. She's a bit dozy though, proper Domey.'

'What about the other assistants?'

'They do their inspections; have meetings with the Mayor's Office and the production people. Everything seems to be ticking over. I've sent some of the worst senior SPs off to Kent on leave –sent some of them on training courses. I've read the Riot Act to the rest – they seemed happy enough to have a new broom around...'

New Broom! Riot Act! I like this Sharpe, Taylor thought.

'How do you come by these old sayings?'

'I like reading. I find these sayings and keep them in a notebook, transfer them later to a file on my wrist. They amuse me; they fit whole tracts of meaning into what would take sentences to explain. '

He put on a stern lecturing voice:

'I have called you here today because I am displeased with your behaviour! I will punish severely any offenders after this briefing who continue in this vein. There are going to be changes and things won't settle down until things go my way and I can stop watching you like a hawk! Or;

'Things have gone down the tubes here lately! - I'm going to read you the Riot Act – I'm the new broom round here! …seems so much simpler!'

'Oho! I like it! - although the tubes reference doesn't cross the gap so well. Now, what I'd like to talk about is how to stop our Scallie friends with as little bloodshed as possible…' Taylor said.

'…the opposite of a bloodless coup then?'

'We're going to get along just fine Mr Sharpe… now…'

And Taylor started to outline his ideas.

***

He took Zill to one side.

'I want to talk to de Klayven…'

'I can get a message to him but no direct line without the heli …'

'Before we do that, how do I talk to Jones?'

She nodded towards the Comms room. They made their way there but were intercepted by Hansen.

'What's happening? Kristen has loaded up Heli-1 with all sorts shit!'

'Just leave it be. I'll want all our helis up and running. Can you speed up the tech guys and girls? Stay close though, I need you for something only you can do!'

'What…?'

Taylor held up his hand. 'Later,' he said and led Zill into the Comms room.

Corporal Evans's face shimmered on Zill's wrist screen.

She had linked it to the high power set they used to communicate with the helis out at extreme range on the tube edge. Her wrist was a superior version of the standard issue, with an extra section Taylor had never noticed before.

'We can see them. He can't see you, just talk!'

'Evans! Taylor here! Is the Sergeant Major about?'

'Hang on I'll get him!' Evans turned, bawled an order; the sound of running feet receding came over Zill's speaker.

'It's been quiet since you went. When you coming back so we can get a bit of excitement going? Megan was asking after you.'

Taylor sensed Zill tense.

'When's she going to marry the Colonel?'

'After that night you ditched the Rover? He'll be on his best behaviour for weeks! He's on jankers for now!'

Zill relaxed. Taylor breathed a sigh of relief. He wasn't sure he had her fully onside. He didn't need any hormones affecting her decision making.

Jones peered into the camera lens.

'What trouble are you in fly boy? Blue jobs only call when they want something...'

'I want to pick your brains, it won't take a minute...'

Jones eyes narrowed. He growled, turned to Evans who was soaking up such priceless gossip. Jones visibly withered him until he got the message and left in a hurry.

Taylor explained what he wanted to do. Jones looked thoughtful, called Evans back, muttered instructions and waved him off. He turned back to the camera.

'Send one of your chariots. I'll be waiting.' He closed the link.

***

Sharpe took his recently promoted seniors around the nettle field perimeter. He had a copy of Taylor's overlays.

'Here, here and here...PTVs with a SWAT team. Check PTVs are fully topped up with dazers. Can we get the lasers swivelled, directable?'

'No problem sir!'

'Do it! We have six hours until dark.'

He posted small teams in the unofficial alleys through the nettle field. Special attention was given to those places Taylor and he had agreed the Scallies would pour out of the ground. He had camouflaged hides erected like the ones Taylor described at Ddihingol Clythrea.

His cavalry, the Litaks and transports, reinforcements were coming in later, were ready to be deployed away from their usual pads. Taylor reckoned their normal dispositions would be general knowledge to every shanty Scallie – assumed to be potential spies. They would be watched, snatched up and dazed when the order came.

Spy bees were programmed to watch the gaps. Teams with the few stasis stunners were under instructions to use them first. He called Taylor

'Ready as we'll ever be!'

'Let's hope you can stand your men down. I'm going to try that something I told you about.'

'What if it fails?'

'Over to you; dulce et decorum est, pro patria mori…'

'How do you spell that…?'

***

Taylor sent Zill with Blair to fetch Jones in the lifter. He gave her a note and asked her to show Jones the ordnance survey maps.

'Tell him we want to stop them not slaughter them. Tell him I have remote controllable seismic charges but I want them boosted. He gave her a sample of the tube skin powder.

'Are you sure you trust me?' she said bitterly.

'Not completely, that will take time, but I told Blair his boyfriend was hostage…besides why would you do anything to interfere?'

She smiled weakly and went to join Blair by the lifter. They took off, the base shaking and rattling as they went straight off overhead.

'Can't you get that bastard to hover gently out of here!?' shouted someone down the row.

259

Chapter Twenty Six

Raoul rejoined his captives. He liked their company; they didn't seem terrified, more curious. He asked them why.

'Taylor will do something,' shrugged Jack.

'You have a lot of faith in him.'

They just looked at him. He started to wonder what he was doing. He was poised on a life-changing event. People would get hurt; they could die. He would give the order to go at midnight. He had nobody to consult on his decision. His own father... what happened to his parents? What happened to everyone's lost parents? ...what would his father say? He imagined him saying something like;

"Do what you want. You always did. Christ! You are nearly fourteen! Stand up for yourself, man. I'm going down the pub, where's your mother's purse...?"

One of his boys came in; beckoned to him. He followed him out; out of earshot.

'Message from the Zill bitch...'

In his command tent, old army canvas with several rooms set up in the old tunnel, he went and sat in front of a screen. Zill's still image flared. Her voice crackled from the speaker.

'Taylor wants to talk. He says he has a demonstration for you. To go outside and watch north west in three to four hours. Depending on your reaction to the demonstration and the next message I send. He will meet you here – graphic follows.'

They looked at a satellite view of a clearing just off the old motorway; not far from where they were sitting hidden in the old railway tunnel.

***

The lifter came in through the water veil and set down. Jones ran out from beneath the running down heli blades. He looked about, squinted up at the now repaired water veil. He took note of the base with its bamboo handrails, the tube skin construction with its harsh edges broken up by planting and flowers. He scowled at people sat about, casually come out of their labs and offices to pretend no interest in what occurred, such as strange visitors bearing packages of strange equipment.

He shook Taylor's hand.

'You didn't say you worked in a Garden Centre, Taylor! Who are

260

these scruffy layabouts sat around?'

'Garden centre?' He looked about. He had to admit as much. Seen through fresh eyes the place had the air of randomness, themes blending from one to the next, bits of half fabricated tube skin, bamboo and nettle stem piled up here and there.

He sat Jones down, gave him water, poured tea and displayed his maps on the wall.

'Who's running this show Taylor? Where're the big bosses? ESO?'

'Exactly. This local lot; who knows what they're thinking? Not nice pleasant things for a start. You should see what they've been doing to the scallie kids…ever looked over your shoulder to see who's behind you, backing you up?'

'Usually some suicide bomber, whenever I looked round. So it's you running the show…who are you? I thought you were some flyboy mechanic who sawed up bits of bamboo and fiddled with wires…'

'So did I Jonesy, so did I. Anyway, this Raoul guy and his boys are coming, the ZI don't care. I've nowhere to run to and hide and my best friends are hostages.'

'Best we do something then. Action! My circulation is starting up again. You're a shit magnet Taylor. Is it infectious?'

'I don't want a mass murder scenario; I want to warn them with this…'

He displayed a sketch diagram of a large container under a parachute, ejected from a hastily sketched heli…

'…set off by a remote controlled charge…' Here he showed Jones the seismic-charges from the rig.

'…we have bio diesel or ethanol and the organic powder Zill showed you…'

'A fuel air bomb? FAE? They used them to clear the Taliban out of the tunnels in the mountains. You're ambitious Taylor…!'

'Yes, but if it doesn't work I want a back up and, and I want some means of getting the other charges to penetrate the tunnels; to be followed by dire results if they don't back off and come to the table…'

Jones whistled between his teeth.

'We're going to need some shaped charges to breach the tunnels. Some cone shapes and – we can make a sort of fertiliser mix with the tube powder and diesel – we haven't got a lot of time. Where can I do a few small scale trials…?'

Taylor showed him his shed where they hunted here and there for suitable pieces of metal.

Jones held up a metal funnel.

'Here's our shaped charge. Got any more?'

Taylor asked a tech to find out. Jones ran tube powder through his fingers. We need wide bore tube – what's that over there by the crate?'

'My seaplane floats…but you can't…'

Taylor handed Jones the saw.

'How long does this tube stuff take to set?' sniffed Jones.

'Half an hour in direct sun…'

***

Jones sketched his idea out with a stick in the dust.

'We cut the spout off the funnel and use it as a former to mould the shape and then graft it onto the tube so we have a reverse rocket head - our shaped charge! We punch a hole into the tunnel. Then we'll have to run in and pour the ethanol. I've got some thermite we can use as a boost incendiary – it'll be an inferno inside…'

***

Blair dropped Jones off with two of his men and Hamid above the first tunnel. Jones squinted at Hamid with suspicion when he heard his origin.

'I have no western blood on my hands if that is what you are thinking, army man!'

Jones was still undergoing some culture shock here in this, this techno world, an hour's flight by heli away from their Welsh stronghold. He'd heard of all this eco stuff and thought it was mainly bollocks but he had to admit to the wisdom of some of it. Taylor's "Shed" was like a mad professor's basement with its wires and boxes and…Using ground up plant dust as fibre glass! While they were waiting for their devices to cure, Taylor had shown him a model helizep, the size of a large dog, from the early development days. It was made from basket work! Taylor demonstrated the strength of the construction by sitting down hard on it. But when he passed it to him, he could lift it with a little finger!

'The old helicopters were like bumble bees. They shouldn't fly! They were expensive, hard to fly. All sorts of tricks and fast reactions were needed to just make simple sorties…look…!'

Taylor got it going. A gas turbine engine from a model wound up and filled the air with noise and fumes. He held a hand held control and demonstrated the controls. A belt gear was engaged and the blades wound themselves up.

'A gyro copter; the jet engine gives thrust as well!' shouted Taylor. He shut it down.

'Add some hydrogen bags in the right place. You've got enough lift for the crew. The rest is available for power and lift A child can fly one straight and level. Needs practise landing exactly where you want though...'

Jones shook his head. Life was confusing enough without being in the presence of a weird wizard.

He'd brought some military explosives with which to boost the improvised powder and bio diesel. Also, a box of his dwindling store of detonators and detonating cord.

What the hell. If I keep it any longer, it won't work. Still, it's for a good cause. I hope Taylor knows what he's doing though, he thought.

***

He set the tube bomb at a stand off to allow the shape to penetrate where they had assessed the firm part of the tunnel lay. He had six of the seismic charges ready to drop into the hole. These could be detonated by a signal sent from the helizep standing off to the side. They would cause a huge bang – even maybe collapse the tunnel arch. The fire bombs would follow on Taylor's signal.

Jones contacted Zill.

'...send the message if the FAE is ready.'

He called Blair back and they climbed aboard. He dropped his two men at a safe distance to fire the charges on his command. They had portable radios with one of Taylor's fuel cells as well as a spare wrist to ensure no loss of communication.

Hamid noticed Jones had a solitary plastic box left unopened. He pointed it out.

'Can we fly over there? Jones asked Blair, showing them a point on the map where an offshoot road of the motorway led into some trees. He tapped the side of his nose to them, a familiar sign for anyone who had worked with Taylor - especially when he had a plan he didn't want to discuss quite yet.

Zill sent the second message.

***

Raoul digested the import of her words. What was Zill doing here? What was Shams thinking? The gist of the message was that any

263

military style action against the Dome would result in unwanted bloodshed. She said the demonstration in thirty minutes would demonstrate this and – if the north western tunnel had any troops inside then they should withdraw to safety…they knew of the tunnels!

***

Taylor, Flynn and Ari were in the lifter. They had staggered into the air carrying the strange contraptions; two of them. The theory, they learned, was to drop the contents in a cloud and then ignite the cloud of vapour and powder at the right time. Taylor told of old mining accidents and gas explosions from before; the force from gas and air explosions was incredible. He was using the seismic charge as a detonating device. He and Jones had fiddled and changed this and that with a furious but agonising patience.

'I want him to think we have easy access to this technology– that we are dropping this one as a warning. I want him to meet me and talk. I want him to leave the Dome out of his plans…'

Chapter Twenty Seven

Raoul and a small guard force had concealed themselves on a small hill. It was still, hot; the air shimmered over the motorway. He looked up. High in the sky a big heli manoeuvred. A container fell from its underside. Even at this distance, it looked big.

A makeshift parachute opened and slowed the descent of the container. The huge dandelion seed like device came down to just about 45 degrees up in the air from their position then burst in a shower of dark particles; a cloud of either liquid or powder. Or both. Whichever, the first droplets at the bottom of the cloud soon reached the ground.

'Hah! A misfire!' He grinned and slapped the backs of the closest of his boys.

Inside the cloud came a bang. The whole world lit up in a blinding flash.

'Jesus!' shouted Raoul and then they were hurled off their feet as the minor quake rippled the ground around them.

***

At the SP Control room, Sharpe heard the bang. The floors trembled with the shock wave. Jeez! That was one hell of an explosion...

Something cold on his cheek. Swivelling in his chair, he found himself face to face with Jarvis holding a Taser. Behind him were two of the senior SPs he'd had sent off to Kent on pretexts.

'Thank you Mr Sharpe! We'll take it from here...' Jarvis turned to his men.

'Whatever Mr Sharpe has been interfering with...undo it.'

Sharpe watched as his dispositions were stood down; listened to Jarvis talking on his Z band.

'No reinforcements needed. We have it all under control. Yes, it was a naïve young officer jumping at shadows...no, no problem – we have the situation in hand. Out'

***

Jones and his mixed crew were back in place ready for Taylor. They had concealed themselves in a ruined building on the edge of the nettle forest. Blair had taken the heli back to a quiet clearing halfway back to the agribase. He was to sit and await the call. Then a call from

Taylor had him flying low over the crops to pick him up. The sun was low down in the western sky when Taylor and Zill joined Jones at their hiding place.

Jones and Taylor walked a little way, Jones pointing out the approximate explosive charge locations. Jones weaved a hand here and there to show his route.

'As soon as we blow the first two we run forward. The fuel and the seismics are concealed nearby.'

Taylor glanced at the green fronds at the side.

'Don't go too near these nettles. At best, you will suffer paralysis like lockjaw. At worst, well, they've been known to kill horses.'

Jones cleared his throat.

'Tender-handed stroke a nettle and it stings you for your pains; Grasp it like a man of mettle and it soft as silk remains.'

Taylor smiled at this uncharacteristic side of Jones.

'I only knew the 'man of mettle' bit, but I'm serious. These are the same as the *Ongaonga* tree from New Zealand. Keep away is my advice.'

Jones looked up.

'They must be six metres or more high. You couldn't take a stick to these once they'd stung you, eh?'

'I did that when I was a boy. I used to ask what use they were; nettles, wasps and so on. Nobody seemed to know or bother to answer.'

'I took a stick to people that stung me. I had the choice. Join the army or go to prison. Well, here we are in another world,' said Jones.

He shrugged off "before" and said:

'… there's another bit…'

'Go on…'

'Tis the same with common natures, use 'em kindly, they rebel; But, be rough as nutmeg-graters and the rogues obey you well. That bit of advice was useful in the Army – and life…'

***

They were back at the hide. The two soldiers hushed them with fingers to lips. Taylor's nerves tingled. He shook Zill's shoulders, hushing her.

'Run! Follow the nettles. Don't touch them! Wait for me!'

Jones drew his pistol too late. He, Hamid and his two men went down under an electro web and a cloud of dazer gas.

The SP sergeant shouted for his men to spread out. He kicked the unconscious Jones in the ribs. The gas had cleared so he took his filter mask off.

'There's one missing! Spread out – find him!'

Taylor's reflex action had saved him. Down, to the side, sense where the danger is, roll away from it; move obliquely so the attacker's own subconscious reflexes could not automatically calculate your path...

Old Kurt! he thought. Old German Kurt! How long is he dead? Taylor was never a fighting sort, preferring to outwit people into a disadvantage, but the self defence had been useful over the years of before; and even recently.

Taylor weaved away from the hide, following in Zill's footsteps.

What has happened at the Dome? No good apparently unless Sharpe was playing games!

He followed the nettle edge; he heard voices. On tiptoe he moved forward to see.

Zill was backed up to the nettle edge. Four Shanty Scallies were taunting her.

'Any further backwards is going to hurt you more than we will, pretty lady!'

The leader grinned in an evil way; his colleagues sniggered in anticipation.

She was very close to a huge nettle leaf.

Taylor shuddered and went cold. This was the time of day they resettled themselves after the heat of the day. She was practically touching one. She only had her thin flight overalls on.

Time for action. Taylor stepped forward, straight armed two of the Scallies into the nettles. They screamed horribly. Taylor whipped the sharp point of his elbow into the nerve ganglion just behind the third one's ear. He went down like a sack of mangoes.

This left Number Four with a Taser at his throat. Frozen with fear he watched the struggles of his former gang members.

'Haven't we met before?' said Taylor.

'You're the bathtard who got me 37 kV! I thtill can't thpeak!'

Number Four's eye gleamed in the red light of Taylor's Taser.

Taylor looked over to Zill. 'Step forward quick! Don't even think!'

Number Four made a bolt for it. Twin barbs caught him between the shoulder blades. He went down twitching and jumping. Taylor looked at the dial – 40kV – it read. Inflation even in these days, thought Taylor and turned to Zill.

The leaf had twitched already. The back of her coverall was like a porcupine of tiny poison hairs. Taylor unzipped the front. He peeled

267

the material from the inside out and ripped it down and off her in practically one fluid motion.

'Taylor! What are you doing? This is neither the time nor the...!'

'Step out of the clothes – slowly!'

He helped her with his knife, cutting the material away from her boot heels. She leaned on his shoulder. He showed her the broken hypodermic like hairs of the nettle clustering along the back of her suit. He turned her round. She was lucky.

She turned back to face him, her firm breasts jutting in the evening light. He noticed she had a cold reaction. It was not cold.

He turned her round again.

'Feel anything?'

'It burns on my shoulder blade.'

He cast about, found a thick leaved plant and broke it open. A milky fluid oozed out. He squeezed it into his palm, came back and rubbed it around the area she had said. For good measure, he rubbed some more all over her back.

'What's that? Aren't you going to do the front?'

'Can't remember the name. Maybe Aloe Vera. Nature often has a cure nearby, my mother used to say...you can do your own front'

He only thought of his mother in dreams; my father had the waking hours shift, he thought. Quickly, he took the outer clothes off the unconscious Scallie.

'Wear these?' she grimaced.

'Wear these or you will be eaten alive and may even be stung by some lesser plant!'

She still looked lovely in the stinking two piece jacket and trousers of the Scallie

'Belle of the Ball!' said Taylor.

She didn't bother to ask.

Number Four groaned. Taylor played the red light over his face.

'What gives? There should be SPs all over rounding you guys up!'

'The top ZI are back; all the pigs are stood down...'

Taylor heard movement, dropped the man and grabbed Zill's arm.

They headed for the ground Jones had pointed out. Taylor tripped on a wire. It was one of Jones's command wires. A back up in case the radio control did not work. Up ahead Taylor could make out the shaped charge.

Now they could hear the SP squad moving their way. Taylor cut the two wires. Taking the ends that led to the charge, he pushed Zill under cover of some bushes.

The SPs were spread out. Two eased past their hiding place.

268

Subconsciously they seemed to be following the contour of the old tunnel. The line of least resistance.

Taylor waited until he heard a shout. The charge was discovered!

He held the two bare ends of the cable to his Taser muzzle prongs.

'Cover your ears Zill,' he hissed, turning one of his own ears into his shoulder

He pressed the trigger. The world erupted around them.

Chapter Twenty Eight

Jones came round as he was thrust into a prison cell. Or so it appeared until he noticed the screens and speakers high up in the wall. Sharpe was there cuffed with a sort of Velcro tube round his arms and legs.. Hamid and his two Welsh boys were still out of it. In the next room, a reception office, the four SPs prepared to leave.

'Who the fuh' all dese? All smokers?' said an Asian guy with medals and shoulder bars. A big SP man scowled.

'Mind your business you fukkin' idiot. Just keep them here quiet until we come back for them.'

'You no right treat me li' tha'!'

The Civil Correction attendant pointed to the sign with his rights and code of socially acceptable behaviour on the wall.

'Want to join them? To join their club, first you need to experience some voltage!'

'OK, I watch…'

The building shook, the ground shivered. The notice fell from the wall and dust trickled down from the roof. The SPs ran out leaving the attendant gazing out into the night in wonder. At a loss what to do, he considered. They didn't seem to be smokers. They looked like trouble. Anti Social Behaviourists? He turned on the ASB hypnovid. He peered in at his charges.

Jones fixed him with a flinty gaze many a recruit had seen and regretted. The attendant's blood ran cold. For some reason he could not define he switched the vid off.

'No trouble from you tonigh'!' he announced but it came out squeaky and without the supreme authority he thought he normally commanded.

***

Taylor was deafened. His right ear rang from the explosion. He peered out from the bushes. A crater smoked where the charge had been. Two SP bodies lay nearby; no sign of the others. He went forward and peered over the crater edge. It had been more successful than they had hoped for. The brickwork of the old tunnel had given way and, if it had not been for the dust, he would have been able to see the rails below.

***

Raoul and Taylor's captive crew were dazed by the explosion. Scallies ran here and there in confusion. The blast had funnelled up and down the tunnel; the tent was in shreds. The effect was more than Taylor had wanted.

'Your faith in your friend seems justified. I must remember to not underestimate people…'

It didn't seem the time or place to say, "I told you so."

'The comms set is still working!' said one of his lieutenants.

'Good! We move to this point here… '

He indicated Taylor's desired meeting point.

'Move the phone base station to safety. Try and keep it high without being seen – oh yes, was anyone hurt?'

'A few bruises – some are deaf…'

'Hmmm, and that was just one blast. He was not bluffing. We must postpone the attack until we know more. Disperse them to their holds! I must hear what this man has to say. He seemed to hint it may be to our advantage.'

'He is an enemy!'

'Maybe, but he is a different enemy to the ones we are used to. We wouldn't be talking to each other now if the SP and ZI had these… explosive talents…these resources. I must think!'

***

Taylor got hold of Blair on his wrist. Blair had seen the SPs and moved his heli back and around.

'Any sign of them?' said Taylor.

'After the bang they withdrew as far as I could see. These night vis goggles of Jones are amazing but the range is limited. I was lucky I wasn't looking through them when it blew!'

'Call Hansen. Tell him we have vasps at point Echo. Heli-2 is ready – point Echo is on his screen. Tell him, fly immediately and to come high and quiet or they will swarm at him! Then come over here and pick us up. Tell him to watch out for SP…'

'Got it, Ben told me the drill. Is he, have you…?'

'He'll be OK. Now get on man! Zill! come, we have an appointment.'

***

Jarvis sat with his feet up, hands behind his head. Z3 came in.

'Bad for your posture; you will have back problems when you are

271

older.'

'Like you care about my health or future,' said Jarvis with a sneer.

The domed intellectual forehead turned to stare at him.

'Let's say I care for at least as long as I get to hear your report.'

Jarvis assumed a more business like position. He opened a screen.

'Seems the agris have gone independent and are taking matters into their own hands. We have the SP back under my control and Sharpe and his cronies are neutralised.'

'So Taylor thinks he is betrayed by the SP he thought he had on his side. Can we get him to think it was Sharpe who played him? Hmmm – maybe.'

Z3 looked at his wrist time.

'De Klayven should attack in two hours. The sub has high explosive missiles targeted on the Dome. Best we make ready to leave…'

'Our story is going to be…?'

'Power struggle. Domeys and agris tried to defend themselves with amateur explosives. The tube powder and ethanol went up and wiped the lot out.'

'There are over a thousand people in and around the Dome…'

'Bah! The experiment is over. We can get all this done again when it all cools down, blows over. We have lost this round. We will never get the high ground back this way and ESO won't give me an army while we have these hick pioneers in their wagon train based here…'

'The sub commander, Armstrong. He has the second command key…'

'I don't even know if Shams will use the other key. Whatever. It is time we made our exit stage left. I told you; I warned you of men like Taylor…'

'I have something I can control Taylor with. I have the Netz girl and… something else he would like to know…'

Z3 studied him. This Jarvis was a smug little shit but was he old enough to be as treacherous as his seniors? Jarvis had his uses though.

'Send me what you have on Taylor. I will consider it. Have the girl strangled or thrown to the nettles; he will know we mean business. I am going to check on our escape arrangements. Let me know when de Klayven makes his move.'

***

The SP sergeant hid behind the partition wall. The Z3 came out of Jarvis's office and out onto the landing. He looked neither right nor left, much to the sergeant's relief. The SP man was tense, fearful but relieved, having overheard such valuable information; life relevant information. So – the rats are leaving are they? Best we make sure the ship doesn't sink. Time for the SPs to move out of here. Who's that troublemaker? Taylor? Yes. A few reinforcements are on the way, Mr Taylor. ZI bastards!

He almost tiptoed down to the barracks.

***

Blair dropped Taylor and Zill off some distance from the meeting point. They made their way on foot and waited.

'What are you going to say, Taylor?'

'I want him to stop this attack. I want to tell him he is being duped, he is doing exactly what is wanted of him; he may even be walking into a trap!'

'How so?'

'Your father's submarine. There were doors with the radiation signs. Did you ever see every part of the boat? Every nook and cranny?

'Well no, but my father is not a megalomaniac. Armstrong and his sailors would not let him…the missiles are conventional, not nuclear, by the way.'

'Armstrong told me it wasn't a warship.'

'It's secret. He didn't know you. You could have been a Soviet mole for all he knew.'

'Mole? You contacted me, remember? Anyway, maybe wouldn't let him, no, but what if he told them it was operational necessity, or he had authority from high up; a coded signal authorising deployment of missiles?'

'I don't understand why anybody would want to commit further acts of destruction.'

'I don't either but what if your father is being duped as well? If the Scallies take over the biomass and biofuel? Headed by a clever resourceful man; what is the next step? Conquest of all the Domes, seizure of the whole of the most efficient agri algae based resources of the Western Hemisphere. The French have the nuclear powered electricity and a lot of agricultural resources but only in the North. It is an oven further down by the Mediterranean but they also have huge refugee camps. They cannot float tubes out into the Atlantic. We have enough trouble with the North Sea.

No; Wales is the geographical barrier which protects what is left of

England. I want to stop this happening regardless of ZI, Shams or de Klayven's ambitions.

'I would never have thought of it that way. You really are not just a flying farmer are you...?'

'Like you said, you approached me. I only wanted a quiet life, find my family...'

Chapter Twenty Nine

In the dark clearing, the moon came from behind a cloud. Wicked crossbows, unwavering bolt ends pointed. Emotionless eyes, tattooed faces with expressions of cold flat dislike, watched him. Fingers tense on triggers; they dared him to make a move,. Taylor looked down at his Taser. It would take two maybe three down but he wouldn't live to enjoy it. He put it away. A familiar face pushed to the front, nodded to Zill, fixed his gaze on Taylor. With almost a smile but not quite, he spoke.

'Devil, or is it imbecile? We meet again.'

'Hello Raoul,' said Zill.

Taylor, shocked, examined the man. Of course! Zill had been asleep, drugged, the last time we met. How odd Shams's surveillance had neglected him dropping the three off on the shore! Taylor's wrist beeped for low signal again. He pressed the cancel alarm button. Crossbows jerked but Raoul waved them down. Taylor pressed another button, dropped his arm to his side.

'Raoul - *the* Raoul - would it be?'

'It would Taylor, it would. I take it you are someone who likes to get to the point. You are either very brave or foolish coming here. Your Dome defences are down, my er, spies tell me the elaborate preparations you made have been dismantled; that Jones is taken. I was impressed with your demonstration, yet here you are. Please enlighten me.'

Taylor studied him. One time creature of Shams, now with his own agenda and his own small ruthless army.

'If you take the Dome, what then? Enslave the workforce? They are already enslaved; you will just make life less comfortable. How will you trade with the outside? Will the ZI treat with you? You know Shams well enough. If he has the resources we have seen, what others exist? It seems to me we are like a sort of lunar colony here. We have material wealth desired by those back home. What do you hope to achieve but a different form of strife, even if you succeed?'

De Klayven looked from him to Zill.

'I want to have a say in ...I...' he turned to include his rough band of guards.

'...I came here to see if I could do some good, naïve as I was. Now I think they are worth it but even more so. If there is going to be persecution, extermination and such then it is time the tables were turned.'

'So you have pushed your button? There is no going back?'

'There is no going back.'

In the distance, Taylor could hear a faint *Voff-voff-voff*. The others did not seem to have noticed it.

De Klayven indicated the watchful guard.

'I would let you leave but these boys here are not keen for the whereabouts of this place to become common knowledge.'

'Shams knows; he can watch all from space.'

Voff-voff-voff - Some of the Scallies started to turn heads towards the sound. Their eyes never left Taylor and his hands.

'These boys are not familiar with this concept. They are not familiar with the god like powers of our great manipulator,' said de Klayven with heavy irony.

'Nor are they yet familiar with such ideas of honour; of debt for favours done in the past. I have been lax in this area of their education, something I will eventually redress. You must come with us.' He started to turn away.

'Wait! Where are my crew?'

'They are here; you will meet them soon'

Voff-voff-voff

'What is that? I see, you think you have reinforcements?' Raoul signalled. From further back fire arrows leapt into the air to illuminate Hansen's heli approaching. He was too high for them; they dropped short, arcing gracefully down to ignite small bush fires where they fell. The heli gently approached and halted directly above their location, hovering barely visible above them, the downdraft wafting faintly around them.

'You there Taylor?' came Hansen's voice over Taylor's wrist.

'Yes; drop the gas on my signal.'

'Are you clear? You look mighty close to me according to your wrist beacon.'

'Yes, I'm clear, but wait for my signal for Christ's sake!'

Raoul ignored the heli, stared at Taylor. His men looked nervous, darting glances from the heli to Taylor.

'My man up there thinks there is a vasp swarm down here. He has cyanide canisters ready to drop on you. So give me my crew members and we'll be on our way.'

'Bluff away. You are not one of these...' Raoul indicated his men. 'You value your life...'

'Drop a sighting flare Hansen...'

They were blinded momentarily by a signal flare burning down amongst them. It set alight to some dried grass, stamped out quickly by Raoul's men. Taylor saw they had a much bigger audience than he first thought.

Raoul stood there, going over his options. He came to a decision, barked orders:

'We are discovered! We move to Base Two! This man is an ally, he will not betray us, bring his people to him!'

Turning to Taylor, he said,

'I don't think for a minute you would cyanide us, but you allow me a way to compromise. You cannot threaten these men with weapons they have never encountered. Breathing cyanide would have been a first and last experience for them. First and last for us all; I though, have seen these cyanide bombs.' He started to turn away.

'Wait! How do I contact you?'

'Why should you want to?'

'We need to stop this madness.'

'Ask her.' He pointed to Zill, rocking back and forth, eyes closed, mentally fleeing the situation.

'She is part of the madness. No, just the two of us; how?'

'Come to the roof of the dogs alone.'

He knows!

'Give me a cell phone.'

Now it was Raoul's turn to look surprised.

'There will be a cell phone on the roof. There may still be ways to track them.' He glanced up, unconsciously referring to the invisible satellites in orbit.

He looked at Zill, her eyes open again; some wordless exchange took place, and then he turned and left them. A scared looking Ben, Marie, Jack and Harry were thrust forward. They were left alone in the clearing.

***

Flying back to base Hansen looked puzzled.

'What was happening back there? I was ready to drop cyanide. In fact it's a good job I checked, some idiot had substituted dazer gas canisters...'

Zill's eyes widened. Taylor went cold, he closed his eyes, thrust his brow between forefinger and thumb and massaged his temples.

'I'll tell the story when we're all together back at Joe's...'

Back at the agri base, they found the place almost deserted. Taylor was surprised to find no SPs. Perhaps the security field was off again.

He got his answer at the comms room. The operator looked curious as he relayed the message.

From SP control – attention Taylor. Zero tolerance cancelled – full tolerance restored. Come home – fatted calf awaits. Hallam. Sgt. SP.

***

Sat in thought in his shed, he played with the red button box, turning it this way and that. A heli approaching. He looked out and up; saw it was the silver helizep returning. He put the box down, stood up to leave, paused, pressed the button hard and then went out to meet them.

Steve and Mick were out of the heli before the rotor even began to run down.

'We got to meet their ZI man; different world or what?'

'Slow down. Easy. Come inside and tell all.'

Seated in the shed they looked about, amused at the junk and half finished projects.

Zill came in and hugs were exchanged. She looked pleased and relieved to see them.

'Their Z2 has called the SP here direct. He told them it would go badly for them if they act on any other orders than his. There is a relief heli force coming; not far behind us…'

'Zill! Get a message to de Klayven. Tell him to hold until I can do something!'

'And if he refuses…?'

'Remind him I've had time for more Devil tricks…'

'Come on, we're going to meet the local ZI. In Shams's heli we have an element of surprise…'

Chapter Thirty

The silver helizep with Taylor and Zill in the front, Ben, Jack, Harry and Hamid in the back, came leisurely in over the nettle fields. Behind were the others in an agri helizep painted up quickly to resemble the first. Touching down, the usual pair of guard SPs actually came forward and gave them a cordial greeting. Flynn and Hamid stayed to stand guard with them; the rest got on the descender down to decontam. The lab techs raised their hands when they saw Tasers levelled.

'Don't hurt us,' one said.

'We are not here to hurt you. Detach your wrists and put them down on that bench! You! The nearest! Show me where the Z3 and the Z6 are!'

The technician scrambled to the screen. She stabbed at the floating photo icons. Her hand shook. One of her colleagues called advice from the other side of the lab; as if it were a routine software problem. Taylor noticed one of the techs had even returned to the holo book he had been reading; flicked the virtual pages idly, all this not his concern. An overview of the Dome zoomed to the Admin area. ZI, Z2 empty, unallocated. Z4 and Z5 the same and, there they were; Z3 and Z6 together in the same room.

'Wait here,' said Taylor and made for the second level descender. Before anyone could react, he was on his way down. Jack and Marie looked down to see the top of his head dropping down, down – too far to jump to join him. 'Typical of him!' snarled Marie. They cast about for another way down. The helpful software tech said, 'one must wait for two to go down on another!'

'Another? Where?' yelled Jack pointing his Taser meaningfully.

'This way,' said the tech, at last showing some alarm.

***

Taylor's tread pulsed micro-volts into the system, harsh red puddles of liquid plasma reforming behind him. He burst in through the paper screen door of Z6-Z9 Assistants. Empty. A door in the back wall was slightly ajar. he kicked it open and dodged back, just in time to avoid a Taser end, wires trailing. The charged ends wrapped themselves round an oxygen orchid which promptly expired in comical surrender. He waited, then glanced quickly round the door frame in time to see the back of Z3 departing through a discreet panel. The Z6 sat at a desk examining his Taser in perplexity. The red discharged light flashing, his wrist warning him that his charge was depleted. Taylor spoke into his own wrist; 'The Z3 is escaping!' He approached Jarvis, went round on his side of the desk and seated himself on the corner, He demonstrated the full charge status of his own weapon and levelled it in his general direction. The lethality light glared green, and then changed to cherry red.

Jarvis seemed to gather his wits.

'Par for the course, eh Taylor? Par for the course...how can we help you today?' he asked brightly.

'Some sort of psychopath you are with all the blood on your hands. There were baddies in the old movies. I always thought they were clichés, but you really are one son of a bitch.'

He nodded to the Taser.

'Dead it may be but I'd feel better if you put that down all the same.'

Jarvis obeyed. 'What are you going to do?' he said in an oddly disinterested way.

'I should hand you over to the authorities but I don't see any about. They seem to have left you in charge.'

He nodded to the exit Z3 had used. Jarvis sneered.

'We wouldn't be having this conversation were it not for him and his ilk.'

Taylor moved closer, reached forward with his Taser, aimed between his eyes.

'Wait; allow me to show you something.'

Taylor nodded, cautious.

Jarvis erected a holo, tapped here, tapped there. A full screen lit up on the wall.

Taylor went rigid, his eyes widened, a camera scene panned across a pleasant sunny room. Enter stage left, his daughter, Rachel; happy, smiling, safe! What was this? a serious little boy about four or five, playing with a model helizep of strange design. A baby sat in a high chair, spattering baby food with a spoon; a happy domestic scene from anywhere or anytime. It was recent; he could see modern hi-tech trappings here and there, a holo screen, a PV jacket hung on the far wall. She looked older, tired, but she was still the little girl on his knee so long ago...

She turned to answer someone, out of view of the camera - a voice, a woman's voice he recognized. Dare he hope? A baby? Rachel must be, what? Eighteen? Nineteen? Or? A four year old? If they think I'm dead, Sally has moved on, found a new partner?

'There's more…' Jarvis tapped again. A new screen appeared. Taylor's son; Andy. Billy Boy - his grandma used to call him that when he was little. Taylor could picture him, bouncing up and down in a sprung contraption hanging from the door frame. Now here he was, in a laboratory; frowning at some experiment; typing in data onto an old type computer. He turned, smiled towards the camera, made an obscene gesture; faded away.

'Send it to me!'

'Why should I?'

'Why did you not let me see this? What sort of creature would withhold this information?'

Jarvis shrugged off such an obvious question.

'Want to see them again Taylor? I mean really, really want to see them again? I can do this…I can send you to the other side of the world.'

Taylor had the Taser hard up against Jarvis's temple. Two spots of blood appeared, little trickles running down, mixing with the sweat now pouring from Jarvis's head.

'Of course I do. Where are they?' Jab.

'That knowledge, for a person in my present situation, is a tradable item.'

Taylor withdrew the gun. He flicked the dial round to zero within the sweating man's view. He flicked it back to 75 kV, to zero and back again to 75. He reapplied the muzzle to Jarvis's head. The red danger light flared. Taylor's wrist spoke out: –

Caution! 75 kilovolts is a lethal ch….

Taylor silenced it.

'Know what 75 kV would do to your brain?'

'I am not devoid of imagination.'

'Send it to me.'

Jarvis tapped the green hued air of his screen; complied.

'You still don't know where they are…'

Behind Taylor, Marie, Jack and Ben appeared. They held back, warily scanning for trouble.

'OK Taylor? We lost Z3 for now. The techs are setting a spy bee on him.'

Then, seeing Jarvis squirming under Taylor's gun,

'What's the score with "Dirt bag" here?'

'Dirt bag here knows where Taylor's long lost family is.' Jarvis laughed unpleasantly.

Taylor looked over to his crew. His friends, colleagues, sharers of experiences, bad days, happy days. They were his family as well; this was his home. This was his life here, now, today. Would they come with me to the other side of the world? He turned back to Jarvis who was now visibly relaxing, even with the discomfort of the Taser probes poking into his skin. Jarvis has won again! read his expression.

Taylor gave him a wry smile.

'I could never have thought it would be you who would make me such a happy man,' he said quietly.

***

Jarvis relaxed fully, sagged in his chair. He exhaled with relief; reached slowly to disengage the sharp muzzle. Politely- easy now. It was hurting but he was out of the woods.

'Taylor, if you don't mind...'

'Not at all...'

Taylor pulled the trigger.

***

When they got back to the heli pad, the Silver heli was gone. Flynn and Hamid looked apologetic.

'Zill took it. She's gone, She said she had an errand for you.'

The lifter was on its way in with Blair, Steve and Mick.

They trooped back down to the techs' room.

'Do you still have a trace on the Z3?'

They all gathered round the screen. The Dome layout zoomed out. They could see the spy bee plot, blip-blip, heading east. Not far behind another blip; Z3's wrist.

'He had a fast float car like a speedboat. We always thought he was a jumped up son of a bitch,' said the helpful tech.

'Can you link into the agribase comms?' said Jack.

It was done and Jack keyed in a code.

The screen was zoomed out to encompass Norfolk and the North Sea. Over the old Wash they saw the silver heli trace heading for a point south of the rig. Another ponderous circular signal made whirlpools on the screen.

'Would that be a low frequency job?' Taylor asked Jack. Jack nodded.

The blips coincided.

Z3 had stopped. In the middle of the sea, the spy bee winked out. Presumably, Z3 had seen it and fired his Dazer at it. He was headed

282

north towards the rig. There was nothing to do but watch the screen. The Z3's boat must be something special, thought Taylor as he watched its rapid progress. They took it in turns, coming and going for refreshments.

Nearly two hours later all three blips coincided. As they watched, the three became one superimposed pulsing centre. A few minutes passed and the larger started moving again south and then east. A smaller dot was left behind. The gap widened. The sub faded.

'Out of range,' murmured Jack.

'I'm amazed it had that much.'

'Well you said to start thinking for ourselves. I put a booster relay running on UV and salt water batteries out on the edge!'

Taylor sighed, looked around his little group. The Techs sat, blinking like owls, wondering what actual drama they had just watched. Life was certainly not routine for them lately.

'I think if you take the lifter out there with a spare pilot you will find a silver helizep riding empty on the sea. Waste not; want not, they used to say,' Taylor said.

They made to leave. Marie held him back.

'He would never have let you find them. He would have betrayed you, and them, like everyone else he dealt with. You were right to do it.'

***

Sharpe peered through the window at the attendant. Jones, Hamid and the two soldiers sat behind him, bored.

'What you want?'

'Why do you talk like that?'

'Like what ?

'Like you are from some Kung Fu movie...I mean you are not old enough to have a Chinese inflection from China or anywhere in Asia.'

The attendant looked uncomfortable. He spoke in a different accent.

'My Mum and Dad said I should talk like this if I wanted to avoid attention. They said it freaked people out if Chinese spoke in an English regional accent. It became a habit, besides, doing this job; if you pretend to be foreign, even now, the customers just think you are a petty bureaucrat. When I take this shit off at night,' he referred to his uniform,' I could speak to someone I'd had locked up here and they never knew it was me...'

'I'd have known it was you...' said Taylor in the doorway.

Chapter Thirty One

Taylor stood waiting on the roof; the roof of the dogs. In the centre was an upturned plastic container weighted down with a brick. He lifted it, half wondering whether if it was a booby trap. He was too tired to care. It was easier.

Underneath, only a hand phone. It had a screensaver of a spinning logo. He pressed one of the keys; saw a picture of him, Harry and their heli. With it was a yellow sticky note with a number written on it. Someone has a sense of humour at last; he smiled.

He started to dial the number. A footfall, a voice behind him. He didn't turn, he waited.

'I thought you'd like that, imbecile!'

Taylor stopped dialling and turned.

Raoul approached, they shook hands. Raoul walked to the edge, stared out across the ruined land. Taylor waited. It seemed an easy silence they shared. He broke it.

'Lord and Master of all he surveys. One day my son, all this will be yours!'

Raoul smiled. These people made him smile. Was it the outdoors that made these people so?

A thought struck him.

'Did you ever fantasise you could be a warlord on another planet, another universe – all you had with you were your innate personal qualities, a keen thirst for fair play, justice, a trademark fetish...a piece of technology from your own, your "before" world' Here he indicated Taylor's cigar, his hand phone.

Taylor joined in the moment. He loved a cliché. You could rely on stereotypes, especially the literary ones.

'Who were you? Flash Gordon? I wasn't athletic and muscle bound enough. For me, someone more technical, maybe Dan Dare or the one in the Time Machine. I would have really liked a picnic basket and some pistols, a hot air balloon, shiny brass and pewter instruments. I'd have been a 19th Century hero myself.'

Raoul turned back to him.

'Would we ever have met if the old world had never changed?'

'Doubt it, kindred spirits only coincide with synchronicity. Without, they drift apart looking for the catalytic voids.'

'Foof! Heavy!'

'I read it somewhere. I've been waiting to use it at an appropriate moment...'

'…an appropriate moment; on a roof. A roof which used to cover a DIY store…still above the water in drowned Jungle England? Their hand tools are rubbish by the way. I prefer the warehouse off Junction Seven; German tools, not Chinese or Korean…until you blew it up that is'

Taylor decided he would not tell him yet of Jones, who, not believing the FAE bomb would definitely work, had attached improvised demolition charges to a nearby butane gas tank, hidden behind trees but in line with Raoul's viewpoint. Taylor thought his bomb had worked but saw no harm in the demoralising effect of the double blast. Jones had not reckoned on the tank actually having so much gas still in it and had fingered his collar and jutted his jaw in his sergeant major way.

'Yeah, but the cheap ones you could throw away when they burnt out; didn't have to mess about trying to repair them, get spares, and you could lend them out and not worry if they didn't come back…'

'When my Dad was sober he would say " the man who lends the tools is on holiday", ' said Raoul.

Taylor thought of his own Dad; wondered what he would have made of all this.

'I used to buy my Dad tools for Christmas and birthday so I could use them myself…'

They laughed, shared the moment but eventually had to move on to business.

'I have a guerrilla army poised if not to conquer the world, well, at least a few English counties. I know what it means to hold them back. What can I do with them Taylor? Conquer Wales? The Romans didn't and Jones not only has a lot of bullets, he makes everyone count.'

'Swords into ploughshares is the obvious answer…'

Taylor pointed out the motorway. He described how would clear off the vehicles, use the scrap, introduce a landing strip for jets, an airport; a Zepp hub.

'…although I don't see myself checking in for a package holiday with your tattooed horrors sat glaring at me.'

'They aren't tattoos. They're only kids. I couldn't work with the older ones, too mad. These, up close, they aren't very scary at all. It's just war paint. War paint from plant dye. I hate tattoos. I always thought they were naff. No Taylor, they will be little angels again in a few months, if I can encourage them to attend to their personal hygiene that is…'

Taylor nodded to himself Yes! The look, the glaring, the offensive unwashed odour had combined to make them quite uncivilised.

He moved forward to take up a commanding view. He continued, waving his arms about expansively, pointing and indicating here and there;

'… clear the roads, build a PTV type rail network, get distribution going, extend the Dome idea inland, round up the older wild ones and treat them; rescue a few rescuables…open discussion channels with the city people…'

Raoul spluttered at the enormity of the task.

'You'd need an army and a superhuman feat of organisation for that…'

'And? Were you doing anything else today?'

'Will you help, Taylor?'

'Later I will, but first I have something to do. Before I go, what does the two finger thing mean?' He tapped his two fingers to his head, then his wrist.'

Raoul smiled. 'Allow us a few secrets…allow us that much.'

***

Back at base, a Dome 1 heli sat on the pad. Taylor was signalled to land on the water. Shutting down he threw a line to Jack, grinning, leaning against the rail. He looked excited as he pulled the heli close so Taylor could jump ashore.

'It's the ZI; from Kent HQ; come to have a word with you. In Wallis's office.'

Taylor made his way in apprehension.; back in the clutches of ZI, he thought.

'Ah, Taylor, I'm Symons, Peter Symons. Z2, Kent Dome.' said a heavy set grey haired man in Wallis's chair. 'Take a pew.'

He stroked and poked the air of the holo screen before him, reading reports, files, grunting from time to time. Taylor sat, silent but askance. The Z2's eyebrows raised.

'You know Livingstone then? Good man; speaks highly of you, one of his doves. For an atheist, he relies on the Bible quite heavily. You also came to the attention of Cartwright and Benson, neither of whom espouse Christianity to any degree, yet called their HQ, Ararat.'

It's all over the place, everywhere I go, Taylor thought. He remembered Livingstone's expression as he spoke of the lightning struck priest. Symons came to the point.

'Don't worry we're not here to arrest you. We opened up Jarvis's files. Not clever that lad, he stored his inner thoughts, his diary, on file. Most of it opium induced fancy, but enough for us to know you were falsely accused. So, forget about that one.'

A lead weight shifted from Taylor's soul. It seemed no amount of innocence could make up for being accused. Now, the accusation was gone. He let his relief show on his face. The Z2, smiled and opened another file on his wrist. Smiling still, he winked.

'Sally, Rachel and Andrew Taylor. Know them?'

Taylor could feel his own heartbeat, like a drum bursting out of his chest. His mouth went dry; a strange ringing started in his ears, his only focus this heavy set grey man sat across the desk from him.

'Only three Taylors? Sorry, go on.'

'In two months' time, the passengers and ship SS Klondike will be released into ESO custody. Thought you might like to be around at the time.'

***

Marie called him.

'One of the junior Z.I came up to me. Told me about the food the Domeys always ate most, the fast food. She thought they didn't eat healthily, wondered if she could change things to get them out of their indifference. One of her duties was to put fluoride and vitamins in the catering water supply. She found out they were opiates and other narcotics. Not only were the Domeys depressed, soporific almost, they were addicted. Odd was that the young women were not particularly affected. We will reduce the dosage slowly. Hopefully she will wean them off without too much… she wanted to stop it dead, stop the secret control but we talked her out of it. That branch of the ZI had a lot to answer for.'

***

In his room at the dome, Taylor uncovered the photocell and threw the cloth into a corner. The small bead grew into a ball with holo buttons dancing just above the surface. His wrist interrogated it and the screen came to life. A tasteful picture, the lifter skimming the surface of the footprint lake, shimmered out at him. Only Zill surely!

Press Show to allow holo message

He did and stepped back. He still found full holos spooky, especially in cramped places.

Zill's image drained into the room down from the top of her head.

She looked weary, casting glances from one side of the room to another. Taylor stepped to one side in order to take a detached view but some trick of the technology allowed her to turn towards the person being addressed and she turned towards him; seemed to look straight into his eyes.

~Taylor – it's me Zill ~. The holo Zill closed her eyes, grimacing at her mistake. She hissed with impatience.

~...of course it's me. You can see it's me. I-er, well you will be thinking I ran because I was guilty. You will think what you like, you do that, but I didn't know everything my father was doing, or why. We always thought we weren't clever enough yet to grasp his big plan.

I knew nothing about the vasp queens. He always said that insects could help mankind more directly, they had helped us build our before world; they had made sure the plants thrived so we could breathe; taken out the trash by eating or carrying away all the rubbish we left about. He has left a message like this for you; it will follow.

I thought he could not stop the ZI, those who were out of ESO control. I did not know he was instrumental. Those poor people on those ships! – he would look sad and turn away. He said there was nothing he could do directly. I cannot forgive him for that but surely, he is not so ill that the victims will not haunt him forever; a punishment even you could not exceed.

It was not until I saw your joke end of the world button that things started to dawn on me. Perhaps you should change the label: Press this button to change the world, Don't Press this button, to change the world. My father had been pressing a red button and could not stop. We were never quite sure why he brought you in. I mean on the surface you were just an agricultural; just getting on with it. No apparent moves on your part to bring about disruptive social change. My father obviously saw more.

He said de Klayven betrayed him but I think he betrayed de Klayven. Raoul was clever and tough but he wasn't you. The time was wrong and by the time you appeared on the scene, you who were always around already, he couldn't exchange you for Raoul. I-I-I ...

Goodbye Taylor, and I hope you find them...'

Zill shrunk into a small dot that flared briefly then winked out, leaving an after image on his retina.

***

His wrist alarmed. It was Marie again.

'Taylor! We've found your – your...we've found Ginny. She's shook up but she's OK. No doubt she'll tell you her adventures in...I'm sorry Taylor, I'm being a bitch aren't I?'

'Thanks. No you're not... I'll catch up with you later. I've got a couple of messages to listen to... I'll let you know what's what soon...'

He closed the link and turned to the screen again.

***

Shams's message followed. His image was of four friends in the years after University; with a little girl with missing front teeth....

He was in his chair. There were no obvious off camera companions; he made no side gestures or glances an accompanied person might make.

~~~

'Thank you for saving my little girl from the God Folk Taylor. You made me realize I was becoming too disconnected. I wanted the youngsters to bring Raoul back. I engineered his capture by the simple expedient of telling the SPs of his whereabouts. That little exercise cost eleven SPs dead and maybe dozens of Scallie ground troops.

I knew the Pastor had taken over, that he was mad and he was doing sacrificial rites. I thought Raoul would escape and sow mayhem himself. I could then take him off and get back inside his head as it were. I still don't understand why he was so passive when you told me of the mysterious leader. Nor why he didn't introduce himself. None of the other three of ours thought to ask about the recording where you dropped the three Scallies off.

I didn't know our young people would be so stupid to go in with no cover, no backup. We shouldn't have to watch them, guide them all the time...I thought the "kids" – if I may borrow your term – would recognize him and take steps to get him back here where I could regain control. You know the outcome very well. Not as I planned, your resourcefulness amazed me and I sat back again to watch, to see how things would pan out...

Well, thank you anyway...

The vasps you ask? Guard creatures of my invention. They would stay below an altitude and were not meant to seek out people. They were meant to attack moving things approaching their nest. To keep SP away from – from places I didn't want them to see. To guard the early building of the dome complexes as well but the creatures were too indiscriminate. Then you brought in the helizep allowing the tubes to extend further and further.

I could have stopped sowing the queens but, apart from a few accidents, your crews soon had the means of destroying them so I just dropped the odd queen module out on the edge. I never considered the nests would be moved in with the harvest programme.

Where I had really lost control? My friend from university, Mark Llewellyn, you know him as Z3, he...well, now I think about it I probably started losing control back then at Aberystwyth. He was very Welsh, hated the English. He was well in with the silly group who burnt the holiday cottages, and then he left them before he got on any government database. I went on to Cambridge with my research; he to Oxford for his politics. It was Mark who encouraged me to work on the spy bees. He got development money from government for the nano technology. The bees could already navigate and store information, return to the hive and communicate that information. Once the audio video chips were small enough and a big enough insect was bred to carry the chip...well - you know.

This sub? What you were told was partly true. There were supposed to be government people carried to safety on board. Mark made sure that didn't happen. Owen and Jones could tell you of a bit of mercenary work one night in the first storms. They were innocent. Mark told them a convoy of armoured vehicles with undesirables on board were under no circumstances to reach the sub base. I think you know Jones's competence now, and Owen's planning ability. It should be obvious then how they came to turn a leisure centre into a small army. They still have no idea who they disposed of.

The rig? It is provisioned for a long occupation. The Navy foresaw no friendly ports. There are domestic floating rigs all over the world that will receive us. If you look on long straight roads left above water, you will find fuel bunkers for RAF jets. You have seen John's hideaway...anyway, the rig will be a good advance warning and weather station for you. The satellites belong to everyone Taylor. Use them wisely. Don't push any buttons without first....well; I'll say no more there. '

He grinned. His chair started to turn. Taylor closed the screen before he had chance to be dismissed.

***

He sighed, found his bed and lay down. He mulled over his days. He had done some good maybe. He had a new before to refer to, he had something to do now; he would be reunited soon. This was his new future. His friends were intact and he seemed to have run out of enemies for the time being.

A knock at the door.

'Come in,' said Taylor.

No response. Another knock. Taylor went to the door and slid it aside. He barely glimpsed a black uniform as two barbs struck him, followed by a jolt of electricity. A gush of dazer gas washed over him and he passed out, crumbling to the floor.

***

He came round. The room swam at first and then cleared. He was trussed up in a nettle cloth sack, unable to move. Collins sat smiling on his bed.

'I've waited very patiently for this, Taylor. I got you off a murder rap so I could sit here now and watch you helpless.

'Murder rap?' said Taylor, appalled. Serves me right to sit back and congratulate myself.

'Oh yes, Jarvis thought you had discovered his little game. He thought your clever lab people would find the source of the incendiaries.'

'How did you know about his...little game?'

'I suggested it to him. An idea I got when we were up in Cumbria. The Scallies were firing their flaming arrows at us from boats. They used boats up there, to get about, you see. We captured some of their crossbows and stuff and ambushed them in return. No big deal for the boats to sink, until the sharks turned up. Lovely stuff. Your new pal Sharpe was surprised to wake up on a wooden boat drifting out into the bay just before dawn. The incendiaries fired up just as the sun came up. He couldn't swim tied up but the sharks came and took pity on him. Put him out of his misery.'

'So, what now?' said Taylor. I can't see a way out of this.

'Awful feeling, to think you are tied up, unable to escape. Any minute your worst fear will materialise and you won't be able to do anything about it. My worst fear is bullies, people stronger, cleverer than me, who don't like me and cause me pain. Sharpe wasn't all those but he got me committed and I had to put my other side to sleep for a while. You see, my other side is stronger and much more clever. He is here now, sitting here waiting patiently for me to finish. He remembers how you humiliated me in front of the others, that time at the evacuation centre. I'm making him wait because I remember how you tied me up and terrified me; telling me exactly when the locks would open. How the drunken looters were angry and would have some "nice fun with someone with a fondness for using his Taser", you said.

"Friends of old George, the old man I shot," you said. What are your worst fears, Taylor? Don't bother, I know. You don't like being confined, in the dark, trapped with no way of escape. Oh yes, I've had time to think about all this. Before I hand over to him I'll give you a taster. Imagine being trapped inside one of your tubes. Imagine your friends in their silly gasbag helicopters towing you out to sea. They wouldn't hear you. They wouldn't imagine anybody would put a person inside a tube. They'll tow you out and leave you and the sun will come up and roast you. The algae will start to grow slowly and the methane will fill up the tube and you will slowly suffocate.'

Did he search me? Taylor looked around his room. He couldn't see any pocket contents lying about. His wrist was there, still turned on, but with the voice turned off. His big Tube knife lay next to it. Collins had made sure of that. Now he was shining his Taser, in turn at his head, heart and genitals. The red light glowed, turned to green, then back to red. Collins got up and went to the door, went out along the corridor and returned dragging Ginny's trolley. He threw its bedding and paraphernalia onto the floor. He produced a large nettle weave sack.

'I'm going to hide you in the sack and take you down the descender on the little Da girl's trolley. Handy to have your own escape door. I bet you never thought it would be so useful.'

Taylor daren't say anything. He had no idea of the psychology he needed to reason with this maniac. It struck him he was, at the moment, in less trouble with the lesser evil of the schizoid creature before him. His wrists were bound. Bound in front of him, a mistake Collins may regret. He had the multi purpose knife in his pocket but he couldn't reach it without a contorted twisting struggle, if at all.

'Time for the sack, Taylor, say goodbye to your nice little tube room.'

The sack went over his head and he was in the dark. Collins had got him wrong. He thought Taylor's phobia was a version of his own madness. Taylor just went limp and made it as awkward as he could for Collins to handle him. Surely, the cameras would pick them up. But no, the side door, his bolthole was chosen just for that, to avoid them. He surrendered himself to Old Kurt and retreated into his core being. Collins would gain no pleasure from an apathetic Taylor. He wanted pleas for mercy, begging. No such luck that he'd get bored and walk away but "many a slip twixt cup and lip" they said. Ah! There! He'd got the knife out of his pocket. For God's sake don't drop it now.

***

Jones and Ben sat in Joe's bar. Jones approved of Joe's; it reminded him of his less sensible youth and old comrades, friends in his dream queue. He wasn't sure of Ben, he didn't seem "over-affectionate", but he kept the table between them.

The others came in, dripping from a sudden cloudburst. Joe's other clients moved away as if the newcomers would shake themselves like dogs any minute.

'Ah, Taylor's band of brothers, and where's the man himself?'

'We thought he was here already. His wrist doesn't answer,' said Jack.

'Where would he go? He was with Raoul earlier but he came back. He said he had a couple of messages to deal with,' said Marie.

'Are all your enemies accounted for?' said Jones. 'I mean, he collects them for a hobby, practically one per friend.'

'Well balanced character, I'd say,' said Jack.

The door burst open. It was Ginny. She was soaked through, gasping for breath and frantic.

'He's been taken away!'

They gathered round.

***

Taylor sawed at his bonds. The knife wasn't sharp and he daren't draw attention to himself. The wheels of the trolley juddered, bumping along the bamboo floor landing, then the sensation of dropping as they went down the descender. The creak of the outer door, then the wash of humid air as they left the Dome. The rain had stopped but the trolley was not designed for rough damp ground and he heard Collins muttering and swearing as he tugged at it. He was dumped onto the ground, the air whooshing out of his lungs. He dropped the knife as Collins decided to drag him over the uneven surface.

He can't be dragging me all the way to the tubes.

A sharp edge against his knee. The knife. He made a grab for it. Hampered by his bound wrists, he struggled to bring it to bear. Two rough bumps pushed the pointed part of the blade into his leg. He was getting angry.

Don't make a single mistake, Collins; not one.

293

He aligned the blade and sawed furiously. He wasn't going to die like this. Collins thought he was scared. To be forcibly confined made him angry; out of control. Maybe why he didn't like being confined. At last, his hands were free. Now for his ankles. Once they were free he was coming out of this sack like a crazed thing. Collins couldn't taser him while he was in contact with him. He couldn't daze him for the same reason. Collins was going to be sorry.

***

Commander Sharpe didn't waste a minute. Jones and the others had Taylor's wrist. The last item on its log file was: "Taser aimed illegally. Taser: Serial number 48510. Logged as missing; last holder Sergeant Nick Sharpe. Deceased; shark attack, Cumbria".

Cold fingers crawled in his stomach. His dear lost dead older brother! Whoever had Taylor must have killed Nick! Nick, who'd befriended a man back then when...

The Taser could be tracked now because of its illegal use. He set the Dome system to search the wi-bands.

'They are in the nettle forest!' he said at last.

***

Taylor was stationary, on his side in the stuffy sack. He strained to hear, strained to establish his whereabouts. More, he ached to his core with the strain of trying to accurately locate Collins by psychic sense alone. Rats ran over the sack; their squealing and chirruping filling him with dread. He waited a few seconds, struggled into a sitting position and then poked an eyehole with the knife through the sack nearest his face. There was moonlight, and then it was cut off by shadow. He heard a chuckle. He jerked back as a much bigger blade entered the eyehole and slit the sack open. The sack was rolled down over his shoulders, effectively pinioning him. Collins moved away and sat on a mound of earth across from him. Taylor looked around. They were in a shanty contraband tunnel. Moonlight filtered through the big nettle leaves above. He looked at Collins, who now wore vasp armour. He chuckled again. It didn't sound right.

'It's me, the other Collins. My other half is not very imaginative. Very melodramatic telling you about sticking you in a tube, but what a faff! I've seen men, and women, die here in the nettles. In fact, I've been quite instrumental on occasion. Cartwright says they can kill a horse. Have you read Cartwright? Of course you have. You would

294

never have got the helizep going without him. I'm going to cut you in a minute Taylor. My alter ego will be disappointed but I love to see the rats at work. They are fond of warm blood just lately. "Missing persons" is my game. No evidence you see. You gave me a fright back at the reservoir. My foolish other one should have never shot the old man. Still, I don't have full control.

So, I'm not wasting any more time. I'm going to daze you a bit first. Oh no, you're not getting close to me. The rats here have a taste for warm meat but they don't like my little sonic box.' He held up a little transmitter and thrust it towards the rats. They retreated, squealing, climbing over each other to escape; but not very far; not far at all.

Taylor's mouth was dry. Collins Two was a much more serious adversary. He could have taken Collins One down maybe, but not this one. He was not going home now. Rat eyes gleamed, like green marbles dancing all around the clearing. They were waiting, peering round Collins as if egging him on.

Collins Two checked his dazer, smiled and stood up. The rats surged forward. Collins turned and waved his device at them again. They shrank back.

'Patience, my lovelies. Patience.'

Taylor started to count. *One...* His world began to slow before his eyes. Collins was close now, he could hear the creak of the nettle-armour, the scrape as he brought up the dazer past his thigh. He could sense Collins's finger tightening, knuckle white, on the trigger. A long knife gleamed in his other hand. Taylor began to close himself down. *Two...*

More rats were gathering behind, apparently quivering with gleeful anticipation. *Thr...* Wait! A thought, a phrase, came to Taylor now; so strong he thought it must be telepathy. *"Grasp it like a man of mettle and it soft as silk remains"*. Collins was not smiling anymore. He was turning in slow motion, jaw dropping, eyes wide in dread; the rats' eye reflections not shining now as they all turned their attention to something to the side, a flinty stare, nearby in the nettle forest...

A distinctive sound; *thub!* Another; *thub!* Collins turned. He was smiling again but somehow distracted, like a drunk. He seemed to have lost interest. A breeze blew in the nettle canopy overhead allowing the moonlight to shine fully on his face. His nettle-armoured body, stiff and robotic, crashed to the ground, but not before Taylor saw two dark holes in the man's forehead.

Jones put his "proper" gun away; his own armour creaked as he kneeled to free Taylor. He looked over at Collins' body.

'Gob-shite,' he said. 'Should have got on with it.'

We travel not for trafficking alone; By hotter winds our fiery hearts are fanned...

The End.

Lightning Source UK Ltd.
Milton Keynes UK
UKOW03f1704070514

231273UK00001B/5/P